The BIRTH MOTHER

SEYMOUR UBELL

ARCHWAY
PUBLISHING

Archway Publishing books may be ordered through booksellers or by contacting:

Archway Publishing
1663 Liberty Drive
Bloomington, IN 47403
www.archwaypublishing.com
1 (888) 242-5904

Because of the dynamic nature of the Internet, any web addresses or
links contained in this book may have changed since publication and
may no longer be valid. The views expressed in this work are solely those
of the author and do not necessarily reflect the views of the publisher,
and the publisher hereby disclaims any responsibility for them.

Cover art created with images from iStockphoto by lambada and exxorian

ISBN: 978-1-4808-7537-1 (sc)
ISBN: 978-1-4808-7535-7 (hc)
ISBN: 978-1-4808-7536-4 (e)

Library of Congress Control Number: 2019907065

Print information available on the last page.

Archway Publishing rev. date: 12/12/2019

Contents

Prologue

As the author, allow me to share with you an important part of this story. It is about a hardworking, successful American businessman and his dedicated wife. In writing this book, the gentleman whose history this tale is about wanted to control my concept of how I write, while sharing his account of twin Eurasian baby girls he and his wife adopted.

His constant interruptions during our interviews and endless direction made it impossible for me to stay the course I planned. In a moment of exasperation, I leaped from my seat at the computer and fought back. I battled with all my intellectual strength. I was determined to tell this amazing saga my way and my way only. He quietly reminded me, without a hint of anger, that it was he who telling the story. In silence, I listened.

Daryl Landsman engaged me to record his and his family's life. He turned out to be an overpowering person. His point of view took on a life of its own. Each day sitting at my computer, the tale flowed with multiple interruptions.

Daryl stood there, looking over my shoulder and reading my words, shaking his head in either disappointment or surprise at my storytelling skills. I knew not which, nor did I care. However, I could not have written this intriguing tale without his help.

When telling the last part of this story, he vanished.

1

A Dream Comes True

"An orphanage?" I questioned, somewhat annoyed. "What's the reason for this visit? What's the purpose?" I turned to my new business partner, sitting beside me in his chauffeur-driven car.

David Chen, a native-born Taiwanese businessman, rolled his eyes and spoke directly to me. He was a no-nonsense guy. Grim faced, he replied, "You Americans — where is your heart? Why must it be business, business *all the time*?" He turned his head, peering out the window of our speeding car. "For your information," he continued, somewhat irritated, "it is a worthwhile charity that I frequently help." His tone was condescending and impatient. I knew in one piercing moment that the comment I'd made was insensitive and foolish "Sorry, David," I apologized. "I understand," I said, backing off. "We, too, support important causes back in the States. It must have been the jet lag that spoke without thinking. Please forgive my careless remark."

Mr. Chen, a man of about forty-five years old, give or take, of medium height compared to other Asian men I knew. A pair of rimless glasses was held tightly at the tip of his nose. I erred when I spoke. I knew he felt that my imprudent sting was unintentional. In his wisdom, he graciously let it go. I sat there without a sound, embarrassed by my unwise aside.

Our sleek black Mercedes pulled up alongside a graying, time-worn stone building. Gazing out the window, I saw one crucifix dominating the front lawn, and another was at the entrance of the ancient edifice. The solemn but antiquated nunnery/orphanage was tucked away in a remote village between Fushun and Guangzhou in China. I stared silently, looking directly into the face of history, speculating the structure had been standing there for perhaps four hundred years or more. It was now a mere two-hour drive from Hong Kong.

David Chen lifted the heavy brass knocker on the ancient front door, allowing it to fall against the massive wooden frame. He did this several times. An echoing thud — in fact, almost a boom — exploded as the antique knocker crashed against the entrance.

On the other side, I could hear someone struggling to open the enormous oak gate, which sang its weary song of a thousand openings and closings. The entryway was studded with brass nails like in a medieval fortress. The old hinges noisily announced access to the archaic building.

A nun, dressed in a white habit, her head uncovered, seemed quite relaxed as she spoke in Mandarin. Chen's assistant, Francis Lee, who accompanied us, translated the conversation for me.

"Welcome, Mr. Chen. It has been too long since we have greeted you," she said in her native tongue.

"It is the same for me. Permit to introduce my friend and new partner, Mr. Daryl Landsman, from New York in the United States. Mr. Landsman, this is Mother Nun Ying," Sister Ying responded in both English and Mandarin. I stood silent, surprised and listening. The sounds of the Chinese words were like a new song waiting to be sung.

"I very pleased meet you, Mr. Landsman. Please join us for tea and baked cakes."

"I am also very happy to meet you," I responded, smiling and a little taken by surprise. I stepped back with some disbelief upon hearing English flowing easily from the nun's lips. I returned to my original position, not wanting to display any disrespect for my new partner.

In an anteroom, tea was served. We all sat as the Mother Superior began the conversation in English, mixed with some idiomatic Mandarin expressions, which Francis easily translated for me.

"May I express to you, Mr. Chen, our gratitude once again for your monthly generous and most gracious gifts?" The Mother Superior humbly stated, looking at Chen and acknowledging me as she simultaneously bowed her head.

"You are most welcome," Chen reciprocated, also bowing slightly. "I am aware of the important work you do here. As a Taiwanese guest in your country, and for much of my family living in China, I appreciate the effort you make and the life you have generously given to ease the pain of these helpless children."

"I pray you enjoy our meager offerings. It is but a tiny gesture for your kindness, and to show our appreciation for God's work that is performed here," she replied.

We sipped the tea and quietly ate the tiny cookies that tasted more like bread to my Anglo taste buds. Nevertheless, I complimented the Mother Superior on the tastiness of her offering.

She smiled and invited us, "Please, join in nursery."

The Mother Superior led us into a small room. Sheer curtains covered the windows. Three ancient oak tables, perhaps a donation from a local resident, surrounded the area. Disposable diapers and sterilized bottles for milk, water, or juice lined the tables, waiting for the infants' demanding cries. Boxes of tissues, paper towels, white cotton, and plastic gloves, and tiny receptacles holding hand-cleaning liquid, lay adjacent to the other baby-care tools. To my surprise, two or three dozen, perhaps more, Gerber baby food jars rested on the table. There was an aroma of talcum powder in the air, and a wet diaper lay in a trash can close by. I pursed my lips and shrugged my shoulders. This was an unexpected adventure.

It was an astonishing scene. I was standing in a room, a nursery, with thirty-three newborn children. Each infant was a girl no more than two or three months old. Every child lay in a rickety bassinet, and these were lined in three rows of eleven. The babies were in tightly swaddled bundles; only their round little faces peeked through the bundling. Most were asleep. Two or three crying children settled quickly as volunteer nurses brought miniature bottles of water and placed them to the babies' softly curled lips, while comforting them with care, cooing, and obvious affection. Several of the teeny tots lay silent with their petite almond-shaped eyes wide open, staring at the ceiling. Perhaps two or three were voicing their opinion of discomfort. A few others were awake but quiet. The infants lay there, eyes wide open and little lips rounded and content.

"Sister, may I walk down the aisles to better see the children?" I asked, turning to Chen with obvious deference. My curiosity had gotten the better of me. Chen nodded his head, approving.

"Yes, Mr. Landsman. Please wear garments." The Mother Superior turned to the ancient table, and made her selection of a white smock, which she held out — a square white hat; a face mask to cover my nose and mouth; and finally, white cotton gloves.

"We protect little ones from unnecessary exposure," Mother Superior explained, turning her head slightly to the right and looking me over carefully. I raised my weary arms for the garment to be placed on my chest. Then I held out my hands for the gloves. I tilted my head forward for the mask. I crouched ever so slightly as the petite nurse, on her tiptoes, placed the white cap on my head.

In hushed steps, I walked alone, silently up the first aisle and down the next. I listened to the rhythmic breathing and the muffled sounds that oozed from the babies' bodies. I turned my head from right to left, taking each muted step while gazing at the babies and feeling an out-of-body experience. I peered with interest as the infants moved their lips or their eyes ever so slightly. Pausing for a moment to look, I admired each child.

"All girls?" I whispered.

"Shh, shh." The nun nodded.

"Why are there only girls here?" I questioned more quietly. "Where are the boys?" I murmured.

"In our country boys have more value than girls. Families keep boys."

"Why?"

"I do not know. But that is how it is. Five thousand years of tradition," the nun responded.

"Very sad, very strange," I said.

One child close to the last cradle caught my eye. She appeared different. She was Asian but not Asian. Her rounder, less Asian-shaped, almost Western eyes were punctuated by her pale complexion.

She was different. I paused, cocking my head to one side and then tilting it the other way. I stared at this unique-looking child for several moments.

She's so beautiful, so angelic, I thought.

The truth was, my heart jumped a little. It was that inner voice signal of instant connection. Or was it my fantasy creeping up on me? Unexpectedly, I trembled at the realization of this child's vulnerability. My thoughts galloped. I confess it was one of my rarest experiences. A feeling of warmth covered my face and body, as if something had just happened. It was a moment of I knew not what. I did not know from where it had come.

Bring this child home? Am I insane? With one word of consent and my signature on a document, I could take this sweet, beautiful infant, this human being, this real person, home with me to New York and change her life forever. She would be our daughter. It feels like magic.

"Doss vellzine ah mitzvah fun Gut," *as my mother would say. This would be a gift from God.* These thoughts raced through me.

"Sister Ying? Mr. Chen?" I said softly. "Would you both join me for a moment?" They approached. I asked, "Why does this most unusual child look so different from the others?"

"Do not comprehend question," Sister Ying responded.

"Her skin is not Asian and not white. She is more Western-looking, and her eyes are less almond-shaped than those of the other babies."

Sister Ying turned to Mr. Chen; they spoke in Chinese.

David looked at me for a moment and then turned his head, looking at the baby girl. He did not lift his face. He only stared at the little girl with saddened eyes as he spoke. A heartbreaking look of pain crossed his face.

"There is shame here with this child in her new life," he began. "She is" — he spoke haltingly — "half Chinese and half European."

Another sister scurried toward them and spoke in Chinese. Sister Ying responded, and Mr. Chen smiled. Sister Ying gave some instructions and the young nurse left. The sister showed us into the adjoining sitting room.

Tea was served once again. For the first time I spoke of the strange feeling I'd had when looking at that beautiful baby. I attempted to explain my feelings; once again a tic nudged my insides. The others just nodded, understanding my encounter.

"You mentioned shame when we spoke earlier. Please explain," I questioned Mr. Chen.

"The child was conceived" — he hesitated — "in an attack on the birth mother by a Westerner."

A pang of pain in my chest. "And the mother?" I questioned.

"She lives. She is well and has recuperated from the assault physically. The rest, we are uncertain." I began to understand the Anglo-Asian look of the baby.

The young nurse returned moments later, carrying another small bundled child in her arms, looking down at her in amazement. She turned the infant to show me another baby with looks similar to those of the first child—white complexion, perhaps slightly lighter, and her eyes clearly with an Asian–Western appearance. The nurse gently pulled the top of the bundle back from the little girl's head to show me a full crown of beautiful golden hair.

"Oh my!" I blurted out, unable to control myself.

Mr. Chen turned to me and said, "This is her twin sister."

2

Ancient Chinese Tradition

"Daryl, you hired me to write your biography. Damn it, you have spoken enough. Let me tell your story. That is why you hired me and why you pay me. I am the so-called author; I am the biographer of your life. You are the subject and the storyteller. It's your life. But I am the translator of your narrative, your pain, and your joy. Let me work.... Please, sit back and be silent."

Daryl sat back in his easy chair as we continued our interview. "You're right," he agreed. "Please do your magic. However, allow me to jump in whenever clarification of the truth is needed."

With the slight misunderstanding settled, I began.

❦

Let me take you to a time two years earlier, in a small village just north of the vast city of Guangzhou, China, in a mud hut. Ling Na Chan sobbed in stabbing convulsions, watching her eldest daughter being led away on that fateful day to the employment broker.

"Please, please," the woman pleaded to her husband, "Shan Di is *our* child. What you are doing is cruel. If you take her to the employment center, we will never see our daughter again," she begged.

"Silence!" Dong Chan commanded. "She is my child as well as yours. Shan Di is the only possession of value we have to offer. And this must be done to save our only son. You know as well as I that we must have the money for the doctor and the hospital," he shouted.

"Please know that I am the father; I too live with much hurt in my heart. Tomorrow I will take our Shan Di to the employment center. I am aware that other families have made this difficult decision for the past many centuries." He ached with the sting of his choice.

"I fear others like us in China and perhaps beyond also cope with much the same decision." He put his hand to his face.

"I am not a stupid man. I am frightened to even think of our daughter's future. And I cannot bear to consider that most likely, as you weep, we will never see her again. I hate the thought of her life being one of struggle with much harshness."

Chan's wife sat in silence, her aching body rocking to and fro as if in prayer.

"Can you even imagine how I am feeling?" he begged. "Soon I must take our daughter to the employment agency. The man there will give me documents to chop and to sign that I cannot read. He will give me money that I cannot count.

"I speak to you with grief in my heart and in my tortured body. When I leave with Shan Di, I will be taking her to an unknown future.

"As your husband, as the father of our children, I sit here in both shame and sorrow that our Shan Di will be the collateral for a loan I must make to save our son. I feel unhappiness for our daughter. My body stings with the thought that our child will work for five years until the debt is repaid. I know her wages will be minimal, perhaps only two hundred yuan each month. The food will be little, and they will give her a place to sleep. Can you not see my body tremble and raw with shame? I hate myself," he shouted.

At the time of this dramatic change in her life, Shan Di was all of fifteen years old. Her family was poor. Everyone slept in one room, a room with a dirt floor covered in straw. It was that tiny, impoverished, improvised mud hut they called home. Here they ate, worked, and slept, and where they would most likely die.

❦

"Poppa, do you think they will like me? I just put on my new white dress that Momma made. She even washed and dried it in yesterday's sun.

"Please, Poppa, look at me. Do not shut your eyes. It is sad for me to see how you tremble. You are in pain, as am I."

Shan Di sat with her eyelids tightly shut. *I must not weep; I must hold back my tears,* she thought.

Her hands covered her ears, so as not to hear the rolling wheels of the rickshaw on the bumpy dirt road.

"Poppa, may I sit close? I'm frightened."

"I too am filled with fear. Come sit nearby, but not too close. It is not fitting for a girl child to be very close to her baba (father)."

A strong-armed man, sweat pouring down his back, pulled a rickshaw sent by the broker. The vehicle moved quickly on the country road.

Shan Di could feel the morning dampness. She felt the touch of a cool breeze as it brushed her face. Silently, she stared at a mist that rose from the earth.

Poppa Dong Chan tried not to look at his child as she quivered by his side. He knew her fate; she would face endless days cooking, cleaning, and washing from dawn until nightfall. She would live in a shed with three or four other women, serving the master in a huge, elegant house. For any errors, which he knew she would make, she would be beaten. In a good home, perhaps beaten once a month; with a cruel master, everyday beatings would be a common ritual. In his mind, Poppa Chan shut his eyes tightly to block the thought of unwelcome sexual commands from the master.

"I too am filled with fear," he said.

Chan forced the nightmare from his head. He understood his life — to forgive himself a thousand times or more for this decision. He could never earn the money to save his only son, who was very ill, the twenty-year-old Leong Chan. This was a necessary choice. It was his only option.

His thoughts persuaded him. *Once I receive payment from the employment agent, I must travel to Putian. There I will find the doctor and the hospital.* Poppa Chan, in a deep private conversation with himself, tried to believe that this was a good decision.

I must save my only son. He has to be saved at all costs. My Shan Di must be the sacrifice. It must be that way. After all, she is only a girl ... only a girl.

Moving along the potholed road, bouncing, bouncing, as they moved every step of the way. Shan Di sank into a moment of hypnotic silence, watching the tiny huts surrounding huge rice fields, a small stream, two women washing clothes, and another woman filling a pail with water. She thought for the first time of the weary life that many people in her village endured. Her mind was blank, not wanting to reflect on or consider her future. Tucked inside her recently developed bosom was a tiny feeling of hope. It was August 8, 1988. *A very good omen, four eights on my departure date.* She smiled. The eighth month and the eighth day, plus the two eights in 1988. The number eight was good luck in Chinese folklore.

Shan Di felt, perhaps this was her lucky day.

How fortunate I am to leave on such a very special four-eight day, she thought. *I will make this come out good. I promise I will work hard, learn, and have a new life.*

A building stood tall, straight, and dark in front of their eyes. Poppa stretched his neck, tilting his head back to see the top of the four-story structure. It looked ominous and unpromising. The letters at the front on a glass entryway, in red calligraphy, glared at the new arrivals and spoke out: Center for Work Placement. Although Poppa Chan could not read or write, he knew in his pained heart that they arrived. Poppa Chan took a deep breath; it left his lips in a deep sigh. On his face was fear, a fright that suddenly struck him directly in his gut like a knife slicing into his flesh. Poppa shuddered as he climbed from the rickshaw, stepping onto a wet, muddy street. He looked up at his daughter, her eyes filled with tears. He knew his daughter's new, beautiful white dress would soon be spoiled and a bad impression made. That was not an option. His paternal protective instincts took over.

He watched as Shan Di stretched her pleading hands out toward him. His arms open and with all his strength, he lifted Shan Di high in a quick and gentle movement, sweeping her from the cart onto the wooden street at the side of the building. He had never touched his daughter that he could remember. He felt her warmth and smelled her smell.

For the first time he realized that Shan Di's child body was gone and that her body was now firm and maturing. Poppa knew she was no longer a girl. He experienced the feeling, much to his surprise, that his daughter would soon be a woman. And in all probability, his little girl was no longer a little girl. She was already a woman. Shan Di's eyes moved swiftly from side to side as she and her poppa stumbled into the offices of the employment center. It was the first time she had ever been to a town or, for that matter, entered a true stone and wooden building.

Straw was the only material used on any structure she had ever seen. Clear and polished windows, like eyes opened wide, welcomed light into the room. Shan saw desks and chairs and a strange machine in front of its own wide window that young women sat in front of and punched finger by finger on buttons that produced she knew not what.

The ceiling, with shining white circular bowls, threw off light — another miracle that was unfamiliar. Suddenly a frightening roar came from outside of the office that she and her father were in. Shan's eyes bulged at the sight of the strange-looking machine with four wheels. In it, a man sat behind yet another wheel, moving quickly out of sight. This young girl had never seen a car in her life.

Surely this visit was filled with wonders of the modern world. Shan Di's life had been one of isolation, with little knowledge of the world that existed. She was uneducated. She could not read a book and had never seen a television screen. The ten or twenty minutes at this office were a staggering experience. Her vision and her brain tried to absorb the labyrinths of puzzlement she viewed. Shan's heart skipped a beat as a tall, Western-dressed woman approached them. She wore a long gray dress with large black buttons running down the front. Her hair was neatly tied in a bun. She smiled and greeted them: *"Nee how (Thank you)."* They responded in kind. Shan bowed slightly as her father introduced her.

The young girl listened carefully as her father explained the arrangements he'd made with the employment broker in his village. His daughter was to be given work in a fine home, where she would earn two hundred yuan each month to pay down the loan for two thousand yuan, over a five-year period.

The woman nodded and took them into another office. She introduced Mr. Chan and Shan to Yang Su Hong, the big boss of the employment agency.

Mr. Hong took out an envelope from his desk, opened it, and removed two thousand yuan, placing the bills neatly on the counter in full view of Poppa Chan and Shan. Neither had ever seen that much money in their lives. It was a tempting sight — a ploy by the agent to keep the father from changing his mind.

Shan sat as the agent smiled and moved the documents close to her father. Her eyes squinted as she tried to understand what was happening.

She watched her father sign the papers with his mark and then place his chop in the proper place as directed. Shan knew that with the stamping of the chop, all the arrangements had been completed. She watched in silence as her father put the tightly bound money into a sack that hung inside his trousers connected to his waist. Shan instinctively recognized that she now belonged to a stranger. Mr. Chan was silent. They both stood hushed looking at each other. Ten seconds, twenty seconds, a half minute; it felt like forever. He could not look at his daughter. She wanted to embrace him, longing for a final hug from her baba. That hug would never happen. Their culture would not allow it.

The young girl shivered an almost unheard murmur, "*Tai tsien*, Poppa," saying goodbye. Tears glazed her eyes. "Tai tsien," she whispered again.

He watched in silence as she was taken away by still another *TaiTai* (housewife). They both understood that they would never see one another again.

3

The Magical City

Daryl Narrates

On my mobile phone, I heard my wife's voice. I responded.

"Hello? Hello? Maxine, I can hardly hear you. Can you speak louder?" I shouted into my BlackBerry while I walked around the small room outside the nursery. I was trying to find the spot where reception might improve. Suddenly there was a signal.

"I can hear you very well here in New York. Is everything all right?"

"Yes, I am fine."

"Where are you?" she asked.

"I'm with Mr. Chen. You remember I told you about him. He and I have agreed to a joint venture here in Canton Province. Our meeting is over. He has taken me to one of his charities. It is an orphanage."

"So, what are you doing there?" my wife questioned.

"I just came along for the ride, but I am having an interesting experience. I've never been to a place like this before."

"So?"

"This is a home for abandoned children. They are almost all girls.... No, no ... all girls. Not a single boy."

"So?" she responded.

"Well, to tell you the truth, I fell in love with one of them."

"Are you insane?" she said in a burst of surprise. "Old age has finally gotten to you. Don't tell me you're thinking ... no, I do not want to hear the word."

"What word?"

"*Adopt.* I do not want to hear it. You will not and cannot bring her home," Maxine firmly stated.

"Sweetheart, you and I have discussed adopting a child for at least a year," I reminded her. "We already have a wonderful boy. We are not getting any younger. I am fifty years old. Having another child will not be easy. I once told you that it's not *your* biological clock; it's my clock that keeps ticking away — and quickly."

Perspiration covered my face. I continued talking and walking, still searching for the area in the room that allowed for the best reception. Her voice was fading. "Let me call you on the landline," I suggested.

"Okay," she answered.

We both hung up. I knew my wife had a smile on her face. I know her angry voice and her happy voice.

My Very Stubborn Author Narrates

At the Landsman apartment in New York City

"What's the grin about?" Nancy, their longtime housekeeper, asked Maxine.

Nancy worked in the Landsman home for more than ten years. Over that decade, she became part of the family. She often went on holidays with them when they took Freddie to Florida or a Caribbean island. They bought a two-bedroom apartment near their home in Manhattan where Nancy and her son could live comfortably. There, in a better neighborhood, Nancy's son, Carlin, could attend a superior school.

Maxine turned to Nancy. "I think Daryl is trying to convince us to adopt a baby girl … from China!!"

"That's not a bad idea. You certainly have plenty of room. You have four — or is it five bedrooms we have here?" Nancy answered. "It's four. You remember — we converted one bedroom into a closet." Maxine was thinking about Daryl's needs as she spoke. *Hmm, another baby. That could mean a raise and at least ten more years with these people. I like it,* Nancy thought.

Maxine's landline rang. It was Daryl. Adopting a baby was still on her mind. "Hello, sweetheart. You are such a kind and generous man," she quickly began. "Do you remember how much work is involved in taking care of a baby? Up early every morning, sometimes four o'clock or earlier. Two hours of sleep, then up again to feed the baby, and again and again to change the baby. It is a major commitment. No sleep for almost a year," she stated in breathless conversation. "Now our lives are easier and more fun and settled. We would have to make a huge sacrifice in our lifestyle. Fred is older; we can take him on holidays, go skiing, and even go to a movie with him or to a restaurant."

"Don't jump the gun," he countered. "We are only having a discussion. I think having another child would give us a longer life. My mom used to say, 'Every child brings his or her own luck to the table.'"

"Your mother, your mother," she exclaimed. "Your mother is long gone, and she never helped us when she was alive. She had four sons and six daughters-in-law, as well as twelve grandchildren. That fact did not make her live a minute longer." She continued, "In fact, the only children she ever loved were her four sons." Zap — an unusual comeback.

"Listen, Daryl, I know we have been talking about adopting. I can hear in your voice a sense of excitement. Here is a thought. It just came to me, and it's only a suggestion. What do you think if I ask Nancy if she could stay for about a week or slightly longer?

And what do you say if I meet you in Shanghai? We can spend a few days together and then go to Guang … something, or other, wherever you say this orphanage is. And like grown-ups, we'll decide together, face-to-face, and not fax to fax or by phone?"

"Is that a question or a suggestion? Sounds like both."

Maxine grinned. "It was both." She imagined that Daryl was also smiling.

"I've always liked your style."

"That's why you married me."

"It was only one itty-bitty part of you that I loved. I can't tell you the rest; they could arrest me in China for telephonic pornography." Maxine beamed with his every word. He was a great salesman.

"Please call Linda at the travel agency. She will take care of all the flight arrangements. I know you are careful with our money but treat yourself: fly business class. When you have your reservations, let me know your flight plans. I will pick you up at the airport. I am very excited."

"I am also sweetheart, but not about the baby." That last was a tiny fib. "I am happy about meeting you in Shanghai. I have wanted to go there for a long time," Maxine replied.

"Oh, I forgot," Daryl said. "There is one more thing I have to tell you."

"What is it?"

"First, travel safe. Second, I love you. And third" — a pause — "that beautiful child?"

"Yes? What is it?" Maxine responded, one eye slightly closed in a quizzical expression.

"She is a twin…. Love you." He heard a gulp just before he hung up.

Maxine sat there, phone in hand, lips apart. "Nancy!" she called out. "Nancy, please come here."

"What is it?" Nancy asked.

"She has a twin. She has a twin sister." Maxine whispered in a bewildered and silent daze, her eyes rolled up to the ceiling. "Oh my, oh my," she said softly.

Nancy's eyes glowed, and her heart smiled.

The Author once again interrupts Daryl, demanding time.

Shan Di Takes Her First Car Ride

She suffered, fear gripped her heart. This was her first car ride. Shan Di held on to the inside handle on the door in terror that she might fall out. Her eyes were wide open as the car swiftly raced by all the townhouses, barns and sheep, cattle, rice paddies, and clear lakes. There were more colorful flowers than she had ever seen in her life. She twisted her neck upward, watching hundreds of workers, like ants atop a hill, placing stones one next to another to prevent mudslides. She sat in the back with Mr. Hi Bo as his chauffer swiftly but carefully brought his passengers to the house where she would be working and living for the next five years. She looked around. The weather was warm, the sky cloudless — both good omens.

The man sitting beside her in the backseat appeared strong and all-knowing. She felt safe in his presence. She had an unknown wishful thought.

Da Loban (Big Boss) Hi Bo was the very successful owner of a shoe factory. He had more than one thousand employees, producing more than twenty-five thousand pairs of shoes each day. Hi Bo was about fifty plus years old. His full head of graying hair gave him an additional distinguished appearance. He was always clean-shaven, and he dressed as a man in his position should dress. His eyes were dark and always searching. He heard everything and said little. He was the master of his community and of his house. Hi Bo treated his staff fairly. While the general salary for factory workers in the late twentieth century was sixty dollars each month, Hi Bo paid sixty-seven dollars. For that reason, he attracted the people with the best skills.

Workers lived on the grounds of the factory in comfortable dormitories. Cleanliness was a must, and health care, a commandment. Hi Bo's wife, Tan Ha, was in her late forties, a woman of elegant style, and she was very knowledgeable and beyond generous.

In the 1980s, China was coming alive; the sleeping giant began to stir after centuries of silence. It was one of the planet's oldest and most isolated empires, reviving its multifaceted muscles. People were working, building, repairing, and prospering. Highways were connecting provinces, bringing the multiple cultures closer together.

Old two-lane gravel roads magically became six- or eight-lane thruways. Western cars and high-speed trucks moving at seventy miles per hour were replacing bicycles, rickshaws, and foot travelers. China had a vast array of natural resources, endless forests, mountains of ore, oil, and natural gas, and most importantly a population of 1.3 billion. Every man, woman, and child were ready and able to join the seemingly limitless army of workers.

A new era, a long-awaited birth, the millennium of the twenty-first century, was quickly approaching. The foundation of an historical adventure was about to begin, not only for Shan Di but also for the entire People's Republic of China — and the rest of the civilized world. A newborn global economy was stretching its arms.

The driver maneuvered the car through a huge iron gate, steering past a small brick gatehouse, moving slowly around a wide, circular driveway paved in stone. Giant oak trees paved the way on both sides of the road, with tall, sharply trimmed bushes guarding the entire grounds. Shan saw at least three strong-looking men standing outside the green-painted stone gatehouse. The men, one by one, saluted as the car passed. All three men trotted alongside the car until it reached the entryway. The men did not look like workers. Shan Di could not tell who they were or what they did. Every move, each view all new to her, never before seen or experienced, her eyes constantly gaping and her lips apart as her young heart beat rapidly, both with a sense of joy and the sharp edge of panic.

Once out of the automobile, Shan Di put her hand out to take her small cloth bag with all her belongings from the chauffer. Mr. Hi Bo ordered the driver to take her bag to the maid's quarters. He planned to personally show Shan Di around the house, an unprecedented, unheard-of act by Hi Bo. They entered through the front door. Here, another unexpected deviation of behavior, as all servants normally entered the house from the back door. Hi Bo wanted Shan Di to know what her job was going to be. He had, within only a few moments, taken a liking to her. His inexplicable behavior and loquaciousness were totally out of character.

"Nee how, Da Loban (Hello, Big Boss)." Hi Bo smiled, tilted his head, removed his hat, and handed it to the maid. He instructed the servant to follow them. As they walked through the entry hall, a huge marble sculpture of a Buddha greeted them. Tall, slender candles burned on each side of the religious icon.

Elegant carpeting covered the room. French doors opened at the left and the right, one set leading into a library and the other into a drawing room. A wide, circular staircase climbed so high that Shan Di, stretching her tiny neck and arching her back, still could not see the top of it. Miniature Buddha statues sat at the foot of the stairs atop two dark oak posts, guarding each side of the staircase.

Sunlight streamed through the sheer-covered windows. The

majesty and obvious wealth easily overwhelmed Shan, as it would have any sophisticated and educated city dweller. The house was still, except for silent steps coming from above.

"Hi Bo?" a high-pitched voiced called out. "Have you returned with the new servant?"

"*Tsie, tsie, TaiTai* (Yes, yes my wife)."

TaiTai Hi Bo was well-dressed and elegantly groomed. She gracefully stepped into the entry hall. She gave Cissy Yu, the waiting maid, instructions. "Please take the new helper to her room and give her direction as to where to begin this evening at dinner. Give advice and lessons for her daily chores. Explain what her day-to-day responsibilities will be." She turned to Shan. There was no welcome, no greeting, and no handshake. It was strictly business.

"Please tell me, what is your name?" Madam Hi Bo asked.

"Shan Di." She bowed slightly.

Madame Hi Bo clenched her eyes and pinched the bridge of her nose. "We will call you Shan." TaiTai Hi Bo nodded as her lips broke into a half smile.

"I am pleased to be here. And I am pleased with my new and shorter name," Shan replied.

"Now run along and begin, both of you. Dinner will be served promptly at six," Madame Hi Bo ordered. "Cissy and you, Shan, have many tasks to complete before the dinner is served."

4

Mysterious China, and Its Queen of Hearts, Shanghai

Maxine was simultaneously exhausted and exhilarated as she exited the business-class cabin. A small leather tote bag hung from her shoulder. Her slender body was neatly dressed in a two-piece navy suit. She moved quickly from the plane.

"Shanghai. Ah, Shanghai," she whispered to herself. Finally, she had made the long-awaited trip that Daryl had been trying to persuade her to take for almost three years. Previously it was an impossible request. How could she have left Fred, or her mom, or her sister, or her brother? She was the family guardian, their protector. She felt that everyone in her family circle was safer when she was but a phone call away.

After the seemingly endless flight across the globe, here she was, in a city she'd only dreamed about. Her prince charming, Daryl, had waved his astonishing magic wand, and in a miracle of breathtaking power, she was swished to Shanghai. Most fantasies never materialize, but this one had.

Maxine moved quickly through immigration as she people-watched, one of her persistent pleasures.

She stared in amazement and curiosity at the distinctively costumed passengers arriving from every part of the globe. She gaped at mothers with three or four children, all traveling as one family. Maxine observed the elderly travelers supporting their aged legs with walkers or canes. Some moved in wheelchairs, assisted by airline attendants.

"There it is," she exclaimed to the porter at the baggage rolling past her, "That's right, the big one, and the small suitcase next to it." Seeing her luggage arrive safely, to Maxine, was like winning the lottery. The middle-aged Asian porter snatched the Missoni luggage. His slightly bent body quickly clutched the two pieces. Maxine knew he had not a clue as to what she had shouted.

The efficient Chinese immigration system moved everyone through Customs without a hitch. Maxine followed the porter as the automatic doors burst open onto a sea of humanity from every walk of life. People were holding signs in multiple languages, greeting VIPs, welcoming friends and relatives. People held signs for car services, with names of clients, wives, and sweethearts, all on the lookout, eyes moving, carefully combing the site, seeking out their welcome arrival, each with their vision squinting and peering. Standing on tiptoe, they searched the throng of people, calling out to their expectant arrival.

Suddenly, from within the midst of all the tumult of people she heard a familiar voice: "Maxine, Maxine!"

Daryl taps my shoulder and he becomes the storyteller.

My smile stretched from ear to ear. I rushed to my bride and held her tightly; we kissed a warm hello. It happened to us every time. We'd been apart for just shy of a week, but it felt like forever to both of us.

"I have a car waiting, sweetheart. Our hotel is in Pudong, not very far from here."

Maxine was breathless. She clutched my hand in hers as we walked toward the waiting limo. My wife and I strode together, arm in arm. I enjoyed her open amazement at the cavernous reception hall. Only a few years earlier, rice paddies had covered the ground, but now it was a giant, modern complex with shops everywhere.

I splurged and ordered a gray Bentley for the ride to the hotel. The car streaked into an eight-lane freeway. Maxine snuggled against my arm, holding my hand. I could feel her hand close, release, close, and release, our secret "I love you" hand signal.

Soon my wife's body collapsed in my arms. I was sure she had begun to feel fatigue from jetlag sinking right to her very toes. I felt that myself often enough. I watched her in the car. I knew that her every bone and her every muscle ached. Her eyes closed. She fell asleep holding my arm and gripping my hand, her head on my shoulder, enjoying the miracle of the Boeing 747 becoming a magic carpet that brought her to her fantasy city in Asia.

We moved swiftly onto the brand-new, smooth highway. In just over thirty-three minutes, we arrived at the Grand Hyatt. The driver, ever efficient, stepped from the car and opened the door. We lifted our aching bodies from the sedan and walked to the revolving doors. The hotel manager greeted us.

"Welcome to the Grand Hyatt, Mr. and Mrs. Landsman. Your suite is ready. You have been preregistered. Permit me to show you the way." Maxine and I looked at each other. The Chinese manager spoke perfect English, as if he'd been educated at Oxford, and probably was.

"How did you know our names?" Maxine questioned. "We have never been here before."

"We always have the driver call us and advise that he is arriving, and he tells us the guests' names. It's simple and courteous," he responded.

The seventy-second-floor suite was fourteen steps to the right of the elevator. The bellman opened the door. The manager stretched his arm forward against the entrance, inviting us to enter the apartment. Once we did, he followed close behind.

"Oh my, this is so beautiful." Maxine whispered, "It must cost a fortune."

I smiled. "It does, but in renminbis (Chinese money)."

She kissed my cheek. "Look at those roses, and the champagne and the goodies." Maxine rushed to the window and pulled the curtain aside, enjoying the view seventy stories high, taking pleasure in the sight of the entire city in all its glowing magnificence. Shanghai shone as if it were Christmastime. She looked at me. "I cannot believe that I am here. If I didn't know I was in Shanghai, I might think, gazing out this window that I was in Paris, New York, or Hong Kong. Thank you so much for this special and exciting gift." Once again, I grinned with pleasure at the sight of my wife so pleased.

"This city is all three of those great cities wrapped up in one unbelievable Asian miracle. But the true miracle is yet to come," I answered. "In just a few days ... you will see a real marvel."

She walked through the living room, through the dining room, and finally into the master bedroom. An extra-large European-style king-size bed sat directly in the center of the room. An oversized armoire with a treated mirror reflected her obvious delight. Maxine glanced into the bathroom. Then she turned to me and said, "Wow, this is so luxurious. The tub is big enough for both of us." She went in, closing the door behind her.

"Anything on the TV?" she called from the bathroom. "I could use a drink, please."

"I think CNN is the only English-speaking station. What would you like Scotch or vodka?"

"No, no, this evening calls for champagne." I heard her happy voice from the bathroom.

An unexpected, thunderous sound came from the electronic flushing mechanism of the toilet — a total surprise. I walked into the bathroom. Maxine was smiling and moved over to the double sink. Her fingers under the faucet, and a flow of warm water streamed onto her knuckles. On a shelf above the tub lay six bath towels, four face towels, and four washcloths. On a glass sill nearby lay bars of soap, bottles of hand and body lotion, and an array of personal toiletries. She dried her hands and patted her face. Gazing into the triple mirror, she looked at her cheeks. Maxine dug into her purse, searching, and pulled out a travel tube of lipstick. She looked at it, shook her head and put it back. She was ready for the great city.

"Let's finish our drinks and shower," I suggested. "Going to bed early would be a good idea. Tomorrow will be busy, busy, and busier."

We slipped into the massive bed. Our bodies were touching at the hips. Her hand was in mine. I have always enjoyed the aroma of her washed body. I smiled to myself, delighting again and again, valuing the closeness of my partner in life.

I put my arm over her shoulder. "I love you," I whispered. My hand deliberately grazed her warm, full breasts.

"What do they look like?" Maxine asked in a low, fatigued voice.

"They continue to look beautiful as always."

"Stop joking. I am talking about the girls."

"The girls? Oh, they're nice too," I teased.

"Come on. Please tell me."

"Well, it's complicated. They're tiny, it's difficult to describe. Let's wait until Wednesday. You'll see for yourself. I have seen them twice, and they change every day. I visited the nursery this past Tuesday, and then when I returned on Friday, they were different."

"What do you mean, different? How different?"

"In barely three days, they got bigger. They had grown. It was amazing."

"I remember Fred when he was born. I experienced the same."

Maxine was exhilarated, but I could hardly keep my eyes

open. My head sank into the pillow. Within moments, I was gone, floating into a yawning, bottomless sleep.

Despite her jet lag, Maxine was beyond excited. She could only think of Wednesday.

My wife turned to me and said, "Will I like them? Is this a mistake? Can I handle such a major commitment? Of course, I can. Or can I? How will Fred be with them?"

She tossed and turned. I felt Maxine rise and leave our bed. She closed the door behind her and silently moved into the living room.

From her window I knew she could see the flickering lights of the city dimming. Shanghai went from bright lights to a darkened, reluctant blue. The city was asleep, only she was awake. I guessed she'd switched on the television, trying to find a station that was not Chinese. After an hour or two, I got up myself to peek into the living room. There she was asleep on the couch. I covered her with a thin woolen scarf that lay on a chair nearby. I returned to my bed.

Hours later, I awoke. I looked at the clock on the night table; it was 2:45 a.m. I opened the bedroom door to the living room. With silent steps, I moved toward my lost-to-the-world wife. In an instant Maxine's eyes flew open. I was somewhat startled.

"Are you okay?" she mumbled.

"I'm good. I was just wondering about you. Come back to bed. It's lonesome."

Smiling, she rose. She slipped back into bed, her arm across my chest. "I love you," she said. I was happy.

5

Da Loban Makes a Serious Mistake

Author Narrates about the Hi Bo Mansion

Cissy and Shan climbed the long, circular staircase to a small bedroom on the top floor of the great house. Shan was breathless when she got to the top. The new maid peeked into a tiny bathroom that was situated very close by. The two girls were going to share the space. In the room were wooden beds with thin mattresses and clean white sheets, each covered by a thin clean woolen blanket. Cissy began to explain what she and Shan's responsibilities were daily.

Breakfast each day was at 6:30 a.m. Sally Nang, the cook, prepared the morning meal of hot rice porridge with soft prunes and green tea. Cissy then went on to discuss their daily chores.

"We begin our day by cleaning the toilets. After that, we go to the bedrooms, make the beds, and sweep and wash the floors. Then we go into the kitchen to remove the trash, as well as the rubbish in each room of the entire house. And finally we clean the back and front yards."

Shan listened. "Do we do that every day?" she asked. Cissy nodded.

"Once a week we wash the windows on the north side of the house, and the week after we clean the windows on the south side." Shan shook her head, wondering if she had the strength to take on so much responsibility.

"It sounds like so much to do," Shan responded. "But I promise you I will try to hold up my end of the chores."

Cissy went on. "In addition, we serve all the meals and clear the table. We wash and dry all the dishes, pots and pans, and chopsticks." Cissy smiled as she saw tears glow in Shan's eyes.

"Don't worry," she said. "You will get used to it. And it is not as hard as it sounds. Remember, there are only two people in the house to serve. But they do have guests often.

"Oh, I forgot this small part of the chores. Two or three times a week, one of us will go to the market with Sally Nang and Mrs. Hi Bo to assist with the bags of food for Da Loban and the staff."

"I think I would like to do that. I have not been to a village often."

"That, my dear Shan, is one of the most difficult jobs. The bags are large and usually very heavy."

"And which one of us does the laundry?" Shan questioned.

"Clothing is washed and ironed by Amy Wu, the laundress. She comes three times each week."

"That makes me happy." Shan smiled, as did Cissy.

"And TaiTai Hi Bo often has her breakfast in her room. At least once a day she inspects different parts of the great house. If an area is inappropriate, the person responsible will have to miss a meal — a reprimand for neglecting the job."

The Never-to-Be-Forgotten Sin

Madame Hi Bo was pleased that Shan was becoming more efficient at her work. She'd only been reprimanded once, thereby missing one meal, in her eight months at the big house. It was obvious to Madame Hi Bo that the new maid was not unhappy with her life. She'd overheard Shan telling Cissy that she was pleased with the regular meals, her own comfortable bed, the clean environment, and the pleasant atmosphere.

Mrs. Hi Bo began to look at Shan in a different way, as did her husband. She was a kind, hardworking young girl. They noticed she was trying to learn how to read and write. Cissy was giving her whatever knowledge she had to offer. It was a custom to keep the servants in their place without learning. Yet Cissy and Shan had become close. They worked together. They bonded, as do friends who have a lifelong history.

Shan was maturing and slowly taking on the appearance of a young and beautiful woman. Despite all the pleasantness surrounding her, during the years that passed, Shan Di missed her family. She thought of them frequently but could hardly remember what her younger sister and older brother looked like. She often wondered if Leong was still alive or well and in good health. She recalled how frail and hollowed out he'd looked. When thinking of her mother, in her mind she could only see an aging woman, unrecognizable to her.

"Cissy and Shan have been good for our family. Much better than previous help," Mrs. Hi Bo said to her husband.

"As you say, I did not notice," he said, pretending.

"It has come to mind that smart people make better workers and, for us, better servants."

"And this new conclusion takes you where?"

"Who do you think is the smarter of the two, Cissy or Shan?" He questioned.

"Please tell me what you have in mind," the husband demanded. Da Loban Hi Bo was getting exasperated. He knew his wife was attempting to manipulate his thinking.

"I have much time on my hands. And most every day I am bored with life. As good as our lives are, I want you to know that I am not with complaint. You are good husband and a smart businessman. I am your wife, and I am very proud of my life in this community."

Now Hi Bo knew there was some serious request on the way. His wife was being too complimentary on her path to getting something she wished for. He shook his head and smiled.

Reaching across the table, he touched her hand.

"I would like to teach Cissy or Shan to read and write. I need advice as to which one of the girls is smarter, in your most educated and experienced opinion." She spoke softly and with much deference, as is the custom for Chinese wives.

"That is out of the question," he said, his voice rising as his right hand flew straight up. "Who has ever heard of teaching maids to read or write?" His traditional point of view was now being challenged. Hi Bo was angry — very angry. "We will be laughed at by neighbors and friends. I will not allow it," Hi Bo bellowed his response in a firm and irritated voice.

His wife remained silent. She bowed.

"You must be losing your mind to take on such a task. You are the wife of Hi Bo, a respected and honored businessman in our community." He rose to pour some water from a pitcher at the bar. He gulped, coughed, and cleared his throat. "It is not proper to teach maids, nor is it face-saving for you, my wife, to engage in such an unthinkable plot. You are a lady of propriety and respect." His tone was strong, his opinion, inflexible.

Mrs. Hi Bo once again bowed in silence. "May I arrange some tea?" she asked. Hi Bo nodded.

The wife rang her little bell. In seconds Shan appeared. She bowed with eyes closed, not looking up, and asked, "May I be of assistance, Madame?"

"Please bring tea service for my husband," she responded coolly.

Shan disappeared into the kitchen. In a few minutes, the obedient maid returned with a cup of green tea, a plate of freshly baked cookies, and a white linen napkin next to a silver spoon. She presented it to Mr. Hi Bo. She bowed, speaking in a soft voice. "I hope Da Loban likes cookies. I baked them myself. Sally, the cook, taught me."

He smiled and looked at Shan in a special way. With tilted head, he placed his hand on a cookie, as he gazed at her girlish grin. She bowed, returned his smile, and departed the room quickly.

Hi Bo knew this was part of his wife's plot to convince him to allow the maid to be taught how to read and write. His wife always gave him tea with one cookie. Now he had tea given by Shan, with three cookies that the maid said she had baked herself. He was no fool. In his head he smiled, but his face remained grim and unshaken as he sipped the tea and slowly enjoyed the two extra delights that were on his plate.

My husband's strong voice is not as strong as it seems when he pretends to speak unkindly to me at times when we do not share the same opinion. His usual kindness toward me and toward everyone makes me realize how difficult it is for him to deviate from his old-fashioned opinions, which were passed down to him from his father and his father's father. Now I must think of how to reverse his decision. You old fool, Hi Bo. Keep your mouth closed when you are angry. Then you will have fewer regrets, her inner voice dictated.

Husband and wife remained silent. After a bit, TaiTai Hi Bo smiled and said, "Shan and Cissy, both good girls. Cissy has knowledge of reading. I would like to teach Shan. She is a fast learner. Forgive me. I just want to improve her and offer a small kindness."

"How much time do you wish to spend in this teaching business with Shan?" Hi Bo questioned.

"Two hours every other day."

"One hour," he said.

"Very well; you are Da Loban." She rose from her chair, took the empty cup and plate, kissed her husband on his forehead, and said, "*Tsitsi* (thank you)." She bowed and left the room.

For six months TaiTai Hi Bo spent an hour every other day teaching Shan.

Cissy was not envious. She was happy that Shan was learning to read and write. It would strengthen their sisterhood. She smiled when she saw her working closely with Madame Hi Bo.

During the teaching hour, Madame Hi Bo never requested anything from Cissy. All were conscious of the simple but considerate decision. From Cissy's point of view, the Hi Bo family's judgments were to be accepted without question. Still, she was aware of the sensitive decision of not asking her to serve Shan.

In February of the following year, Shan was reading books and writing letters to her brother, who, unbeknownst to Shan, had returned from the hospital cured of all his fevers and rashes. And though she wrote frequently, no answer ever came back to her. *Perhaps he died from his illness?* She thought.

Shan, in her selflessness, began to share her small education with Cissy. She devoured every word, and Cissy was also able to improve her reading and writing skills. In moments of mutual caring, they would embrace with a sense of love and sisterhood and then break away in laughter. They had become family. Cissy missed the closeness of her own sister and little brother back home.

March was a very busy month for the family of Hi Bo. Many guests came to their home from all parts of the world. Important clients of giant shoe companies came from Asia, Europe, and South America.

Each evening during the heavy buying and selling seasons, the great house was filled with guests. Extra servants were hired during these times. A helper was hired for Sally, the cook, and a cleaner was hired for the kitchen. Often there were as many as twelve or fourteen people for dinner.

The extra servants were guided by Cissy, who had been promoted to house manager, and Shan, both of whom taught them how to serve and patiently showed the staff where everything was. Cissy tended bar as Shan and the others helped with hors d'oeuvres, warmed, moist hand towels, cigars, and drinks of the guests' choosing. And though the girls worked hard, they enjoyed the parties. Hi Bo and TaiTai were always at their best as host and hostess. When the selling season was complete and guests no longer came, the house cleaned and spotless, both Cissy and Shan were given two hundred renminbi (Chinese money) as a bonus gift.

Hans Leopold was one of Hi Bo's largest customers from Zurich, Switzerland. During his visit, he stayed at the big house. Sang Ye Piao, a close colleague and a powerful Chinese business investor, gambler, and friend, joined the couple three or four times a year for meetings of business and investments. He was a man of silent strength, with great friendship and loyalty toward Hi Bo.

Herr Leopold, the owner of the largest footwear agency in all of Europe, Africa, and parts of the Middle East, would place orders four times each season during the year, totaling more than three million pairs of shoes. He would stay at the big house in a guest room on the second floor. It was spacious with a large bath, which was perfect for Hans; he was a huge man. He was tall and good-looking, with a smattering of gray hair in his sideburns and a small Van Dyke beard that was also turning gray. Hans was quiet and polite. He had excellent manners. He ate enormous portions of fish and vegetables and several cakes for dessert. He drank wine and beer in considerable quantities, more than anyone at the great house had ever seen. He was not boisterous but polite and soft-spoken. Though his lifestyle and eating and drinking habits were Swiss, he was always the gentleman, never rude or impolite.

Piao was the opposite of Hans. He enjoyed his privacy. For

the few days he was visiting Hi Bo, he stayed at the famous White Swan Hotel in Guangzhou. He ate and drank carefully. He seldom spoke, and instead he listened. He could hear and observe the expression on a face, the modification in the sound of a voice — features most people would ignore. He spoke four languages: Mandarin (his mother tongue), English, Russian, and Arabic. Piao's powerful connections throughout the world were an important asset. When Piao needed something or asked a favor, no one ever refused him. And the good turn was never forgotten. In private corners he was known as "the unspoken Asian godfather." Three times each year Piao would come to Guangzhou to visit his friend Hi Bo and conduct business in the city and Hong Kong. Piao was Chinese and lived far in the north.

Once a year Hi Bo would visit Hans in Switzerland and bring the many samples he'd developed for the meeting. Hans would place orders. Last year, of the more than three million pairs of shoes that were made in the Hi Bo factory, almost one-third were bought by Hans. This year the projection was for about 30 percent more. Business was good for both men and mutual respect was obvious.

Hi Bo's relationship with Sang Ye Piao differed significantly from the one he had with Hans. He and Piao would also meet in Macau for a few days of fun and gambling. Piao was well-known on the former Portuguese gambling island, now a territory of the People's Republic of China. When Piao entered a casino or a restaurant, his presence was treated with respect and deference. The two men discussed the business and new investments that Sang Ye brought to the table. Hi Bo knew that Piao was a clever and ruthless adversary. With this knowledge, he preferred to be the man's ally and a partner in the ventures his special friend presented to him as opportunities. In the early days of their friendship, Hi Bo made his position clear that he would never take part in any illegal business ventures. Thus their relationship yielded private opportunities that were not open to others. As a result, both men became wealthy.

In the morning, Hans and Da Loban drove to the shoe factory, just twenty kilometers from the big house. They spent the day reviewing the production of all the shoes Hans was going to order. Each day they poured over every design, testing the leather and assessing the fit with a young local girl trying the shoes on. They reviewed every detail again before the order was placed.

At the end of the day, the two friends retired to Da Loban's men's club, which included a bar, a casino, and a small restaurant. The guests played mah-jongg, poker, and a dice game called Over and Under. In this game, three dice were rolled. The player could bet in yuan that the total number rolled would be under six, excluding a two or three and over seven, excluding a twelve. It was the game that always saw the highest amount of money wagered. Many players were at that table. The room was filled with laughter, shouting, and cigar and cigarette smoke, and, of course, there was much to drink. The club rule was that members could bring only one guest. No women were ever allowed apart from the dealers, all seriously trained and well behaved, as the rules of the club called for.

The women dealers enjoyed the many generous tips and boisterous laughter rolling their way from the winners. Losers were also open-handed.

At 7:00 p.m., both men returned to Hi Bo's home for dinner. Everyone sat quietly at the dining room table. Cissy and Shan served these private dinners with care and respect. During the meal, as each course was meticulously served, Hans looked at both well-groomed servers with a careful but casual eye. The girls were young, pleasant, and very polite.

Hi Bo watched his guest's smiling glare at Cissy. He instructed Cissy, in Chinese, to stay in the kitchen to help the cook. Hi Bo was suspicious of Leopold's casual look. He had never seen that before. It was not an unusual incident. It had happened often with other guests. The two women were young and innocent in appearance. Neither was unattractive.

When dinner was over, the two men sat in the living room, smoking — a Havana cigar from Hi Bo's own humidor for Hans and an Asian pipe with Jamaican tobacco for the host. The conversation was about business and life in China and in Zurich. Hans spoke about his son, Bernhard, at the university, and his daughter, Nora, still in high school. The boy took after the mother's side of the family. The girl favored Hans and his side. Nora was smart and handsome like her father. She was more favored because of her good work ethic.

"My son, Bernhard, is a fine student. Unfortunately, like his maternal grandfather, he practically prays over each detail and every minor roadblock. I hoped he would be more like me and have my aggressive need to lunge after a goal. He is young; perhaps he will mature into a more determined man with our Swiss drive for completion and success."

"Tell me about your daughter."

"Ah, my Nora. She is an angel and a pest. I adore her. She is very similar to my mother: smart and sensitive, and she will weep at the drop of a hat. She speaks constantly, hardly taking a breath. And the girl makes me laugh. But most of all, I admire her work and business skills."

After an hour, Hans yawned. "We will have another full day tomorrow. I think it is important for me to rest now and read a little before retiring."

Mrs. Hi Bo asked Hans if he wanted a cup of tea before leaving for his room.

"May I have it in my room?" he asked.

"Of course, you can," Da Loban answered, wishing his longtime customer and friend a good night.

Cissy came out of the kitchen and helped Shan clean up the

table and the dining room. Cissy prepared tea and cookies for Mr. Leopold. Shan carefully took the tray up the stairs. She knocked on Mr. Leopold's door.

"Enter," he called out.

Shan Di, in hushed steps, carried the tray to a miniature table next to the bed. Hans was already half asleep. She put the tray down and looked at Hans with her eyes closed and her head bowed.

In one swift instant, and with a frightened shriek from Shan, Hans leaped from under the covers, totally nude. With an iron grip on her, he pulled Shan to the bed. She felt the power of his entire body as he thrust his hand toward her face, covering her mouth. Shan continued her muffled screams. With all his power, Hans forced her down on her back. In a frantic move, her nail dug into his face, grabbed his hair, pulling with all her strength. His hand was like a vice over her lips. Still she had the strength to tear the skin on the hand gagging her mouth. She bit deep with a piercing force, creating a huge gash. Instantly her face was covered with a spray of blood. He wrenched his hand from her mouth and wrapped a part of the bed sheet around it to stop the spurting blood. For that millisecond, Shan screamed.

Cissy, up in her room, clenched her hands over her ears and threw her face into the pillow, weeping hysterically.

Mrs. Hi Bo turned to her husband, shouting, "Do something. *Now!*" She pushed him wildly from their bed. She could not recall a single moment in their many years of marriage that she had spoken so disrespectfully to her husband. She felt shame and fear.

Within seconds, Hans forced his way into Shan's young body. After a few moments of thrashing, with her hands flailing at his body and face and her nails digging into his back, it was over … he was finished. He pushed Shan off the bed onto the floor like some foul piece of trash. She screamed in pain. Blood oozed from between her legs. Hans collapsed on the bed, facedown. His naked body was covered with scratches. Blood dribbled from his back and face.

Hi Bo rushed into the room, rifle in hand. He pointed the gun at Hans's head. Cissy and TaiTai followed. Lo Ban ordered the women to take Shan and help her. They quickly moved Shan's curled-up, sobbing body to the next-door bathroom.

Hi Bo looked at Hans with hatred in his eyes, pointing the gun first at his head, then moving it to his throat.

From the bathroom, Shan could be heard sobbing, "Oh Momma, oh Momma. He hurt me, he hurt me. I hate that animal." Her body convulsed in sobs as she moaned.

Hi Bo, his eyes open wide, screamed, "You come to my house as my guest. You have dishonored me and yourself. You have an insane mind to attack a harmless, innocent housemaid.

"My wife and I were sleeping below. You disgust me. You are an animal to hurt such a helpless child, no older than your own daughter. You are an inhuman disgrace. Take your things and leave my home this minute, before I kill you. I will not take your business ever again. I want you to leave right now — and never, ever return," he shouted in anger as never before.

Hans looked at Hi Bo in amazement. "Why are you in such an uproar? She is only a maid. You are a foolish man. I am your best customer. Are you prepared to make such a sacrifice? You will suffer if you lose my business over a mere ignorant servant … and a Chinese one at that. Don't you know that their kind love that treatment?"

Hi Bo could not believe his ears. *What is this man talking about? What is he doing in my house? I exposed my wife and my staff to this maniac. How could I have been so blind?* Hi Bo could hear the young girl in the next room weeping. He could not bear the pain she was experiencing.

In one swift blow, Hi Bo smashed the rifle into Hans's head, causing a deep wound. Blood streamed over the bed. "Get up and get out before I become a murderer!" he shouted.

"Move!" Da Loban commanded. "*Move!*" He smashed another blow with the butt of the gun into Hans's head, and another into his stomach. Hans fell back onto the bed in pain. "Move before I kill you," his breaking, gravel voice ordered.

"You are such a disgusting lowlife. You are an animal! You do not have the slightest clue of what sin you have committed against another helpless human being."

Suddenly two of the men from the gatehouse, having heard the commotion, rushed into the room. They took the gun from Hi Bo. Then they grabbed Hans, dragged him to the Iron Gate at the entrance of the property, and tossed him, nude, onto the dirt road. Moments later, a third man threw Hans's luggage and clothes at him as he lay on the bitter-cold, windblown road.

"You will regret this. This is not over," Hans shouted to the house. "I shall have my way with you, as I had with your little slut."

"No, it is not over," Hi Bo whispered to himself. *"Somehow you shall be severely punished."*

Upstairs, Shan lay in her room with her body twisted, curled up. The child was hysterical, a towel between her legs, red with blood.

"Help me, help me." She wept. "I feel dizzy." She placed her head into Madame Hi Bo's chest.

Madame Hi Bo held her close to her own body. "We must take her to the doctor, to the hospital."

"No, no," Shan shouted, crying. "I will be shamed. I will not allow anyone to see me this way. Please, Madame, please. I feel dirty. I am disgraced for the rest of my life. Oh my God. Oh my God." Her sobbing voice and her tears were uncontrollable. "Please, please, Poppa Hi Bo," she cried, "do not allow my life to be shamed."

Hi Bo commanded, "Get the guard staff to carry her to our car. We will take her at once. We do not want her to die." Then he whispered, "Do not worry, my dear child. I will arrange and demand everyone's silence."

Shan, in all her pain, said, "Thank you ... thank you." She wept with pulsating gasps of breath.

6

A Woman's Love Is the Most Powerful of All Life's Experiences

The Author Narrates

Guangzhou is no Shanghai. It is much different. Shanghai is a cosmopolitan metropolis, filled with both Asian and Western cultures. Its busy streets are packed with taxis and buses. There are shops of every size, selling thousands of different items, gadgets, and delicacies. Theaters, museums, extraordinary galleries, and restaurants fill its zigzag of streets and neighborhoods. There are multiple skyscraper office buildings and an equal number of luxury hotels.

You can hear the symphony of voices in many languages that include Italian, Swiss, English, and Mandarin and more as you stroll the boulevards.

Guangzhou is different. It is not as glamorous but has its own culture and is a highly populated province — approximately fifteen million people in a totally industrialized area.

The city is surrounded by factories with tens of thousands of workers producing clothing, auto parts, telephones, shoes, and countless consumer demands throughout the world. Ships are loaded with tons of containers filled to the brim, bringing product to all parts of the earth.

Maxine and Daryl, after their flight from Shanghai, were taken from the airport to the White Swan Hotel in Mr. Chen's car. The White Swan is a very comfortable residence for travelers doing business in this industrious province of Guangzhou, the province that hosts the Canton Fair. Daryl had attended the fair many times. It is an amazing presentation. This mind-blowing expo caters to tens of thousands of business people from every corner of the world. Each visitor, similar in their search, is hunting for that special product, the one with an unusually marketable price. The Canton Fair is known to manufacturers, retailers, and merchants throughout the entire global marketplace. It is impossible to cover the entire convention in one or two days. Four days to one week is a normal visit for foreigners. Daryl spent four days and was able to see just a little more than half the exposition.

Twice a year businesspeople come from every sphere of industry, filling each hotel, every restaurant, and each bus traveling to and from the fair. Reservations to attend the expo are made a year or more in advance. Daryl's reservation was made almost six months prior to the meeting he attended.

The thoroughfares of Guangzhou are lined with a forest of maple trees. They cover both sides of the many boulevards throughout the city, all carefully pruned. Scenic bushes trimmed in circular designs rest at each traffic intersection. It is not surprising to see older people with overlapping straw hats, protecting them from the sun, slowly sweeping each street. Motorcycles substitute for traditional taxis, with one or two passengers sitting behind the driver, zipping through the streets to their specific destinations. Daryl attempted to be a passenger on a speedy motorcycle once; it was, to say the least, frightening. And once was enough.

Avenues and side streets are crowded with cars and trucks. Buses filled with passengers on their way to work weave through the labyrinth of the city. This is another great Chinese municipality with millions of people working every day. It is not Shanghai, but it is a bustling environment jammed with busy lives everywhere. Although smog-covered, Guangzhou continues to amaze its foreign visitors and guests.

Maxine and Daryl rested that first morning. They ordered breakfast to be brought to their room. Both were experiencing impatience and an unfamiliar sense of anxiety.

"What time do we have an appointment to see the girls?" Maxine asked Daryl, looking out the hotel window.

"Mr. Chen will be sending his car to pick us up and take us to the orphanage by ten a.m."

Chen arrived exactly on time. He sat in the front with the driver, while Maxine and Daryl sat tensed up in the backseat. Within thirty minutes the car arrived at the orphanage. Chen's driver pulled up in front of the old building.

Maxine saw the ancient crucifix out front. "I am surprised that this is exactly the same as the one in my old neighborhood church in the Bushwick section of Brooklyn," she commented to Mr. Chen. "My mother was Jewish and my dad, Catholic."

"A very complicated match," Chen replied. "How much difficulty is there when children grow up with two different philosophies?" Mr. Chen questioned.

"On the Jewish holidays, we went to synagogue with my mom and grandparents. After synagogue we would go to my Grandma Hilda for some of the most wonderful dinners. During Christmas we went to church with dad, ending up at the home of Grandma Angie. Her house was happy and filled with a charming Christmas tree, glowing, wrapped gifts surrounding it. I have happy memories of both homes. When I was a child, we weren't rich, and hadn't a clue about money. I was a happy little girl having a great time."

Mr. Chen listened to the soft-spoken Maxine, enjoying her story and the gentle sound of her voice.

They stepped from the car and walked to the huge entrance door.

David Chen lifted the heavy knocker outside the massive oak door. As it collapsed against the entry, Maxine's face and nose twitched up. The sister greeted them with her soft voice, saying, "Welcome" in English and in Mandarin, "Nee how." They were invited into the orphanage. The building had a strange odor. Was it baby smells, or food cooking in the galley? It was unfamiliar.

Maxine, thinking, *I can hear my heart beating. I promise I will not to make any instant decisions. My mind's primary thoughts are of the children and their fit into our family. In spite of my inner-voice signals for caution, my head is slightly spinning. Oh, please stop.* "Please stop," she commanded her brain and her body.

"Did you say anything?" Daryl asked.

"No, I didn't. I was just thinking out loud."

Maxine's instincts continued to whisper: *We must think this commitment over very carefully. It is a major step that will affect everyone in our lives. Adopting will change things for Fred, for my brother and sister, and the rest of the family. It is huge, beyond huge. It cannot be decided upon instantly. We will go slowly. It is something that requires serious thought. And perhaps we may have to return to New York to think this over thoroughly, and even come back if we decide to adopt. I know in my heart that this is the only way. I am committed to going slowly and decisively. It must be well thought out. We should not make an instant decision that will affect our lives forever.* Maxine's brain and her heart were on a roller-coaster.

Daryl's mind was buzzing with apprehension; his teeth were clenched. It was an experience he'd never had before. There was a clutching, heart-pounding angst surrounding his body.

Maxine, Daryl, and Mr. Chen sat in the anteroom outside the nursery. Maxine searched the room. She saw the slightest touch of dust everywhere, dust that neither Mr. Chen nor Daryl would ever see. Her sudden sharp instinct could hear the tiny tots in the adjacent room breathing and gurgling. The sounds were like musical instruments, a classical sonata of life awakening. When the door opened occasionally, she could see the nurse nuns feeding, changing, and turning the babies. Her heart beat rapidly with each new scene. She involuntarily gulped. Her eyes blinked and blinked.

A young, delicate-looking girl, like a flower bending with the wind, came toward the guests. She entered as if floating — light as a breeze. She brought green tea and fresh-baked breads on a scratched but very clean old wooden tray. They all sat, quietly sipping. Mr. Chen reached for a tiny bread cake.

Mother Ting entered the room. They all stood. Mr. Chen bowed. Daryl put his hand forward to shake. Mother Superior accepted.

After introductions, in broken English, Mother Superior began. "Taking the lives of two girl-children is a challenging, much easier said than done decision. The children are gifts from God." The nun gazed deeply into Maxine's eyes. She took a deep breath, knowing how important her words were for the safety of the twins. She also knew this moment was an important lesson passed to the potential mother, if the meeting was successful.

"This moment in your life and the lives of the children cannot be thought of lightly. Mother and father must think with care on decision. Know that, Mr. Chen, we see very well." Turning to Maxine, she said, "He speaks highly of your husband. He said he's never met Mrs. Landsman, but that Mr. Landsman always speak of you in highest of good words about character and kindness. You are good wife to husband and good mother to son. I pleased that you have come long way to see children. Should you adopt girls and they be part of your family, God will bless your lives. Two children are much work, much worry, and much energy, usually for parents of much less age." A young nun ran in short, rapid steps with a chair and placed it behind Mother Superior, who sat quietly, waiting for a response.

"Thank you, Mother, for your warm greeting, your kindness, and your valued advice and wisdom," Maxine replied.

"Should you agree, from this day, much effort will be taken by you and by our ancient responsibility to assure children of good life and safe travel. You will have many documents to complete. It is required you go to American Embassy for visas, two for baby girls, and two for student nurses we send with you to help on your trip back to America. The students will return in five days, and you will have to promise all their expenses and safety. There are few other details. We can speak to them after you and Mr. Landsman make important decision."

Maxine sat in a daze, her head spinning. She did not hear most of what Mother Ting was saying. She heard the words and got the gist of them, but she was focusing on only one thing: she wanted to see the children. *Be calm, be calm,* she urged herself. *No hurried decisions. Oh God help me. I can't believe I am in China doing this. Why, why?*

Two young nurse nuns gave Maxine and Daryl each a white coat, a white mask, and a white hat, plus a pair of white gloves.

"Soon children come. You will see," Mother Superior muttered, unsmiling, serious, and cautious. She had been in this position many times. Often the hopeful mother did not like the child's looks, or the shape of the baby's head or feet, and the meeting would abruptly end.

Five minutes passed, then five more. It seemed like a century. Maxine was very nervous. *So, where are they? I will scream in another minute.* She held her breath; her chest was about to explode.

Maxine could not wait to see the children. Five more minutes, three minutes. Still they sat in silence, wondering, *where are they? When, when....* Finally, she could see from down the hall two nurse nuns approaching. Each carrying a child. Maxine, almost choking in fear, her throat dry; she gulped for air. *Oh my God*, she thought, while she masked her excitement in a high tension of total silence. There they were. She saw both children. They were tightly swaddled from the tops of their heads to their tiny toes. Her first clue was the sight of their perfect little round faces peeking through the swaddling. All she could see were eyes and their tiny noses. Her teeth and lips crushed against each other.

Maxine rose slowly from her chair, bracing herself with all her strength on her arms and wrists. With all her force, she balanced herself on the arms of the chair, her head just a bit dizzy, her breathing short and quick. One nurse held out a child toward her. Maxine trembled and felt she was going to faint. The nurses, with wide-open eyes, stared at her with a puzzled, almost frightened look, not knowing if this was going to be.

Mother Superior nodded toward Maxine. It was a silent signal for her to come forward from where she was standing to better see the children. In one brief, explosive moment, there they were. She saw the faces of both children and their teeny features. Two beautiful expressions peeked from the oval openings in their swaddling. Their eyes were wide open. Their tiny lips curled, and just a wee bit apart, as if to whisper and say to Maxine, *"Hello, Momma."* She could hear those words in her heart, in her head. Her arms reached out. One nun placed a child in her right arm. Maxine gazed down. The second nurse placed the twin child in her left arm. Maxine took a swallow of air; her chest heaved, and a deep gasp escaped her lips. The scene surrounding her was a shadow. Her focus was solely on the glowing that came from the little girls in her arms. Her eyes became blurred. And as swiftly as that feeling came, it disappeared.

Not a single word was uttered. The stillness was mysterious. The scene was hushed. With eyes wide open, the twins, both still, knew that this was an important moment in their lives. The

Momma trembled, looking from right to left and left to right, not lifting her head for a second. She stared at the girls. Gently a nurse nudged the swaddling from their heads to expose these two little blond children. Maxine flinched.

"Oh my," she gasped in surprise. A huge grin covered her face. The grin turned into laughter as she lifted her head and looked at Daryl. He smiled back to her and began laughing.

Daryl moved his lips. Maxine recognized the words often said. *I love you.*

"I love you back," she whispered.

Her heart was thundering. She was sure everyone could hear it. Again, she looked up. She gazed into Daryl's eyes. He stared directly at her in frozen silence, no grin, no laugh. Without warning, she burst into tears. Daryl wept with her.

"They are so beautiful, so beautiful," Maxine whispered. "I can't take my eyes from these two little girls," she sobbed.

Daryl looked at his wife. She held the children close to her breast, her voice wavering. "I knew instantly these two angels were my children, as if I had just given birth to them myself."

Tears tumbled from her eyes. She smiled, sobbed, and smiled again, taking in swallows of air. She paused, looking at the two helpless, adorable children. She held them tightly to her chest. The feelings that poured from her body told her that these two girls were not strangers. She was emotionally overwhelmed with a mountain of joy and happiness. Her senses were lost; only her overpowering maternal instincts ruled. *I am a woman; I am the mother of these children.* She looked at Daryl, the love of her life, who had also totally surrendered to the magic moment.

Maxine peered directly into her husband's eyes and uttered, "I love them."

"I love them with you," Daryl said. She held the infants close to her body. The twins continued to glow. They knew that their momma was holding them.

The new poppa turned to Mr. Chen. "David, do they take American Express here?" He asked, misty-eyed, with a proud grin breaking his ashen face. He moved toward Maxine and gently kissed her tiny left earlobe. She was weeping. Daryl whispered into her ear, "*Mazel tov (Congratulations)*, my love, mommy of our new twin *mishpachah* (family members)."

Daryl turned to Mr. Chen and Mother Superior. "It looks like we have found our own two beautiful daughters."

Mother Superior's lips quivered. She reached out for Mr. Chen's hand. He in turn grasped Daryl's hand as his friend simultaneously put his arm around Maxine's shoulders. Mr. Chen, Mother Superior, and Daryl silently, in a connected circle of life, surrounded the new mother and her daughters.

"Hello, my darlings. Welcome. Welcome to the Landsman family," Maxine cooed.

The sudden movements of each child were obvious: eyes alert, bodies in motion. Somehow, the children knew, they felt, that something wonderful had just happened. The three nurses standing close by began sobbing quietly. Two middle-aged people changed their lives as well as the lives of the two very blonde infants whom Maxine held tightly in her arms. They were hers and she was theirs; she was never going to let them go. God had smiled and blessed all of them.

"'Every child brings its own luck to the family,' my mother always said. *God must be a woman.*" Daryl smiled.

7

The Disappearance

On the morning of the second day after the attack on Shan, she turned her head toward the window. Each movement brought stinging pain, which twisted its tight, ugly web throughout her body. She lay in a bed at the People's Hospital in Dongguan. On the sill, a flowering plant raised its face to the painted sunlight. Shan's lips curved upward, not in a smile but in acknowledgment of another day. Her back ached from lying in one position for more than sixteen hours in a deep, welcome sleep of forgetfulness. She wished she could bury the memory of the violence she had experienced. The recall was reluctant. It would not leave her mind for an instant.

Shan Di lay motionless above and beneath a set of clean white sheets. Her toes were warmed by a blue woolen blanket folded at the bottom of her bed.

The bleeding from between her legs stopped. The rape trauma remained vivid, a mentally cruel picture — an experience never to be forgotten, nor forgiven.

Shan's face was inflamed from an apparent blow; her ribs ached. The area between her legs raw; the tenderness diminished by soothing vaginal cream. Her young brow furrowed as her mind sought unknown answers to mysterious questions. *Why me? Why me?* Her lips felt chapped. Seed-like particles filled the corners of her eyes. She breathed in and out, catching her breath, trying to understand the brutal attack. No answer came. Shan lay motionless, placing the back of her wrist on her eyes to block the constant vision of the assault streaming through her memory.

Dr. Ta Sun, a woman of about forty years old, with dark hair pulled back in a bun; her features were plain and expressionless. A white coat covered her dark suit. She turned to Mr. and Mrs. Hi Bo and spoke in soft tones. Her lips were tight. A grim look crossed her face.

"I am satisfied that she has slept for many hours. It will help her recuperate. I must confess, I have seen many such cases, but I shuttered when I saw strands of his blonde hair on her fingernails." Her voice turned to a whisper. The doctor, an obstetric specialist and surgeon, offered simple, understandable explanations. She attempted not to be overbearing, but her appearance demonstrated a twist of unspoken despair.

As Shan lay in her bed, she did not hear what was being said.

"There was complete penetration, with definite evidence of sperm within. We have no clue as to whether she was ovulating. How old is she?" the doctor questioned.

"Perhaps fifteen or sixteen years old is my guess," Hi Bo responded.

"Is she not your daughter?" the doctor questioned, slightly puzzled.

"Thank Buddha, no. Shan is our servant girl and has been working for our family for about a year."

"I have seen this before. The only wound will be the mental and emotional one. I do not believe that science has a cure for that. Let us hope that there will be no … lifelong evidence of this horrific moment in her young life."

"Is it possible that she…?" Da Loban's voice wandered off, unable to finish his sentence.

"Anything is possible. She is young and healthy. It is a rare result, but it could happen. Try not to worry about it. Be kind and gentle. It will help her return to health rapidly. However, much rest is needed," the doctor advised, standing tall and mournful.

❧

At the big house, after having spent a week in the hospital, Shan began her chores, despite the fact Da Loban and his TaiTai suggested that she rest as the doctor ordered.

"I must take care of my responsibilities. Doing my share helps me. May I ask if you would continue with my lessons? I appreciate what you are doing for me," Shan said.

Mrs. Hi Bo dropped her head slowly as an expression of assent.

Autumn leaves had turned golden orange. The fall was in its height, preparing to pass into winter.

Four months flew by. Shan had gone through a period of nausea every day for a month. She sat near the toilet puking on an empty stomach. When she arose and returned to her room, Mrs. Hi Bo was there. She recognized the symptoms. "Have you had your monthly woman time?" She questioned.

"No, I had not noticed," Shan responded in total innocence. Madame Hi Bo left the young woman, who then lay quiet in her room.

With her face tightly clenched, and feelings of fear and despair, the mistress of the house walked into her husband's office, experiencing sympathetic nausea and vaginal pain.

"We must be prepared," TaiTai addressed her husband.

"Prepared for what?" he asked.

"Please sit down next to me."

"Yes, what is it that we must be prepared for?" he questioned again as he sat.

"I am positive that our little Shan is with child."

The vast room became silent. You could hear the early spring leaves rustle on the trees. A floorboard groaned upstairs, and there was water flowing in Sally's kitchen. Hi Bo cleared his throat. "Are you actually telling me that Shan is going to have a baby?" His puzzled eyes pleaded. He pushed his twisting finger into his ear, as if to gain clarity for what was about to be explained.

"I am not only telling you, my honored husband; I am insisting that we recognize this coming event."

"How can you be so certain? You have had no children; what makes you an expert?" he demanded.

"I am not a trained person. However, my lack of experience and firsthand knowledge does not prevent me from recognizing the signs that are so obviously clear."

"What are those clues you so willingly accept?"

The wife sat facing her husband. Involuntarily clenching and opening her hands, she rang the bell to call for Cissy. "Please get wine for me and whiskey for Da Loban." Cissy returned quickly with drinks on a tray. TaiTai sipped the wine; her husband put his whiskey glass to his lips, threw his head back, and swallowed, all in one movement.

"A few months ago, I remember," TaiTai began, "our Shan began experiencing frequent nausea. This is a first sign, but not a definite one. I also noticed her breasts had enlarged. Another signal, but she is maturing, I thought. Finally I asked her when she'd had her last period. She could not remember. I have put all those simple but accurate facts together, while adding to those truths the horror of that night. I am positive that our lovely, intelligent young housemaid will have a child sometime in June or early July. If I recall accurately, that villain Hans was here in mid-October."

"What are we to do? What can we do?" Hi Bo asked, his voice filled with anxiety.

"We must help her, talk to her about what is happening to her body, and prepare her for whatever is in store for her," she answered.

"What do we know about a woman with child? We have no experience," he said.

"No one knows what to do the first time. We will deal with each change as it happens."

"That horrible, disgusting animal; I should have shot him on the spot." Hi Bo spat out his enraged, furious words.

One night, as Shan wretched and wept, Cissy sat next to her on the floor of the toilet. Neither spoke a word. When Shan was calm again, Cissy helped her up and led her back to her room. Cissy crawled into the bed beside Shan, put her arms around her, and held her close to her body.

"Oh, what am I to do? I am going to have a child. How will I care for it? I have not a clue."

"You and I will manage together, right here in this house. Mr. and Mrs. Hi Bo are generous people. I have heard them speak of you and offer some solutions. They are concerned for both you and the child. Try not to worry; the future is in God's hands." Cissy, as kind and caring as a sister, tried to comfort her friend and partner.

"I know my God. I know She will not abandon me." They slept quietly together in a sisterly embrace, the elder comforting the younger sister.

A baby is about to have a baby, Cissy thought just before falling asleep.

On June 24, Shan Di gave birth to twin girls.

Without hesitation, and without discussion with the new mother or anyone else, Hi Bo and his TaiTai, in a moment of unthinking desperation and fear, took the infants to the Catholic orphanage and knocked on the heavy door. A nun responded. Madame Hi Bo spoke in quick, breathless sentences.

"Please take these two helpless and abandoned children. Take care of them. We are too old to be responsible. Here in this envelope is seven thousand yuan," she said, handing over approximately one thousand American dollars. The couple turned and left. The young student nun held the children, one in each arm, with the envelope in her teeth. She stood helplessly holding the infants.

Frightened to death and with eyes wide open, she turned and took the girls into the orphanage, kicking the door closed. Hi Bo and TaiTai drove off in the early-morning mist covering the road, their hearts beating, their eyes teary, their minds plagued with torment and shame.

How could we have done what we just did to two actual human beings? For sure we will be punished. These thoughts swept through the mind of Madame Hi Bo.

"I see the pain on your face. Remember, they are only girls, only girls," her husband said.

"But what if they had been boys?"

"I do not know, I do not know. For sure we will be penalized." He tortured himself, glaring into the early morning light, not clear in his mind and unsure of himself as he nervously drove for the first time in more than twenty years.

"I'm convinced we will be condemned to death with me behind the wheel."

Both sat in silence with their sense of judgment as their car moved slowly back to the iron-gated house. One man stepped out from the little guardhouse, opened the gate, and saluted. "Good morning, sir. Good morning, Madame Hi Bo. Hope you have a very nice morning. Good to see you behind the wheel again, Da Loban." The guard bowed.

Hi Bo and his wife sat dishonored in Shan's room. They

remained there, holding each other's hands. Hi Bo whispered to his wife, "This is my fault. I am to blame. I should have been wiser. I endangered everyone in the family. Our poor Shan suffered the most. My business blinded me. Oh mighty Buddha, please forgive me."

Shan stirred. "Thank you for helping me, Momma," she whispered. The couple looked at each other, startled, but did not answer.

"The baby has gone to a safe place," Madame Hi Bo began.

"To heaven?" she questioned.

"Like heaven."

"I do not understand. I always dreamed that God loved me. Why has She done this?" Her words drifted as her body began throbbing into tiny sobs.

Hi Bo and his wife stared at each other in disbelief. "God is a She?" He was puzzled. "Our Shan is no doubt delirious."

After a week had passed, Shan was ready to return to the big house. She sat up in her hospital bed and looked at TaiTai and Hi Bo. *They look so serious and worried. What are they going to tell me? Are they going to dismiss me before my loan is paid? Has my shame caused them to be angry? Oh please, my God, let this not be,* she prayed.

"We know you are Christian. And you know we are Buddhists. Our teaching is that there are Four Noble Truths that exist in the life of man and woman. My child, at this moment in your life you should only think of one truth that we believe in. It is the Third Noble Truth. It is called, *nirodha,* the cessation of suffering, which means an end to grief and all anguish."

Hi Bo spoke tenderly, with sympathy and kindness. "The Buddha taught us that the way to extinguish desire and bodily pain, causing misery, is to liberate oneself from attachment. It means to clear your mind of any evil, revenge, or hatred. Once you do this, the pain and distress will end."

Shan looked up at Da Loban. She heard his voice and his words. She reached out to him and touched his hand. He turned his head ever so slightly and gazed at his TaiTai. Madame Hi Bo leaned toward the girl and kissed her forehead. "Stay quiet and try to get well, my little Shan."

Shan fixed her eyes on Hi Bo, trying to absorb the words. The sounds that came from him were a puzzle. She turned to the closet and took her bag. The three, as one, left the room.

The car moved slowly to the front door of the great house. Hi Bo sat in the front seat next to the driver. TaiTai and Shan sat in the back. The driver was confused.

8

The Power of the Chinese Government

Daryl Narrates

Our car pulled into the Delta Airlines terminal at the Beijing airport. Sally, Chinese nanny number one, held the littlest twin child, Sing Ye, while Tami, nanny number two, cradled LangPi, who was a bit stronger and more awake than her sister. The car behind us was filled with diapers, baby powder, and dozens of bottles filled with boiled formula.

Maxine and I stepped from the sedan, helping the nannies with our two new American citizens.

In an hour and a half we would be off to New York's JFK airport. Sixteen and a half plus hours later, we'd finally be at home with our daughters.

We presented the travel documents to the Chinese immigration clerk: US passports, adoption documents, visas, and immunization papers, plus visas for the nannies' five-day stay. The clerk inside the customs cage eyed each of us with a suspicious look, and perhaps a look of anger. He requested that Maxine and I remove our sunglasses. He examined our passports and stared at our photos and faces, finally thumping our documents with a huge leather stamp.

We were not finished yet. Carefully, he examined our

credentials and stamped them one by one. With every approval of departure, the immigration agent sharpened his eyes, scrutinizing all of us. We arrived as two, and now, as if some magic wand passed over us, we were returning home as six.

It was a miracle we'd never expected, an unbelievable moment for Maxine and me. I knew that I would never experience the feelings that rushed through my heart, my brain, and the very essence of my existence again. This was me, myself, and my wife, bringing two children I had only seen them for the first time less than two weeks ago ... and I was madly in love with them.

The customs official worked slowly with a curious sense of accuracy and care. A long line of passengers stood behind our new family. The agent counted six people, six visas, and six passports and finally asked the two nannies why they were going to the United States with our family. Each explained separately in Mandarin that they work as nurses at the Catholic Center for Distressed Children in Guangzhou, adding that they'd been hired to assist with the adopted children, after which point they'd return to China.

The immigration agent stamped the visas and passports and finally instructed all of us to proceed through security and then go on to the departure gate. Because there was still one hour prior to departure, I led my new family to the Delta First Class Lounge.

Weary travelers oohed and ahhed at our precious twins. "Congratulations" and "Good luck" greeted us wherever we stopped. Waiting passengers asked to take photos. This scene was repeated by many other travelers, mostly Americans. We smiled and nodded at each kind and warm gesture. Suddenly baby LangPi began to cry with all her energy. Nanny Sally quickly moved into action, removing a bottle of formula from the overstuffed carry pack with all the baby paraphernalia packed for the flight. Sally, unhurriedly, with poise, changed the baby's diaper. It took only a moment or two for little LangPi to resume her happy, quiet disposition. Sally was an angel and a magician.

Maxine turned to me. "I wish we could take the nannies with us forever. They are so efficient, and the girls would learn to speak Mandarin."

"They too have family and ties here in China. It would be okay for a few months, but we agreed that they would return in one week, and not longer," I answered. "We will find proper assistance. We'd better. I'm too old for this." I was happy. "The girls will definitely learn to speak Chinese. That's a promise."

An announcement came over the loudspeaker: "Thirty minutes to board. Families with children may board first." We all left the lounge, thanking everyone for their good wishes and kind words. At the gate we offered our boarding passes and showed our passports.

As we were about to enter the Boeing 747, from out of nowhere, two police officers and one soldier, the latter armed with an automatic rifle, stepped up to the boarding gate. In perfect English, the officer who appeared to be in command said directly to me, "Sir, may I examine your departure documents?" I reached into my inside breast pocket and showed all the papers that we had procured from the Catholic agency and the Chinese People's Republic of Immigration.

The officer slowly viewed each and every piece of paper stamped with an official chop and signed by the Catholic Church and other Chinese adoption department officials. All were in order.

The officer demanded, "You do not have departure documents for the children. I cannot allow you to remove Chinese children from the sovereign state of the People's Republic of China without the official departure documents." He stood there, still, firm, and erect. The other men stood down. They waited. Our quiet fear became sheer fright for a moment. I remained silent. *I do not want to antagonize him. Let's try a little politeness.*

"Officer, is it possible that you may be mistaken? According to all Chinese adoption rules and regulations, we have everything we require, co-signed by the official mayor of Guangdong. I insist you reconsider and allow us to board."

"You insist? You can insist on nothing. Trying to cajole me is a Western custom that I am quite familiar with. While I am in command, only I can insist," he stated, his voice sounding like an oncoming storm, harsh and intimidating. The officer looked at us with scorn on his face.

I was not frightened. I returned his look, and said, "You have no idea who I am." I bluffed. "Are you sure you want to go through with this tactic and delay our departure?" I demanded.

"I do not appreciate your tone of voice. You, sir, are in my country. You will follow the rules and the laws of China. And you will speak respectfully." Maxine turned to the officer. "Please, sir, we have worked and traveled far for this moment to be able to take our daughters home with us." I looked into my wife's eyes; they were flooded with tears. Her face was ashen, and in a moment of explosive feelings, she began to sob uncontrollably.

"Crying will not help you or these children; only the document of departure will," the commander asserted. His face was ice. He stood there, posturing, with his hand at his side resting on his revolver. My poor Maxine's release of emotion did not move him.

The captain of the plane came from the cockpit. "This is not the first time this has happened on my flight," he whispered to me.

"The Chinese resent when foreigners take children from their country. It is not easy. How would you feel if Chinese people were taking American children to live with them in this country? Not so good, I would guess." The officer gave his approval for Maxine and the nannies to board. All did so with the exception of my two little Chinese children. I stood there, cautious, unafraid, but a little concerned, holding the babies, one in each arm.

The captain put his hand under my arm and pulled me aside. "I think a few hundred US dollars would do the trick, and make this go away."

"Thank you," I replied. "But I will not give him a single cent. I have been doing business in China for many years, and I have never given anyone a bribe. I will not start with his refusal for us to legally take our children home."

"You're the boss." The captain returned to his plane.

This son of a bitch wants me to give him a few hundred dollars? That would make all this easy. I am not going to do that. He may be setting a trap that could cost thousands and perhaps land me in jail. No bribes today, my friend, my inner voice instructed. My strategy and my tone changed. I had a plan. Or I thought I had a plan. I became more solicitous. I moved from my tough business character to my winning people skills. They had always rewarded me with the goal I wanted to achieve. "I am sorry that I do not have the departure documents. It was most likely an oversight by the staff that assisted me. Please have someone hold the children while I look once more through all my papers. Maybe they are in this bag that we carry for the children's travel needs."

The officer called one of the soldiers and another police officer to the scene. I carefully put a child into the arms of each man. I began to rummage through everything, knowing full well that no such documents existed. After a few moments, I looked up at the officer. "No luck. That being the fact, we cannot take our children with us until we get their departure documents. Am I correct?"

"You are precisely correct," the Chinese commander responded in a clipped voice, still in a frozen, rigid position.

In a quiet and composed manner, I said, "Here, then, is the only solution I can offer. In this bag are diapers, milk in bottles, water, and everything else the children require. I will return to

Beijing in six weeks with the departure documents and take the children with me at that time. Please take good care of them. We love them very much." My heart was exploding. My head was spinning. I was not solid on my feet.

That said, unruffled, I turned my back to the officer and gave my boarding pass to the Delta agent. She placed her hand to her lips and gasped. I could hear her say, "Oh my, sir, do not do that. Do as our captain suggested."

I politely ignored her plea. Upon entering the plane, I sat down in the first row of the first-class section, seat 1A, next to Maxine, who was in seat 1B. I strapped myself in and sat back next to a startled, disbelieving Maxine. I looked into the cockpit and saw a gasping pilot and flight crew.

"What have you done? What have you done? Are you insane? Have you left our children in China?" Maxine cried, gritting her teeth, punching my shoulder. My heart was pounding, but my poker face remained unchanged.

The flight attendants announced the departure and explained the usual safety rituals. One of the attendants requested that everyone make certain they were strapped in and had all electronic devices shut off.

Maxine, pale and trembling, a deluge of tears flowing from her eyes, clutched my hand with all her strength. She opened her purse reaching for money. I pressed my hand against hers.

The flight attendant approached the door to shut it. In a few moments the plane was to depart, leaving the twins abandoned in the care of the Chinese officer and his aides.

As the plane door was inches from being closed, two officers appeared and pushed the door back with a thrust. The children were in their arms, tiny smiles on their handsome Asian faces. They saw me, placed the girls in my arms, and put the bag with all the children's needs next to me. They looked at ne, a glimmer of a smile on their faces. I took a hundred-dollar bill I had hidden in my hand and gave it to one of the soldiers. He saluted and clicked his heels with a quick bow.

The cabin remained silent. Every passenger was aware of this tense moment. In a burst of excitement, many of them applauded. Others cheered. One called out, "Congratulations" in Swedish; another said the same in French. A skull-capped passenger said the familiar words to my ears, "*Mazel tov.*" Unbeknownst to everyone, I almost had a heart attack.

Their mother turned to me. "You took the risk that the officer would not want to take care of our girls?"

I turned to all the first-class passengers and announced, "Drinks and dinner are on me." Everyone laughed and applauded. All the passengers knew that in first class, dinner and drinks are included in the price of the ticket. I moved my shoulder close to Maxine and explained his motives.

"I felt that SOB wanted a bribe. He did not want the children. He wanted me to give him five hundred dollars or more. I was not going to do that. The captain told me that this type of incident has happened before. The twins were only a ploy. The officer wanted money. He had a choice: explain his actions to his superiors or return the girls to us. He did not want to tell his supervisors his make-believe story of departure documents. He knew they did not exist. I took the risk that he would back down. I knew the odds were in our favor. And we won." I hesitated for a moment and then got up from my seat. "Maxine, will you hold the girls for a while?" I quietly and very calmly asked.

"Where are you going now? We are about to take off," she pleaded.

"I am going to the toilet to do two things. One of them is ... throwing up."

9

What's in a Name? Everything.

The Author Narrates

Everyone was there. Not a single member of the family was absent when the Landsman clan arrived at JFK airport. Nancy, the housekeeper, and her handsome son stood there excited. Also glowing with anticipation were Maxine's sister, Yvette; brother, Irv; and mother, Shirley. The most important greeter was little Fred. He wrapped his arms around his mom's legs, hugging her. Daryl lifted his son high off the ground.

Each friend and family member greeted the new household with feelings of amazement. There were many tears. In everyone's mind was the courage and insanity of this fifty-five-year-old man and his forty-eight-year-old wife, changing everyone's lives, above all, their own. It was a morning engulfed in total pleasure, smiling tears, and nervous laughter. The moment was a *simcha* (joyous event). One could see the happy but skeptical look in Grandma Shirley's eyes. She knew the work, the heartbreak, the colds, and the fevers that were yet to come. For that brief moment she rejected the bliss and the love that children bring to a parent and thought instead of often heartbreak.

"What are their names?" Fred asked, now the eldest child and given the new title of big brother. Eight-year-old Fred was swimming in his own personal enthusiasm. He had been an only child, safe and loved, and was not aware of the changes to come. It was as if someone had clicked on a light in his room, and poof, he became one of three children in the family. His young mind explained that they were a basketball team of five, believing he was still the star and the twins were on the bench, for now. He felt something inside him, a signal he could not explain; it was new and strange, an unknown sense of responsibility at the age of eight.

"What are their names?" he asked again.

"We have not decided yet. We thought that you would help us with that. And whatever we choose, we must find the Chinese translation. They will know their heritage."

"What is heritage?" Fred questioned his dad.

"It is your background. Like Grandma and Grandpa are Jewish from Lithuania and Poland. That is my culture, my heritage," Daryl explained.

"Am I Polish also?" Fred continued to probe.

"Part of your background and mine is. Mostly our culture is Jewish American. Just like Italians are called Italian Americans and black people are called African Americans. Got it?"

"Got it!" the little guy responded.

"But," Daryl said, hesitating, "and this is a big but: in our Jewish culture a child is what the mother is."

"Why?"

"There is never any doubt about who the mother is."

"Why?" Fred questioned again.

"The answer to that question will come when you are older. When we arrive at home, we will all sit down and think of some appropriate names," responded the proud father of the twin girls and their eight-year-old brother.

How can I explain to Fred the philosophy and the absolute truth? We know who the mother is 100 percent of the time. We can see the child in the act of birth, there is no question. But who the father is has historically been in question. Daryl smiled with his thoughts.

"Daddy, Mom's father is Irish. Am I Irish also?"

"You know, that's an interesting question. Come to think of it, you are part Irish."

"Wow, I am part Jewish, part Irish, and don't forget, part Polish and that other country. I can't remember the name." The little guy grinned.

Daryl looked down at his son. He smiled at the sudden realization his boy was experiencing. "You got it, my boy. You are all four, which includes Lithuanian. And you know what that makes you?"

"What, Dad?"

"It makes you a real American."

"And don't forget, I am also a Mets fan. That's real American. Can we name one of my new sisters Mookie, after Mookie Wilson the ball player?"

Daryl and Maxine's son, Freddie, was an unusual child. Over the past eight years they had watched as he overcame some child-learning issues. Maxine jumped in like a lioness caring for her cubs. Slowly but assuredly, with professional guidance, they noticed the tiny leaps their son was making in his knowledge stream. The boy knew most of the names of the players on the New York Mets. He could also recite verbatim news capsules he listened to on the television. His grades in literature were increasing to a new level of intelligence. His math skills and comprehension were showing signs of serious growth. He was on his way to brilliance. That's the father talking.

Fred knew from his own name, after his grandfather, the value and importance of naming someone. He did not yet understand the tradition, but he knew its value.

Daryl grinned. Hugging his son, he reached out to Maxine, grasping her extended hand. Both beamed and gazed at each other, grateful for the moment. *This is going to be … well, we will see,* Daryl thought as a complete flow of pleasure surged through him. The adoration of his son was at maximum. As Daryl looked around the room at his newly arrived daughters and his son, he was pleased and thankful. He experienced total love for his three children. It was all embracing and a never before encounter with his feelings. It was complete, without the slightest doubt. Daryl never thought a parent could love so absolutely.

He turned to Maxine. "I wonder if my mother loved me as much I love our kids."

"I think you are getting signs of dementia in your old age. Of course she did. And if not" — she paused — "you got me, honey."

They both laughed. He hugged her and planted a kiss on her welcoming lips.

Daryl's driver was waiting for the family at the airport when they arrived. The driver invited a friend of his to bring another car so everyone and the luggage could arrive home comfortably.

The two cars, fighting their way through New York City traffic, finally arrived at their home on Central Park West. The doormen rushed to their aid, taking cases and packages from the cars. Words of congratulations came from everyone in the lobby. It did not take long for all the Landsman's friends and neighbors to enjoy the news that twins had just moved into the Landsman home.

Neighbors gossiped. "I didn't know Mrs. Landsman was pregnant."

"How old is she?" Another neighbor whispered.

"Aren't they too old to have kids?" A third questioned.

Janet from the top floor said, "You are all so unkind. Mr. and Mrs. Landsman adopted twins from China. Isn't that wonderful? Just think of it. In their seventies they will have children still at home. They are very smart people."

Daryl and Maxine's apartment had taken on a different look.

No, not different — it was new, and the atmosphere had changed. It was now a home with little children, filled with a twins' carriage, a double stroller, two cribs, tons of diapers from Costco, and every conceivable baby requirement times two. All the baby needs filled an empty bedroom.

"Maxine," Daryl called, "a friend of mine suggested that a small ad in the New York Chinese newspaper might ensure that we get people to help who are bilingual. Do you think it's a good idea?"

"It can't hurt," she agreed.

A few days later, Daryl and Maxine spoke at dinner.

"That was valued advice. It brought us ten résumés and many telephone calls. I think it will not take long to find two Chinese women to be nannies."

A few days later, Daryl said, "Can you believe that in three days we found sisters who are both experienced and have excellent twin care references?"

The new parents decided that each nanny would work a shift of eight hours spanning seven days overlapping, with different days off.

"Now I am at ease that the children have ample care every day," Daryl announced.

"Sweetheart," he said to Maxine, "I am leaving it all in your hands. Ensure that the aides are each given comfortable beds and a new TV. Do you agree?" he asked.

"I have already purchased a new TV for the room adjoining the nursery. And I told Nancy that she was in charge. I also gave her a twenty-five dollar a week raise." Maxine shook her head. "He always thinks that he is the boss taking care of everything." she murmured.

Daryl grinned. "You are the best. And I want to tell you how pleased I am that the nannies speak to the girls in a Chinese dialect, whispering to them in a loving way."

He knew that his girls would be bilingual, a plus for a lifetime. The aides were not totally fluent in English, but their language skills were sufficient. Their daughters would have a valuable tool throughout their lives. He also recognized that the future was in both the United States and China. Having the skills of speaking Mandarin and English would give his children a head start, placing them far ahead of their peers.

Two weeks quickly passed. The family and many friends gathered at the Central Park West Synagogue close to their home on a sunny Sabbath morning for the traditional naming ceremony.

The rabbi recited the prayers of health and happiness and discussed the joys of being a good Jewish woman. He repeated the prayers from the Torah, kissed the ancient scriptures while wearing his prayer shawl, turned to Maxine, and asked the name of the child she was holding.

"Samantha Sing Ye Landsman," she recited.

"And your other daughter?" he asked the father.

"Lauren LangPi Landsman," he answered.

"What are their Jewish names?" the rabbi asked.

Maxine and Daryl looked at each other. They had forgotten this part of the ritual.

Silence filled the podium. "Sarah." Maxine grasped the first Jewish name she thought of.

In a whisper, Daryl added, "And Rachel," remembering his grandmother's name.

Two more prayers were spoken. The rabbi asked Daryl to recite a few Hebrew words from the Torah, and for Maxine to repeat the rabbi's prayer from the holy book for the children, one word at a time. He presented them with an official naming certificate for each girl.

"*Mazel tov*," the rabbi concluded.

Grandma Shirley had tears in her eyes. Her husband, a nonpracticing Catholic, smiled with delight at the event. At the age of seventy-eight, it was the start of a new beginning. Still working every day at his job, Grandpa was an amazing man. A deafening "*mazel tov*" was shouted by the entire congregation. Everyone cheered.

Little Fred looked up at his dad. "Pop, did they name one of my sisters Mookie?"

The entire assembly left the synagogue and gathered in a reception room. An oval-shaped wooden table was filled with traditional kosher food: gefilte fish (stuffed white fish), red horseradish, roasted chicken, rugelach (little cakes), wine, soft drinks, and a huge challah (kosher-style bread). Maxine frowned just a bit; outside the clouds blocked the sun-filled day. As quickly as they came, rays of sunlight peaked through the overcast and into the synagogue windows. The twins slept through the entire ceremony and celebration, but they already had their own blessing: three weeks earlier in an orphanage in Guangzhou eight thousand miles away.

10

The Brother of Shan Di

Leong Chan had not seen Shan Di for perhaps fifteen years or longer. It was a time when she was a child and he a very sick youngster. His sister was a mystery to him. His illness over such a long period as a boy made his memory imprecise. If he were to pass his baby sister on the street, he doubted he would recognize her. His memory of Shan Di was almost nonexistent. In his mind she was a young girl, helpless and ignorant. Lately, she was on his mind. Now at the age of twenty-seven, he calculated that Shan was about twenty-three years old. Her sweet and innocent face that he recalled was now just a shadow in his memory. She'd been about twelve or thirteen years old. He was not clear when last he'd seen her. It was the time when he left for the clinic where he was diagnosed with scarlet fever. After years of treatment, he'd finally recovered. It was indeed a miracle, as many died from the epidemic at that time in China.

Education is free in China at the university to those students who earn a minimum grade of a B– average. Leong was one of those fortunate students.

He'd studied and worked hard as an undergraduate, completing his education with a degree in languages. Leong spoke

French and English fluently and had learned about fifty words of Spanish.

After graduation he hounded company after company, persistent in his search for the right position. He was relentless in seeking out the job most suited to his skills and personality.

Six months passed. The young graduate student was finally hired as a trainee at an import-export company in Guangzhou. His total commitment to his job, working six full days each week, successfully fulfilling his assignments, listening and learning, resulted in a special position after two and a half years at Asia Wholesale Corporation (AWC). Management appreciated his ambitious energy and talent. He turned out to be the go-to person for problem solving for all their Western customers. His language skills enhanced his business acumen. The company sent him everywhere in Europe and Asia. He also traveled throughout China, as far north as Mongolia. He was physically strong, smart, charming, and attractive. He had been blessed. Leong was a welcome sight to the isolated businessmen and factory owners in the far-flung corners of China and Mongolia.

He possessed a keen sense of his value to AWC. He was constantly invited to the homes of many factory owners for dinner and casual conversation. On numerous occasions, he was offered a room to stay for the night. The underlying ploy of the factory owners and businessmen was to introduce this smart professional to an unmarried daughter or niece. Leong was no fool. A good marriage would be helpful for his life and career. It was the tradition in China for thousands of years for the father to select a husband for his daughter. On his decision she had no choice but to obey. The father could select a fifty-year-old man for his fifteen-year-old daughter — or even an older man.

Leong was an achiever, negotiating and traveling as he worked relentlessly and brought to his employers a plethora of new financially strong suppliers and customers. These contacts and new clients were a powerful tool of great interest to the owners and managers, as they benefited AWC. This empowered Leong as a valued employee, with his constant dream of the time when he might be offered a partnership, a rare opportunity in China with its culture steeped in nepotism. He was not the son or nephew of any of the higher-ups at his company, which narrowed his opportunities. It was the entrepreneurs who envisioned him as a family asset, a possible convenient match to one of their own.

Leong was a traditional and responsible son. Each month he sent two thousand yuan (about $175) to his mother and youngest sister, who were still living in their small village. It was a great help to them. He knew how difficult their lives were. His mother was getting older, and his father was not well. Leong was constantly aware of the sacrifice they'd made in giving up their daughter Shan Di in exchange for the money they needed to improve his health. They never spoke about their daughter; her name was never brought up. It was as if she did not exist. She'd become an invisible memory. Still he felt that his sister was the true victim. He secretly felt ashamed of the ancient tradition of valuing a son more than a daughter. *Where is she? What has her life been like? Is she married? Does she have children?* For Leong the mystery of his sister was constant. Would he ever see Shan Di again? Would he recognize her if he did? There was a piece of him that wanted to thank her for putting her life aside in favor of his.

He prepared for his return home to Guangzhou after a long and exhausting business trip in Upper Mongolia, a wearying thirty-plus-hour train ride, depending on the weather. Leong purchased a lower-berth sleep cabin with a bed that he might rest in — what was termed a businessman's seat. The train car he was in had very little heat and offered zero comfort. Cold wind and chill seeped into every corner of his coach. Leong's fur-lined shearling coat and his fleece-lined boots were a valued comfort. Still, there was little escape from the freezing weather lashing constantly outside the train. His palm against the window became affixed to the freezing pane and had to be pulled carefully from the icy glass. Leong bought a small pack of food and water to last him at least two days. He felt comfortable with his stash — and last but not least, ample toilet tissue, never again to be forgotten, as he'd made the painful mistake of forgetting it on his last trip home.

The train chugged along the steep, snow-packed slopes. Leong gazed at the two dim light bulbs on the ceiling flickering on and off. His sleep was fitful.

He boarded the train at the ancient, dreary city of Ulaanbaatar in Upper Mongolia.

As the train sped along the tracks, he stared through the window. The terrain was covered with mountains of white. Leafless trees flew by. He saw an occasional pack of wild dogs scouting the landscape for a morsel of food. The sky was painted gray, with intermittent streams of sunlight breaking through the clouds. As daylight drifted from the landscape, he turned in his bed. In his broken sleep on the lower bunk, Leong's back ached and his head swam. He tried to retain a sense of where he was.

Six hours of sleepless torture. The eight cars sped rapidly south into Qinghai Province, with an unusual three-and-a-half-hour stop at the city of Xining. The engine had to be changed, and the entire train had to be cleaned and somehow sanitized.

Very few buildings surrounded the downtown area of Xining. Small shops were tightly squeezed together side by side, each bartering and selling its own specialty. There were plumbing supplies, building materials, shoes and clothing shops, a quick-meal restaurant, and others, too many to mention. The town was a labyrinth of closely knit streets.

The downtown was surprisingly clean. Elderly men and some women wrapped in weighty blankets, wearing heavy woolen caps with earflaps, swept the streets, picking up parcels of dirt. Each appeared tired. Hawkers offered bottles of juice or water for sale to the people in cars that paused at each corner. Others had hats to sell. One or two offered toys from a local factory.

Several three- or four-story buildings with terraces displayed washed clothes hanging out to dry; several appeared to be frozen. It was a cold and tired town, with little to do except work, eat, and sleep. Televisions were absent. If you wanted to see a movie, you had to travel four hundred miles south. It was a pre-millennial town of one hundred and fifty thousand people, all of whom had nothing to do. There were hundreds of villages and towns like this throughout China.

Leong cautiously stepped from the snow-covered train. A crush of frozen wind stabbed his face — cold like he had never experienced. But it was important to get some fresh air. He also had to buy a large jar of clear water for the next part of the journey.

He searched the open-air station; passengers were waiting to board the next local. Travelers were protecting themselves with heavy coats, fur-lined boots, and long woolen scarves wrapped and rewrapped around their fire-red cheeks. It was astonishing to see a wall of snow nearest the tracks to the right of the station. And the view toward the left appeared as if he were standing at the face of a tunnel of ice. Only the tracks peeked out as they rolled into the distance of the glowing whiteness that surrounded all that the eye could see. He could only guess that the temperature was -2° Celsius (about -18° Fahrenheit).

On the station platform, Leong extended his body, raising his arms skyward in an effort to lighten the backache he was experiencing. He twisted his torso from left to right in an attempt to shake his fatigue. A cold shiver streaked through him. A toilet in the station was, for a change, reasonably clean, but it still had the foul and stale smell of urine. Taking his time, he washed his face using the jar of water he had bought in the small comfort shop in the station. The young man touched his stubble-covered chin, twisting his head in a circular motion to view what he thought was a fair-looking man. *I will shave when I return to my own place.* Dark rings circled his eyes, adding to the look of weariness his body felt.

His stretching had been to no avail, as his back experienced no relief from the ache he suffered from sleeping in the painful, too expensive berth. Much to his disappointment, the bed was about four inches too short for his long legs. The bed was five feet, seven inches long, just right for the average Chinese traveler, but too short for Leong, who stretched out to five feet, ten inches, plus the extra inches of his boots and hat.

Slowly he came alive again; his aches diminished. It occurred to him that a business colleague lived in Xining. With more than a three-hour delay and waiting time, he thought that it might be a good opportunity for a quick visit, one that could further strengthen his bond with the powerful and respected Mr. Sang Ye Piao.

Leong was soon in a taxi, cruising along the quiet road, surrounded by a veneer of white, which concealed the frozen, comatose trees. It was only a four-mile ride, but it felt like fifty miles. The cab pulled up to the offices of Global Trading International. Leong stepped from the car and entered the small but well-heated office. The warmth of the room rolled slowly into his body and into every bone and every pore of his skin.

A young receptionist asked, in Mandarin, "May I help you?"

"Yes, I would like to see Mr. Piao, please. Advise him that Leong Chan has come for a visit," Leong answered in his mother-tongue. It took only a moment for a slight-built man with rimless glasses to appear. "Leong, Leong, this is a happy surprise. What brings you to our humble city?" The two men bowed their heads and smiled.

"I have a three-hour layover; I thought it would be an added pleasure to my difficult travels to visit a most respected friend."

Both entered Piao's office. In a moment, a bottle of Scotch, twelve-year-old Johnnie Walker Black, was brought to the desk. Two glasses were wiped clean and the whiskey poured. The men clicked glasses, and each took a deep swallow. The burning liquid quickly flowed; the sensation gave Leong's body a surging sense of warmth that he welcomed. He looked up at Piao, "May I?" he asked, and unhesitatingly poured a second drink into his glass, along with another for Mr. Piao.

Sang Ye Piao was a man of significant wealth. His business investments included legitimate as well as many underground ventures. Piao was well-connected to powerful families in many Asian and European cities. He was not a man to be toyed with. If he was your friend, he was steadfast; if an enemy, dangerous. He was a frequent open-handed benefactor for causes assisting the poor and the sick. When Piao walked into a room, forceful voices muted. Silent greetings were shared as heads bowed, acknowledging respect.

Sang Ye was a frequent guest at the casinos in Macau and a recurrent guest passenger on a private jet bound for Caesar's Palace in Las Vegas.

Leong was pleased with himself for having taken the time to make the unscheduled visit. Piao welcomed the young man. He scratched his chin slowly, observing Leong and wondering if he might be a trusted ally. They drank for a while, and then freshly baked cookies and other refreshments were served. The conversation was comfortable for both. Leong was a charming and educated young man. To have a one-on-one conversation with Piao was a master class with one of Asia's most powerful men. It took no longer than ten or fifteen minutes with Leong for Piao, the master, to come to his decision.

"Is it possible for you to help with a special favor?" Piao asked.

Leong was surprised, but he remained silent. He considered

the question. *Perhaps this is an opportunity to strengthen my relationship with Piao.* "You honor me, sir. How may I help you?"

A smile crossed the elder gentleman's face, his eyes ablaze with a twinge of excitement. He rose from his chair and invited Leong to join him as he walked into another office. A huge safe stood against the wall. Piao put eyeglasses on as he spun the dials. The huge door hummed an aching cry of age as it opened slowly. Piao searched through the upper compartment, rummaging and rifling through several envelopes, and finally uncovering the one he was searching for.

"I have an envelope that I want you to personally deliver to a client of mine. His offices are in Guangzhou. Not to worry, it is perfectly legitimate. I would never put you in harm's way. My client's name and address are on the envelope face. I would be grateful. Just deliver. No conversation, no sales pitch."

This was a term used many times by the master Piao. "You are just a messenger, nothing more. Before I seal it, I must write a message." He pulled a pen from his pocket, went to the computer printer, extracted a sheet of blank paper, and wrote his communication. Piao folded the paper, inserted the sheet into the envelope, licked the glued edge, and sealed it.

"I am happy to be of service to you, Master Piao," the visitor answered in a cautious voice. He bowed, then placed the envelope in the inside breast pocket of his coat, pulled the flap down, and buttoned the pocket.

"Thank you very much. Your cooperation will not be forgotten." The two men chatted for another hour or so. It was time for Leong to depart. They shook hands with strength. Leong gulped the drink that was on the table. "May I have the cookies on the table as my reward?" Both laughed. Goodbyes were exchanged. They bowed to each other. Leong left. Mr. Piao instructed his driver take the welcome but silent guest to the train station.

The screeching train whistle blew for "All aboard." Quickly, Leong moved back to his sleeping car and into his berth. He was stunned. There before his eyes dangling from the upper bed were legs. They were attached to a young girl. Beyond her in the berth lay an older woman, curled up and asleep. He blinked, studying the young woman all bundled in a woolen scarf, her arms wrapped around her slender shoulders; shivers slipped from her lips. She tried to smile, but it appeared she was about to weep.

"N-n-nee how," she shivered, saying hello. "It looks like m-m-my aunt and I are your r-r-roommates."

Leong was silent.

"W-w-we are on our way to Guangdong Province. We will be visiting my nana. W-w-where are you going?"

Leong was digesting the situation. *How could this happen? A young girl, perhaps eighteen or nineteen, and her aunt? Can I believe this?*

"The train was f-f-fully booked. This was all they h-h-had, an upper in your compartment."

"Are you both prepared to sleep together in a single berth?" he questioned.

"W-w-we have not figured that out yet. We have about twenty-two hours of a train ride. We thought my aunt should s-s-sleep first, and when she awakens, it will be my turn and I will take some rest. Like I said, the train was completely sold out. This was the only berth available."

"An interesting plan," he said. "Good night and good luck." Leong lay down, rolled over, and shut his eyes, as if wanting to escape the sudden, unexpected complication.

Once Leong put his head down on the pillow, he lifted his feet at the far end, as they were slightly longer than his bunk. His eyes opened and slowly closed as sleep moved its chilly hand across his face and body. The train continued up a mountain, exerting all the power the new engine offered. It moved at a snail's pace.

Blizzard-like flakes fell heavily outside the chugging train. All one could see through the snow-painted window was a mantle of white. The temperature may have tumbled to three or four degrees.

Leong curled up in a fetal position, thus giving additional warmth to his body. Somewhere in the distance, not too far away, he heard a murmur, or perhaps a whimper. Unsure, he lifted his head just slightly. An ache quivered down his neck. The young woman with the dangling feet sat on a suitcase. Wrapped in a thin sweater, she was trembling. A deep sigh slipped from Leong's slightly parted lips. His head rose another inch or two; the twinge ran down his back. The young man listened as the train whistled once and then twice. The engine thundered on its way through a narrow mountain pass, finally clearing the peak, and at long last came the new motion of speed. Leong laid his head down and shut his eyes once again, trying to force sleep. Slumber was reluctant to come; distress filled his thoughts. He was thinking about the freezing girl sitting on the suitcase, chattering away.

"Excuse me," he whispered. The feet-dangling girl glanced up. "You look like you will freeze to death sitting there. Please take my coat."

"I am n-n-not cold," she whispered. "I cannot d-d-do that. I will—"

Leong interrupted her. "Don't tell me you are not cold. I can see your entire body shivering." He slipped from his berth, moving a few steps toward her. "Please, take my bed. My blankets and coat will warm you."

"I cannot do that. You do not know me. I cannot take advantage."

Leong, in a brotherly way, put his arm around her shoulder, pulling her toward him. He could feel her chilled body as it touched him. He opened his coat and swallowed her tiny, trembling frame into his shearling cocoon. They stood there. He made no gesture or the slightest move so as not to frighten the young woman.

"Why are you doing this?" she asked.

"We are both human beings. I offer you the help of a fellow traveler. If I ignored you and as a result you froze, or at the very least became ill, it would distress me."

He led the girl to his bunk, climbed in, and gently drew her reluctant body next to his.

Oh my God, what have I gotten myself into? Leong thought. *Have I made a serious mistake?* "I promise, I will not hurt you. Please do not be frightened. We just want to keep warm," he assured her. She listened and trusted him with some trepidation.

He covered the girl with his coat and wrapped her trembling figure with the two blankets he had. They tried to sleep together in a spoon like position, neither moving an inch. Leong was careful not to accidently make an inappropriate move or touch. He heard the silent rhythm of her breathing. He finally surrendered himself to a deep sleep.

The train was now hurtling forward at a high speed, the ride bumpy, interrupted only by an occasional slowdown at a bypass. He heard somewhere in the far-off distance of his sleep a whistle blow. A momentary reduction in speed was followed by a lurch forward, as steel wheels screeched their resistance.

11

The Birth Mother's Life-Changing Gift

Shan Di, deep in her heart, pretended she was the adopted daughter of the childless Hi Bo family. Now she was at the age of twenty-two. After almost seven years together, the three, Da Loban, TaiTai, and their maid, found that it was osmosis. With very few words of feeling or overt affection, they'd turned into a family. The young housemaid, who'd arrived years ago, was no longer a servant. She'd become a member of the Hi Bo clan. She did not sleep in the servants' quarters, she did not wear the maid uniform, and she did not clean or do dishes or sweep or run errands. Shan, after years of private tutoring, was at university to study, as befitted her new station in life, to become educated. She was now living a life she'd never dreamed of. She was given a small allowance of spending money. Madame Hi Bo's earlier lessons had taught Shan Di the value of finances, including a respect for all possessions. With permission from the Madame, once a month Shan sent a small portion of the funds to her birth family, the Chans. This was the family that had become a distant, cloudy illusion. They were a dream that was slowly slipping away. Shan barely acknowledged the feeling of responsibility to that part of her life, a time when she was little. Her strongest memory was that singular moment when her father lifted her from the rickshaw — the look of anguish on his face and his hands on her body while he gently guided her to safety. She'd seen that scene in her mind's eye hundreds of times.

Shan selected a time in October, during the celebration of Autumn Festival, as the week of her twenty-second birthday, seeing as she had no record of her birth. Shan returned to her new home, the Hi Bo mansion, from university for a brief holiday visit. She returned home with two girlfriends from her dormitory. Her companions marveled at the splendor of the house. No one was home except for the servants. The three young women walked around viewing the rooms, the art, the magnificent Buddha sculptures, and the elegance of Shan's home. Settling in her spacious bedroom, the three young women gossiped, laughed, drank tea, and devoured the tiny sandwiches brought to them by Sally Yu, the new housemaid. An hour passed.

"Shan, Shan!" an urgent voice called out from downstairs on the main floor.

"Come quickly," the young hostess told her friends. They rapidly left the room and dashed down the steps, screaming with laughter, almost tripping over one another.

A woman, beautifully dressed, her smiling eyes glowing, and carrying many gifts as if it were Christmas, greeted the girls. "Hello, everyone."

Shan ran to her, hugged her, kissed her cheek, and said, "Momma, these are my friends from school, Pia and Sasi." Madame Hi Bo, after setting down her parcels, shook their hands, and then collapsed into a huge chair. Her eyes filled with tears. She looked at Shan with a love that was pure and natural. Shan and she knew exactly what happened in that instant, in that special flash of excitement.

In that split second of spontaneity, the long-concealed hope and prayer of both Shan and Madame Hi Bo materialized. Shan had finally addressed Madame Hi Bo as "Momma." Shan knew that inside TaiTai were the heart and the love of a mother, the mother she'd always wanted and never spoken of. The connection had finally arrived. It had transformed two loving women into mother and daughter. Now at long last she was the daughter she'd wanted to be.

Shan spun to her friends and said, "Please, call my momma by her first name. It's TanHa. Is that all right, Mother? Or would you prefer 'Madame Hi Bo'?"

"No, no, please call me TanHa. That was my name when I was your age." She blushed.

Da Loban Hi Bo arrived later that evening. He appeared a little tired. A worried look crossed his face. The maid took his cloak and hat. He entered the sitting room. The four women stood and bowed. Shan walked to him, bowed again, and said, "Poppa, these are my friends from school."

He turned to the girls, smiled, tilted his head politely, reached out, and gently touched Shan's cheek with his open palm. It was done. That stroke on her cheek, simple as it was, meant that Shan had been given the blessing. She was now the official daughter of the Hi Bo family.

When Shan's friends left for an early return to school, the new family was at last alone. Hi Bo called his wife and his new daughter into the library.

"Yes, Poppa, what is it?"

Madame Hi Bo sat directly next to her husband. "Please, sit here, next to me as well," Hi Bo said to Shan Di. "Mother and I want to discuss something that is important to me."

Shan looked up into her poppa's eyes without fear and without skipping a heartbeat.

"Since you are now officially our daughter, at the end of the term at university, Mother and I want to arrange a gala introducing you to all our friends as our new and official adopted daughter.

Is that all right?" Da Loban looked at his daughter, waiting for a response.

A voice of ecstatic delight exploded from Shan. "May I invite my friends from school? Can I get a new dress and new shoes to look beautiful for all your friends?"

Both Hi Bo and Madame Hi Bo smiled with joy. All three embraced each other. It was a moment filled with promise for a future that would bring unexpected events.

Hi Bo looked at his new adult child. "There is one more request that we have. Now that you are our daughter, I would like to honor my long-gone mother. I ask you to discard the name of Shan Di and take my mother's name. Her name was Jan Yee Hi Bo."

Shan Di sat quietly and began to sob. She could not control her convulsive weeping. After moments, some calm came to her. She fixed her eyes, first on Madame Hi Bo and then to Da Loban Hi Bo.

"You honor me. You are my true and loving parents. And I will respect and reciprocate this blessing you have bestowed upon me. From this day forward I am now Jan Yee Hi Bo, the proud daughter of two of the kindest, most wonderful parents any daughter could have to honor and respect."

"It is vital — very important — that you never forget your biological parents. They have blessed us all by sending you to us. We must always honor them and provide for them," Hi Bo announced. "In our religion, we honor an adopted child by encouraging the child to continue to worship in the religion they were born into. Your birth religion is Christianity. Ours is Buddhism."

"But Poppa, it is difficult for me to remember my religion or my parents. As much as I try, I cannot bring up a vision of them. My only recollection is being lifted from the rickshaw and placed on the wooden street in our village, when, by God's gift, She brought me to this house."

"So be it. It is done." Hi Bo gazed at his lovely daughter. She looked into her new father's eyes. She wanted him to embrace her, but such a thing was not done. Mother embraced her daughter and brushed a hair from her child's forehead. Poppa touched his lips to her forehead, a rare act of affection.

In a swift moment of joy and love, Jan threw her arms around Hi Bo and pressed her head to his chest, whispering, "I love you." His eyes filled with moisture. His chest heaved with the exceptional gift he had just been given: this precious child. For the first time in his life, he saw the future for all his efforts.

Jan Yee left for her room to prepare for dinner. Hi Bo turned to his wife. "Jan Yee said 'She' when she spoke of God."

TaiTai Hi Bo shrugged her shoulders, her palms open. "I noticed a speck in your eyes," she whispered. He removed a handkerchief from his pocket, using it to dab first his left and then his right eye.

12

The Twins Growing Up Quickly

"I cannot believe that our girls are celebrating their eighth birthday," Maxine said out loud to herself. As Daryl walked into the kitchen, Maxine continued. "It's a miracle that the years have zipped by. And now I snap my fingers and our daughters are in third grade.

"I would go into their room and often stare at them lying asleep in their beds, and whisper, 'You two are a miracle in our lives.' Our decision" — she took hold of Daryl's hand — "has brought more than we ever expected." She kissed his cheek. Daryl wrapped his arms around his wife, kissed her full on the mouth, and touched her breast slightly with his right hand.

"Is that a message?" she questioned. They both laughed.

"I love you," she said.

"I love you back … and your front," he replied. The laughter continued.

❦

The chilly days of autumn quickly arrived. It was almost Thanksgiving. Mommy Maxine had taken her three children to Bloomingdale's for a Saturday afternoon of lunch and shopping;

cold-weather clothes would soon be needed. "My children grow faster than trees."

Warm winter jackets, boots, and sweaters were carefully selected, tried on, and bought. There was lots of teasing, running around the store, looking, and touching. The children were privileged; they knew it and loved it ... and their parents knew it. Still, school work had to be finished, reading was a must, and Nancy was not their maid. All clothes had to be hung up. At dinner, it was an absolute, at the very least, that dishes were cleared and placed in the dishwasher. Above all, fresh talk was not allowed, and the reciprocation of polite greetings to guests was uncompromised. Thank-you messages were sent for all gifts received. No deviation was permitted by Mom or Dad. The same rules existed for Fred. They were privileged children, but not totally spoiled.

For one scary moment, no one knew where Fred was. He had disappeared somewhere in the store. The boy had taken an elevator ride to the eighth floor and forgot where he had left his family. Finally, and much to everyone's relief, he returned laughing. "Where were you?" his mom demanded.

"I just took a ride. I knew exactly where I was. Mom, I am not a baby. Remember, I am fifteen years old."

That's a boy for you, Maxine thought, smiling with relief.

Maxine, with Nancy's help, gathered the children and all their new goodies, plus a warm jacket and boots for Nancy's son. They returned home to attend the planned birthday party for the twins. It was to be a surprise.

Maxine and Daryl, much to their constant amazement, found that although they were twins, the girls were not the same. They were both interestingly different. Each had her own point of view. Sing enjoyed her American name, Sammy, while Lauren insisted on being called by her traditional Chinese name, LangPi. That's how it was. Lauren liked colorful dresses and clothes; Sammy was more conservative, wearing only navy and gray, and an occasional red scarf or sweater. Samantha was a reader. More thoughtful, she asked many questions. If her head was not in a book, her nose was in the computer her parents had given her. The girls never dressed alike. They also had different undergarments. They were twins, but they were different.

LangPi valued the difference between her and her sister; being a twin was not her idea of specialness. To anyone who would ask her, "Are you twins?" She felt the need to casually reply, "No. Sammy has brown eyes. I have one brown eye and one hazel eye. That makes us different, so we are not exact twins." She grinned. "We like different things. We do not dress alike, and the only time you can tell that we are true twins is when we both have no clothes on. That is the only time we look exactly alike." She would then offer a smile, perhaps more of a smirk, to the listener.

Despite the minor physical variations and the diversity in their personalities and interests, the twins recognized, as young as eight years old, that they were bound by their powerful genetic ties. Their link lay deep inside them. At the age of eight years they, in unsaid words, were able to distinguish their feelings for each other. Their simultaneous thoughts and sentences brought laughter and high fives. It was how each kept the other safe. They were facing their lives together with a unique feeling, protecting each from loneliness. The girls did not have an intellectual understanding of the twin bond. It was never discussed. It just felt right, a liaison that would continue without end.

Occasionally, in whispered tones, the conversation turned to their uncertainty about their birth mother. "Do you think she was pretty? How old is she now? I wonder if she thinks about us." The questions were casual, spoken only in Chinese, not thoroughly thought out, but persisting as an unsolved equation.

At home, Paul, the elevator man, greeted them. "Happy birthday, Samantha," he said, looking at Ling. "Happy birthday,

Lauren," he said to Samantha. Everyone laughed. It was an error made often by friends and family, and especially by Paul and Ray, the latter being the second-shift elevator man.

Their apartment door opened. *"Happy birthday to you,"* sang all the family members and the ten children invited from Riverdale Country School, where the three Landsman children attended.

Aunts, uncles, cousins, and, of course, Grandma Shirley, with smiles and tears, all looked on. Hugs and kisses were exchanged. Balloons filled the room, along with confetti and spangles all aglow. The twins had their eyes wide open in awe and surprise. This was followed by an immediate charge to all the gifts piled on the ebony baby grand piano.

"No gifts now," Maxine instructed. "Please be polite and say hello to all your guests." Faces sulked; disappointment engulfed her daughters and young guests.

"This is not a time for rules or manners. No, it is a time for freedom, fun, and smiles," Samantha complained.

"This is happy birthday time. Mommy, please...." Lauren finished.

The room was silent. Everyone waited for Mom to decide. "Okay, okay ... you win. Gifts first. Nancy, please help them."

The children screamed with delight. Sammy dashed to Maxine and Daryl. "Thank you, Daddy. Love you, Mommy." She was off to the frenzy surrounding the piano.

Lauren walked toward her parents. "We are so lucky," she said, giving them powerful hugs and kisses. "Thank you," Lauren whispered, and rushed off to the avalanche of birthday gifts.

Maxine went into the kitchen. Daryl followed her. She investigated his face and put her arms around his neck. "Why are you so smart? I never dreamed my life would be like this. I am so happy I listened to you, married you, and let you kiss me on our first date." She looked into his eyes, kissed his lips, touched the front of his trousers, and felt his immediate response.

"I may be smart," Daryl responded, "but this would never have happened if you hadn't had the courage. You were able to take the risk for more happiness. This was your gift to all of us. It was not an easy decision to make, accepting responsibility for the lives of two human beings."

"We are partners and made the right decision together. I often tremble at the thought of the lives our daughters may have endured if we'd passed." Tears flushed her eyes.

"Let's not dwell on what-ifs. Let's enjoy what we have. They are growing fast. Before we turn around, it will be college. And I shudder to say that at long last we will be alone."

"They will have success and disappointments. That is life. Our Freddy will have the same. He told me only yesterday that there is a girl in his geometry class whom he likes very much. He also asked me to attend his lacrosse match on Thursday." The serious part of the conversation at an end, he continued, "And don't forget that special tease you gave me a minute ago. That will have to be finished later." Both laughed. He touched her backside and then rejoined the party.

Suddenly she asked, "Did we forget Freddy?"

"How could we forget Freddy? Of course not. I got him a new pair of skis, boots, and goggles. He will go bananas. I wouldn't be surprised if he is in his room trying everything on … including the skis."

13

The Surprise

The train finally arrived at its destination. The city of Guangzhou — Leong wished his traveling companions well. He bowed and said goodbye to Ying Tang and her aunt. "Thank you so very much for your kindness to us." She too bowed.

As the pair walked away, Auntie said, "He is a very interesting gentleman. I am so pleased we met him. Did you like him?"

"I was so tired, I did not notice," the young woman responded, covering her true feelings.

Leong stepped into a waiting taxi, which took him to his apartment in a recently built twenty-five-story modern apartment building. He moved his luggage into the elevator, which carried him up to apartment eight on the seventeenth floor. He chose his new home because the number eight and the numbers one and seven sums to eight. In China, the number eight is a lucky number. The sleek structure was built only five-years earlier. He bought his home two short years ago with assistance from his firm. Not a gift, it was a loan he was repaying every month with part of his salary. The owner of his company said, "Mr. Chan, we make this special accommodation to you as a reward for the effort you have put into your commitment to our firm."

"I am very lucky to be a part of this firm," Chan stated in appreciation.

Chan's senior company owner advised, "You will find, as you gain more experience in your career, usually, the hardest workers are the luckiest people."

The late afternoon light shone into his living room window as he wheeled his luggage into an expansive bedroom. The room was filled with a king-size bed. Two silver and glass lamps with twisting necks stood warmly on either side of the bed. Three large closets, side by side like soldiers, sat within a wall and were filled with suits, jackets, shirts, and shoes. A comfortable black leather chair with a tall reading lamp at its back, both atop a gray and white tweed carpet, completed his bachelor bedroom. A small but comfortable living room/office, filled with art, books, a large television, and a small antique desk, all contributing to the masculine appearance of his relaxing home. There was a bathtub and shower in the fair-sized bathroom. White tiles covered the floor and walls. A huge mirrored medicine cabinet completed the washroom.

An extraordinary home like this one for a single person was very rare in China, where apartments were usually tiny and utilitarian. In China as many as three or four people would live in a space similar to Leong's.

He peeked into his small but adequate office. A pile of mail lay upon his desk, all clean and tidy. His twice-a-week housekeeper had done her job.

He did not unpack. He showered, shaved, and wrapped himself with a navy terrycloth bathrobe without toweling himself dry, a lazy habit. He enjoyed the terry robe drying experience. Leong plopped down onto his bed. A sigh of relief escaped from his slightly open mouth, as his eyes closed. A warm, welcome sleep came swiftly. The thirty-hour train trip had not been easy.

The reward of rest and quiet quickly enveloped him. He was completely fatigued.

Two hours slipped by. His eyes opened. He was in the same flat position he'd been in when his body hit the bed. He looked at the ceiling. His lids hung heavily as he tried to figure out where he was. His mind was floating. *Where am I? What day is it?*

Leong's sense of himself slowly eased back into his brain. *It's good to be back in my own bed. Back to work at the office tomorrow, or a day off? I'll think about it.*

The girl on the train, very nice.... Ah yes, two new potential clients in Mongolia and one in Tibet. Good visit with Sang Ye Piao. All these thoughts raced through his mind.

In a burst of strength, he sat up quickly. "Sang Ye Piao!" he shouted. "Where is that envelope? Where is that envelope?"

He jumped from the bed and began a frantic search for Piao's written message. He went through his briefcase and his luggage. He found nothing. *Oh my God! I hope I didn't lose it. Piao will be very upset.* He ran from room to room, searching tables, desk drawers, and the kitchen. He searched his brief case and his luggage. His heart beat rapidly. The memory of where he'd left Piao's important envelope was nowhere. He simply could not remember what he'd done with it. He felt the biting claw of panic. *Could I have left it on the train, or in the taxi going home? Could I have left it in Piao's car?* He pushed his hands to his head, searching his memory, shaking his head. *No, no, I could not have lost the Piao envelope that he trusted me with. That girl, she distracted me. You are such a fool,* he rebuked himself.

Leong rushed into the kitchen. *A cold drink of water might help.* He twisted the cap of the water bottle and gulped the fresh, cool liquid. In one final desperate attempt, he rushed to the coat closet near his front door. Reaching for his shearling coat he slipped his hand deep into its pockets. "Nothing!" He fumed, and with a final thrust, he searched the inside breast pocket, reaching down, down, with a prayer: *Please be there, please.* He felt perspiration dampen his chest. And then suddenly his fingers danced at the touch of a paper envelope. *That was close.* He pulled the document from the coat and said out loud, with a sigh of relief, "It would be safer for me to be the messenger as soon as possible. *Like, right now.*"

In less than an hour Mr. Leong Chan was greeted at the green gatehouse of the vast Hi Bo mansion by two men, who, after he'd shown them the addressed envelope and offered a simple explanation, took him to the front door. The leader touched the bell. A maid opened the door. Telling Leong to wait a moment, she walked away, soon returning from the sitting room, followed by Da Loban Hi Bo.

"What is so urgent that I am disturbed in my home on a Sunday evening? Could this not have waited until tomorrow at my office?" he commanded.

Leong made a step forward. The two guards immediately moved between him and Hi Bo. Looking straight into Hi Bo's eyes without flinching, Leong replied, "No, sir, it could not wait. I was instructed that it was urgent and that I deliver this to you in person as soon as I returned to Guangzhou."

"And who, may I ask, gave you these orders?" The two men relaxed a little.

"Sang Ye Piao!" he answered in a firm voice. About ten seconds of silence followed.

Hi Bo nodded to his two gate guards. They turned and left.

"Please come in," he said in a respectful tone.

Leong followed slowly. *I cannot believe the power of Sang Ye Piao. Here I stand in front of one of the wealthiest men in all of Southern China, and at the mention of Piao's name, he becomes different. I wonder why. Be patient and see what happens next.* Leong and Hi Bo walked into the sitting room. "Please sit ... here in my chair. It is the most comfortable."

"Sir, I do not want to be rude and reject your polite offer of comfort. Truthfully, I would be most comfortable sitting on the sofa, with you sitting in your own chair."

"And tell me, young man," Da Loban began, "what is your name, and how does a young person like you enjoy the trust and friendship of the master Sang Ye Piao?"

Should I share the history of Piao and me with Hi Bo? He is a man of prestige and wealth. Will my talking too much backfire? Be careful, very careful.

The visitor bowed. "My name is Leong Chan, and I am employed by a trading company here in Guangzhou. I met Master Piao at a business convention in Shanghai two years ago. We were both enjoying a drink of Scotch, relaxing after a day of work, and we struck up a conversation. I am not exactly sure whether he or I began our exchange. I told him about myself. And to tell the truth, now that I think of it, he told me very little ... practically nothing."

"That is Piao." Hi Bo smiled.

"He apparently found something in me that interested him, but for sure he only guessed that I was trustworthy. He took a chance and gave me a business assignment in Mongolia, where I was going for my firm. I was given some shoe samples, plus an envelope, which may have had prices and delivery dates. I cannot remember. On my return from my business dealings in Mongolia, I delivered the package to his customer. And that was it. A month later I received a wire transfer to my bank for one thousand US dollars.

"This month on my way back home from a business trip, my train had a three-and-a-half-hour layover in Piao's town of Xining. I went to surprise him with a visit."

Hi Bo closed his eyes. He pushed himself back in his seat, head down, and clasped his hands together. He opened his eyes and looked at Leong. "On your business card here, it reads, 'Leong Chan.' May I call you Leong?"

"I welcome that, sir. You honor me."

"Then allow me to invite you to dinner tonight. My daughter is home from college, and my wife's niece is visiting."

"Please, sir, I cannot impose."

"I insist."

Hi Bo sat in his chair, thinking; *he is a very clever young man. He was careful in his conversation. He did not divulge anything important. Attractive, lives up to his commitments, and appears to have a good work ethic. Perhaps a match for Ting or Jan Yee.*

My trusted friend Piao was right to suggest this young man as a consideration for a match, as his letter stated, he thought, contemplating this quiet and interesting new person in his life.

Leong considered; *having dinner with the Hi Bo family is not a terrible reward for helping Piao. In such a short time I have formed an intimate friendship with two very important men. I will do it. I will stay for dinner.*

"Sir, you honor me with the invitation to have dinner with your family. I accept your generous offer." He bowed his head.

"Dinner is within the hour. Please let me show you to the washroom so you may freshen up. We will meet in the library for cocktails."

The Surprise Meeting

Leong sat comfortably in the library, sinking deep into a rich brown leather sofa. A maid placed a Scotch with ice upon a tiny yellow-striped napkin at the corner of a huge oak coffee table adjacent to the sofa.

Six carved wooden legs supporting the massive table resembled huge lion paws. A small vase of pink flowers made the scene more festive. At right angles were a set of leather chairs matching the couches. Each seat was gracefully covered with a dozen or more large silken pillows, placed perfectly. On the floor lay a huge Persian rug, imported from Iran. Leong sat comfortably sipping his Scotch. Hi Bo asked the maid to prepare his usual vodka martini. He joined Leong. Both men mused and stirred their drinks in silence.

Leong viewed the full wood-paneled bookcases. Although mostly filled with Mandarin books, there were volumes from the United States, Spain, France, and other countries around the world. The cases covered three walls, with spaced sections for a painting or a photo. Leong's interest was piqued by an entire section of Buddhist literature. He hoped that sometime soon he would have the opportunity to examine those ancient tomes.

"Where were you born?" Hi Bo asked, breaking the silence.

"It was a small town between Foshan and this very village. My parents were poor, hardworking people. I am the eldest of three children."

"So it appears that you have lifted yourself up in the world."

"Not exactly. I still have much to learn and a mountain to conquer. Sir, at this moment I am a novice."

"I myself came from a working-class family. My father drove a taxi part-time, and my mother was a schoolteacher. Because of her, I went to university in the United States, in Michigan."

The door opened, and a young woman walked in. "Good evening, Uncle. I hope I am not disturbing you."

"No, you are not. Let me introduce you to a new friend, Mr. Leong Chan."

"Ting! Is that you?" Leong said, his eyes close to bursting.

"Yes it is."

Leong immediately rose and bowed with profound respect.

"You two know each other?" Hi Bo questioned.

"We do, sir. We met on the train traveling to Guangzhou. She was accompanied by her aunt. Please forgive my boldness, but I must say you look very beautiful. I am pleased to see you in a setting that is much different from our train experience." He smiled.

"Thank you for your compliment. You too look different, Mr. Chan, and also very handsome," Ting responded, as she reciprocated with a bow and a simple smile.

All three stood in silence at the surprise meeting.

"Why is everyone so quiet?" the lovely Jan Yee asked as she entered. All eyes quickly moved. There she was, Hi Bo's radiant daughter, standing in the glow of the leaping flames in the fireplace. The light shone through her sheer dress. Leong could see for an instant an exciting shape. He caught himself, stood up, and bowed.

"This is Jan Yee Hi Bo, my daughter. Allow me, Mr. Chan, to give you a more formal introduction to my niece Ting Asan, from Xining. And permit me" — he turned to his daughter — "to make a formal introduction of Mr. Leong Chan from Foshan, a friend of Sang Ye Piao. Please, everyone, sit." He called to the maid. "Amy, please prepare some drinks for everyone." The young woman nodded and quickly moved to the liquor cabinet.

Leong looked at both women in amazement, his host's daughter and his niece, one more lovely than the other. Leong guessed that Yee was a woman of twenty-eight or thirty years old. Her expression was elegant and proud. Ting, petite Ting, had a sparkling young face and an impeccable feminine shape.

Leong stared at Jan Yee. She reciprocated his attentive look. He knew her — her face seemed familiar — but he could not remember from where.

What did Poppa say our guest's name was? Oh my, I cannot remember it, Jan Yee mused.

Madame Hi Bo entered with Auntie Sun. Everyone stood and bowed. The acknowledgment was returned. The two stylishly dressed women were seated. No one spoke. The room became a tomb as each person gazed at the other. Hi Bo turned to his

TaiTai. "This is Leong Chan, a friend of Sang Ye Piao from Xining," Hi Bo said, addressing both TaiTai and Auntie.

"I remember this young man from our recent journey to Guangzhou." Auntie added, "It is so good to see you again."

Jan Yee could not believe her ears. *He has the same name as my brother. Is it possible? What shall I do? Oh, how I wish I could remember what my brother looked like. Close your eyes. Do not look at him. Do not like him. This is impossible. He betrays himself by looking at me with intensity. Please, please do not like me or think of me. Please, I beg you to like Ting, to love her if you can. I can only pray that she will help.*

During dinner Leong sat next to Ting. She was on his left, and Auntie was on his right. He chatted quietly with both women, interrupted intermittently by general conversation from the table. Leong intentionally focused his conversation on Madame Hi Bo, an approach to win her approval. However, the young man found Jan Yee the most interesting of the group. She appeared more educated and was quite striking. He was beginning to feel slightly interested in her. He knew Ting was young, available, and charming. At dinner Ting frequently touched Leong's arm when speaking to him. It made Leong feel warm but still mostly confused.

I wonder what Hi Bo has in mind, bringing me together with his daughter and his niece. Perhaps he has another gentleman in mind and I am just being egotistical. No, that could not be. When he opened the envelope and looked at me.... Is it possible that Piao arranged all of this, acting as a matchmaker? Oh, Master Piao, my new friend, you are a clever one.

14

Hans Must Pay for His Crime

The snow tumbled onto the streets of Zurich, Switzerland. Hans Leopold was signing the final checks for the month's payments. Completing his task, he gazed at an unopened letter.

The company bank balances were diminishing. His business was experiencing a serious loss of customers.

In his vast office, letter in hand, he glanced around the room, looking down through the balcony window at the staff; there were more than fifty clerks, accountants, merchandisers, and buyers, plus his assistant and two other senior officers of the firm.

The Leopold Footwear Company had enjoyed more than twenty-five years of success. They had more than two hundred retail stores, including at least one in every city in Europe, plus two in China and one in Japan. Hans was satisfied, content with his accomplishment of a lifetime of work and success.

Slowly he edged his finger through the envelope flap and lifted it, throwing the small piece of paper into the brass wastebasket beneath his desk. He unfolded the letter and began to read.

My Dear Mr. Leopold,

Your shipment of twelve hundred pairs of the women's collection arrived this week. My staff and

I were very disappointed to see the poor quality of the ladies' group of shoes as compared to those of last season.

The sizing, the fit, and the quality of leather have seriously diminished. We plan to return the shoes by no later than tomorrow. Please issue a credit and a charge back for shipping.

Sincerely,
Jacques Michel, President

Leopold, a man in his early fifties, sank into his chair at his desk. A sudden, stinging lurch struck his heart. *Hi Bo, you son of a bitch. This is your fault for abandoning me in favor of that slut. I cannot believe that the incident with that whore maid still haunts me!*

Leopold felt the hurt and the pain of his agonizing memory. *What did I do wrong? Isn't it true that those Asian types love the attention? Why can I not forget that moment? Why do I feel that I am being punished for nothing serious? I cannot understand this chastisement. What wrong have I done? I am not a murderer or a thief. What crime have I committed?*

He couldn't imagine that he was guilty of any offense. Leopold did not know what all the fuss was about. *As for Hi Bo, such a stupid man, he rejected the business from my company over an incident with a worthless maid. Our business together was always so profitable, and now it is over and we both suffer. Why could it not be business as usual? I have four maids at home and three young women at the office, and I touch them at my pleasure. What is this hassle all about?* Hans Leopold, in all his old world ignorance, was unable to comprehend his sinful habits.

Leopold left for home in a state of anxiety. He had to figure out how to solve the disaster he faced.

At the Leopold residence, his eight-year-old son leaped up to greet him. "Daddy, Daddy, I am so happy you're home. I want you to see the new picture I drew for you." For a few brief hours, Leopold enjoyed a little rest. It gave him time to think and find a solution to the catastrophic business problem he faced.

The dinner table was silent as he ate and drank, overwhelmed by the enormous problems the company was facing. Mrs. Leopold knew her husband was troubled about something serious. "Hans, is there anything wrong? Can I help?"

"Do not meddle in my affairs. There is nothing anyone can do, except I, who can solve all issues," he shouted. There was a crushing sound as he smashed his fist on the table.

In his office at home, he pondered for hours the path he had no choice but to take. It was the decision he dreaded, as he dialed a private number in Asia.

"Hello," the voice answered.

"This is Hans Leopold."

"How are you, Hans?" Piao questioned.

"I am perfectly well other than a small business problem. I need your guidance and help."

"Tell me, my friend, and I will see if I can be of service to you."

"For many years, I have successfully been doing business with the Hi Bo shoe factory in Guangzhou. Over some silly misunderstanding, Hi Bo has refused to work with my firm. You have strong connections in Asia, and you know him personally. I need some advice and some assistance."

"Hans, my friend, I had expected this call from you years ago. I know the whole story. You made a serious mistake. You are a very wealthy man, able to purchase anything you want, even a woman if you so desire. Why such bad behavior? You should know better," Sang Ye Piao said. "In a man's home in China, to betray his trust is to dishonor him. Hi Bo has lost face with his family and his employees. His responsibility is to protect his people and his property. A maid, my friend, is a person under his protection."

Silence followed for a few moments. Hans continued. "I have shamed myself, and my family will be in disgrace if this incident is ever exposed. I plead, Master Piao, how can I make things right?" Piao knew from the moment Leopold spoke that his pleas were insincere and totally untrue.

"It is going to be very expensive. Are you prepared to pay the price?"

"Whatever you say, Master Piao. I will do as you command." Leopold's voice was cracking. His usual arrogant behavior had lessened. He was almost pleading.

Piao recognized weakness and decided he was going make Leopold pay dearly for his horrendous, aberrant behavior.

"How much will this cost me?" Hans queried.

"I will get back to you in a week or two," Piao said. *Despicable animal,* he thought as he hung up the phone.

Several weeks passed. Finally, a meeting was arranged between the two conspirators. Hi Bo greeted Piao at the Guangzhou airport. "Welcome, my friend. I am so pleased to see you again. My driver is outside." Piao nodded.

"Do not tell me you will not be staying at my home," Hi Bo implored.

"I am sorry, my most trusted comrade; I prefer my own suite at a hotel. I appreciate your gracious offer. I have many appointments here in Guangzhou. I must be free to come and go as I please. For sure we will have dinner at your home. This in no way is meant as an insult. It is my own idiosyncratic need. I beg you to understand and forgive me."

Hi Bo tipped his head graciously, with total appreciation for

Piao's direct style of speaking. He knew that Master Piao was a ladies' man. On their visits to Macau and Las Vegas, Piao did not conceal his vigor for women who were available. Guangzhou was a city that was no different. Hi Bo was a religious person and approached life differently. Still, a man is a man, and he enjoyed the vicarious experience he had as Piao's friend. Hi Bo's masculinity was demonstrated by his morals, by the huge company he had built, and by his loyalty and commitment to his partner in life and best friend, TaiTai Hi Bo.

Three nights passed before Piao came to the mansion for dinner. The guests included Da Loban's niece, Ting; his daughter, Jan Yee; Auntie; his TaiTai and the young man, Leong Chan.

Piao gazed around the room and nodded to Leong, tilting his head in a polite bow. He looked at Auntie, rose, walked over to her, bowed, and extended his hand. "I am so sorry, I do not remember your name, but I recognize your most charming face as a friend of my wife, Tyne Ya. You have been to our home. Am I correct?"

Auntie Sun remembered how stunned she was to hear Leong was doing business with Sang Ye Piao, a notorious man with a horrid reputation for dishonest ventures. TaiTai Piao was part of a charity that Auntie was involved with. The wife was nice but very pushy.

The Crime and the Chinese punishment

"Tan Ha," Hi Bo said quietly, turning to his wife, "when will dinner be served?"

She gazed at her watch, stared a moment, and replied, "In about forty-five minutes. Would you like another cocktail?"

"Not now, my love. Please forgive me. Piao, Leong, and I are going to have a private conversation in the library for a very short time. Leong, please join us." Everyone looked at each other in utter surprise. This situation had never happened before when guests were being entertained at the big house.

As Piao left with the other men, he had other things on his mind as well. Piao knew what he was doing. He knew of his wife's pain when she was rejected by other women in her peer group. He was intent on fixing it when they returned to the dinner table. He was going to put it right. From this day forward, his wife would be welcomed and respected by her neighbors. It was only a beginning with Auntie Sun.

The three men entered the library, took seats, and sipped the drinks that had been waiting for them on the coffee table. Leong could not believe that he was invited to be an onlooker of a very private matter with two of the most powerful businessmen in South China and most of Europe. His heart beat rapidly, and a flash of redness covered his face.

"Since this is your meeting, my friend, how can I be of service to you?" Hi Bo began, looking directly into Piao's face.

"The issue here," Piao replied, "is how I can be of service to you and help your business."

"I do not understand," Hi Bo answered.

"It is not a secret that your factories have suffered since you ended your relationship with Hans Leopold. Is that not true?"

"You are correct. But we are managing. Our cash flow is adequate. We have experienced slight volume problems, but we are slowly adding new clients."

"Leopold came to me. His company is also suffering because of the horrible, unforgivable incident. He asked how he can make amends and repair the relationship. He admits to his guilt," Piao stated quickly.

"I do not believe for one moment that Leopold will ever acknowledge he did anything wrong. He believes that I am the guilty party and I deserve to be punished for taking the side of a maid girl instead of that of a most valued customer. I will never consider working with that animal again. My honor tarnished, my trust betrayed." Hi Bo's voice rose, demonstrating his intense agitation.

"Never is a very long time. You are getting older, and restructuring your business has not been, nor will it be, easy. I offer that Leopold must pay, and pay dearly, for his terrible transgression. To that, every right-minded person agrees," Piao explained.

"There is not enough money in all of Switzerland or China to pay for his crime against my daughter."

"She was not your daughter at the time."

Hi Bo glared at Piao. This was the first time he'd felt an insult from a man he trusted. "She is now. I shall always honor her and respect her privacy."

Piao realized his error and quickly tried to correct what he'd said. "I understand your feelings totally. I too have a daughter. And I am not trying to diminish your pain or your anger and your need for revenge."

"You cannot imagine what is in my mind for retribution. I should have shot him when I had the chance. But I am not a killer or a rapist."

"You threw Leopold out of your home, banished him from your life, and exorcized him from your business for that horrid encounter with your housemaid. That young woman is now your beloved adopted daughter. I understand your pain; I can only imagine your feelings." Everyone remained silent. Piao had salvaged his misstep. The three men clicked glasses, and all was understood.

"Permit me to share my thoughts with you. I have a plan for revenge that may interest you."

Leong listened to the conversation, digesting all the shocking information. He kept silent. He had nothing to contribute yet; he simply sipped his Scotch.

"Here is my proposal, my plan." Piao stood up. He walked around the room to the liquor cabinet and poured a little soda water.

"Money is everything to Leopold. It is his god. Destroying his treasure would be like taking his children from him. Even worse, the loss of affluence will diminish the legacy he has planned for his family. It will inflict a great deal of pain, yet he is prepared to pay you and your daughter a substantial fine."

The thought of fining Hans for his transgression amused Hi Bo.

"I knew you could not, you would not, agree to a payoff. You are one of the most honorable businessmen in all of South China. You shall never accept a bribe, nor will you ever pay anyone for their business. I admire and respect your ethics. That is why I trust you and why I am here. I want you to earn the vengeance you rightly deserve."

"Sir, if I may say so," Hi Bo interrupted, "I do not seek revenge. I pursue retribution for my daughter. And now where does this lead us?" There was a silent pause for a moment of reflection. Everyone in the room was thinking. "How much of a fine do you have in mind?" Piao was caught off guard by his friend's surprise response. He was not expecting an agreement or even the idea of such a solution so soon. He thought for a moment and responded.

"I was considering in the area of two million euros. That number is equivalent to more than thirteen million yuan, or equal to two and a half million US dollars. It will not only be pain for Leopold; it will also be a lifetime of torture."

No one spoke. Hi Bo stood up. He walked to the liquor cabinet. He filled his glass, not with water but with Scotch and two ice cubes. He stirred.

Leong sat still, just watching and listening. *I wonder how Hi Bo is going to come to some conclusion and decide.*

"You speak of a great deal of money. Is that the price you put on my honor or that of my daughter? You and I have often said to each other that everyone has a number. Why do you offer my family such a windfall? What is your gain with this enormous gift, or as you put it, a fine? Why are we so fortunate to have you as our benefactor? You are a businessman; you must have some profit or some sort of percentage in mind."

"Just our friendship and any tiny, thoughtful gift you wish to bestow on me. Or nothing at all, if you so desire. I am here on a mission of friendship, not with a commitment to profit."

This is an amazing experience. It is a master class, watching two giants negotiating while speaking in a tone of friendship, Leong thought, keeping his lips shut and finding his hands cold and damp.

"You are a true friend," Hi Bo said. "I appreciate your interest. I want to think on this overnight. I will speak to you tomorrow of my decision." Hi Bo excused himself and left the two men, joining the women in the dining room.

Piao and Leong sat there silent, each in his own space with his private thoughts.

"What decision will Hi Bo make?" Leong questioned.

"I will not guess," Piao responded. "Our host is a very learned man — a lifetime of decisions. A solution will come. I trust him. He believes in mending, not destroying. Let us adjourn to the dining room and have dinner with our hosts." They followed Hi Bo, joining the others for dinner.

The evening was quiet and Da Loban very thoughtful. Hi Bo was not his usual talkative self. He sat quietly sipping his whiskey, mulling over the composition and the opus he had orchestrated to avenge his daughter's childhood pain.

Piao dined quietly with grace and etiquette, focusing on Auntie Sun. He knew she did not find him or his wife welcome among her circle of friends. He was determined to reverse her opinion of him and his family.

"It has been difficult for you since your husband passed," Piao began.

Auntie nodded.

"Perhaps you would honor us by joining my wife and me for dinner at our home one month from Thursday. My cousin from Beijing will be visiting. You are a very intelligent and attractive woman. He is successful and very creative. I am confident you would find his company interesting."

"Why would you suggest that?" she queried in a tone almost of anger.

"He, too, had a similar experience."

"What was that?" Auntie replied with uncertainty.

"His wife died of breast cancer two years ago. He shared his loneliness with me. I thought you may be experiencing the same."

Auntie Sun tapped her lips with her handkerchief, her eyes looking down at the table. Then she looked directly into Piao's eyes. She replied, "Yes, that is true. I too am experiencing loneliness. It is thoughtful of you to be so considerate. I would be honored."

His mission was accomplished. He bowed deeply.

Hi Bo lay in his bed. Sleep eluded him. He was not seeking an escape from the conversation with Piao earlier that evening; he was unraveling the revenge puzzle presented to him. Hi Bo gazed at the clock: 10:00 p.m., midnight, then 1:00 a.m., and seeming only a few moments later, 3:00 a.m.

Unexpectedly an idea, a clue, for solving the Leopold dilemma seeped into his brain ever so slowly. It began to surround him. He considered the pros and the cons, evaluating each possibility, searching for clarification of fairness and justice to all parties. He sought retribution not for himself, only for his daughter. A moment of respite came as he considered the possibility of his beautiful Jan Yee and the young Leong marrying each other. He would capture all the birds with a single swoosh; a sense of calm came to him as a tiny smile crossed his lips.

Hi Bo's eyes closed as sleep arrived with its gentle brush across his lids....

The next morning, Hi Bo, Piao, and Leong met at the club for drinks and conversation.

Hi Bo and Piao ordered tea, and Leong ordered coffee. Da Loban appeared tired, as a result of a sleepless night.

Leong looked awake and alert, as did Piao. They sat there waiting for Hi Bo to articulate his strategy.

"Have you arrived at some reasonable answer to, or rejection of, my offer?" Mr. Piao solicited.

"I have been contemplating your proposal. I believe there is nothing to gain from endless rage. Revenge has its purpose, but my religion teaches that we must put anger aside. Once that is done, suffering subsides, and we experience rest and tranquility. My philosophy is that the angry person suffers more than the one with whom he is angry.

"I agree with your astute observation. An added plus of diminishing Leopold's capital will be the enormous anguish it will inflict, resulting in a different lifestyle for him and his family. I regret that part. I am not an animal like our adversary.

"Here is my proposition," Hi Bo began. "I slept little last night. The solution is a complicated challenge. Saving face is secondary. I loathe being a party to hurting another human being. Yet my anger toward our enemy goes beyond the pale. Much to my embarrassment, you are correct: money is his god. Its loss would cause him much grief. He is used to the good life. If we somehow could diminish that lifestyle or take it away completely, that would be a harsh punishment. As a result, his power and the respect he receives from his community, which he neither has earned nor deserves, would lessen, and perhaps vanish."

Piao and Leong sat hushed, listening to Da Loban. Leong
drank his coffee; Piao sipped tea. Hi Bo continued.

Da Loban pulled a sheet of paper from his inside jacket pocket
and unhurriedly opened it, focusing on Piao. "I estimate that Mr.
Leopold's company is worth ten million US dollars. If I wanted
to buy it as a sign of forgiveness, I would insist on a two-million-
dollar forgiveness discount as an opening penalty for his filthy
transgression. He must — and this a deal breaker if he refuses —
he must apologize to my daughter in front of our entire family,
including the servants who witnessed this horror." Da Loban
peered down at his notes and resumed.

"In a negotiation I will buy his debilitated company for eight
million dollars. The buyout will be paid with five million dollars
cash, and the balance will be paid over a five-year period. I will
take over his accounts receivable and payable."

He turned to Piao. "And to you, my good friend, since this is
your idea, I want to include you, sir. You, Master Piao, will put up
two and a half million, and I will put up another two and a half
million. We will pay off the balance as I mentioned, including
a two percent interest charge for the unpaid balance. You and I
will be equal partners, and perhaps Mr. Chan here will run the
business in Switzerland with a small equity position. Leong's part
will come from your half and my half of our equity investment.
And finally, we will offer a sales position to Leopold so that he
may continue to work and perhaps no one will know about the
changes to the company. That, sir, is my offer to Leopold, and my
reward to you for arranging this apology."

Piao stroked his chin, remaining silent, considering the
offer. "May Buddha forgive me and not interpret my sentence on
Leopold as greed." Hi Bo stared at his friend Piao. A significant
sense of calm swathed Hi Bo. He drank the last drops of tea that
had settled in his cup. He motioned for the waiter, nodding for

another, and then sat back in his chair, satisfied. He nodded his head to Leong, assured of his plan.

As he looked at Leong, Hi Bo was deep in thought. *You, my young man, may not understand what is going on here. You are not married to my daughter yet. Still, I want to set the scene for providing for my daughter's future should you and Jan Yee find the path to be as one. It appears that the clever Piao has miscalculated what my conclusive offer might be. My best guess is that Piao has underestimated me. The choice is now in his hands. Should he reject me, or accept, or come up with another solution, now it is I who will wait for my friend's response.*

Piao smiled. *A very clever negotiator, this Hi Bo.* "Now I am convinced why we are friends. It has always been my pleasure to be surrounded by intelligent and selfless colleagues."

Piao took a quiet reflective moment, carefully scanning his own deep deliberations. "I think your plan is an excellent form of retribution or, should I say, an apology. It will restore your daughter's honor and simultaneously strengthen your company. However, I have a different thought in mind. Please listen to my view of the situation. I am not an entrepreneur. I do not know the first thing about running a business. I, sir, am a deal maker, a broker. I bring people together and take a little commission off the top. I am always satisfied with just a trivial taste to keep me happy. And one, two, three, I depart. I leave the businessmen to figure out how to make a success of an unusual opportunity. That is my goal. And if my plan is of interest to you, I shall pursue it in the hope that we will all benefit at the expense of the villain, who will receive his deserved penalty."

Hi Bo sat silently. *So clever this Piao is. He wants to have his cake and eat it too. He hits and runs with the cash in his pocket, leaving the burden of success on me. Still, it is a plan I shall not refuse.* "Please, sir, having you as a colleague and business partner would honor me. I ask that you accept."

"You are my trusted brother, Hi Bo. A baker kneads and rolls his dough; a shoemaker makes shoes. I, sir, am a deal maker, and a good one at that. I must continue to do what I do best. I cannot accept your offer, even if not a single cent fills my pockets."

My God, Piao is brilliant and persuasive, Leong thought. *He knows what he wants and asks for it — and gets it. He is someone to learn from. Still, this remains an exciting conundrum,* Leong mused. *How this transaction will come to an end remains to be seen.*

"I, with much disappointment, now throw down the gauntlet to you, my colleague. You have accepted the challenge. The great Sang Ye Piao is standing here before me. Sir, you are my hero. And I am confident that you will succeed. However, there is a single caveat."

"And that stipulation is, my friend?"

"You, sir, if you are to conclude this arrangement, must find a partner for me, one whom I can trust and who is honest and hardworking." Hi Bo put his hand forward as Piao reached across the table. Leong gazed in surprise as they shook in agreement.

Check and mate. Young Leong's brain whizzed.

❦

Daryl Narrates

On Monday night at ten o'clock, my phone rang. It was David Chen. "How are you, David?" I paused. "To what do I owe the pleasure of this call?"

"First, how is Maxine? And, of course, how are your beautiful daughters and your clever son Fred?" Chen asked me in his most polite Asian style.

"The girls are in fifth grade. Fred is in high school. He is working his butt off," I politely responded.

What is all this idle talk? What could be on Chen's mind that he has telephoned me from Guangzhou, when he watches every penny?

"How is your business? Going well, I hope," Chen persisted.

"Yes, it is." I said, "What's on your mind, David? You never call unless it's very important."

"A very interesting opportunity has been brought to my attention by a trusted friend. It is one that comes rarely, or should I say once in a lifetime."

"Please explain." My curiosity took over.

"A huge shoe distributor, who sells footwear worldwide, in the millions, perhaps fifteen million to twenty million pairs, has gotten himself into trouble with a major shoemaker. The manufacturer refuses to make product for his company. Wherever the distributor goes for quality shoe making, the door is closed to him."

"What did he do that was so terrible?"

"No one wants to discuss it. I do not even know his transgression. Nor do I want to know. He is being forced to sell his business at a deep discount. The major shoemaker mentioned earlier is the potential buyer. He wants and needs a smart partner to put up half the money."

I remained silent … thinking. "How much money are we talking about?"

"We are talking about two and a half million US dollars."

"What is the big deal? You can do that alone. Why does Mr. Big Shoemaker need a partner?"

"I would commit to this opportunity in a minute, but it is not what I do. I am a manufacturer, not an entrepreneur. That is why you and I joined hands. You are the best, the very best seller I know or have ever worked with. Most important, you are honest.

"The buyer doesn't want to run the new business. He only wants to make shoes for the bad guy's company after he buys it. It is a situation that offers great potential. He wants a partner he can trust. The synergy of the plot is fascinating. Both companies will have the same financial team, the same sales organization, and an identical production group. The distributor will just do sales and service the customers. I called you because you are an expert in sales and service. All you must do is create a stronger client base and bring back the old buyers who left because of poor quality and customer cooperation. And let me add, the purchaser who is seeking a partner is a very honorable man."

I stopped and thought for a moment. "Where is this company he wants to buy located? Is there a projection sheet, a balance sheet, and a P&L statement I can read?"

"The company is in Zurich, Switzerland. I can send all the numbers to you by FedEx."

"Why not email?" I questioned.

"Email is not confidential. If you decide to take this opportunity, you will be among a group of some of the most powerful businessmen in all of China. Capiche?"

I smiled, immediately understanding the powerful connections the Chinese shoemaker must have. We said our goodbyes. I hung up.

"Who was that on the phone?" Maxine asked me.

"David Chen from Guangzhou," I answered.

"What did he want?"

"He had a crazy proposal for a new business in China and Switzerland. He is sending some information to me."

"You're not thinking of another business? Don't you have enough on your plate and so far away in Switzerland?"

"I want to see the plan and the potential upside. I want to know the margins and the volume and see the profit and loss statement and the balance sheet."

"I have no idea what you're talking about."

I smiled at my wife's reaction to the business vernacular as if it were gibberish. Maxine was very smart. Before I married her she was a senior vice president of a major fashion company. She knew exactly what I was talking about. With so much on her mind about our family, she permitted words to fly by her — not her usual style.

"While David was speaking, it occurred to me that if we invested in a company with a Chinese partner, our daughters, or at least one of them, could take a summer job at our new firm. It would give her an opportunity to hone her Mandarin and perhaps learn some French, German, and Italian, as well as get a taste of being an entrepreneur."

"The girls are only thirteen years old. Why are you thinking so far into the future?"

"My dearest of all my partners, the British thought they were the smartest empire on the face of the earth. They made a deal with China to lease Hong Kong for ninety-nine years. To the English, ninety-nine years sounded like forever. To the Chinese the time agreed upon was only one or one and half lifetimes. Now, today, who controls Hong Kong, England or China? Not a single shot fired, not a single person killed. Those endless ninety-nine years flew by, and who do you think made the better deal, the brilliant king of England or the challenged Chinese emperor? It was the shrewd emperor of China, with his wise understanding of time and its value. And ninety-nine years from now, no one will ever remember that the British once owned Hong Kong. It's amusing because it was one of the great real estate deals of the century. Well ... almost as good as the Louisiana Purchase."

"What does all that history have to do with this transaction you are considering?"

"Before you know it, those two delicious daughters we have will be twenty-plus years old. Fred will be in his thirties. China and the United States will be the future world economic powers. And maybe, just maybe, our children will be in the midst of the most prosperous trade and industry boom in history, able to live anywhere in the world they want."

"What if this is not what they want?"

"I still believe, if the numbers prove interesting, it could be an excellent investment." I walked into the kitchen, opened the refrigerator, plucked a shiny apple from a bowl, and dug my teeth into its crisp, fresh coolness.

❦

The Plot Thickens

Leong was a welcome and frequent visitor to the big house. He was puzzled and much disappointed by Jan Yee's coolness. *Did I say something offensive? Was I too aggressive in my overtures to Hi Bo's daughter? Does her father regret thinking of me as a potential suitor?*

Jan Yee sat in the library reading, as Leong watched local news on the television. All Leong could think about was holding this beautiful woman in his arms as she sat close by. He wanted to embrace her and perhaps gently kiss her. *Why is she so distant? Does she not care for me? I must find out.*

"Jan Yee," Leong said in a soft tone, "you know I am very fond of you. I can only guess that it is obvious. And yet, and yet...." He fumbled for a moment. "You are so distant. Have I said something or acted in any way that offended you?"

She remained silent, pretending not to hear, her eyes fixed on the pages of the book. Yet sadly and intently, she listened to every word he whispered.

"You must answer," he pleaded.

"I like you very much," she responded. "But I am guessing that there is some connection between you and I that blocks the relationship you may have on your mind."

"Tell me what you are talking about." He was mystified by her answer.

"I am Madame Hi Bo and Da Loban Hi Bo's adopted

daughter. I came here as a housemaid. My parents gave me up so they could get the money to help my sick brother. Your last name is Chan. You were born in Fushun. My last name is also Chan; I too was born in Fushun. I believe we are brother and sister." Jan Yee sat hushed, her head tilted down to one side.

"Your name is Jan Yee," Leong argued. "My sister's name is Shan Di."

"That is true. Shan Di was my birth name, my name as a maid in this very house. My adoptive father requested that I change my name from Shan Di to Jan Yee to honor his deceased mother. Without hesitation, I agreed. I felt it was my way of reciprocating the joy and safety he had bestowed upon me."

Leong looked at her in total silence. *Could this be true? Is this lovely young woman my true sister? Oh God, please forgive me. I feel unbearably ashamed of my disgraceful, lascivious thoughts.* Leong put his head down, placing his forehead into his open hands. He sobbed and gritted his teeth, trying to block out his humiliation.

The two young people sat for more than an hour sharing memories of their childhood. The startling coincidental matching truths confirmed what they were loath to accept. The evidence was clear: they *were* brother and sister. They embraced, holding each other close as tears ran down their cheeks. It was a moment of joy for Jan Yee and a quicksand of disappointment and dishonor for Leong. Still he felt a trickle of joy to be finally united with his sister.

"What shall we do?" she asked. "What shall we do?"

"I must think," he replied.

"There is one more part of my life I have not disclosed to you."

"What is that? Please do not leave anything out. I must know everything," he begged.

"I was a young girl." She hesitated, rethinking her confession. "I was fifteen or sixteen years old. A business guest of my father assaulted me here in this house. It was a horror. I was young and did not understand the implications. I became pregnant and gave birth to a child. I do not know if it was a boy or a girl. My parents gave the child up for adoption. That was it. I thought they did the right thing. I was young and helpless. I was not able to make any decisions. I just wanted to forget the entire incident. But, but" — she stammered — "at night in my bed, when I am reading or perhaps doing absolutely nothing, the memory returns. It pains me, my memory of the attack, and the thought that I may have a child growing up destitute, homeless, and struggling. Often I put my hands over my eyes to push the ugly vision of that horrific moment far away from me."

Leong touched his sister's hand and pulled her close to him. With his arms around her, she wept deep, painful sobs. They both rocked slowly, Jan Yee with shame, Leong with sorrow.

"My disgrace, my pain, I had no answer. I questioned, why me? I am a good person, a kind and careful woman, respectful to my parents. Somehow, She and She alone knew that my lifelong anguish was unwarranted. She rescued me. She gave me a good life with caring, gentle mother and father. And now She returns to me my brother." They sat quietly in an embrace, trying to bring comfort to one another.

"Oh! Excuse me," Hi Bo said as he walked into the library. "I should have knocked." A smile crossed his lips. What he had been hoping for appeared to be happening. The look he saw on their faces was gratifying. *This will be a good match.* He left the room.

"Oh my," Jan Yee uttered, "Now my father thinks we are something we are not."

15

The Complication Continues

Daryl continues to tell his version of the story

I placed the documents that came from China on my desk. I was satisfied for the moment, but now it was time for the twins' birthday party. Maxine had invited their classmates and their parents to join us in celebrating our daughters' thirteenth birthday party. And a b'not mitzvah to follow next week. Fred, now a grown man at the age of twenty-one, stood silently to the side listening to the screams, laughter, and giggles as his sisters sifted their way through the mountain of gifts everyone had brought. All those beautiful gold and silver packages tied with silk bows were a redundancy in their lives, since they already had everything.

The moms stood around gossiping, focused on themselves, smiling, pointing, critical of one another, all of them sipping wine and quietly enjoying the few hours we'd offered them.

I called Fred aside. We left for the guest room/office in the apartment.

I sat in my easy chair and Fred on the couch. "One of my customers has invited me on a fishing trip to the North Pole." I paused and sipped my Pellegrino. "I suggested that my son join us. What do you think?"

Fred stared and was silent, and then he burst out with, "You're kidding?"

"It's not a joke. It is a real invitation. We fly to Chicago and change planes to a private jet that will take us and a few other guests to a lodge in the Northwest Territory about two hundred miles south of the North Pole. I hear it is great. Mostly guys, all businesspeople taking a break. Good food, make some new friends."

"Let's do it, Dad," Fred replied.

We both sat there quietly. I noticed that Fred was now just a half inch taller than I. There was stubble on my son's chin, a pack of Chesterfields in his shirt pocket. I closed my eyes for a moment in disappointment. There was nothing to be said; both of us were silent. The young man looked down at his pocket, searched my eyes, and saw a tiny disapproving glimpse. He shrugged, as if to say, *I'm grown up now.*

"Thank you, Dad, for making my sisters' birthday a good day for me as well." I loved his being polite. His mother had taught him well. I felt proud. *Fred knows exactly how to express his needs. It must be a gift from his mother's genes. I wish I had that from my parents.*

"Love you, Fred."

"Love you too, Dad."

I clicked my phone. It was now 7:30 p.m. — 8:30 a.m. in China. *I'll wait another half hour and then call David.*

At 9:00 p.m. I dialed. There was one ring, and then a second. "*Wei* (Hello)?" I heard his voice.

"David? It's Daryl. How are you, my friend? I didn't want to call you too early. Is it all right?"

"I've been up for hours. I start jogging at six thirty. How may I help you?"

"I reviewed the documents of the Chinese/Swiss opportunity you sent. My people here say it looks interesting. It may be an opening for us to have a new toehold in China. It will also be an opportunity for my children and their future. What also pleases me is my being a full partner in one company. Somewhat important is having one of the most powerful men in China as a business colleague. It makes me feel confident about the future. I'm very grateful that you have brought this prospect to me. And I thank you. My premonition is that the strong global economy will be shared almost equally by China and the United States. My family will be in both countries. That is, if the financial commitments are similar."

I spoke slowly and cautiously, trying not to show the slightest eagerness.

"When you and your associates are more certain of yourselves, may I suggest you come to Guangzhou and meet with Mr. Hi Bo, the gentleman who is the other side of this deal?"

"Sounds like a plan," I responded. "Give me a few days, and I will get back to you."

I clicked the off button, ending our conversation.

❦

About ten days later at the airport in Hong Kong, Tang, the same driver who had taken us to the orphanage almost twelve years ago, still on the job for David Chen, awaited my arrival.

"Long time, no see," the chauffeur said as I got into the car.

"Yes, Tang, it has been quite a while. How are you and your family?"

"They are well. And how are the twins and Mr. Daryl's very kind wife?"

"TaiTai good and twins, thirteen years old last month."

"So quickly the time passes."

"How much time to Guangzhou?"

"About one and a half hour. New road now, directly from

Hong Kong to Guangzhou. No more ferry. You get sleep. When you wake, we be at hotel."

My eyelids heard the suggestion and obeyed, closing. "Thank you."

❦

The Entrepreneurial Courtship

My first evening at the White Swan Hotel in Guangzhou was a restless night, trying to shake off and adjust to the jet lag. Still, I was grateful for the four hours of uninterrupted slumber. At four in the morning, I stretched my still-sleeping arm toward the phone, picked it up, and telephoned my office in New York. The staff was ready and waiting for the communication, giving me a full report of the past two days' activities. I made a few mental notes about the office call, and I was ready for my meeting.

A moment later the phone rang. It was Maxine, with loving maternal instructions for me to rest, drink bottled water only, use no ice, avoid raw fish, and "please don't work too hard." I easily accepted all her counsel and care, except for her request that I not work too hard. That was impossible. My work ethic was the master; I was its obedient messenger. I knew it, and Maxine recognized it. My wife was not aware of how many people have said to me how fortunate I have been in my business ventures. No one knew that I had discovered early in my career the fact that the harder I worked … the luckier I got.

❦

I peered out the car window as Tang slowly pulled the vehicle around the massive driveway in front of the big house. Tang opened the back door of the car and assisted me as I exited. Walking to the house, I saw an elegant gentleman standing tall and straight at the door. On the first or second step, I stretched out my hand, greeting my host with a handshake. "I am Daryl Landsman."

Hi Bo extended his hand to me with a bow. I reached forward. We firmly pressed our palms together. I was very impressed immediately as I looked intently into the face of my probable new business associate. We both exchanged a true and honest smile. A good feeling of trust and welcome linked us in a strange but knowing way. Each was familiar with the inner voice we valued. Good vibes passed between me and Mr. Hi Bo, a positive beginning to a new business enterprise.

David Chen stepped forward and put his right hand into Hi Bo's as he placed his left arm on my shoulder, and said, "This a very important and momentous meeting. You are both my very valued friends.

"Mr. Hi Bo, permit me to introduce my friend and a former partner, Mr. Daryl Landsman, from New York City."

We walked into Hi Bo's home and into the library. I do not surprise easily, but the elegance of the massive home caught me off guard. I turned my head from right to left, scanning every inch, enjoying the signs of great Asian wealth and ultimate success.

Hi Bo and I looked at each other, both of us in silence. Not a word passed. I admired the room. The art was both Asian and Western. The magnificent Buddha was dazzling, as were the multiple sculptures, bronze and marble, tastefully filling the entryway and the library. I was impressed. My possible new partner looked like a true global businessman. Dressed in a gray-striped double-breasted suit, a starched white shirt, and a well-knotted burgundy silk tie, he carried himself with elegance.

We all remained standing, waiting for Hi Bo to sit in his huge leather chair that appeared to be his private spot. "Please, gentlemen, please sit. Let's not be so formal. We are about to become friends." A young woman came into the room and bowed.

"Cissy, please arrange for my guests, Mr. Landsman and Mr. Chen, the refreshments of their choice."

The young woman moved toward me, once again a very slight bow, and looked into my eyes. "How I serve you, sir?"

"Coffee, black, one sugar, *Cie, cie* (Thank you),"I responded.

"Bukertzie (You're welcome)." I nodded. Everyone was surprised to hear my limited Chinese vocabulary. This was a singular moment of bonding between me and each person in the room. It was simple, polite, and effective. I had accomplished this on many occasions when speaking the few Chinese words I knew during my career in Asia.

"You speak Mandarin?" Hi Bo questioned.

"I have a small vocabulary of about fifty or sixty words."

"That is quite good. When did you learn?"

"Many years ago, when David and I were partners, I used to visit Dongguan, here in Southern China and felt a responsibility to have some measure of polite communication."

"Excellent." Hi Bo smiled.

"I did go to Macau once, to the casinos."

Cissy returned and brought the fresh coffee, a soft drink for David, and a tomato juice for Da Loban. I sipped the strong brew, clenching my eyes.

Here, my dear reader, is a strange moment in this story and the history of the lives of two able businessmen.

I shared this tale with the author. I hadn't planned this moment, nor had I imagined it could occur.

Here in one room, Hi Bo and I were sitting together in a social setting. A bizarre meeting was taking place. Hi Bo was the adoptive father of Jan Yee (the biological mother of the twins that Maxine and I adopted). This was an impossible moment, but the story is true — very true.

Guess who was coming down the stairs? The striking Jan Yee, the birth mother of my twins. "Good morning, everyone. I hope I am not disturbing your meeting. I was about to get my morning tea. May I get any of you gentlemen something from the kitchen?" She inquired.

Everyone stood. Jan Yee looked dazzling in a simple black pantsuit, a white blouse peeking out of the buttoned jacket, and a red scarf tossed around her neck.

"May I introduce my daughter, Jan Yee? This is Mr. Landsman from New York in the USA."

"Oh, I have always wanted to visit New York; it's my dream. I have heard and read so much about that wonderful city. Please forgive me, Father. I did not mean to interrupt you." The charming Jan Yee backed up with a slight bow.

"You have met Mr. Chen before. Please join us. Have Cissy bring your tea."

She sat in the chair next to her father. *And once again, my reader, please believe me — you cannot make this story up. Trust me that it is true.*

The business opportunity was not discussed. It was idle banter, of family and politics of the West and Asia. After lunch, I was hoping there would be another occasion to discuss the details of the partnership deal, or later that day — perhaps tomorrow.

"Do you play golf, Mr. Landsman?" Hi Bo questioned.

"No I do not. I prefer tennis," I responded.

"Why is that? Here in China, golf has become a tradition."

In my most diplomatic style, I said, "I tried my hand at your traditional sport. I found it too time-consuming. At tennis, we play about an hour or an hour and a half. The schedule gives us more time to spend with our families. Golf is an all-day affair."

"You do have a family?" Hi Bo asked.

"Yes, I do. I'm very much married. I have three children, a son and twin daughters." I sipped my coffee.

"I'm impressed that a busy man like you thinks of the importance that family has in his life."

Slow and easy, it's the Chinese way. Get to know the person first; the deal will follow. The Chinese tradition is unhurried, relaxed, and gradual, consisting of more measured conversation. I felt somewhat impatient and wanted to begin. But I was a guest in the man's house, and Mr. Hi Bo would set the pace, the time, and the agenda. When my turn arrived, I would know how to make my position clear and acceptable.

As we sat and spoke, I was fascinated by this very attractive young woman. She must be twenty-eight or twenty-nine years old, I guessed. Very well-spoken and well educated. Her English was right out of the book with just a tiny twinge of Asian accent.

Cissy quietly entered the room, and like a hummingbird, in one single position so as not to disturb Hi Bo and his guests, she waited for the conversation to end. At an opportune moment, she announced, "Lunch is being served."

The dining area was filled with orchids of every color. On the paneled walls close to the windows there hung more than twenty varieties in extraordinary planters. The oak floor was partially covered by a small Persian rug. I looked everywhere in complete fascination.

"We have a greenhouse on the back patio where my wife raises these orchids. Many have been prizewinners. Look at each individual transmutation of black and turquoise, orange and purple. As they say in America, my wife has a green thumb. Many of the plants you see are first-place award winners at Shanghai and Beijing floral pavilions," Hi Bo explained.

The astonishing color of the orchids was, without doubt, an incredible sight for all. We three men sat there silently, staring at the array of shades and variations.

I rose from my seat, stepping closer to the hanging plants. I moved slowly around the windows. My face, no doubt, showed my admiration for the talented Madame Hi Bo. Those sitting at the table glanced at one another and nodded, impressed with my interest and observations.

The midday meal was served on the huge oaken table covered by a white glistening Swiss cotton cloth, on which lay an oversized silver Lazy Susan. The platters of food were placed onto the huge circular serving dish. Each person in turn gently pushed the turntable until the choice arrived in front of his or her plate. First to arrive was a platter of drunken shrimp on a sizzling serving dish.

I was told that the shrimp, while alive, are tossed into a bowl of sweet Chinese wine. It takes an hour for them to ingest the wine. After that, the shrimp are grilled. The flavors swimming across the backs of the shrimp and the magic of the wine mix become a taste never to be forgotten. This course was followed by lightly fried calamari with a special dipping sauce. Each person had his or her own bowl of white rice. Wine stood on a small serving table, along with two bottles of water, one plain and the other sparkling. Chopsticks lay neatly on a tiny white glass holder. Western utensils were available at my position. In an instant, chopsticks were my only choice.

"May I be so bold as to ask if you are currently involved in other enterprises?" Hi Bo began.

"May I be even bolder, sir, and ask to fill our glasses with some wine, so I can make a toast honoring my host and hostess, as well as to my new friends, the Hi Bo family?"

I looked around the room. I was pleased by Hi Bo's nod and Jan Yee's smile.

I stood at my seat and said, "Please accept my sincere thank you to the entire Hi Bo family for welcoming me into your most elegant and most gracious home. Thank you for introducing your daughter, Jan Yee. I am also grateful for the thought of joining our two families together in an interesting business opportunity; and a special appreciation to our friend David Chen for the introduction." I sat and sipped my wine. All the others clicked glasses.

David Chen said, "Amen."

I heard, with much surprise, Jan Yee whisper under her breath, "Awomen."

The group began their lunch. I turned to Hi Bo.

"I've been married for twenty-five years to my soul mate. It was love at first sight," I said.

Jan Yee smiled, obviously enjoying the openness of a Western man. Few Chinese men speak their minds, and hardly, if ever, discuss their personal feelings. Most Asian men I know have the wisdom to listen, rather than speak. You learn more from the former and less from the latter.

As I uttered those words describing the affection I have for my wife, suddenly I saw a strange but familiar look. It was cheek movements, on Jan Yee. It was only by instinct I recognized and knew that slight twitch. It reminded me of something familiar I could not recall.

"I want to express my appreciation of your toast to my wife, who remains upstairs showering now," Hi Bo added. "She will join our luncheon soon. She asked that we begin without her. I expect her in a few moments. She extends her apology."

Ten minutes slipped quickly by as the guests ate and drank, engaged in quiet conversation about Chinese economics in the Middle East. "Not a safe political choice," Hi Bo commented.

I very much agree with this observant gentleman, but I will keep silent. I bided my time.

"Ah ... here she comes. Tan Ha Hi Bo, welcome. Please join us," her husband said. We all rose from the table. After introductions, we returned to our seats to resume our lunch.

"I can see where your daughter inherited her beauty," I said in a flattering tone.

"My daughter is much more beautiful than I," Madame Hi

Bo responded. "Still, I am very grateful for the compliment, coming from so handsome a gentleman." I suddenly realized I was sitting with a very sophisticated family.

Eyes moved from right to left. A grin on David's face indicated something that he refrained from voicing so as not to embarrass me, a well-meaning guest.

A huge bronze platter arrived filled with a massive steamed white fish recently netted in the China Sea. The succulent aroma seeped into my nostrils. The fish was covered with fresh greens and tiny slivers of garlic. At the bottom of the dish, mushrooms swam in an unforgettable Chinese sauce. A huge bowl of fried rice and a side dish of pea pods were in the center of the table. Though only six people were there to dine, the food was plentiful enough for ten.

In a moment of lightheartedness, with the wine in me, I commented, "The cuisine was most delicious, so much so," I commented, "I could run off with the cook." The guests around the table were speechless. I instantly recognized that my joke had not been well-taken. My face flushed. It was a first lesson in Asian manners: just the suggestion of taking a friend's employee is forbidden and unacceptable behavior.

"If I may ask," I said, turning to Jan Yee, "what is your business?" I was trying to continue the conversation. Another error; I was sinking quickly. I clenched my teeth. My body felt the heat of embarrassment. My eyes shut. *Oh no, oh no. I better just listen. This is China, not New York. This deal may be dead already.*

Jan Yee gazed at her father. He nodded, giving her permission to answer my poor selection of inquiries.

"I work at my father's company, assisting him with anything he needs done. I host and conduct meetings with customers, developing styles, which I enjoy the most. I follow up production, and I am, as you say in America, my father's girl Friday. I participate in just about everything, including collecting late payments when necessary."

"My kind of woman," I said. "You should be proud of her." I turned to Hi Bo, trying to compensate for my errors, only to have made another blunder with "my kind of woman."

"Do you have children?" Hi Bo asked in his subtle interview.

"I do, sir. I am proud of all of them."

"*Your* children, do they participate in your business?"

"Not yet. My son is still in college. He is only twenty-one years old. My daughters are thirteen." Again, I experienced a slight jolt in my head. *There goes that twist of Jan Yee's cheek again. I am puzzled. The cheek tic stirs a memory, a memory I cannot remember. Not important.*

"Actually, my daughters are twins."

"Giving birth to twins has to be a difficult task," Mrs. Hi Bo added.

"It is certainly more arduous than a single childbirth, but my wife did not have that choice." Silence fell over the room, looks of puzzlement painted on everyone's face. The guests around the table were baffled, with one exception, David Chen. He knew exactly what was about to be revealed.

"My wife was not the birth mother. We adopted our daughters. In fact, it happened right here in Guangzhou. Our good friend and partner David Chen was kind enough to introduce me to the Catholic orphanage just about twelve years ago. At that sacred institution, much to our good fortune, I met our two beautiful children and brought them home with us to New York. That was thirteen years ago. Now they live happily as Chinese American children, true members of our family. I am only guessing, but not more than a ten-minute drive from this very house is the orphanage."

16

The Birthing History

The car swiftly moved toward the city of Fushun. Jan and Leong were trying to find their mom's little house. They struggled to remember it from their childhood experiences. Both knew their mother's new house was close by. The children, with a major assist from Hi Bo, had been able to help their mother purchase a tiny house. She and her remaining daughter, now seventeen years old, lived in the downstairs apartment. A tenant with one child lived upstairs, paying rent of just over 600 renminbi each month, equivalent to about one hundred dollars.

Will I remember my mom or my little sister? My vision of what Momma looks like has disappeared. I have forgotten how her voice sounds. If she called out to me, would I know this stranger speaking? This is totally unbearable. It is impossible to believe. Will she remember me? Will she recognize her daughter's face or anything about me?

"My heart is beating. I can hear it. I can feel it. Are you nervous?" Leong whispered to Jan Yee.

"We are in rhythm. I am frightened. My insides feel nauseous. My mouth is dry. This may be dreadful for both of us."

"I hope not. I hope not," he replied.

The small brown and white cottage was in sight. A red brick chimney rose ten feet above the roof and opened at the main-floor level in the family room. A black wire fence surrounded the property. Two scraggly trees stood at either side of the house. Tiny bushes inside the fence struggled to reach out to the sun and to whatever little rain fell around their thirsty roots. Occasionally Momma Chan gave some boys a few yuan to bring water from the river to feed the parched bushes.

Two entrances, one at the front and another at the side of the house, welcomed visitors. The side, no doubt, was the entrance for the tenant.

Both young people sat silently in the car. It was going to take mettle to meet their mom again, to return to the squalor and poverty they recalled. They looked at each other. Hesitantly, Leong said, "I wish I had a whiskey."

"I wish I drank," Jan Yee replied. For a moment they each smiled, frightened.

"Okay, let's do it."

The front door opened. A young girl peered out, dressed in blue jeans, a sweater, and sneakers, her hair combed to the back and neatly tied in a bun. She was pretty and seemed curious.

"Nee how (Hello)," she called out.

"Nee how back to you," Jan called. Hand in hand, she and Leong walked slowly toward the open door.

"I am Leong, and this is Shan Di. Are you Tan Ta?"

"Yes, yes!" she screamed. "Momma, Momma, come quickly. Look who has come to visit us."

There she was, Momma, at the age of about fifty-eight, still looking healthy and firm. Her face was not wrinkled or aged as they had expected. It was stoic, with no smile and no sense of excitement. She was staring, perhaps in disbelief.

"Shan Di, my child. I do not recognize you. You are a grown woman, a grown and beautiful woman. Is this your husband?" She pointed to Leong; he stood stunned like a stone. His eyes glistened with moisture. He could not believe his own mother could not recognize him.

"No, Momma, this is your son, Leong." Jan Yee could see Momma unsteady on her feet. Momma stretched her arms forward, out into empty space, trying to catch herself from falling to the ground. All three children ran to her. They supported Momma Chan and helped her to a rocking chair at the right of the fireplace inside the house.

Oh my God, how could I have forgotten what my son looks like? Momma Chan placed her face in her hands, weeping with deep, uncontrollable sobs. All stood around watching their mother struggle with the reality that two of her children had finally come home.

She lifted her head, rubbing her eyes with the edge of her sleeve, stood, and embraced her daughter and her son. "I am so happy to see you both. I cannot believe that this is happening. My children back. It's a miracle." Her voice struggled. She cleared her throat. "Tan Ta, go get water, and boil a kettle for tea for your sister and brother. This is a time for celebration."

Inside the compact, tidy residence, all three children sat sipping the tea that Tan Ta had brought to the table, along with some freshly baked crackers. There were few possessions, but the home was clean and very livable. Through the window they saw an outhouse for the two families living in the cottage.

"How are you feeling, Momma? How is your health?"

"I feel well. A few aches and pains, but nothing I prefer to complain about. I work three days a week as a cook for a bookstore owner. He pays me fifteen dollars each week, which helps a great deal. Plus, what you and Leong send every month is a big help. We are both so grateful. You have made our lives bearable."

"And you, Caren" — their sister's English name — "are you going to school?"

"I will graduate this year, and then I hope to go to university. I have very good grades and plan to study medicine in college."

The two guests looked at each other, nodding in approval. They were happy that everyone was healthy and reasonably comfortable.

"Where is Poppa?" Leong questioned.

In an almost whispering voice, Caren answered, "Poppa passed almost three years ago."

"What happened?" Jan Yee and Leong said almost simultaneously.

"He died of tuberculosis. It was a long illness. He was in pain, unhappy. Maybe he is happier now," Momma answered.

Jan Yee reached out toward her mother's hands and enclosed them in hers. Saddened eyes faced each other. There were no tears and no words, only an acknowledgment of regret for the time lost and the distance between them.

"Why the surprise visit? What is happening in your lives? How did you two discover each other?"

"Do you remember — Poppa sent me off to be a housemaid for a loan he took to help Leong with his health?"

"Yes, yes ... please, let us not speak of the worst day of my life. Can you ever forgive me?"

"It turned out to be good for everyone. She has watched over us. My Da Loban was so taken with me that he and his wife adopted me. I am your child, but I am their daughter. I am treated like a daughter, and they have spoiled me with love and education. They have given me affection and a fine life."

"And I too am well," Leong began. "I am also educated. I have a good job. That is why I can send money every month. I am healthy, and at this moment very happy. Well, sort of."

"You have not answered my question. Why have you come to see me after all these years? Is there something I can help you with?" the intuitive mother asked.

"We want to know the history of our family. When I was born, what did our father do to earn a living? What are our exact ages, and where we were raised? Where were we educated, if at all?" Leong questioned.

Silence filled the room. Momma looked with intensity into Shan Di's and Leong's faces. She saw as no one but a mother can see. A momma recognizes what no one else can detect; her son and her daughter had a connection that was not as brother and sister. She smiled and touched her brow. Her eyelids closed for an instant. Then she reached out to the table, fingered the teacup, and sipped. She uttered a deep sigh as if unloading a burden.

She began, "In 1989, during the horror in Tiananmen Square and the silencing of all China, fear replaced calm and peace. It ripped families apart. You were born," she said, turning to Leong, "almost thirty years ago.

"You were my first child, a son. It was a blessing. Poppa and I had prayed for a son. We valued your life more than our own. In those dark days, the law allowed a family only one child unless a tax was paid. We had no money, and fate bestowed on Poppa and me that you would be our only child."

"You became ill when you were eight years old. It was a strange disease, no known cure. Your father tried very hard to work and accumulate the money needed for the hospital. It was an impossible, inhuman task. He was paid two dollars a day. It was barely enough to eat."

Everyone listened intently. They could hear the wind brush the hopeless bushes outside.

"From our hovel, we saw federal police and soldiers come to a neighbor's hut. We heard screams, and we hid. We saw the police and soldiers drag the man out and take him away. Your father ran to the nearby hut. The mother was lying on the ground, a pool of blood surrounding her legs and stomach. She begged your poppa to take Shan Di — and to leave her to die — before the soldiers returned."

Momma Chan stood up and walked to the sink. She poured another cup of water from a pitcher and then put the cover back on. She rinsed her mouth and throat and spit the water into the sink. She took a deep breath and returned to her chair. Tears rimmed her eyes. She breathed deeply through her nose, filling her lungs with oxygen, and with a deep sigh, expelled the air. Momma Chan sat quietly, gathering her thoughts, and she continued.

"The little girl was about six or seven years old. We took her as our own. Our worry was that we were only allowed to have a single child. To say Shan Di was our maid would be a lie. To tell someone she was the daughter of a revolutionary would certainly bring trouble to us and to her."

"What happened?" Jan Yee asked.

"Soon after Shan Di came to us, you became ill, my son, and our neighbors moved in and moved out. It appeared that Shan Di was *our* daughter. And in fact, she was our daughter. She was a child whom we loved very much, especially Poppa. However, I became pregnant." She pointed to Tan Ta. "We could not have three children in our home. We would be fined and imprisoned and lose the three of you. That was an impossible and unacceptable choice.

"Poppa went to Guangzhou and took a loan from an employment agency. We sent Shan Di off to work as a housemaid. With the loan, we sent you to a health center," she said, pointing at Leong, "finally perhaps to find a cure. Now with my son and daughter away, everyone was safe. Shan Di was safe in Guangzhou, you were in a health center, and Caren here arrived at a childless home."

"Oh my, oh my." Shan Di clutched her blouse with two hands and wept. "How awful for you and Poppa; let me ask you one question, an urgent question that must be answered in complete truth. Please do not try to make us feel good with tiny lies. We want and need the truth, no matter how painful. This is important for our future and our lives.

"Momma, I beg you for certainty. Are you telling us that I am not your daughter, or is the story made up? Momma, this is a very important question. What you and Poppa had to do, you had to do. It was a terrible time. Swear on all our lives that you are telling the truth."

"I swear to you, every word is true. Leong is my son, and you, Shan Di, are not my daughter. I swear on the lives of each of you. The only thing I am not able to swear to is your birth date and Leong's."

Jan Yee and Leong stood up and looked into each other's eyes with the realization that they were not biological children of the same parents. They could not believe that their wish and dream was about to come true. Momma Chan had just given them a gift. It was the best news that could come out of a very sad story. They clasped hands and touched foreheads, their eyes peering at one another.

Jan Yee bowed and kissed her mother goodbye, and she hugged her sister. Jan and Leong offered help for when their little sister was ready to go to the university. Leong took some bills from his wallet and passed them to Tan Ta. Jan Yee took money from her purse and placed the money into her mom's dress pocket. They walked to the door, went outside, waved from the car, and left. Shouts of "Tai tsien, tai tsien (goodbye, goodbye)" were heard as the car noisily pulled away on the gravel road.

They were cautiously happy. Perhaps they were called brother and sister because they'd lived together since childhood. Everyone had assumed that was the case. Suddenly a new story had emanated from the past. Their mother had told them she was not Jan Yee's birth mother, that Jan Yee was the child of the woman in the hut next door. This would absolutely be good news to her adoring adoptive parents.

In the car, they spoke straightforward to each other.

"I cannot stop the feeling stirring inside of me that you are my sister. But that is not stopping me from loving you."

"I, too, feel that you are my brother." They gently touched their lips together.

"I honestly do not care, but let's do the DNA test anyway, just to be absolutely certain," Leong said.

"I agree, the test is a must. As much as we trust our momma, she is getting old. I believe she is telling the truth but let us be positive. This is too important a matter; there is no room for error," Jan Yee responded.

Leong drove as they held hands, feeling happy, finally connected with the freedom to go forward. He put his right hand on Jan Yee's knee. The touch felt good. They both laughed because it was the first flirtatious move Leong had attempted with his newfound love. "I have a lovely apartment in town. May I invite you up to see it? Perhaps if all goes well, we can stay there at first."

"I would love to. I dream about that." She laughed. "But we want to be absolutely sure. We shouldn't wait too long for our test. Once that is behind us, we can let go, and you may court me. I do want to be courted."

He put his arm around her shoulder, pulled her close, and promised, "You shall have the most exciting courtship in all of Guangzhou — no, in all of China."

Jan Yee was happy. "Leong, please drive with two hands." They laughed.

17

The Deal Is Done

Now Daryl Tells His Story

Hi Bo and I ended our negotiation and signed a mutually agreed-upon document outlining our business arrangement. I wire-transferred the total investment as I had promised. Hi Bo did his part. Piao received his commission of 6 percent, 3 percent from me and 3 percent from Hi Bo. Piao told me he had offered David Chen a fee for his participation, but Chen refused it. As he said, it was an honor to have assisted his valued friends. Everyone was satisfied, though Hi Bo and I thought the price was too high and Leopold thought the price too low. We all understood that a perfect business negotiation result is when all parties are dissatisfied.

David Chen called me in New York and told me that when they were alone at dinner, Master Piao said to him, "You are a most principled man. Please consider Piao a friend always. Your contribution was the key to the successful arrangement we have accomplished."

"Piao is a true gentleman," I replied to David.

"Life is long," David said. "Someday in the future, I may have a need to come to you for guidance and assistance." I replied that he could depend on me to reciprocate any time.

We both understood the meaning of our friendship.

18

The Power of Genetics

Author Continues

Three months passed after the visit to their mother and the subsequent tests for the genetic evaluation. The relationship between Jan Yee and Leong grew stronger, as did the love they felt for each other; still no test results. "What is taking so long?" Jan Yee murmured to herself.

The crushing news came: the DNA was a positive match; Leong and Jan Yee *were* genetically bound. The doctors explained that the match may have been the result of a fragment of genetic strain that settled into a parent years ago at his or her birth.

The genetic test result was unacceptable to Jan Yee. She, along with Leong, returned to her mother's home and, in a raging, accusatory argument, reproached her mother for lying. Finally, exhausted, reluctant, and filled with disgrace, Momma confessed that Poppa, in a moment of weakness, had an affair with the neighbor. She, Shan Di, was born as a result.

"You and your brother have the same father. Forgive me," she pleaded. "I did not want to bring dishonor and humiliation to you, to Poppa, or to me. I told you the truth when I said that I was not your birth mother." In silence Jan Yee and Leong left. Driving home, they pulled to the side of the road, wept, and embraced.

"What shall we do? What can we do?" Jan Yee whispered with tears streaming down her cheeks.

"We will try to find an answer. There must a solution." They closed their eyes and fell into a deep, escaping sleep.

❦

Alone in their library, Jan Yee sat quietly with her father. He was sipping his usual evening whiskey and his daughter, a bit of wine.

"Why is there no longer a relationship between you and Leong? He is such a fine man. He is hardworking and honest, and he wants to make something of himself. Are you no longer interested in him? It was my impression that you both cared for each other."

"We do care, my father, we do. There are issues and customs that forbid us to have an alliance."

"Is it a class issue? He is a Christian and we are Buddhists?" Hi Bo asked.

"If that was all it was, we would be together, Poppa."

"You must tell me so I can understand and perhaps help the situation."

"The situation is set in stone. No one can do anything!" She sobbed.

"I cannot believe that it can be so difficult that something cannot be corrected."

"Poppa, please hear me carefully. When Leong first came to our home, I found him very attractive. The more he was around, the more I liked and admired him. Yet there was a part of him that I found familiar. I could not place that strange, cloud-like experience."

Her father was quiet. His eyes were fixed upon his daughter, his hand behind his right ear, his head tilted to allow him to hear more sharply, and his brow furrowed.

"Then it occurred to me in an inexplicable and strange way," she continued, "that his last name was the same as mine before I became your daughter. But that was not unusual; there are many Chan families in China. After long, intimate, exploring discussions, we were amazed to find that we had been raised in the same town near the same village, and surprise of surprises, we were shocked to discover ... we are brother and sister."

Hi Bo's mouth dropped open. He took a deep breath and then gulped the whiskey in his glass. As he looked at his daughter, he tilted his head as if trying to hear correctly.

"To add more flames to our fire," Jan Yee continued, "we fell in love. That's right, Poppa: we fell in love. We fell in love not like a brother loves a sister, but like a man and a woman falls in love. Oh, Poppa, what shall we do? What shall we do?"

Her father's eyes squinted; perspiration appeared on his forehead. The two were silent. A twenty-second-long pregnant quiet moment hung over them. He was in disbelief.

"Yet we understood that our bloodlines forbade us to take it any further. It would be an unforgivable sin for us to be intimate. We wanted that so much that we fled from each other to protect ourselves and our families."

"Did you take blood tests?"

"Yes, we did. They proved our DNA matched. We are related, with matching genetic lines."

"Cousins are related and often they wed."

"We are *not* cousins; we are half-bother and half-sister," she said in an unusually emphatic voice, not her usual tone to her much-respected father.

"Who told you this story?" he asked, almost whispering.

"Leong's biological mother and my stepmother is one and the same person."

"Who is the father?"

"We were told we both have the same father."

Hi Bo sat quietly shaking his head. He bent over, pressing his clenched fists against his forehead, and pondered this complex situation. "This is truly a problem," he whispered, and rose unsteadily in a dizzying daze from his chair, almost limping.

Daryl Narrates from Zurich

"Hello, Maxine. How are you? Is everything okay?" I was holding my cell phone tight against my left ear.

"LangPi is not feeling well. I called the doctor, and she said our daughter must have a touch of the flu. The doctor called the pharmacy and prescribed some antibiotic medicine."

"How is our baby now?"

"Mostly she is asleep. But her temperature is one hundred and three."

"I would give her some aspirin also to keep the fever down."

"We are doing that."

"Keep me posted. I want to know every detail. Goodbye, darling," Daryl said.

"Be well, my love." I clicked my phone off.

Hi Bo suggested that I take Leong with me to Zurich and get a look at the new investment. We agreed that I would train Leong in the skills of running a company, dealing with employees, vendors, sales, accounts receivable, and all day-to-day issues that need constant attention.

Leong was a salesperson with a passion, a man with excellent people skills. Although I love to sell, I was more of an entrepreneur. I demonstrated to Leong that sales were important, but that was the easy part. The stressful extension of the sale is scheduling on-time production and delivery, performing quality maintenance, providing customer service, and most important, getting paid from the buyer. All these steps combined are just the tip of the corporate iceberg when it comes to a successful conclusion to the fiscal year and a favorable annual report. I tried to demonstrate in detail the power and importance of the most valued asset of any company: the customer base, the essential worth of any firm.

I shared a lifetime's expertise of customer care and how it works to grow the company. "All companies make errors. A smart businessman can take a company blip and convert the blunder by providing a rapid response to the clients' requirements."

"How do we do that?" Leong inquired.

"The smart manager corrects the error immediately, blames no one, and gets the situation back to normal."

"How does that help the company?"

"You have made the error disappear. And it confirmed the buyer's judgment in selecting the right vendor." Leong laughed; he grasped the nuances of a tightly held rein on a new, maturing company. Once the organization was under his leadership, old customers began to return. New purchasers came calling for the quality footwear and au courant designs.

The staff was transformed rapidly. New designers and experienced quality control managers moved from shoe factory to shoe factory. A small team of customer service people visited the offices and retail shops of as many clients as possible. The goal: for each customer to understand and welcome the attention to detail they were now getting. It was a great old company, now being transformed into a new twenty-first-century footwear organization with two dynamic leaders at the head: the wise and experienced older man, Daryl, and the energetic and hungry younger man, Leong.

As an American, I viewed the relationship as Leong being the quarterback and I the coach.

The numbers at Hi Bo's division in Guangzhou were spiraling upward, and the profits in Switzerland were above expectations. The marriage of the two once-hostile firms had turned the two struggling companies into a behemoth producer of better women's footwear, the premier supplier to the entire footwear industry in all of Europe.

Hans Leopold was shown some mercy. He was given a position as a sales assistant to maintain what was left of the old customer base of the original company. Perhaps undeserved, this saved him some dignity — a merciful gift from Hi Bo.

I gave eight weeks of nonstop work, including weekends.

The pressure and the commitment enveloped me. Inside my belly, a flame burned with the excitement of a new adventure. The new company required my total pledge and obligation. I was tired and simultaneously gratified. Strangely, I experienced anger with myself for the sacrifice I had made for a new business I could do without. Bizarre as it sounds, I wanted it, and I needed it. The ambiguity of my new love affair was its challenge, and this test was the undeniable compulsion of my life. I was not in control. This was my strength and my weakness. I did not drink or smoke or do drugs. Still I knew, inside my brain and my body, that I was an addict. I had no power over my wants and my compulsion to go to work every day. It was my life, and I was helpless to restrain myself.

Two months is a long time to be away from your wife and your children. I tried to convince myself that I would never take on this type of obligation again. My next venture will be a grocery store on the next street. It was a promise I'd made to myself on several occasions. I nodded. "Sure, sure, stop bullshitting yourself," I whispered.

Returning home with gifts does not count. They have little

or no value to relationships — empty gestures. What is valued is being there, showing up. Emotional support validates a father's responsibility to his family. Yet the strength of the relationships I had with Maxine and my son and daughters found forgiveness and a strong welcome once I returned home. Their hugs and kisses were nonstop. Once again, I was happy for my many blessings, including the love I had for my family and my new business, and the fresh excitement.

"This is my last foray into a new undertaking, unless my next office is around the corner." Everyone laughed.

"Yeah, sure, you are never going anywhere in the world again for some exciting new grocery store. Poor old daddy is going to retire," they all teased me.

Maxine put her arms around my waist and held me close. "Do you remember the Jacques Brel song you loved so much?" I looked at my wife. I was puzzled, not recalling anything. And suddenly she sang, "And if you stay, I'll make you a night like no night has been or will be again." The kids cheered. I smiled and kissed Maxine.

Sing Ye sang out, "Mommy is kissing Daddy. Mommy is kissing Daddy." Sammy put her hand over her eyes.

I stared at my children and wife, at their unique wonderful faces; they were everything to me. I was comfortable beyond my insane imagination. I looked in silence. Everyone was quiet, waiting for their father to say something funny. My eyes fixed on everyone, I raised my glass of seltzer, "To all of you," I began. "You are the treasure of my time and my life's true accomplishment. I value nothing more than you guys here right now. For a change, this is not going to be a lecture."

Not a word, not a murmur came from their lips. Maxine, serene, was listening with calmness on her face. "You all are not truly conscious of the accomplishments that your mother and I have made. We two, as a happy team, have put together the most valuable gift for any child. You all have a family, a safety net, and a home filled with love and caring. Make notes and do the same for your own lives and your own children." The calm continued. There were no jokes or wise remarks. Quiet and respect were on their faces.

"Well said." My bride joined in.

"Bravo, Daddy."

"I am not finished," I interrupted. "All that said, now here is what I want," I said in a softer voice. "I want you ladies and gentlemen to clear the table and help Nancy with the dishes!" I shouted in a jokingly cross voice.

"Daddy is home," Sammy said, laughing.

"The big boss is finally back," Fred said with a laugh. They all dashed from the table, taking dishes and napkins in to the kitchen and shouting, "Welcome home, Daddy."

I shouted an actor's shout. "*Da Loban* means 'big boss' in Chinese – learn it!"

They all jumped, running from the dining room to the kitchen, emptying the table of all the dishes, silverware, soiled napkins, and glasses, plus a very empty bottle of club soda.

Maxine added, "When you get through in the kitchen, I want you all to go to your rooms and finish your homework. The welcome party is over."

Maxine turned to me. "I will unpack your bag. Go to our bathroom and take a shower. You girls as well, please take showers. Sammy, you have been ill. Please take it easy. Fred, I need you to go to the store. Take the car."

"Wow! You bet. Where is the store, Upstate New York?"

"Is that boy okay?" I asked.

"He just likes to drive." Mom grinned.

With the children in their rooms, all was quiet in the house. I undressed and got into my pajamas. Maxine came out of the bathroom. I could not take my eyes off her sexy nude body. She smiled. "Hello, stranger. What did you say your name was?" she joked. We both laughed.

"Don't be funny," I said. "This is a serious moment. I want to enjoy your loving me. I want to relish the touch of your delicious body."

"Come and get it." She grinned. I left one light on, a dimmed glow.

The Discovery, Daryl Continues

Two days later, sitting in my office looking over figures from our Honda car agency, the packaging company, the small restaurant, and the shoe company partnership, I enjoyed a feeling of satisfaction to be involved in so many endeavors. The profits for the first quarter were about 18 percent higher than the previous year. I sat back, pleased. Notwithstanding the income or the return on my investments, I was thinking of what new venture I might consider. I smiled. *Maxine is right, I must be losing it. Seventy-two is not old but it isn't young either.*

The phone rang. I reached over. "Hello, Daryl speaking," I answered.

"Daryl? Nee how, this is Hi Bo. How are you?"

"I'm good," I responded. "Are you calling from Guangzhou?"

"Yes, my friend."

"Is everyone okay?

"Yes, all is well, and we are fine."

"What can I do for you?"

"Daryl, I would like to know if you will be in New York next week. I need to come and speak to you in person. It has nothing to do with our business together. That investment, as you have seen in the figures we sent, is doing very well."

"Yes, I know. It was a good move to put Leong in charge of

our new joint venture. He is a fast learner. And judging from his emails, I think he is continuing to grow and mature."

Hi Bo listened with patience. Then he said, "I plan to arrive on Sunday afternoon and stay for about four days. Does that fit into your schedule?"

"I will make myself available anytime you arrive."

"Is there a hotel you would suggest that I go to?"

"Please stay with us. We have much room."

"Daryl, forgive me, and thank you. I prefer my privacy and I am not comfortable in someone else's home," he explained.

"My assistant will arrange a hotel for you. It will be either the Carlisle or the Regency. Both are close to my office and close to our apartment. Not to worry. I will send you an email. May I send a car to pick you up?"

"Thank you, I am taken care of. I will be at your office first thing Monday morning."

"Excellent. See you then. Safe travels, partner."

Later that evening, Maxine and I were having dinner alone. Nancy had prepared my favorite, Dover sole.

"This so good and so healthy," Maxine mused. "When something is good, you know two things: it's fattening and it's not good for you. However, fish is the opposite."

I added, "Once in a while a good steak isn't harmful. We hardly ever eat meat."

"My goal is to keep you healthy and have you around for a long life," Maxine lovingly whispered. "So far, so good. My main frustration with your diet is ice cream."

We knew and understood each other. After thirty-five years, we still had a sex life and were in love with one another. We were fortunate to have a happy, healthy marriage.

"Guess who called from Guangzhou?"

"I hope it was not Mr. Chen with another deal," my wife moaned.

I laughed. "No, no, I wish it were true. No, it was Hi Bo. He is coming to New York on Sunday. We have an appointment at my office on Monday morning."

"That sounds serious. I wonder what is on his mind," Maxine said.

"I have no idea. I think we should plan dinner either here or at a restaurant."

"Whatever you wish; he is your partner. I've never met him. Perhaps we should go to a great restaurant. It would be a treat for him. Or," she said with a smile "a Chinese restaurant?" Maxine suggested kiddingly.

"Stop fooling around." I responded.

"I will make a reservation at the Leopard. We like that spot. Is he alone?" She was in charge and would take care of all the plans.

"I don't have a clue why he is coming. He didn't mention that he was bringing anyone."

On the following Monday, at work, my assistant Sally came to the door of my office and said, "Mr. Hi Bo is here, Daryl. Shall I show him into your office?"

"No, I'll come out to greet him."

I stepped into my front office. There he was, Da Loban, my partner, one of the most respected businessmen in China. It always amazed me how he oversaw more than three thousand employees with fairness and care.

"Welcome, my friend. You must be a bit jet lagged from your long trip."

He bowed slightly. His face was grim. He always had a serious look, but this morning was different. "I happen to be feeling better than expected." He looked around. "Handsome office," Hi Bo said, glancing around my home away from home.

"Come into my workplace." I turned to my assistant, "Sally, no calls, and no interruptions. I do not want to be disturbed, except for Maxine or Fred and the twins."

I pointed Hi Bo to a black leather chair. I sat in my very old brown leather seat with wrinkles and cracks. "I hope you understand how hard it is to get rid of this heirloom from my first office almost thirty-five years ago or more. I'm superstitious. This was with me during the bad times; let it enjoy the good times."

Sally took Hi Bo's coat and hung it up next to mine on a long, ancient wooden pole with old-fashioned bronze hooks.

An antique oak coffee table from the days of the Revolutionary War sat between us. The *New York Times*, the *Wall Street Journal*, and an assortment of magazines lay atop the table. I got up to close the blinds as the morning sun streamed in from the eastern window. It had rained that morning. My umbrella in the stand and rubbers lay tumbled in a corner.

There was a knock on the door. "Excuse me, Daryl. May I bring in two fresh bottles of water?"

"Thanks Sally. Good idea. Or would you prefer tea or coffee, Da Loban?" I asked as a sign of respect, learned in Asia.

"Water is fine. Thank you."

"Now, my friend, how can I be of service to you?"

Hi Bo sat back. He lifted the water bottle to his lips, taking a deep sip and then another, ending with a satisfying, "Ah."

My intuition signaled that this was going to be a difficult conversation.

Da Loban pulled glasses from his inner pocket and then took a tissue from a box on the coffee table. He put his head down, wiping the glasses clean, and he looked up at me. He was grim as he began, "I find your office quite interesting. In fact, it is exactly as I pictured it — full of life and amusing. I am not surprised to see all the photos of your family. I would guess there are at least fifty or sixty. Are they all relatives?"

"You are quite observant. No, these twelve in the front are family. The others are photos of customers, who are impressed, surprised, and pleased when they visit me here. I usually ask a new client, when we meet, to show me a photo of a grandchild, or a son or daughter. I follow with a request to email the photo to me. I then ask my staff to reproduce a larger copy on our printer. We have frames here. I send a framed photo as a gift to the customer. It is a very important and low-cost gift that pleases everyone," Daryl concluded.

"I knew you were different when I first met you in our home and you made every effort to impress us and failed badly. However, I was not surprised that you recovered with your comfortable, self-assured style. And as my wife said, you were charming."

"You flatter me. Thank you. Now tell me, sir, how may I assist you or give you my input? You did not travel halfway around the world for a bottle of water."

"Life is a strange road we travel. Situations happen to us that we cannot foresee. Yet despite some twists and turns, we who are strong manage our lives. Often issues are not within our control or in our best interests. They are in the hands of God and for me, Buddha. We pray that all will end in peace and happiness." The room was quiet. "Sometimes, yes, they have a happy conclusion, but frequently the story does not have, as Americans often say, a Hollywood ending."

I sat, focusing only on my partner. Hi Bo was serious. I listened to the wisdom of this Chinese sage, who again lifted his water bottle and drank. He took a swallow and sat back in his seat.

"There is a history to the business we joined together to buy. The original owner, Leopold, was one of my best customers. You met him when you were in Zurich. I treated him with respect and fairness. He was, in fact, my best customer. When in China, he resided in my home, ate there, slept there. He appeared to be the perfect gentleman.

"I was very intense in valuing the huge amount of business he gave us. Much to my stupidity and regret, I did not see that he was a scoundrel."

"What did he do that has so disappointed you?" I questioned.

"He raped one of my maids."

"Oh my, that son of a bitch." I gasped in disbelief. "Excuse me," I apologized.

"Now let me get to the point of my visit here. The maid became pregnant. She gave birth to twins."

I interrupted in anger. I stood up and turned to the office window looking out onto Madison Avenue in total silence. My head was pounding. A swift pain lurched from my side. I whipped around and glared at Hi Bo. "Don't tell me that you think my daughters ... I cannot believe this story. Is that why you came here?" I demanded in anger.

"Please, please, be calm and let me finish," Hi Bo said, holding his hand up. "When the children were born, my wife and I took them to the same Catholic orphanage where you adopted your children. I pried the information from the nuns that the adoptive parents were Mr. and Mrs. Daryl Landsman."

I sat in my chair. My heart was crushing my chest ... I was furious. I stood up, walked over to Hi Bo, and pushed my face into his. "How dare you come here and tell me this cockamamie story? I have been a good friend and partner. Are you here to destroy my family?" I shouted. "How dare you! Have you no decency?"

"No! No! The girls *are* your children." Hi Bo raised his hands as he retreated. "They are never to be taken away from you, except by their husbands. That I swear and promise you; you are my friend and partner. I come to you and plead for you to help *my* daughter, Jan Yee."

I tried to calm down. I went back to my seat. It was 10:00 a.m. I removed a bottle of Scotch from the shelf of a bookcase and poured some into a New York Mets cup that had been in the same spot for ten years. I swallowed. "So tell me, what is the true purpose of your visit?" My eyes peered at Hi Bo; I tried to control the anger in my voice.

"I apologize for causing you much distress. It is only my lack of expression and the shallowness of my English that is the source of my long-winded explanation. Permit me to finish the story," Hi Bo defensively responded. "It gets even more complicated. The birth mother, my maid, is now *my* adopted daughter. Her name is Jan Yee, after my beloved mother. On your visit to my home you met her. She is beautiful and intelligent and has a great mind."

I knew it, I knew it. That twitch in her cheek was familiar. It is the same as Lauren's, who for some unknown reason insists on being called by her Chinese name. Hmm, genes?

"I came as a friend. I think it is important for adoptive parents to know the genetics and the background of the birth mother. Finding the father is usually impossible, but here we also know the father. I say that to you because I know nothing of my own daughter's background, except for poverty and no education."

As Hi Bo told his story, I became considerably more comfortable. *Maxine and I have always wondered who the birth mother was.*

"My story gets more complicated. My daughter has fallen in love with Leong."

"Very good; he is a fine young man," I answered.

"They are brother and sister," Hi Bo calmly said.

"*What?* What are you saying to me? Are you telling me that they are related, and they never knew? That is hard to swallow." I sat there, my eyes staring in disbelief, my mouth open wide. I was astonished by the story.

"That is why I have come to you. Their DNA shows they are genetically linked. I need to know how closely related and if it would be safe for them to marry."

"What can I do? I am not a doctor, and I know zero about genetics."

"I came to you because I need your help. I want you to assist me in finding a doctor here in America. I want the most brilliant mind in the United States who has the talent and the expertise to test my daughter and Leong and give an opinion we can trust. Cost, of course, is not an issue. My need is to find out, should they marry and have a baby, what the chances are of birthing a normal child."

"Wow, that is a tall order. I have to think about this." I sat there in silence. "But I promise I will try." *I am not a scientist; I do not know even where to start. This is a tall order.*

I sat stunned by this news. I was thinking of my daughters, of Maxine, and of their future. For the first time in my life, I was startled and alarmed. No, I trembled. I was filled with fear.

Oh my God, how can this be? Is my business relationship with Hi Bo a penalty or chastisement? Has my life been too easy? Have I taken too much for granted?

We both stood. I took Hi Bo's hand in a firm grip. "Forgive my instant reaction. I was taken by surprise and frightened. You are correct that it is good for adoptive parents to know a little about the birth mother. For this, I thank you. I will get back to you as soon as possible. May we invite you to dinner tonight?"

"I am sorry. First I must go downtown to NYU's medical school."

"May I have my car and driver take you downtown?" I inquired.

"Truthfully, on the many business trips I have made to New York City, I have never taken the subway. Today I will do so." Hi Bo grinned. "After that appointment, I leave for Chicago — this afternoon. I have a meeting with a famous professor of genetics. Perhaps he can help me. After that, I fly to San Francisco to see another expert and get her opinion."

I accompanied Hi Bo to the elevator. He pressed the down button. In a few minutes, the elevator door opened. We shook hands again. "Good luck, my friend." As the door began to close, Hi Bo put his hand on it, preventing it from shutting. He gazed straight into my eyes, and in a quiet voice, he asked me, "What does *cockamamie* mean?" The door closed. I shook my head, totally confused.

❦

That night at dinner, I told the entire story to Maxine. She listened intently. Her reaction was a surprise, much different from mine. Maxine shook her head and took a deep breath. "It is so very sad for his daughter to have lost the privilege and the pleasure of knowing our children. We must invite her to visit someday." I sat there in silence. A thousand thoughts flowed through my mind.

Women are unbelievable human beings. I am always astonished by my wife's talent of putting everything into perspective. She is an amazing person. I wonder if our thoughts are similar about knowing our children's biological mother.

The next day, by 11:00 a.m., I was on the phone to my internist and urologist, a very special doctor and friend, Dr. Frank Freid, a brilliant surgical specialist who knows everything about everything.

Dr. Freid's response to my call disappointed me. The doctor said, "I am busy with patients now. I will call you at home tonight."

"Okay, Frank. Please make a note that it's important. *I'll call him again tomorrow if he forgets.*

The phone rang at 8:00 p.m. "Hi, Daryl, it's Frank Freid. How can I help you, my friend? Peeing stronger these days?"

I smiled. "I need some advice for my Chinese partner and my good friend."

"Are you still making those ball-breaking trips to Asia?"

"Not as frequently." I grinned.

I told Frank the entire story, including the DNA results and how the two young people wanted to get married.

"That is a tough one. Let me think … let me think. I know two brilliant experts in that field. And they are both here in New York. Dr. Samuel Beckerman is one, and the other is Dr. Helen Bandersen. He is at Columbia Presbyterian, and she is at New York Cornell. I will email their contact information to you and drop them a note saying that you will be calling them. I wish good luck to your Chinese friend's daughter and the love of her life. I am not optimistic."

"Thanks, Frank. I appreciate the effort."

The Author Narrates

In Zurich at the office, Leong submerged himself into his work at the new company. His goal was success, both for himself and for the two owners who had entrusted him to make their investment worthwhile. He had to be in total control of his emotions and his energy, with no distractions. Still, he could not erase Jan Yee from his thoughts….

I don't care about this sister-brother genetic nonsense. I love her like a lover. I want her, and I will never give her up. I am not her brother. We are soul mates. There has to have been many times in this world, in this life, when half-brother and half-sister, without knowing it, married, had children, and lived a quiet and happy life. I will find out the truth somewhere, somehow. I will never give up.

Leong found Daryl to be a superior mentor. Patiently, Daryl had explained in detail how to develop the skills to manage a big company and a staff of 250 people. The process was painstakingly detailed, from the original sale to production, quality, design, shipping, and invoicing, as well as payment collection. His every step had to be vigilantly watched. It was the only path to the success of the company.

People skills with customers were always a priority. That came naturally to Leong. He had a gift for words. He was attractive, smart, and charming. But much to Leong's surprise, what Daryl failed to warn him about was the bottomless pit of problem solving. Complications, small and large, snags that led to sleepless nights, glitches that were annoying — each had to be resolved for the benefit of the customer and the company.

The labyrinth of issues, mostly insignificant, had to have solutions. Each hitch took time and effort, sapping Leong's strength and patience day by day. He made a conscious effort to keep his temper under control for those careless employees who required his powerful direction and correction of their negligence. Leong fought a tendency to be thin-skinned when an employee committed the same stupid and thoughtless error more than once.

His most difficult job was discharging an employee for incompetence. In Switzerland it is not so easy to fire a member of the staff. The boss has to present a truthful account and an ample amount of evidence for a dismissal. Leong developed his own style, which began with a warning letter sent to the worker. If there was a second letter, the employee had to sign it and acknowledge the caution. And finally came a report from the union for dismissal.

Leong sat in his office, his chin resting in the palm of his left hand, a bottle of Evian in his right. He'd had no idea how hard a boss works. He smiled with pride. He had become the master of his fate. And most important, the company had turned a profit.

19

Solving the Genetic Mystery

Daryl Narrates

The alarm at my elbow shook me awake at 6:30 am; I was off to the gym for my daily workout. Once I was finished, I quickly showered, shaved, and dressed. I slipped into the backseat of my waiting car and was on my way to the office. I arrived at 9:30 a.m. Quickly I scanned my morning reports in an open basket at the upper corner of my desk, including cash in, accounts payable and receivable, and the orders and business of the day. I signed about a dozen checks and thought, *Time to call Dr. Beckerman.*

I rose from my chair, closed and latched my door, and dialed. One ring, a second, and then...

"Hello, Dr. Beckerman?"

"Yes. Beckerman speaking." Much to my surprise, there he was, Beckerman himself answering the phone.

"This is Daryl Landsman. Dr. Frank Freid suggested I contact you."

"I have been expecting your call. How can I help?"

"Just briefly, my partner in China adopted a young woman many years ago. Recently she met a young man, and they have fallen in love and want to marry."

"*Mazel tov.* What is the problem that I might be able to help with?"

"They have the same father and different mothers. Is the marriage of these two people an impossible situation? And furthermore, what is the danger if they were to have children?"

"Daryl," the doctor began, "I see problems like your friend's daughter has, two or three times a month. My advice to the young people: Do what will make you both happy, get married and decide not to have children; adopt or do not adopt and have a full and happy life."

I sat quietly, somewhat surprised by Beckerman's simple answer. "So, if I understand what you have just said, having a child, even if they are half-siblings, could possibly mean a troubled, unhealthy infant. Am I correct?"

"This couple will be taking a risk if they conceived. What I just said is the only acceptable advice I can give. There is no other. Let me add a hypothetical situation. A couple meets. They are for all matters normal and healthy. They have zero biological history of any illness or unknown genetic issues like the couple you are referring to. They have a child. For some strange genetic twist of fate, their offspring is physically or mentally in the minus column. That can happen with a healthy couple. The couple you described to me has a much greater chance of birthing a genetically impaired baby. For the couple we are discussing, to have an infant offers greater risk. If they love each other and want a family, they should marry and adopt.

"Forgive me, Mr. Landsman; I have a patient waiting in my outer office. Call me again if I can be of any help. Please give my best regards to Frank. Bye." The doctor hung up the phone.

I sat there, puzzled. "He did not answer my question, or did he?" I whispered to myself.

This issue is not so difficult. They love each other. They should adopt. It's as simple as that. We adopted and we have a biological son,

and we love all three equally. What is the big deal about adopting?
Dr. Beckerman's response made sense, and it was reasonable.

The remainder of the day was filled with phone calls, two other meetings, and three or four questions tossed at me by my staff.

Back at home, my daughters ran to greet me with hugs and tugs. Maxine called out, "Is that you, Daryl? I'm in our room." The three of us marched into the master bedroom.

I turned to my daughters and asked, "Will you two sweethearts please leave your mother and me alone for a few minutes? See you at dinner." My kids begrudgingly left. I flopped down on the huge king-size bed, shoes on, briefcase in my hand.

"What a day. What a day. I am exhausted."

"Was it that bad? Tell me. Big customer gone, restaurant burned down, Leong quit in Zurich?"

"None of the above. Worse — I spoke to that genius doctor. He was very matter-of-fact and very cold. He gave me the facts in less than five minutes and then said goodbye. Very disappointing." I thought I would be a hero to Hi Bo with a real solution to his daughter's problem.

"Did you also speak to the other doctor? What's her name, Helen, or something like that?"

"What's the sense? She will probably tell me the same biological, genetic bull crap."

"Since when do you take the first no as a final answer? You, my big successful earner, you've always told me your philosophy is that the word *no* has nothing to do with you. You're always advising everyone the word *no* is of no importance and is only a temporary response." Maxine spoke from experience, having lived with me for almost half her life.

"Get on the phone tomorrow and call the other doctor. Your internist has already told her you would call."

"Okay, okay ... I will, tomorrow." I shut my eyes to take my daily twenty-minute nap. Maxine pulled my shoes from my feet and gently opened the grasp on my briefcase.

Our author writes. It's his turn.

Leong stared at the company statements in his office late Friday afternoon. He was looking, not seeing. His concentration was both nowhere and everywhere. His mind was a blank yet flooded with thought. He gazed out the window; the early evening darkness began to settle on the miraculous white-topped Swiss mountains on the horizon. He wanted to reach out and touch them. Winter would soon come. He looked forward to moving swiftly down the Matterhorn on the Swiss side, enjoying a sense of freedom on his skis. His mind wandered and then swiftly returned to his desk and papers. He thrust his head into his upheld palms, muttering, "No, no, why can it not be different. My life, this pain, this sense of loss; I cannot believe this is my life. Someone, please, please help me."

Karl, a favorite among Leong's many colleagues, popped his head into Leong's office. "Good night, Leong. Anything you need before I'm gone for the weekend?"

Leong shook his head in silence. "No, thank you." Karl could hardly hear the voice.

"Anything wrong? You're not yourself."

"I guess I am just a little drained. We have all been working hard these past few weeks."

"No, sir, that is not the same Leong Chan I know. You are always full of energy, having a great time at work." Karl stepped into the office and closed the door. "Please tell me. It always makes me feel better when I tell a friend something that irks me. And the one I speak to is usually my wife."

Leong took a deep breath, letting the air rush from his lungs. "To tell the truth, I'm lonesome."

"Is it the girl waiting for you in China?

"Yes, it is."

"Go to see her. You owe yourself a week off. Patricia, Hans, and I can cover for a week. And there is always the telephone and email. Give yourself a break."

"It's more than that." Leong paused, a very long pause. "It's not possible."

"Why not?" Karl asked.

"I am in love with her."

"What's wrong with that? It sounds wonderful and sexy."

"She is my sister — my half-sister." His head bowed in shame.

Karl gasped; he felt his Adam's apple in the swallow. He was overcome in silence. Leong's friend sat down in a chair next to him.

"Wow, that is a problem. Have you ... have you both ... uh...?"

"No, no. That's what is so difficult. We both want to, and we are afraid we will not be able to stop. It is so complicated."

"No, it is not complicated. There are all kinds of new birth control methods, for you and for her."

"Birth control is not what we want. We want everything. We want a life together. We want children. We want it all. And we know it is a crime. It is illegal in almost every country on this planet for siblings to marry and have children."

"You said almost every country. In which country is it legal?"

"Only in Sweden may half-brother and half-sister marry and have children."

"Half-brother and half-sister can marry in Sweden? Perhaps that is your choice. It's only a one-hour flight from Zurich. Maybe that could work out. Have you seen an obstetrician or a specialist in genetics?"

How did I think of that so quickly? Karl thought. "You say you want children. Not everyone is that fortunate. Maybe she, or you, are not able to conceive. Couples marry. They are in love. They make all kinds of plans and, without warning, come to face the truth that they are incapable of having children. It's just bad luck."

"We never did investigate our ability to have kids. The only thing we did was get a disappointing DNA test, which confirmed our relationship, our connected blood line."

"What are you, a detective, like on TV? Do something; go find a specialist who knows about your problem. Google it," Karl suggested. "You always talk to me about our big boss, Daryl. You told me a hundred times, 'Daryl never gives up.' If you learned anything from him, it should be that you should never stop. My dad used to say, 'Never is a long time.'"

"You are an idiot," Leong said with a chuckle, "but for sure, not a stupid one. Maybe you are right." He smiled. "Perhaps Jan Yee and I should get more information."

"By the way," Karl said, on a roll, "throw in a psychiatrist and a marriage counselor. And you know that old saying, 'Maybe the dog will talk.'" Karl was on top of his game. "Let me tell you a great story that my dad always told me and my three brothers." He decided quickly to tell that old joke again to ease Leong's pain.

"A king orders a slave to be beheaded. The slave pleads for his life, 'Your Majesty, I am training a dog to talk. Please let me live until the dog speaks.' The king thinks, slowly and carefully and asks how long it will take. The slave also weighs his thoughts and answers, 'Just another two and a half years.' The king smiles and agrees not to behead the slave. Back in his dungeon, the slave's friends hear the good and bad news and tell him that he will surely die because the dog will never talk. The slave looks at his friends and answers, 'Two and a half years is a long time. Maybe I will die, or maybe the king will die. And for your information, you never know, maybe … the dog might talk.'"

They both laughed. Leong understood the old joke about the

dog talking. Both men embraced. "I guess you're a smarter idiot than I am. Have a restful weekend. Join me in a whiskey before you leave?"

"Sorry, boss, I'm driving." Karl turned and walked out of the office, shaking his head, a grin on his face. *Maybe Leong's smarts are contagious.*

20

A Comprehensive Lesson in Genetics — the Risks, the Results, and the Truth

The telephone rang.

"Dr. Helen Bandersen's office, how may I help you?" A staccato voice with a British accent answered.

"My name is Daryl Landsman. Dr. Francois Freid suggested I telephone and speak to Dr. Bandersen."

"Dr. Bandersen is traveling now. She is lecturing to the European Union Medical Association in Amsterdam. She will return next Monday. May I make an appointment for some time next week?"

I flicked my intercom. "Sally," I called to my secretary, "what is my schedule for next week?"

"Just lunch on Wednesday at the Aqua Grill, with your brothers, Al and Bob," she replied.

I turned to my phone and told the British voice that I was available any day next week except Wednesday from noon until 2:00 p.m.

We agreed: Wednesday at 4:00 p.m. at Dr. Bandersen's office in the New York Hospital, East Seventieth Street and York Avenue, third floor.

There couldn't be a better place to get the information Hi Bo needs. Maybe I will be lucky. Perhaps we will all be lucky.

I Googled Dr. Bandersen and was not surprised to discover all the awards she had received during her illustrious career, as follows:

- Graduated Johns Hopkins medical school, top of her class
- Internist, pediatric specialist
- Cornell Medicine genetics professor
- Former head of pediatric genetics at New York Hospital
- Director of human inbreeding studies for Lawrence Medical Association
- Lecturer, teacher, and professor of human inbreeding

This is the right person. If anyone knows about what can happen if you marry a kangaroo or your cousin, she knows.

For the life of me I could not understand why my mind raced as I recalled a visit I'd made to a factory I did business with just outside Florence, Italy. I remembered my special residence when I traveled with Maxine in Italy, the Lungarno, a luxurious five-star hotel owned and managed by the Ferragamo family. The hotel sat proudly overlooking the Arno in central Florence.

Back then, I was alone on business. I was enjoying a cappuccino sitting on a huge sofa in the living-room-style lobby. The room was filled with photos and paintings of famous stars from old movies and theater, each celebrated actress wearing the famous Ferragamo shoes. I studied the old photos, some in black-and-white, of legendary movie stars, people like Bette Davis, Marilyn Monroe, Marlene Dietrich, and Grace Kelly. All were beautiful and fascinating.

I am never shy about speaking to strangers. Close by a young couple, perhaps in their early to mid-twenties, were sharing cocktails, being affectionate, and having a wonderful, happy time, like two puppies.

"Are you from the States?" I asked. They looked, smiled, touched hands, and nodded.

"We come from Biloxi, Mississippi, sir," the young man responded. "Are y'all from the USA also?" he asked in a noticeable Southern accent.

"No," I replied.

"What country do y'all come from?"

"New York City," I responded.

They laughed. "You are right as rain," the young man said. "New York is not in the United States. It's a great country unto itself. Wow! New York. We love that town, right, honey?"

"Uh-huh," she politely replied.

"Are you here on a holiday?" I continued.

"Yup. We is with our parents, celebrating our engagement. We're gonna be married in October."

"Congratulations. You're from Mississippi, right?"

"Right as rain."

"You guys cousins?"

"Uh-huh. How'd y'all know that?" the young woman asked.

"Just a lucky guess." I sipped my cappuccino and looked down at the *New York Herald Tribune* on the table, a smile in my head.

❦

A week after I'd made the appointment with the geneticist, my driver took me to the New York Cornell hospital. He made a slow right turn onto East Seventieth Street, turning east out of the heavy traffic on York Avenue. The car cruised slowly downhill to the entrance of the hospital. Assane moved swiftly to open the car door for me. I moved through the entrance, directly to the reception desk. "Dr. Helen Bandersen, Genetics, please?"

"Take that elevator on the right." The receptionist pointed. "Third floor and turn right."

The door opened to an obvious sign reading, "Genetics." An arrow pointed to the right. Inside the office, I was greeted by the British-sounding voice. "Good afternoon, sir. May I help you?"

"I am Daryl Landsman," I began.

I was interrupted. "Oh yes, please follow me. Dr. Bandersen has been expecting you."

"My goodness, this is the first time I've not had to wait for a doctor."

"You're fortunate; the doctor's last patient left five minutes ago."

"Today's my lucky day."

"It is. She is usually very busy here until after six thirty p.m. Dr. Bandersen, Mr. Landsman is here. He is your last appointment."

On Ms. British's desk, I eyed a small bowl filled with chocolate candy kisses. As we walked into the doctor's office, I slipped two of my favorite candies into my pocket.

The doctor's tiny office surprised me. One desk, one chair, another for a patient, papers all over her working space, a half-filled glass of water, a single photo of a man and two little boys, and documents indicating accomplishments, all framed and impressive, completed the room.

Dr. Bandersen welcomed me, pointed to the empty seat facing her, and asked me to sit. Her phone rang. She told the caller that she was in a meeting and would return the call within the hour.

She appeared to be in her mid- to late forties, perhaps forty-seven, maybe a little older. Her light-colored hair was a bit tousled over the right side of her forehead. In front of me was a strong, sculptured nose, great smile, and sparkling greenish-blue eyes. In fact, I would go so far as to say to myself, *very attractive.*

"How do you do?" Dr. Bandersen began. "Welcome to my little cave."

"You come highly recommended," I politely responded.

"Dr. Freid and I interned together at Johns Hopkins. He is a wonderful man and a brilliant surgeon." There was a pause. I felt like I was a buyer and she the seller. "You have some issues with which Frank thought I could be of some assistance."

"Thank you for seeing me," I began. "Dr. Freid said that you are an expert in genetics. I need a simple answer to a simple question."

"There are no simple answers when it comes to genetics." She smiled.

I told the entire story, point by point, about the half-brother-half-sister affair. I also included that the woman was the birth mother of our adopted twin daughters. The doctor tilted her head, acknowledging my tale, but I believe she had a keen understanding of my story. I saw a strange, perhaps smiling look in her eyes.

"I am only the messenger for a close friend. Can you help?"

"Mr. Landsman," she began, "the options in these relationships are never easy. Very often children with true severe genetic matches do not survive past five years old.

"In my experience," she went on, "the choices that a couple has to make are not medical or genetic decisions. All are very personal judgments. Yes, couples with an inherited match also fall in love. They desperately want to marry and have a normal life. They want children, desiring to grow old with them and educate them, and to enjoy the totality of family living. Often, that scenario is quite possible. But there is a risk. The risk comes from the chance that some *bad* gene that may go back two or three generations, or more, continues to be present in both parties. How often that happens, very few of us know."

Bandersen sipped a little water from the half-filled glass on her desk. She continued.

"There are research studies of populations who do practice inbreeding, which is done more often because of geographical or religious reasons. Many people know the history of royalty throughout the kingdoms of Europe and parts of Asia. The royal courts of many European empires have a history of hemophilia because of inbreeding. The princess of Austria marries the prince of France. All that is now history, but the genetics still exist. Currently many royals are marrying regular citizens that they have fallen in love with. It is healthier."

The doctor moved back in her chair, trying to be certain that her guest understood. She guessed I did.

"Geography, for example. Take a small village in the mountains somewhere, anywhere in the world. Families and neighbors become relatives because there is no one else to copulate with. Tibet many years ago is a good example. As for religious interfamily marriage, the Amish or the Mennonites, for example, are religious groups who tend to live quietly among themselves, where inbreeding is frequent and dominant.

"Groups of the population in southeastern Quebec have a carrier frequency similar to that seen in Ashkenazi Jews. It is called Tay-Sachs. Cajuns of southern Louisiana carry the same mutation. Why? We have no clue.

"All this said, it is the result of tightly held communities where marrying outside the religion is forbidden. Because of this, inbreeding is difficult to halt."

I took a deep breath and gave a sigh of defeat, figuring that I was about to hear the bad news.

"Out breeding makes our society healthier. It diminishes the chances of unwelcome genes, causing serious issues, not just for the couple, but also for generations to come.

"So that brings us to your question and my answer. Should this couple marry, they can risk having a child, or" — she paused — "they can adopt a child. The adoption choice is the much safer course for them. Adopted children, like the two girls in your life, as you told me in your story, are yours as if you and your wife were the biological parents. And you love them as much as you adore your son, of whom your wife was the birth mother. You love all three as I love my two adopted sons." She pointed to the photo on her desk.

My eyes opened wide. I peered more closely at the photo. *I knew I liked her the minute I saw her.*

"My sons were born here in the USA. We know the birth mother. She is a young Guatemalan woman from a fine family. In her seventh month we brought her to New York. We arranged to rent an apartment for several months. When her time came, our sons were born right here in this hospital."

"What happened to the birth mother?"

"Her parents came here and then took her home. She went back to school and now lives a full life. And everyone lived happily ever after."

"Have your sons ever met their birth mother?"

"Not yet. But my wife and I have been talking about it."

In a flash, my mind went to, *is Dr. Bandersen gay? Life is strange. A first for me.*

She continued, "We think they are still too young to grasp the history of their genetic background. But I do believe we will someday work a meeting out. Just like you and your wife have thought or may be thinking about?"

We both laughed. I shook her hand, and without thinking, like some automatic move, I kissed her cheek. "You're great. Thank you." Dr. Bandersen's cheek reddened slightly.

"Before you leave, let me strongly advise you that marriage among siblings is illegal in most of the world, except for Sweden. Or ... if the couple decides to go forward, I urge them to keep it a deep, dark family secret." The conversation was over. I felt a welcome calmness. The doctor concluded the visit with, "Please excuse me. I must return the call I had when you first arrived. I hope our chat was helpful and informative."

"It was not what I wanted to hear, but I learned a great deal."
She is wonderful, smart, and sensitive.

Once out the door, I gave my business card to "British."
"Here's my card. Please send me a bill. Are the two-chocolate candy kisses I secretly took from the plate on your desk covered by Blue Cross? Thank you for your assistance in the appointment process." The young woman looked into my eyes. Her cheeks reddened a wee bit. She recognized my flirtation.

At home I shared the doctor's visit with Maxine.

"Maxine, I had a very interesting experience today. Dr. Bandersen talked about her and her wife adopting twins. They are a gay couple living the life that we are. It's wonderful." However, I was unhappy and frustrated about my lack of control, being accustomed to having total influence over any issue in my life and the lives of my young family. I thought the situation through; we must collaborate, compromise, and solve it. I recalled my father saying, "A smart man can control everything in his life, with two exceptions: his birth and his death. The rest he has to figure out."

"Let's talk about *our* daughters' birth mother," Maxine began from out of nowhere.

"What about her?"

"I think we should meet her."

A deafening silence filled the room. She sat looking into my face, her legs crossed and arms akimbo, affirmative and convinced, with a sense of strength. Her inner voice, coupled with her female intuition, overcame any doubts she may have previously had. The meeting was on her agenda.

Maxine did not sleep well that night. She tossed and turned, until she turned off the air conditioner in the bedroom, got up, took her pillow and a blanket, and tried to find rest on the couch in the living room.

I was asleep before my head hit the pillow and awoke to tiny snores issuing from my nose, plus small coughing sounds from my throat, as usual.

It was early Saturday morning — no office, no gym, just a relaxing few hours at home, and perhaps an afternoon movie with the kids.

At about 9:30 a.m., I crawled out of bed, reached for my robe, and went to the bathroom.

Maxine was just about finished blow-drying her hair after her shower.

She turned to me as I began brushing my teeth. "Did you sleep well?" she asked.

"It was too warm in our room. Otherwise I did sleep well. But I was thinking about our conversation last night."

"So, have you come to any serious conclusions?" Maxine questioned.

"I think you should know that I did meet Jan Yee, our birth mother. I didn't know all the facts at the time of our meeting."

"You never told me that. What is she like?" There was a slight detection of annoyance in Maxine's voice.

"What I saw was a beautiful Asian woman who was charming and well educated. Hi Bo is very proud and protective of his daughter. At least I thought she was his daughter."

"She *is his* daughter," Maxine responded firmly.

"Oh, you know what I mean." I was beginning to hear anger.

"I believe we would be better parents to our daughters if we knew more about their birth mother," my wife said, applying pressure.

"I don't know ... I don't know. We may be opening a hornets' nest. There could be serious repercussions."

"Well ... let's think about it. Okay?" she calmly replied.

I nodded in silence, with some trepidation.

"I do recall seeing an infrequent muscle twitch on Jan Yee very similar to our Sammy's."

Maxine looked away, thinking in silence, her eyes squinting.

⸿

Leong tortured himself about taking time off. It was not his style to have his personal needs interfere in the progress of the company and commitments to its daily requirements. Because of his feelings of loneliness for Jan Yee and his want to be with her, difficult as it was, he decided to take a holiday. He would return to Guangzhou and spend some polite time with the love of his life.

Polite was the term he'd sold himself on, denying his secret wish. His brain and his body wanted her very much. His body knew only longing whereas his brain battled the consequences of ultimately surrendering to each confrontation with his spirit of decency and respect.

His silent voice, the most powerful of Leong's instincts, more sensitive than his heart, more insightful than his brain, told him that for now he knew better. Sitting quietly on the Swiss Air flight to Shenzhen, his feelings of confusion were mixed with love and the conflicts of nature and his sense of morality.

The plane touched down on the runway twenty minutes early. Instantly he clicked his cell phone. "Hi, I'm here. I just landed," Leong announced.

"Thank goodness you're safe. Planes frighten me," Jan Yee answered.

"I feel the same way."

"See you soon," she whispered.

"Can't wait," Leong replied.

Over the loudspeaker came the voice of a flight attendant: "Please remain in your seats with your seat belt fastened until we arrive at the gate." Leong could not wait any longer.

21

A Bad Person Returns

The Author Narrates

Hans parked his 1998 Volkswagen at the assigned private spot. He seldom came into the office on Saturday, but today was different. Leong was away. He felt a sense of old-fashioned responsibility, a rare and satisfying experience since the company's change of ownership. Walking into the office, his limp was more exaggerated today as he dragged his leg to the front door. He put his key in to open the entrance.

He greeted the few people present, saying, "*Guten morgen (Good morning)*, Karl. *Guten morgen*, Gretta."

He nodded coolly to Patricia in her cubical. Hans dragged his body up the stairs to his office; he could hear the packing machines humming from the warehouse. Here they loaded hundreds of pairs of shoes into shipping cartons to be dispatched first thing Monday morning. He knew the difference of the new company's current success and the past failure. Now machines packed shoes twelve hours a day. It was a huge change from loading every other day when he ran the company.

Karl did not like Hans Leopold. He didn't know why. There was just something about him that did not fit. In his mind the man was a puzzle.

In his office, Hans looked at his messages and checked the sales report and the sheet listing some of the prospective customers whom Leong was in negotiations with. Hans bemoaned his fate. His agreement only allowed him to speak to or visit his old and loyal friends, those he had been doing business with for many years. He was sadly conscious of the reality that these old ties would soon end as he got older and his customers retired, or perhaps closed and sold their businesses. He was experiencing the sentence he'd received for his never-to-be-forgiven act years ago in China.

In the outer office Karl's cell phone rang. "Good morning, Hi Bo — Landsman Footwear," he said into the receiver.

"Good morning, Karl. Leong here."

"What are you doing working on a Sunday afternoon? It's Sunday in China, am I correct?" Karl questioned.

"Karl, my friend, bosses never stop working ... I need some specs and pricing for Danshel Shoes. Would you please fax that information to me? It's important. I need it urgently."

"Isn't that Hans's account?"

"Yes, but Mr. Danshel called me directly on my mobile here in China and asked me to take care of it ... personally."

"Will do." *Click, click* ... and then silence.

Karl placed his phone face down on his desk. He called Patricia to his office and explained what he wanted. The young woman knew exactly how to download the information. Karl suggested that she print out the data and show the documents to Hans in case any statistics were left out or by accident deleted. Patricia sat at her computer, rapidly did a Web search, and found the Danshel Shoes portfolio. She printed it out, turned in her swivel chair, and handed it to her supervisor. Karl placed the pages on his desk. He continued with his work as he sipped his black coffee. His phone rang again. This time it was his wife, Karolin.

He listened, shook his head, smiled, and said, "Okay, I know its Saturday. I will be home by one, and then we can go for lunch and a movie."

In a moment of almost forgetfulness, he saw the Danshel file near his right elbow. He ran his finger down all six pages, reached for the ballpoint pen at his left, and made three or four corrections. Karl looked once again, but this time with more care to be sure he had not forgotten anything.

He nodded in silence and called, "Patricia!" She was immediately at his desk. "Please give these to Leopold to review. After he okays everything, ask him to initial each page and add today's date."

Patricia knocked on Hans's door. "Open!" he commanded.

"Sorry to disturb you, Mr. Leopold. Karl asked me to give you these documents. It's the Danshel file. Karl wants you to review and okay each page with your initials and the date at the bottom, please."

"Danshel?" he shouted. "What is Karl doing with my customer?" he demanded.

"I think he has to send the information to Leong in China."

"That stupid, arrogant yellow asshole," Hans grumbled. "What is he doing with my lifelong friend Marvin Danshel? Leong was in diapers when I met Danshel."

Patricia placed the file on his desk and left. She had no idea why Mr. Leopold was always angry. In a way she felt very sympathetic toward this lonely man and his behavior at the office.

22

The First Kiss

Jan Yee and Leong hiked hand in hand in Baiyun White Mountain Park. He, serious and full of thought, carried a small backpack, and she had a glow of happiness. The park, a national treasure maintained by the People's Republic of China, is situated outside Guangzhou City. The young couple planned to take the cable car to the summit and breathe fresh air into their lungs. Many tourists and visitors trekked two by two up the winding path to the top. There they would rest, appreciate the view, and enjoy the treats they'd brought for themselves. It was the Autumn Festival national holiday custom.

At the summit they sat on a small blanket, quiet, with only their thoughts and concerns. An unknown and unsettled future lived in their everyday reflections. Jan Yee spoke first.

"How is the business in Zurich?" she began.

"Good business. Each day we are busy with the issues of work decisions and old customers returning as new accounts.

"Mostly, Switzerland is beautiful with all its glorious mountains and forests. But I am so happy here in China, being close to you Jan."

"I am the same. Being with you is my best time." She ran her fingers gently across his face.

And the city of Zurich is filled with museums, concerts, and many cultural attractions. There is a group of mountains that are so very beautiful. They are breathtaking, they are called the Alps. One is called Zermatt, also known as the Matterhorn; it stands there like a silent giant. It protects the people, it guards them, and it helps them. The magnificence of this brilliant piece of nature is a sight to see. Visitors come from every part of the globe. The mountain brings wealth and economy to that small village lying at the foot of this colossus.

"In ski season, you board a crowded train; that is how you reach the top. People climb or ski down into a tiny beautiful village in Italy called Cervinia from the Swiss side. In the tiny Italian village, the food is delicious, and the wines are excellent. After lunch the skiers board a cable car, returning up, and swoosh down once again into Zermatt on the Swiss side. At the end of the trip, it is time for rest, a shower and then dinner. We, you and I, must go together someday. I know you will fall in love with it. And especially the wonder of its delicious cakes filled with schlag."

"Schlag, what is that?" she questioned.

"It is luscious whipped cream." He laughed. Jan Yee smiled.

And then her head turned down, her face saddened, and bemoaned her fate, "But I cannot ski. How will I do that? Besides falling in love with Zermatt, I am certain I will also fall when I ski." They giggled, like two happy children.

"An instructor will teach you. It is not difficult. I learned in a little over a month."

"It could be a happy time for us." This was a special day dream for Jan Yee; she felt that tiny drop of fear as her heart accelerated.

Leong's mind raced from one issue to another. He wanted to begin a conversation but had not a clue as to which concern, which matter, to begin with. There was more than enough to deal with. He did not want to engulf Jan Yee with additional obstacles. What he did not know yet about Jan Yee was that she was a woman of boundless strength and wisdom. There was a silent ten minutes. Both were quiet, each thinking their own thoughts.

"Leong, my love," Jan Yee began. She leaned toward him, placing her hand playfully on his. "You appear to be so deep in thought. Have you vanished from our autumn walk already?"

She called me "my love" and touched me. Leong looked into her eyes. "No, my sweet, I am only thinking of us and our future."

"I too have given our life together much reflection and investigation. Shall I speak first, or do you wish to begin?"

Leong feared that Jan Yee had concluded that there was little or no future for them. He did not want to hear that she had decided to end their relationship and their love for one another. He dreaded the thought that she would leave for a life without him. He could not bear to hear her possible painful decision. *Do not speak, please, please,* he pleaded in his mind. *I do not want to hear that we are ending.* He felt like crushing his hands over his ears. He did not want to listen to the rejection of his life. Leong's head slumped. *I must speak first. It is crucial.*

Jan Yee reached for his chin and gently lifted his face toward her eyes, about to speak. Leong interrupted. "I have done considerable research into our situation. I have visited several genetic specialists who have experience with people in our situation," Leong stated with confidence. He pulled a bottle of water from the sack, took a deep gulp, and continued.

"Our partner Daryl Landsman has been to see the best genetics specialists in New York. Every doctor explained that for couples who have one parent that is the same, as you and I have — the same father and different mothers — there is always the possibility that a child conceived by the half-siblings could inherit the same weak or bad gene from each. It is possible that we have a gene that may have a history going back years before we were born, having nothing to do with us or our biological father. The odds are that nothing bad will happen. I am told all could be normal. However, each doctor convincingly said it was a risk one must consider seriously. And each advised not to take that risk. That said, one hundred percent of them mentioned that there is no reason why we cannot marry and be happy in our love for each other."

Leong continued, "We believe we have a genetic tie because we have the same biological father. I say biological, because in true life, we did not know him. And he never truly knew us. What if his gene that swims through our veins represents one half of one percent of our biological connection, or perhaps one hundredth of one percent? That totally reduces the statement, 'half-brother, half-sister' to almost zero."

Jan Yee sat in her silence. She bowed her head, turning her face slowly from left to right. They stopped speaking. She reached inside his sack, took out another bottle of water, unscrewed the cap, and poured several drops on her tongue. With her eyes shut, she held the bottle in her hand, twisting the cap until it was refastened.

"My dear Leong, could you be happy without your own biological children? Could you be happy adopting children?"

"My partner Mr. Landsman has two adopted daughters and has an older biological son. He loves all three equally. I could do the same."

"Are you absolutely sure?" Jan Yee questioned.

"More than you know. I want to be with you. I want to make a life with you. I want to adopt ten children if that will make you happy. Whatever you want, I want. You know what Mr. Landsman once advised me?"

"What?" She cocked her head to one side.

"He told me straight to my face, 'Happy wife, happy life,'" he answered Jan Yee with a big grin.

She put her lips to his. There in that swift emotional moment they had their very first kiss.

"I love you very much." He sighed.

"You always make me happy. I love you more each moment," she whispered. Leong could not hold back his happy laughter.

They walked over to the summit and looked at the horizon, holding each other's hands tightly. Jan Yee had her head on Leong's shoulder. Tears filled her eyes — tears of joy and happiness. Both had happy hearts; they were filled with contentment. A decision had been made, and their future was now secure.

Leong turned to her and suggested they return to the cable car, go back to her home, and tell her parents.

"Let's do it. You know, my dearest," she said, "you make my heart smile." She embraced him, feeling the hold of his body next to hers. It was good.

They held on to each other for a long time. The decision and the gamble decided.

"My colleague Karl suggested that I stop feeling sorry for myself. He ordered me to come here to you and resolve this. He is indeed a very smart partner."

"Give him a raise!" she ordered, with smile on her face.

"Well … he's not that smart." They both laughed.

"You have become a combination of Da Loban and Mr. Landsman," she whispered as they boarded the funicular.

A Tragic Moment Back in Switzerland

"Patricia," Karl shouted, "did Leopold give you back the Danshel file?"

Karl disliked Hans very much. The village they all lived in was very small. Karl knew from the talk of some local men that Hans was still an angry man, especially toward women. Karl's position with women was the opposite. He was a shy lover, a gentle person. He thought only of making his wife happy and their lives together loving and easy. And like his father, who loved and adored his mother, he and his wife, Ingrid, lived a simple and happy life. He felt that he and his high school sweetheart were not only husband and wife, but most important, they were partners and bound together at the hip.

He often said, "Inge is my best friend."

Patricia moved from her desk and walked directly to Hans's office. She knocked. "Mr. Leopold, do you have the documents ready for Karl?"

Hans sat in his office, reviewing with reluctance the Danshel history with the company. Thoughts swirled inside him with unresolved anger toward anyone and everyone. *Oh, how I despise Leong, that yellow piece of dreck (shit) ... And Karl, that sniveling ass kisser; I can't stand to look at him. I hate his voice, I hate his face. And Patricia ... bitch. I hate her vulgar perfume. She is a horrid slut with those whorish, extreme high heels and the slutty clothes she wears.*

He reached into his bottom drawer, took out a small whiskey bottle, slowly pulled out the cork, and took a gulp. He shut his eyes tight and swallowed the fire-filled liquid.

His mind was a whirlwind, filled with pain and remorse for the behavior that he had no control over. Hans knew that an evil partner existed in his soul. It was only lately that he'd experienced both guilt and shame. Still this wicked master of his emotions was often a welcome collaborator. The evil cohort filled his addictive passion and led to a joyous release in his mind and in his body — only to be followed by the torture and anguish of his sin. Patricia pushed the door open.

"Come in, come in," he said, his voice somewhat softened. "They're here on my desk. Let's look and see if I have initialed all the pages. Ah, yes, yes," he replied, a calm smile on his face. "Here they are. Come, take them to Karl."

Patricia walked rapidly to his desk and reached for his outstretched hand, holding the file. In a split second he seized

her wrist and jerked her with all his strength down toward him
and jabbed his right hand beneath her skirt. Releasing her wrist,
he plunged his left hand toward her buttock, moving quickly,
tearing at her panties and thrusting his hand between her legs.
Oh my god, I cannot allow him to hurt me or perhaps kill me, her
mind screamed.

With all her strength, she wrenched herself from his grip; she
grasped the marble penholder on his desk and slammed it into
his head, and swinging back with all strength, she smashed the
marble block into his jaw, knocking two teeth from his mouth.
Patricia shrieked, "Let me go! Let me go, you son of a bitch!"
Blood gushed from the open wound on his skull and from his
mouth. He moaned in heart-pounding pain. He collapsed and
crashed to the floor, semiconscious.

The young woman rushed from the room, limping, holding
on to the wall, sobbing. Karl jumped up from his desk. His head
jerked in two directions. Seeing Patricia, he ran from his office,
and held her firmly by the shoulders. "What happened? Are you
hurt?" he blurted.

"That man, that disgusting animal. He lunged at me and
shoved his hand up my skirt, touching me all over," she shrieked
in pain and fear.

"What? What did you say? Did Hans attack you?" he shouted.

"Yes. Yes." She moaned and wept uncontrollably. Her knees
buckling, she collapsed to the floor.

He called to Sally, the receptionist, and to Gretta. "Help
Patricia," he pleaded.

Karl tore into Leopold's office. The man lay on the floor,
facedown, hardly breathing, choking, and gasping for air. Karl
gently rolled Hans over until he was facing up. Then he covered
him with the blanket that was found lying on the chair. He
stretched for some paper towels and tried to stop the bleeding.
"What happened in here?" Karl grilled in a harsh, menacing

voice. "What have you done to that young woman?" he shouted in disbelief.

In a breathless voice Hans gasped, "That insane woman, that filthy bitch" — he coughed and choked — "came into my office pretending she needed the Danshel records, and without reason struck me in the head." He could hardly speak. "And she deliberately smashed it into my mouth. She must be insane. Get her out of this office. She is a danger to everyone and should be fired — or worse. Call the police and have her arrested … immediately." Hans panted, struggling to breathe; his eyes closed.

Karl could not believe he heard two different stories. *It's the Rashomon effect.* He stood there baffled. He sensed that Patricia was telling the truth.

An ambulance came and took Mr. Leopold to the hospital. Karl and Patricia got into his car and drove behind the ambulance.

Several hours passed before the doctor came into the waiting room and spoke to Karl. "That elderly gentleman has a bad bruise on his head, like he was struck with a hammer. We gave him three stitches and some painkillers. We think he should stay overnight and rest. He can go home in the morning."

"And the young woman — how is she?" Karl asked.

"She has a black-and-blue mark on her arm, a small scratch on her vulva, and a slight bruise on her anus. Her physical injuries are minimal. I cannot diagnose the emotional damage. She has been severely frightened and perhaps psychologically scarred. How did all this start?" the young doctor asked.

"Two totally different stories."

"I know." The doctor said, "They both told me their perception of the incident."

"Who is telling the truth?" Karl questioned.

"We found a tiny piece of fabric under the man's fingernail. It matches her undergarment. "And one more thing," the doctor resumed. "This is not just an incident. This is a rape, and the police will be contacted." The young doctor turned and walked into his office.

❦

Two Days Later

Karl sipped his morning cappuccino as his wife, Karolin, fussed with their two boys, getting them ready for school and preparing their breakfast. His mind was wandering, thinking that his boss was returning from China. Leong was due to arrive late that night or the next morning.

As Karl sipped, he gazed at the television in front of him, listening, but not hearing the local news and the weather. Unexpectedly a news reporter interrupted the program, announcing in clipped tones, "Good morning, ladies and gentlemen. Here is a flash report from our news desk. Hans Leopold, a well-known businessman and philanthropist in our great city, was found dead last night in his home of an apparent heart attack. The Leopold family has a long history of business development and generosity in our city. Their footwear imprint has given employment to hundreds of families here in Zurich for more than four generations. Mr. Leopold was one of Zurich's preeminent citizens. He was a faithful organizer of the young women's college, giving generous scholarships to many of its students. He was known by many of the young women as an outstanding mentor with a sympathetic ear. I am confident that the entire student body and many of the alumnae will share the loss of a close and feeling friend. Our sympathies and the thoughts of our entire community go out to the Leopold family."

Karl listened in shock. He turned to his phone.

Sure, he had feelings; he would feel any girl he could get his dirty hands on.

He reached for his phone, remembering that Leong was on a plane returning to Zurich.

"Karolin, Karolin!"

"Yes, what is it?"

"Hans Leopold is dead, of a heart attack."

"After what you told me, God please forgive me for saying, good riddance!"

Daryl Interrupts the Author

Daryl tapped the author on his shoulder, "Go take a coffee break. It's my turn to tell this part."

I snapped my fingers, and our daughters were going to college. It was impossible to believe how quickly time had passed. And believe it or not, I just had my sixty-fourth birthday.

Samantha and LangPi were about to take their SAT examinations. The frightening event was just around the corner. Maxine was doing her best to help them. It was exhausting. She hired a special teacher to assist. In one month, they would be taking their tests and soon after applying to colleges for the fall semester.

At the dinner table I asked if the girls had given any thought to which college they wished to attend. And I suggested, "Don't forget to pick a safe school."

Sammy chose Smith College and NYU, the first being her real choice with early decision. Sammy was thrilled with her acceptance to both schools.

LangPi, as usual, was much different. She chose five schools, just to be safe.

Her first choice, with an early decision, was Johns Hopkins; her second choices were Yale, Dartmouth, Harvard, and Bennington.

Time was running out. Everyone was feeling nervous. She

waited, Mom waited, and I waited. The first five days flew by. The sixth day, there was no response. In anxious despair, the seventh day passed. It was eight days before graduation, and finally Lauren was notified that she'd been put on the wait list for Harvard. "Oh shit," she said, weeping. Being accepted at Bennington was good, but no consolation. She was happy, but not deliriously so. Her first choice had not answered. To be wait-listed at Harvard was okay but not a cause for celebration. Both Maxine and I were a little startled by the, "Oh shit." It was a first for us, hearing one of our children speak that way.

I put my arm around my LangPi. "Sweetheart, being wait-listed at Harvard is pretty good. If you plan to study medicine, they have one of the finest schools in the world. I think you will get an answer very soon. And being accepted at Bennington is not too shabby."

The next day, two letters arrived, from Dartmouth and Johns Hopkins.

She quickly opened the letter from Hopkins, her first choice. "We regret to inform you," etc. LangPi fell back into her chair. Tears covered her face. She was not disappointed; she was devastated.

Maxine came into the room. "Momma, I was not accepted at Johns Hopkins. Are they rejecting me because I am Asian, or because I am Jewish; perhaps both." She wept.

"Please do not speak that way. You know that cannot be true." Maxine spoke angrily. And in a softening tone she said, "I am so sorry, baby ... so sorry. But what are these other envelopes that also arrived today?"

"I don't care. I don't care." The child bemoaned her fate.

"Shall I open them, or would you like to and see what they say?"

"*No!* I don't care what they've written. You open them. *I don't care!*" Lauren angrily answered.

Maxine slowly opened the first envelope from Yale. Slowly she read the results of her daughter's application. "Hmm, would you like to hear what Yale wrote?"

"I don't care, I don't care."

"I regret to advise you." Maxine paused for ten seconds.... "You were accepted to Yale, one of the best, may I add, one of the most expensive." LangPi picked her head up from the bed. She tried not to smile. But she could not hold back the grin that crossed her face. She closed her eyes in mild embarrassment.

"Let's look at the one from Dartmouth." Momma suggested.

Slowly she opened the second envelope, a very large one that had come from the university.

She read it quietly with hesitation, and then turned to LangPi, who lay there in total silence. The child's eyes opened widely as her mother read, "We are pleased to invite to join the graduating class of 2028."

"Oh my God!" the young woman screamed in delight. "Yale and Dartmouth! Are you fooling me? Oh my God, my God. Momma, Dartmouth was my secret first choice. I thought I would never have a chance to get into that school. Momma, I am so happy." Now all was quiet. Lauren shut her eyes, quivering. "Momma, I don't know what to do. I am so confused, what shall I do? Dartmouth or Yale; what do you think? Please help me."

"Well," her mother replied, "when you are in such a dilemma about which great school to pick from, this is a serious problem. Let's call Daddy and see what he advises." She grinned.

"No, Momma, you and I can decide and tell Daddy when he comes home from work," she said in a childish voice.

"Dartmouth is one of the best schools in the United States. You are my lucky star." Maxine wept, holding her daughter in a tight hug. "I love you, my darling." As mother and daughter lay on the bed in an all-consuming embrace, they both wept a happy cry of relief.

For the first time in their young lives, the twins would be in their own separate worlds. Sammy chose Smith, much to her parents' surprise. LangPi would be at Dartmouth. Each young woman would be pursuing her own interests and her individual goals. Sammy would follow her dream of studying literature, writing, and journalism. LangPi was more interested in chemistry and biology, and perhaps a career in medicine.

Fred, their older brother, was already making his mark on his conglomerate of investments. He himself was a graduate of Bennington.

That evening, I returned home from work. "Hi Daryl," Maxine greeted me, with a tiny kiss on my cheek.

"What have I done to deserve such a warm welcome?" I asked.

"I have good news and bad news for you. Which do you want first?

"Give me the good news first," I replied.

"The good news is that Lauren has been accepted at Dartmouth and Yale. And she has decided on Dartmouth."

"So tell me, what is the bad news?"

"You, my dear 'big earner,' are going to have to earn more money. Smith and Dartmouth are very expensive."

We both hugged, with smiles. "We are very lucky. Our son, a graduate from Bennington, our daughters accepted to Smith and Dartmouth. That is an accomplishment. And look at me," I said with pride, "I never went to college."

❦

I lay quietly in my bed listening to the Beethoven violin concerto, my Bose earphones connected to my cell phone. At last, after a long day, it was relaxation time. Maxine was reading her Kindle, and the girls were preparing for their move to school during the next few weeks. Fred was at his own apartment and promised to take time from his hectic social life to return the next day for a family dinner. He rarely attended family meals anymore.

With my eyes closed, I was listening to Anne-Sophie Mutter playing the concerto. Now tranquil, I heard nothing except the violin masterpiece. Classical music had been an integral part of my life since my early high school days. I also enjoyed Frank Sinatra and Jimmy Durante, and pop singers of my generation, like Shirley Bassey, Simon and Garfunkel, and John Denver.

"Daryl, do you hear me?" Maxine lightly prodded on my shoulder.

I pulled the earphones from my head and shut the cell. "What's happening? Is everything okay?" I had been in my own world; now, back to reality, hearing my wife's voice.

"Yes, everything is just fine. I am sorry I disturbed you," she said to me. "I was just considering that we should plan to have the girls meet their birth mother before they leave for college."

I fell silent. I was reluctant to answer. I had my doubts about a meeting with Jan Yee. I still wasn't convinced that a meeting was in the best interests of our daughters or the family. A whirlwind of thoughts raced through my mind as I reasoned with myself. I knew the arrangements would be complicated. I would have to contact Hi Bo and discuss a meeting to get his approval and cooperation. The birth mother had to approve and decide for herself if she had any desire to meet the twins. Perhaps a meeting would stir up complex feelings in her. Possibly she did not want to have to remember that horrid moment in her life with dreadful Hans. I considered all the costs of transportation, accommodations, and entertainment. My focus on the cost was not an issue, only a thought. I secretly envisioned that during the time Jan Yee would visit with us in New York, it would involve a firm commitment to be away from work and all my obligations.

Of course, I thought, *Fred is now capable of handling most everything at the office.*

"Why is a meeting with the birth mother for you and our children suddenly such a priority? What would the benefits be? And have you considered the downside?"

Maxine lay unmoving on her side of the bed. "You have always preached about risk and reward. I can understand your feelings about taking this gamble, but my inner voice, the one you told me I have, is urging me to take a chance on this for the sake of our daughters."

"Risk and reward, my love, is only about making money. It is not about life."

"Was adopting the girls a gamble? And now that they are ours, is it not a magnificent reward in our lives for the chance we took?"

This was not a discussion or a debate for husband and wife, not a matter of winning or losing, or of who was wrong and who was right. The question was, would this decision help our daughters? Would meeting their birth mother enhance their lives, or conceivably be trouble once this exercise was over? It was a task I continued to have serious doubts about. It was a Y turn in the road, a decision I found dangerous.

In our bed, Maxine moved closer to me. "Sweetheart," she whispered, "you know that inner signal we always talk about? Let's sit down and ask our children if they have any interest in their birth mother."

I nodded. "That's reasonable." I remained unconvinced.

That wife of mine, that woman is such an amazing person. She takes my philosophy, my father's concept of life and what he taught me, and she feeds it back to me when she needs to. She is much like my dad. I have always been similar to my mom's temperament. You can't push Maxine around. I am never sure if she plans these conversations. Is it possible they are spontaneous?

"That's a fair idea. No, in fact, it is a very good idea. Does tomorrow evening after dinner work for you? They will be finished with their packing, and Fred will be coming over. We can hear his opinion. He is smarter than all of us."

She kissed my extended cheek and dimmed the lights.

What a great woman, constantly thinking and planning. She never stops giving our kids every opportunity to grow with each experience. I am not sure meeting their birth mother will be good. I hope so. I can't erase my nervous feeling.

The next evening went as planned.

Dinner was noisy — plates clicking, silverware singing, food was passing, Fred talking nonstop about the family business and his job. Sammy talked about her prom dress, and LangPi discussed the school she would begin in September. Maxine and I sat back as we sipped our wine and enjoyed the animated conversation that continued for about half an hour.

Fred spoke up. "Mom, Dad, you guys are so quiet. What's up? I can see those looks on your faces that we are all here for a special announcement."

"I didn't notice it. You're right, Fred; they do have a mission tonight," Sammy interrupted.

"We do have things on our mind," said Maxine. "Dad and I have something serious we want to discuss and share with all of you to get your feedback and, of course, your honest evaluation.

"I believe that it would be a very special experience for you two to meet and get to know your birth mother." Maxine was never one to hem and haw; she came right to the point and put it all on the table. There it was, open and ready for comments.

Sammy and Lauren looked at each other and then to Maxine. It was a challenge for them to comprehend what their mother had just said. Nancy came into the dining room to clear the table. Both girls jumped up to help. They did not hear the, "No, no" that their mom and Nancy spoke. They moved quickly around the table. In unusual silence, they carried dishes into the kitchen, where they rinsed the plates, silverware, cups, and saucers and then placed them all into the dishwasher.

"What is Mom talking about?" Sammy whispered, loud enough for everyone to hear.

"You know we've often talked about who our birth mother was, and where she is now, and if she has more children," Lauren whispered.

"True. But this is serious. Do we want to do this?"

"I don't know. Let's go back and hear what Mom has to say."

"What about our biological father?"

"It's scary."

"Uh-huh."

"You guys finished with your conference?" Fred called into the kitchen.

"Oh, be quiet," his sisters angrily shouted in one voice.

The girls were back in their seats; no one spoke. Eyes went from one person to another. Finally, Lauren asked, "Mom, what is this all about?"

"Most biological children know their mother and their father. Those children were born to them. The boys and girls recognize their parents' skills and behavioral idiosyncrasies. We are familiar with the actions and performance patterns that we see in Fred from the social and communication styles of his biological mom and dad. These experiences are never conscious; they are just part of everyday life. I have always believed, even today as I speak, in total truth, that both of you do so many things that you have learned from Dad and me. We enjoy knowing where you got them from. And often we convince ourselves that this home, the schools you go to, and the friends you care about have shaped your lives. And often your behavior and your thinking come from having us as your parents and Fred as your brother. To us that is no mystery."

"So, what are you getting at?" Fred asked in his newfound commanding voice.

Daryl gazed at his son, with just a hint of scorn; the sound of Fred's voice was unacceptable.

"Sorry, Dad." Fred nodded.

Maxine gazed directly at the girls, ignoring Fred's comment. "Occasionally Dad and I see a strange reaction to something we hear either of you say or do. It is a look on your face, or the raising of your voice, or an unfamiliar smile. I believe that if you met your birth mother, it would help you. It would also help us know our children better. The point I am trying to make is you may be surprised to recognize things in her that you have in yourself. It will give you a healthier understanding of who you are as individuals and as sisters and as women. There is a possibility that you may experience disappointment. I must add this is how I feel. Dad has his doubts. However, I do think it is worth it."

The three children, Maxine, and I sat in silence. Mom had been eloquent, which was no surprise.

"Anyone want dessert? I've got apple pie a la mode — baked it myself," Nancy interrupted. No one answered at first.

"I'll have a piece," Fred murmured.

"Me too," I agreed.

"To tell the truth," Sammy began, "LangPi and I have often spoken about this very thing, about who our birth mother was or is. Is she pretty? Is she smart? Is she still alive, and does she have other children? Occasionally we spoke about our biological father, but not often."

"That's right," LangPi joined in, "we seldom talk about it. But we think about it time and again. Our most frequent shared thought is why she didn't keep us? Why did she give us up for adoption? And more important, how did we get so lucky to have you and Dad as our parents? It's puzzling."

"What should we do?" LangPi looked at her parents with pleading eyes. She was perplexed.

"I met your birth mother once," I interrupted. The startled children hushed for twenty seconds. My words were a lightning bolt. Everyone was astonished.

Each turned their heads to one another. Maxine shut her eyes in slight anguish.

"Why haven't you told us about this before?" LangPi questioned, confused.

"Yes, Daddy, why is this coming out now? You could have told us about our birth mother a long time ago."

I sat silently, contemplating the answers to my children. I looked at my wife. *Help me* was in my pleading eyes.

You're on your own, her face silently answered. I understood instantly.

"They're right, Dad; you've always been above board with everyone," Fred added in a tone of authority.

I gave my son another glance, which translated meant, "Quiet!"

"The answer is not so simple." I paused. "Fathers are not the smartest people in the world." I glanced down, deep in thought. "We often make mistakes. I was never sure that the information would be in anyone's best interest." I took a deep breath and exhaled. "I watched you both grow up. You are smart, healthy, and in my eyes the most beautiful girls a dad could have."

"Please, please, tell us about our birth mother — as much as you can remember."

I sipped a little water in a glass nearby, "Her name is Jan Yee Hi Bo. She is the daughter of one my business partners. It was only by coincidence that I found this out, when I told them the story of how you became our children."

"Tell us about our *mother*," Sammy cut in with a hug around Daryl's neck.

"First, young lady," he said in a slightly firmer voice, "*your mother* is sitting right here. This woman in that seat is your true and only mother. Remember that." Sammy realized her error; her eyes and brows crunched together. She breathed a sigh of knowingness.

"Sorry, Mom."

Maxine mouthed in silence, "I love you."

"You are Jewish children. It is our belief, as written in the Talmud, that the law clearly and unmistakably states that the mother and the father are the people who raise the child or children. And no one else has the title of mom and dad."

I sat back in my chair, trying to collect myself. I leaned over and took a sip of my drink. Everyone was quiet. They observed that I was a little upset because Sammy had called her birth mother "mother."

"A birth mother is a different kind of mother. The phrase *birth mother* is a mere technical term. Please, I want to clarify one important fact: she is our birth mother. That means all of us in this room, me and Mom and Fred and you two. Jan Yee is ours, all of us. She is a part of this family. She does not know us, does not love us, and does not care about us. We are strangers to her. And she is an unknown person to us." My voice had changed; at the beginning it had been firm, but at the conclusion, it was gentler. My shoulders ached, and I began to feel pain in my lower back. This was more difficult than I'd anticipated. Age was creeping up on me.

Sammy and LangPi were misty-eyed. Maxine went to her twins and put her arms around them. "This is a difficult subject. We are all going to learn. It is important. I want this event to make you happier, or at the very least, smarter about yourselves. You'll be able to understand why you have blonde hair when most people of Chinese heritage have dark hair. I want you to know why you are smart. Is it a combination of genes and family surroundings? It is important for you to know why you are thin and tall. All those things have to do with genetics."

"So sorry, my precious, I am so very sorry if my voice has frightened you. I understand. I understand. I too am frightened. I did not want to hurt your feelings. I would never do that," I spoke softly.

I turned to Maxine and shrugged my shoulders. My wife nodded. She knew the discussion was finished; they were going to make a serious effort to meet the birth mother.

"How many times have you heard your father say, 'No risk, no reward'?" Mom questioned.

"A thousand times," all three children replied in unison. They ran to their daddy and hugged him. Each whispered, "Love you, Dad. Love you." He held them in his arms, close and tight. He looked up at Maxine. They both were pale and teary-eyed.

"Well said, and a very good story," the author said to me.

"Okay," I replied. "Now you take over and start writing."

Back from the Mountain in Guangzhou

Leong and Jan Yee rushed into the Hi Bo house. "Momma, Baba, we have some news for you." Jan Yee placed her hand into Leong's. She turned to her parents, with red cheeks and a radiant smile. She burst out in laughter. "Leong has asked me to be his wife. I have agreed."

Hi Bo and his TaiTai were silent. They looked at each other and then stared at their daughter and Leong. No smile, no sign of any emotion. No one moved. Neither parent spoke. There were no words of congratulations. Leong placed his arm around Jan Yee's waist.

Without announcement, Cissy walked into the room. The

servant looked around, not knowing what to say to anyone. "May I bring some refreshment, my Da Loban?"

"Yes," he ordered. "Bring us a bottle of our best champagne. We must celebrate the great news that our beloved daughter and Leong are going to become engaged and make plans to marry." He called to Jan Yee, "Come to me, my child."

His arms reached out, welcoming her embrace. In a single simultaneous moment, the family joined together in a happy encirclement. Jan Yee stretched her arms around her father, holding him close to her — a rare experience for father and daughter in the Hi Bo family.

"Oh my child," he whispered to her, "you have made my life, you make *our* life, your mother and I, worth living, and you make my heart so very happy, like it never has before."

"Poppa, I love you. It is She and only She we should thank for this moment in our lives." Jan Yee looked into her father's eyes and kissed his head and his cheek. She turned to her mother, dropped to her knees in front of her, and lay her head on mother's lap. "Thank you, Momma, for all your kindness to me and for being the woman you are. I want to be exactly like you."

"We must have a great engagement party, and announce your marriage plans," he stated, joy in his strong voice. Momma Hi Bo sat quietly sucking in the air. *How blessed my life has been to have my Hi Bo, to have lost a woman's natural gift of birthing a child. And from nowhere this child, my daughter, walks innocently into our lives. Thank you, my Buddha.*

"Poppa," Jan Yee interrupted, "before we plan any parties or make any announcements, we have confessions to make. We have decided that we will never keep secrets from our parents. We have vowed to be open and honest. Leong and I love each other. Yes, we will be engaged, and yes, we will marry." The happy moment disappeared. "Unfortunately," she explained after a deep sigh, "we will never have any children. If we are fortunate, and when we are ready, we will make every effort to adopt a child, as you did for me. And you love me as I love you both."

"What are you talking about?" Momma Hi Bo looked puzzled. She continued, "Please tell me what is happening here, my child. Why are you speaking about adoption? Is there something that is going on that I do not know? If there is, I want to know, I must know ... now!

"Do you think that after twenty years living with Hi Bo there is something I won't be able to handle? What is it that you are frightened to tell me? I am a strong woman. I will handle what it is you all are too shy to share with me," Momma explained in a low but strong voice.

"Forgive me, my TaiTai. I thought, foolishly, that it would be too painful for you to accept. Still, I know from all these years with you as my TaiTai that you are very smart and very strong woman," Hi Bo said. "Please, stand here next to me."

Madame Hi Bo paled as she listened, "Tell me, tell me," she pleaded. "Has someone we love passed?"

"Our children are half-brother and half-sister," he whispered and finally confessed.

The new family gazed at each other. No one uttered a sound. Leong looked into Jan Yee's tear-filled eyes. She put her hands to her face as Hi Bo's eyes closed, tilting his head down.

"Madame Hi Bo," Leong began, "Jan Yee and I discovered that we have the same father and different mothers. We are half-brother and half-sister. When we met, we were as strangers. We did not have a clue, but Jan Yee, with her secret God-given instincts, was suspicious. Our history is very complex. On the first day we met, here in this house, there was an immediate connection. It was love at first sight for me. We did not recognize one another. Remember, we had not seen each other since we were little children. For more than half our lives, I had vanished into the labyrinth of doctors and hospitals. Jan Yee was given to a broker and fortunately came here to work, where you, in all your kindness, adopted this beautiful person whom you now call your daughter. I knew my sister, or rather half-sister, by her birth name, not as Jan Yee Hi Bo, but as Shan Di Chan. Still, your brilliant daughter put it all together. My name is Chan. She remembered my first name. She did not remember my face."

Hi Bo and his TaiTai, in fear and unease, were listening intently as Leong told the story. "We had, from the time we were little children, not seen each other or ever been in contact. It was like we came from different families. Somehow God has brought us together. For better or for worse, here we are. We love each other, not like a brother loves his sister or a sister loves her brother. We love each other like a man loves a woman and like a woman loves a man."

Momma Hi Bo rose and walked to her daughter; she reached out one arm to Jan Yee and the other arm to Leong. "I always knew it. I recognized the similarity in your faces. Then there is the same name, and your mutual kindness to everyone. There was no doubt in my mind that you did not know about your history. I'd only guessed. But I did not want to tell your baba and hurt him." She moved her hand from Jan Yee, touched her husband's forehead, and turned to the embracing couple. "And you two, from the bottom of my heart, you have my blessing." She kissed her daughter and then embraced her future son-in-law. Her arms around Hi Bo, TaiTai Hi Bo offered peace and acceptance. There was now a new harmony in the great house. Added to this was the excitement of an engagement and a wedding celebration soon to come, and the next generation on its way.

Leong returned to his office in Zurich, all smiles, and received a warm but solemn greeting from Karl.

"What's the matter, Karl? Is everything all right?" Leong sensed something going on.

"Well, yes and no," Karl responded.

"What are you talking about?"

"Leopold is dead."

"Dead — what happened?" Leong asked in shock.

"Had a heart attack."

"When?"

"Two days ago."

Leong asked, "Have you gone to their house to pay our respects?"

"We were waiting for you to return from China."

"Karl, please get the car. Let's go. We must help the family."

Once they were in the car, Leong began. "I didn't have a clue that Hans had a heart condition. He always looked healthy to me."

Karl, with his foot heavy on the pedal, raced to the Leopold home. "Let me bring you up to date. You will not like what I am about to tell you."

"Tell me," Leong answered impatiently.

"A few days ago, he attacked Patricia sexually."

"What?" Leong exploded.

"She gave him a heavy chop to his head with the marble penholder on his desk. He was almost unconscious when I flew into his office. I helped him as much as I could. We called an ambulance, and they took Hans to the hospital. I took Patricia in my car."

"I knew that guy would bring us trouble. He was always a bad person — very bad," Leong added.

"He denied everything and accused Patricia of attacking him for no reason."

"He is a liar and a disgusting animal," Leong replied in anger.

"Each had their own story," Karl continued. "It was so confusing, until the doctor found a small piece of Patricia's panties under Hans's fingernail."

"Is that it?" Leong questioned.

"That is the whole story. The doctor discovered the panty cloth."

"Hans is the worst person I ever met," Leong responded.

Leong and Karl arrived at the Leopold house. The housekeeper came to the door. She wept as she asked them to come in. There were eight people sitting in the parlor: a doctor, the local minister, Leopold's sister, Mrs. Leopold, Leopold's older daughter, and a man whom Leong did not know. His children, Nora and Bernhard, were there as well.

"I am so pleased you have come to our home. Thank you, Mr. Chan, so much for coming. I appreciate it."

Leong remained silent, looking into the sorrowful eyes of Mrs. Leopold.

"So sad to hear about Hans, I never knew he had a heart condition," he answered her.

"He never had any trouble with his heart. He was as healthy as any man his age."

"How old was he?"

"He just turned sixty-three," the widow answered.

"Young, very young," Leong said, sighing.

The man whom Leong did not know, tall and trim with a head of well-groomed gray hair, walked over to them and introduced himself.

"I am Chief Inspector Meinshaft of the Zurich government police."

"I am Leong Chan. Leopold and I worked together. What is this all about?"

"May we step outside to speak for a moment?"

On the cold patio, Inspector Meinshaft, with stern, piercing eyes, scanned Leong. Neither man said anything. The inspector began.

"Leopold did not die of a heart attack. He took his own life."

"He did what?" Leong exclaimed.

"Leopold committed suicide. He was a very good husband and father, an honored and generous citizen of this community," Meinshaft explained.

Leong stood there next to Karl, both in total surprise and shock. The two men were speechless.

"We know your firm has an excellent reputation here in our city, always caring for its employees. You should be proud of the status you have earned in our community." The inspector viewed Leong with a slight attitude of contempt. "It is also known the firm has a very good life insurance policy for all your staff, including, of course, Hans." His voice was a touch arrogant.

Leong was confused. *Where is this inspector going with this kind and complimentary story about Hans?*

"The Leopold family was good to the people who worked at the company. He and the firm was very generous for more than three generations to many institutions here in Zurich. They were strong supporters of the women's college and many of the charities in this community. We want his death to go down as a heart attack, so his wife and children can benefit. We are adamant that you cooperate." The inspector modified his voice just slightly when speaking the word *adamant*.

It was cold and windy. The leafless trees bent slightly in the blustery weather. The men stood close to each other, huddled secretly in an atmosphere of privacy and confidentiality. Leong stood tall, Karl only inches away. Leong looked the inspector straight into his eyes. He moved his face closer, almost nose touching and without the slightest hesitation, using a calm, even-tempered voice, he said, "Inspector, I am sorry to advise you, Hans was not a very good person. In fact he was a horrid human being. He was a predator of women — a history so horrific I need not tell you the details. I believe you know his history and have no doubt memorized the facts." The inspector only listened. He made no sign of being surprised at hearing the information from Leong or the tone of Leong's voice.

"I know two women personally whom he attacked. He raped a young helpless woman and impregnated her. It was his friend's maid. Leopold's friend almost shot him on the spot. Your so-called honored citizen was his business colleague and had been his trusted associate for almost twenty years. Permit me to add to that piece of information. Your philanthropic and most generous citizen of this community, Mr. Hans Leopold, also just last week attacked one of our employees." Leong put his hands together, rubbing them, creating a bit of warmth. He continued. "Yes, this happened only last week. I am surprised that the blow to the head he received from the woman defending herself didn't kill him.

"Now hear me, Inspector," he said in a much stronger voice, "we will not now or ever be a party to a fraudulent scheme. If you want to have a terrible scandal in this community, then try to force our firm into a conspiracy to defraud the insurance company. We have undeniable proof of, along with witnesses to, Hans's character and disgusting actions." Leong was fixed and unswerving as he continued. "If you are smart, you will wash your hands of this. Your career will be at stake. I am willing to wager, if the scandal begins, that other women in this community and at the women's college he endowed will come forward declaring their contempt and hatred for his behavior over the years. They will be seeking vengeance and restitution from the family."

The three men stood in silence. The Inspector did not take to Leong's response kindly. "You are a very clever young man. I appeal to your charity. I am confident you value your position and your company. Your employers in the United States and China will be very disappointed by your decision. May I strongly urge you to reconsider your attitude and your intransigent position? We are a small city; we can make living and working here most uncomfortable."

Leong did not retreat. And suddenly a powerful calmness overcame him. In a very quiet voice, he said, "Inspector, our firm is very charitable to our employees and to the community, but I resent your tone. It sounds like you are threatening me. May I respond to your evaluation of this situation and to your suggestion?"

Leong stepped back and opened a little black book he had inside his breast pocket. He wrote a few notes of the confrontation. Then he gazed directly into Meinshaft's face.

Gusts of breath tumbled from Leong's mouth. His head rose, and his voice was filled with determination.

"Inspector Meinshaft, should you even attempt to give us the slightest, the tiniest, bit of difficulty, or threaten me or my firm in any way: Should a window break by accident; or perhaps a small fire be started by lightning; any of my employees be arrested for speeding; or a fire inspector show up; or our business be interrupted, even slightly, in any way, believe what I say to you: I will move our company to Romania instantly, where employees are plentiful and wages are very competitive. And sir, you will be responsible for putting hundreds of people out of a job."

A pause; both men were silent. Leong scrutinized the inspector, and in a very nonthreatening voice concluded with, "I do feel sorry for his children. They are punished for the deeds of their parents. I have little or no feelings for Mrs. Leopold. I have no doubt that she knew all about her husband's wickedness and transgressions but had little or no power to change him. I am confident that if a professional officer were to question her, she would confess that she too had been raped by her husband — not once, but many times."

"Do you have any suggestions for how to help the children?" the inspector answered, his voice now more compliant. "Would you consider one year's salary?"

"Not one cent!" Leong responded firmly. "Hans was a horrible person, a very sick person. And you know it better than I do. But what I will do? I will ask the owners of the company if they have any interest. Perhaps we could find a position for either the son or the daughter. Please know, this is not a promise."

"Thank you for that consideration. Good afternoon." Inspector Meinshaft put his hand forward for a handshake. Leong demurred and in a very icy moment, turned away.

"By the way, when is the funeral? The firm will send flowers. Is there going to be an open casket?"

"There will be a memorial service next week — no coffin. It was Hans's wish. In his will he stated he was to be cremated. That was done yesterday."

Back in the Leopold's parlor, Leong approached Hans's wife. He extended his condolences and welcomed her to call if she needed any assistance. Then he and Karl left for the office.

In the car, Karl said, "You were tough on the inspector. Do you think he will give us any trouble? You know, he is a powerful man here in this city."

"Karl, that man is a bully and a thief. He is conditioned; it's a game he plays, bullying people around. They cower under their Swiss ways of never questioning the police."

Leong continued, "Guess what happened to him today? From nowhere he was confronted, for the first time in his career, by a mild-looking Asian man who, to his total surprise, did not respond to his aggressiveness, his condescending tone, or his manipulation. This man sitting here next to you is someone who did not accept his intimidating tone of voice, his arrogance, or his threats. Like all loudmouth tyrants, he put his tail between his legs and slunk off when confronted with strength — and the truth."

"How were you so sure that he would back down?"

"Just think what history we have about Leopold. The Inspector did not know that we had the true knowledge of the kind of man Leopold was. I only guessed his collaboration with Hans. I was right; that was luck. Leopold was a disgusting, never-to-be-forgiven rapist. He deserves no sympathy. On top of that, he was a coward. That is why he took his own life. The cremation is a puzzle to me. Do you know of any Swiss being cremated? I am glad he is out of our hair and gone forever."

"We can promote someone to his position," Karl hinted. Leong nodded.

❦

Hi Bo set the telephone down. He raised the martini-filled glass to his lips, drank, and exhaled in a sigh, which somehow diminished his new apprehension. His eyes glassy from the drink, he blinked his lids several times, attempting to clear his vision.

Without warning, his body sank deep into the leather chair. He placed the back of his wrist to his forehead and shut his eyes, descending into deep thought and serious consideration. Within moments his body relaxed, succumbing to the heaven-sent reprieve from the distress of the unexpected telephone call.

Outside the winter light faded, a gentle wind crossed the trees, and some of the late autumn leaves floated to the ground. Soon the comfort of spring weather will be welcomed by everyone.

He slept no longer than ten, perhaps fifteen, minutes, when his TaiTai nudged his shoulder. Startled, he awoke, dazed for a moment, with no sense of where he was. He had no clue of neither the time nor the day. He felt he had slept for hours.

"What happened?" He gasped.

"Nothing, my dear," she murmured. "It is five o'clock. We have a dinner appointment this evening at six thirty."

"I cannot think of dinner now. We must talk, we must talk … we must talk this very moment," Hi Bo insisted.

"What is so urgent? Can it not wait until after dinner?"

"No, it is most pressing and vital to our lives and our family."

"Oh my goodness, please explain. You're frightening me."

"Sometime late this afternoon, Daryl Landsman — you know him — he is my partner —"

"Yes, yes, continue."

"— he requested a time to arrange for him and his family, including his twin daughters, to come here to Guangzhou and meet Jan Yee, his daughters' birth mother."

TaiTai sat hushed. She reached down to the coffee table and picked up the unfinished martini her husband had set down for a moment. She gulped it down in one swallow.

"What are we to do? What can we do? Most important, what is the right course of action?"

They both sat there gazing at one another, together searching their thoughts and their memories, trying to recall that horrid morning, and now attempting to find a solution to the riddle that interrupted their lives. They could not contemplate a single way to unlock the answer.

"We must consider this very carefully. I had an intuition after I met with Daryl at dinner here in our home. I was very surprised to find, after you and he had become partners, that his twins were children from our Jan Yee. I will tell you, my most respected husband, I had a premonition, a voice that whispered, *the twins will return*. The coincidence is no surprise. I was warned." She shook her head, betraying her shame. "I regret not listening to that silent inner voice in my bosom."

"Tell me all that you are considering. This situation never, ever occurred to me," he whispered.

Madame Hi Bo continued. "When we took the babies from the hospital all those years ago, never saying a word about it to Jan Yee, we knew it was a mistake. We knew it was wrong then, and we know it is wrong now. We felt we were evil and that

Buddha would punish us. This is the penalty for our grave error that morning."

"How can you arrive at such a conclusion? What is your reasoning? The actual truth is that Jan Yee's twins are now part of a wonderful family. They are well educated, healthy, and much loved. They have a happy existence because of our actions. Jan Yee equally has a wonderful life as our adopted daughter. We are pleased to have her as part of our family, connected to us forever. All parties have, in a strange way, been given gifts because of our impetuous action. Yes, it was a very bad decision, but it has turned out good. Thank Buddha."

For Hi Bo, it did not matter what he said to his wife or to himself; he was not convinced. He knew in his heart and his mind that their taking the babies from Jan Yee was an error. Somehow a solution must be found. In the secret corner of his brain, he thought, *perhaps we should have kept the twins. Jan Yee would still be our adopted daughter and the mother of the two girls. Buddha forgive me for the misdeed upon our daughter and our grandchildren.*

On the other hand, Mrs. Hi Bo knew the answer. She could not bring herself to say it. She knew her position in life as a wife. She was not permitted to come to conclusions, make suggestions, or give opinions. Hi Bo was the man of the house. It was his responsibility to make all the choices. And as she had been taught by her mother, and her mother before her, her only duty was to obey her husband, carry out his wishes, and please him.

"What path should we now take, my most honored wife?" Hi Bo questioned.

"I will do as you wish," she responded.

"I will require your help. This is more a woman's issue than a man's. I am a man of business, not of children or of the heart. I beg you to give me your thoughts. I will honor them," he pleaded.

"I am not as wise as you," she responded. "You are the master of the house, my lord, my husband. It is my duty to obey what my husband wants."

"It is I who now stands before my most trusted friend, and it is I who asks you to forgo our thousand-year custom that the woman lives an obedient life. History has changed many things, and most of all, the wisdom of the wife. Please," Hi Bo pleaded, "give me your woman's thoughts that come from your heart and your mind for the correct path. Although I have the heart and the brain for my company, you, my TaiTai, have the heart and the mind for life, feeling, love, and caring as all women do. Please search the wisdom of your mother and your mother's mother to find the right course, the proper mixture of heart and intellect, to solve our dilemma."

Such a statement by the male of the Hi Bo family was never voiced in the history of his ancestors. He felt his lips moving, he heard the words he recited, his heart was calm, his brain attentive, waiting as he did, in silence for the words and the wisdom of his wife.

His lifelong spouse sat hushed, thinking with care and caution of which words to choose. After taking a deep breath, she began. "I recall that terrifying day when we took the children to the mission and left them with the caring nuns. We asked no one. We told no one. We never shared our actions with anyone. Not even our beloved Jan Yee. Please advise if I am correct in saying that we cannot make the same error for a second time."

"You are truthful." Hi Bo nodded.

"We must proceed with caution as we do not want to blunder again," Madame Hi Bo explained. "This time we should speak to Jan Yee and ask what *she* wants and how *she* feels. Our daughter is now a grown woman. It is we who must give support and respect her wishes." A silence enveloped the room. Hi Bo looked at his empty glass. The martini was gone. His eyes were closed. *No more drink. Tonight, I must be 100 percent.*

"My most honored husband, for many years I have known of your cleverness in matters of the brain. Now with same power and intellect, you must rise to attend to the business of the heart and what is the best for our daughter and our family." Mrs. Hi Bo smiled and touched her husband's cheek with her hand and then with her lips

"Yes," he agreed, "we should speak to our daughter and request her guidance."

Hi Bo stood up, thinking that his decision to listen to his wife was the correct path to the solution. He walked from the room and prepared himself for their dinner appointment.

A knowing, confident smile crossed the wife's face. She was satisfied with the result. Her husband's decision was as she guided him. It was a first in her life, when a man took the advice instead of giving it. She lived through, as never before, a sense of assurance, a new self-respect. With eyes slightly closed, she experienced the moment.

⸙

Daryl took the cell phone lying on his desk and slipped it into his pocket. He sat in his vast corporate office in midtown Manhattan. The sills and shelves were filled with photos of his family and of the children of clients and friends. He relished the pleasure and surprise customers experienced when they visited him at the office, each searching for the photo, that special picture of their son or daughter. Upon discovering it, their faces light up. It was the best gift they could ever be given by their friend and business colleague.

The walls were selectively covered by art Daryl had bought in Hong Kong, China, and India. A photo of a fishing trip to the North Pole with Fred and a giant map of China hung on another wall facing his desk.

He relaxed in his leather chair in front of a hand-me-down desk, a gift from a former friend who had retired. The top of the desk was covered with documents, folders, paper clips, and pens. Earphones connected to both his cell and his landline, allowing him privacy in conversations. Seldom did he use speakerphones. Against the wall facing Madison Avenue rested a three-piece black leather sectional sofa. Adjacent to the couch was an antique coffee table that was a relic from his bachelor days. All the furniture was resting on a thick beige carpet. It was a room to work in or to have private meetings with clients or employees. That room was his sanctuary for reflection and decision. It was the heartbeat and brain of his corporate existence.

Daryl understood how many people loathe going to work each day. He also recognized that much of his success was attributed to his joy of going to his office daily. The other half of the equation was the pleasure of returning home to the woman he loved.

Maxine, without reservation, was Daryl's priority. He also knew that the children he cared about would someday leave. They would have their own lives, and then it would be just him and Maxine. He smiled, remembering a joke Maxine made: "When I am old and if you should decide to leave me, I am going with you." He enjoyed that moment. He'd responded, "And the same for me." They'd hugged and kissed. "Number six for the day ... and every day," he'd said. "Who's counting?" she'd replied.

Daryl took a deep breath. Now came the moment of decision. Hi Bo had agreed to the meeting, but there were conditions. The telephone call was an hour of uninterrupted sharing of unease and hopes, and explanations from the Landsman side. Hi Bo wanted to know why this meeting of birth mother and twins was important to the Landsman family. Daryl planned to answer all the questions posed. For now, his choice was either to take the risk, postpone the meeting, or reject it completely.

He knew it was time to discuss the details with Maxine. He

took out his cell phone and dialed. "Where are you now?" he inquired.

"I am uptown shopping. What's on your mind?"

"Let me send the car to pick you up and bring you to my office. We can go home together."

His very smart wife knew this was a ploy. She had no doubt that Daryl had something important on his mind.

"Absolutely, I would like that very much. Please tell the driver to pick me up at the Fifth Avenue entrance of Bergdorf's. I will be there at three-thirty."

❦

Jan Yee descended the winding staircase, taking one step at a time. She was thinking about her rapidly approaching engagement party the following weekend. Her parents had invited guests from everywhere. Young men and women from college and family friends from Guangzhou were coming, as were many relatives and business colleagues, some from distant points of China and some from the USA and Europe. It had become the most talked about ball of the year.

She was pleased. Still, a touch of guilt lingered in her heart. Her mother and her sister had not been included on the guest list. She felt a deep regret and remorse.

She shared her feelings with Leong. He felt the same, but told her, "It could be risky." They had been speaking to Momma Chan and Nina on their newly installed phone, and writing to each other daily by mail.

Jan Yee and Leong decided to find a way to agree on the matter and put it behind them. They were troubled by the uncertainty. Was it their mother's poverty and lack of education? Would Leong and his bride be ashamed or embarrassed? They had no clue. It had to be examined honestly and resolved. This was a joyful occasion. No stain should be permitted to tarnish their celebration.

With all the pros and cons having been examined, at last they both came to an honest understanding of their reluctance. It was not that Jan Yee or Leong did not want their mother and sister at the wedding. Instead, it was a convenient oversight. In all their excitement they had totally forgotten this detail.

The decision was made by the bride and groom: this problem would be corrected quickly. Let the chips fall where they may. They understood their duty; inviting their mother and sister was part of their responsibility to show respect. Their only deep concern was an accidental slip of the tongue, exposing to everyone that Leong and Jan Yee were half brother and sister. It was a risk they had no choice but to take.

Momma Chan and their sister Nina were coming. They received an invitation carefully written in Chinese by Jan Yee's own hand. She'd inserted ¥3,000 for her mother and sister to buy new dresses and other clothes befitting the stepmother of the bride and birth mother of the groom. She shared her decision with her adopted parents, and they agreed. Hi Bo and his TaiTai were proud of their daughter. They added another ¥3,000 so that their daughter and future son-in-law would be comfortable.

The special letter of invitation had been hand-delivered to their mother and Nina.

❧

"Oh my God, my God," Jan Yee said when she awakened on the day of the engagement party. The sky was gray, and a steady rain fell. Jan Yee prayed that She would bless her with clear skies and a warm evening. The clouds had burst open. It rained all morning and did not stop until 3:00 p.m.

She lay on her bed, tears flooding her pillow. Sleep had

deserted her. But she was overpowered by her need for rest and surrendered to the welcome nap her body begged for.

At 4:00 p.m. she awakened. The first engagement offering came. It was Her gift: the downpour had disappeared. Sighing in relief, Jan Yee murmured, "Thank You, my Sister. You are my true God."

Jan Yee called to her mother, "Mother, Mother, come see. The sky is clearing. It is going to be a beautiful evening. Our staff and all the people you hired are now arriving."

"Yes, my love, I see them."

"Mother, if you do not need me, I am going to prepare for this evening."

"Leave it to me and Cissy."

The bride-to-be disappeared up the stairs just as thirty people who had been retained for that evening, including two chefs, their crew, waiters, bartenders, cleaners, coat checkers, two photographers, and the musicians arrived.

Jan's choice of orchids from Madame Hi Bo's own greenhouse covered the entire main floor and the garden at the rear of the home. She stood at the window of her room and looked down. "Oh my, I cannot believe my good fortune. How blessed I am."

Not a single detail had been left to chance. A clear plastic roof stood ready to install, should there be another shower. Fortunately, a moonlit sky graced the evening.

With a happy smile, Jan looked into the heavens and whispered, "Thank You."

❦

"We are so fortunate to have such a beautiful evening." Jan Yee rested her head on Leong's shoulder.

"My love," he began, "it would never rain at the party of Jan

Yee Hi Bo! Our Da Loban would never allow it." The young couple laughed.

Momma Chan and Sister Nina were brought to the big house by the Hi Bo driver. Their excitement was beyond comprehension. Sitting in a car being driven was unbelievable to them. Nina had insisted on riding in the front seat.

Every other minute Nina looked at her mom; her eyes were filled with joy, and she blew kisses at her. Their mutual silence contributed to the amazement they felt during the drive. The anticipation of the moment was incredible. Giggles, laughter, and oohs and ahs poured from them.

On arrival at the big house, Momma Chan and Nina were welcomed by Hi Bo and his TaiTai. They were offered refreshments, but they declined. Then they were shown to their rooms to rest. They would bathe and dress for the party at 7:00 p.m.

A special maid was engaged to assist them with their every wish. "Momma, I feel like I am in paradise." No response came except for a knowing smile.

Nina could not rest. She had never in her life been alone in a bed. She was frightened and when all was silent, she quietly tip-toed into Momma Chan's room, slipped under the covers, and slept like a baby.

Once Nina awoke, a smile of pride spread across her face. This was the home of her brother and sister. Nina could not help but fantasize about her sister's good fortune. *Will I have such good luck to meet and fall in love with a man like Leong? I must study. I must go to college. I want a better life, not only for myself but for my children. May God bless me with these silent prayers? I swear to you, my Buddha. I swear with all my heart that I will be the woman I was destined to be.*

The evening of the celebration arrived quickly. The maid helped Momma Chan and Nina to dress. She applied just a tiny bit of lip rouge to Nina's trembling lips. This young, lovely child could not stop gazing into the full-length mirror in their room. Nina quivered in this ecstatic moment in her life. Her teenage eyes fixated on her hair, the lip rouge, the fine-looking dress. It was like a dream. It was heaven. Momma would have none of it. She was a simple, very proud woman. All the glamour and luxuries meant nothing to her. Her happiness came only from her family's joy on this special day. Being welcomed to witness her son's happy moment was truly a miracle. It was time to join the party. The maid led Mrs. Chan and Nina slowly down the circular staircase. She held the trembling Madame Chan tightly.

Leong's sister was at the age where she was beginning to blossom into the woman she would grow to be. Momma Chan, his handsome mother, was walking steadily entering the party. Leong moved quickly to his mother's and sister's side. He received them with open arms and warmly embraced them. He walked with them arm in arm, tall and proud. The music changed; it was if a welcoming cadenza announced the arrival of an important guest.

Friends greeted Leong. "Permit me to introduce my mother and my sister, Madame Chan and Nina." All bowed, treating his family with complete respect.

Leong watched as his mother and Nina smiled. He felt a sense of pride upon seeing them enjoying their dignity as they reciprocated the multiple welcomes.

He watched, experiencing the happiest, most exciting moment in his life, and was delighted to share it with his mom and sister. He saw in their eyes how pleased his long-forgotten family was by the splendor of the house and the elegantly dressed men and women attending. It was going to be an evening never to be forgotten by Momma and Nina, or anyone.

Leong from afar saw Jan Yee as she entered the reception room. He called to her. She smiled and rapidly moved to her fiancé. With eyes closed, she brushed his cheek with her lips, while Leong presented Jan to his mother. Jan Yee smiled and bowed. "Honored Mother, I am so very pleased that you and Nina will share this moment with us to meet my friends and my parents." A few of the guests who'd overheard Jan Yee's kind words were surprised by her greeting. Two couples listening solved the confusion.

One woman in a long silken gown leaned over to a friend and said, "She is already calling her mother-in-law-to-be 'honored Mother.' How respectful. It is refreshing to see young people revering our traditions."

The other responded, "I understand she comes from a very respectable family."

The first woman, smiling, knew the Hi Bo family very well, and responded, "That stunning bride comes from the very best family in Guangzhou, perhaps all of China." Leong nudged Nina, who was gazing at her stepsister. Jan Yee was the most beautiful woman at the ball.

Each and every guest shared in the gala. Longtime friends congratulated the engaged couple, embraced one another, and shared many jeroboams of champagne. A five-piece orchestra played Western and Asian music continuously. Atop a small platform, a mature Asian woman sang, with her extraordinary voice, many time-honored Chinese love songs. A young man dressed in a tuxedo offered songs by Frank Sinatra, the Beatles, and other Western well-known music, to which everyone gathered on the dance floor.

As the guests sat dining, a tinkling of a glass called everyone to attention. The room quieted. Poppa Da Loban Hi Bo stood to speak.

"My friends, and Momma and Nina Chan, welcome to our home. This is an evening neither I nor my TaiTai, Madame Hi Bo, ever dreamed we would experience. A young girl came into our lives. She was fifteen years old. In time we grew to love her dearly. We asked this child for permission to adopt her." The room hushed as Hi Bo sipped a little water. "She returned our love in equal proportion, honoring us by taking my mother's name. Though she is adopted, make no mistake; she is the same to us as if we were her biological momma and baba. Our love is deep, unconditional, and without reservation."

Everyone applauded. He raised his hand, hushing his guests. They marveled at a dynasty being born right before their eyes. Generations of Guangzhou would be economically safe. They understood that the marriage of Hi Bo's daughter to Leong Chan and their heirs would create a place for the community to work in his great factory, supporting their families for years to come. Many people agreed with what a reporter from the local Guangzhou newspaper wrote in an editorial: an economic miracle had been bestowed on the people and the city. This giant shoe factory employing thousands of residents would now prosper and live respectable lives as the local economy would grow for generations. Today was truly a celebration, and a blessing for the province of Guangdong and the city of Guangzhou.

"Now, ladies and gentlemen, the next step to our happiness was the blessed meeting of two young people who subsequently fell in love. It is with pride and pleasure that I introduce my son-in-law-to-be, Leong Chan. He is a young man who has all the qualities every father dreams of for his daughter." He hesitated again and touched his glasses. "Mostly I do not judge a man by his wealth or his accomplishments. I reach my understanding of a man and of my future son by his integrity and the dreams he has for himself and my daughter. And now I am pleased to announce that both Leong and Jan Yee are soon to marry and build a family that we hope will carry the Hi Bo name long into our Chinese history." Cheers rang through the room again. There was a deafening ovation with bravos and congratulations.

Piao and his wife stood quietly in a corner. He smiled, turned to his wife, and whispered with pride, "I am the maker of this union." David Chen sat close by with his two children, Chin Ha and Tat Ya. His Western wife, Laura, glowed with delight. They were happy for the well-deserving, well-respected Hi Bo family.

"Please, my friends, raise your glasses and join me in a toast to celebrate the union of two families."

"Hi Bo," a guest called out, "we honor you and your family. And now you ask us to drink a toast, which I must withhold until you address the vicious, unsubstantiated rumor that your daughter and her groom are brother and sister. I pray you have an explanation, with all due respect." The entire assembly sat in shocked speechlessness. A hum of quiet murmurs filled the congregation.

Hi Bo stood in his place frozen and silenced by this question. His face was grim. He glared at the woman. He felt attacked. But he remained composed and began. "Madame Choy," he said, his voice strong with a slight tone of anger, "I may advise you and all our guests that — " another strong woman's voice interrupted the evening.

Momma Chan stood. "Forgive me, my Da Loban." The room silenced. All eyes focused on Mrs. Chan as she slowly rose and began to speak in a commanding voice with the mighty force of a male. Her voice echoed like that no other Chinese woman had ever used to address such an audience. The room quieted as everyone experienced a moment of shock. The guests could not believe their ears.

"Honored Hi Bo, Madame Hi Bo, and guests," Momma Chan began. "I have been invited to this celebration to honor the engagement of my son and his bride, Jan Yee. Please note that I used the term *my son*. I did not call Jan Yee my daughter. What mother could ever deny the birthright of her own child?" She pointed her finger at the woman who rudely spoke earlier.

"Could you, Madame Choy, deny your child's birthright? Tell

me. Could you?" She questioned in a raised voice. "Ah, you are silent now. I know your answer. Shame on you." Momma Chan thundered.

"To you mothers sitting in this room for this celebration, could any of you publicly deny that your child is your child in front of your child? I think not." A hum of agreement and appreciation swept through the room.

"Leong and Nina are my only birth children. Shan Di, now called Jan Yee to honor Mr. Hi Bo's mother, is my stepdaughter." She paused and took a deep breath, giving everyone a moment to understand the significance of her statement. "I am *not* Jan Yee's birth mother." She stressed again, "I am *not* her birth mother. I am only the birth mother to Leong and Nina. On this I swear." Mrs. Chan continued with energy and strength. She spoke as if she'd just been emancipated after years of confinement, having now burst into the freedom she'd yearned for during her lifetime.

"Her birth mother died of an illness. My husband and I took your Jan Yee into our home. Her true birth mother was a neighbor and a dear friend." All the guests were still quiet, amazed; this woman, tiny in stature, was able to hypnotize the entire room with her simple, clear narrative. Never before had they seen a woman with such authority rising to the occasion and telling her story to a large and powerful audience. Such a thing was unheard of for a Chinese woman. For Mother Chan, it was a luxury to speak with the power of a man and remain in the body, and the voice of, a woman. She knew not from where her new voice emerged.

But speak she did, saying, "I pray to Buddha that my daughter-in-law's first child will have the beauty of her birth mother and the intellect of her father.

"On this I swear," she concluded, "Leong and Jan Yee are not brother and sister. Would a mother wish ill-born children for her child? Would I as a future grandmother want such a fate? I ask each and every one of you, as Buddha is my witness, on this I swear." She waved to Nina, who came to her mother's side. Momma Chan placed her arm around her and led Nina to Madame Choy. Everyone watched. "My dear Madame, this beautiful child is my only daughter. You have brought shame to yourself and to your husband and your family." No one spoke. No one breathed. "You are a silly woman, but I forgive you, my son forgives you, and most certainly, the Hi Bo family forgives you."

Silence filled the room. Then, in a burst of elation, the guests exploded with cheers and applause. It was not the previously untold story that Mrs. Chan had just shared that moved the guests to this peak of emotion. No, not at all. It was the commanding voice and tone of one who spoke with the love of a mother and authority of a man. The applause rang out in response to the sound of a woman declaring her story to all present in a voice miraculously confident and dominant in a single flash. Mrs. Chan had roused the feelings of every woman in the room, as all had experienced oppression throughout their entire lives, as did their mothers and their mother's mothers. They all knew that their existence was determined by men, and that they all lived in a man's world. They also recognized that change was coming for their daughters and granddaughters, where their voices would be heard and honored.

"Please, please, everyone." Hi Bo stood up. "Let us continue our celebration and raise our glasses to honor long life to Momma Chan and to good health and many children for my daughter and Leong," he toasted.

Continuing, he said, "Let us all stand and once again be grateful for the powerful blood that flows through the veins of my daughter's mother-in-law, Momma Chan. And we pray to Buddha to allow that blood continue its journey into the minds and bodies of my forthcoming grandchildren."

The guests smiled and nodded. Every woman in the room felt the clout contained in *that* woman, something they had never before experienced or seen. It was a moment that made each woman in that setting reflect silently on the strength Mama Chan had in her voice. Each mother understood the feelings of pain and the anger in their heart. Is it an inner gift to muster the courage, to stand strong before such an audience for the sake of her children? *Yes, yes, it is possible when we have to protect our children,* their inner voices whispered. *We must have courage, the daring, and the guts to speak truth to power.*

Much too quickly for the hosts and the guests, the dining, the dancing, and the music came to an end. It was past midnight when each guest respectfully approached Da Loban Hi Bo, Madame Hi Bo, and Mrs. Chan and their family. Each deeply bowed and paid their respects. They offered congratulations befitting such a wonderful match, with special compliments to Leong's mother for her unusual bravery in taking on the role of the father and standing up for her children.

One elderly woman, with cane in her hand approached Leong's mother and said in an unusually strong voice, "My dear Mrs. Chan, you are not only a very brave woman; you are a most powerful person blessed with the highest character to stand there and defend your children." Mrs. Chan bowed; the woman kissed her cheek and blessed her. The lovely sister Nina smiled with a pride in her mother she had never experienced.

The party came to an end. All the invitees departed. Tranquility returned to the big house.

The family sat in the study, exhausted. Tea was served as they reminisced about the events of the wedding reception. Madame Hi Bo spoke directly to Mrs. Chan, congratulating her on having two wonderful children in Leong and Nina.

Momma Chan, a simple, uneducated woman, a woman who could not read or write — this uncomplicated lady was a mountain of street smarts. She had come to the party with her own plan in mind: if needed, to clarify the relationships and tell her semi-fictional but believable story to put an end to all doubts about Shan Di and Leong's relationship. It was now done, for the family and the community.

Mrs. Hi Bo rose from her seat and walked over to Mrs. Chan. They faced one another and embraced. "Welcome to our family. You honor us with your son, Leong, your daughter, Nina, and your presence. We are now one family." She held her hand out to Nina. Leong and Jan Yee joined hands, as did Hi Bo. They stood in a circle, holding each other, joyful and weeping. The moment was one of harmony and triumph.

The fears that Jan Yee and Leong had, that their mother would mistakenly tell someone that they were half brother and sister, totally disappeared.

Mother Chan was a very intelligent woman. She knew what she was doing. She wanted to protect her children. It was a clever, well-thought-out scheme. It was the only part of her plan that was a surprise: she'd never expected to tell her story to such a vast audience.

23

An Emergency

"Daryl, I am worried to death. Lauren's voice on the phone was not her own. It had the tone and the sound of a stranger. Something is wrong." Maxine insisted.

"Sweetheart, I think you are overreacting. When kids go away to school, they work hard and play hard. That's all it is. She must be very tired." Maxine remained silent. She sat in a chair near the window looking out at the park below, and then turned to her husband.

"Daryl, listen to me and pay attention carefully: a mother's instincts are better than any doctor's diagnosis, better than a CAT scan or an x-ray machine. A mother knows her child." She trembled.

"I could hear something in the sound of her voice, just as I can tell when something is wrong by the way her eyes look, or how I'm able to detect a tiny rash that no one else sees." This mother did not have to see her daughter to know that there was a serious problem with her child.

For a week, Daryl and Maxine tossed around possible scenarios to explain Lauren's infrequent calls and changed tone of voice. They speculated that she was homesick; or she was rejected by a boyfriend; or she was struggling with her academic load at college.

There had not been a single phone call from Lauren for almost eight days; her lack of communication was a bad omen. Maxine decided to call her. Her baby's voice was unrecognizable.

"Daryl, that's it. It may be only my intuition, but I don't need any further proof or diagnosis. The voice that I heard on the phone had the sound of, 'Momma, I need you now!'"

Distance did not dull her maternal antenna. A few hours later Maxine called again. Sammy's roommate answered. "I am so glad you called, Mrs. Landsman. Lauren seems very sick. I am her roommate, Claudine."

"What's the matter?" Maxine asked.

"No one knows. I think you should come as soon as possible."

Daryl and Maxine were in a panic. They both moved quickly to their car. Daryl left a note in the garage for Assane, their driver.

It took several hours to drive from New York to New Hampshire. At the Dartmouth reception center, they introduced themselves. Within minutes they were at the college infirmary.

Daryl Narrates — Listen to the Voice of a Frightened Father

The attending nurse greeted us. "We think Lauren has the flu," the woman said. "We gave her penicillin and two Tylenol. It brought her temperature down. She still has a temperature of a hundred and two."

We walked into the infirmary. Our daughter was asleep. Maxine put her lips to Lauren's forehead. She looked at me. "She's on fire. Let's get her to a hospital."

"Where is the nearest hospital?" I demanded of the nurse.

"It's in Lebanon, about ten miles. You will have to sign her out first."

"Give the paperwork to my wife. I am getting the car. What's the name of the hospital?" I asked.

"It's the Mary Hitchcock Memorial Hospital. It's the best we've got," the nurse responded in a slightly frightened voice.

In one day, I had driven our car more than I had driven in ten years. I had become too accustomed to my driver; I experienced memory loss and had forgotten what to do behind the wheel. I was suffering through a feeling I seldom had before: panic.

We carried Lauren into the emergency room. A young Asian doctor greeted us. Without hesitation Maxine spoke.

"Our daughter appears to be very ill. She has a high temperature after a flu shot and some Tylenol. I also noticed a bit of blood around her nose, as if she has been bleeding," Maxine said, explaining Lauren's symptoms.

"Let me help you put her down here on this bed. I will examine her." He called a nurse to help him take our daughter to an examination room.

"My name is Dr. Hsu. I am the attending physician on duty today. Please tell me more about your daughter. Can you tell me about her health or health issues or any other symptoms you know about?"

"She is nineteen years old. Generally, she has been very healthy. She had occasional colds and headaches and also the measles at a young age. I have noticed fatigue more frequently. She did mention she had a backache before she left for the second semester," Maxine answered.

"Oh, she is at the college?"

"Yes, a freshman."

"We often see this with freshmen, their first experience with total freedom. Most are great kids, but still they often burn the candle at both ends, working till late and partying till dawn. She is probably like the hundreds of other kids we get in here every year. I do not think there is much to worry about. She will probably be okay in a day or two. Please wait outside while the nurse and I examine her."

"Thank you, Doctor." We both moved to the waiting area and sat in silence.

"*Kinder, kinder* (children). My mom used to say, 'little children, little worries; big children, big worries,'" I said, exasperated.

"Why is it whenever there is some stressful incident, you're always quoting some silly thing your mother used to say?" Maxine responded, slightly short. "To tell you the truth" — she reexamined her anxiety — "your mother was very accurate with the phrase you just gave me."

I reached out and took her hand. "I am sure everything will be all right." It took about thirty minutes for the young doctor to return from the examining room. He appeared calm and did not look upset.

"My first guess was fairly accurate. Her blood pressure is normal. Cardiogram: normal. Her nosebleed is a puzzle. She has four tiny blood clots on her neck and below her breasts. I took a blood sample. It will be a couple of hours before we get the test result. We'll send that out to a local lab. I saw no bruises."

"What's the blood test for, Doctor?" Maxine asked.

"It's our method of diagnosing any infection in her system, and of finding out if there are drugs in her bloodstream, which I doubt. Occasionally a kid away from home has a slip of carelessness. It happens. We can never tell without the blood test. Always better to be safe than sorry. I have my doubts though."

"Do you think Lauren is taking drugs?" Maxine's voice trembled.

"No, I think no such thing. Forget it. I really hope not. She is not stupid," I said, thinking of the danger.

My mobile phone rang.

"Who was that?" Maxine questioned after I'd hung up.

"It was our driver. He read my note in the garage and took the first train up here to help."

An hour went by, no doctor. We drank coffee; another hour, no doctor. We sat there, as fear crushed our senses. After another hour, the door finally opened.

"What took so long?" Maxine spoke, teary eyed. The doctor did not respond.

"There is no infection, and no drugs. But her blood count is very low. She is strong enough to travel. I suggest you take her home to your own physician. I think you will need an expert."

"What do you mean an expert? Are you saying we will need to see a specialist?"

"That is exactly what I mean."

"Please, Doctor, I promise I will not hold you to it. Give me your best guess," I pleaded.

Dr. Hsu stood there, his hand on his chin. He was quiet, pondering his answer, an answer he was reluctant to offer.

"Take the child home tonight. Tomorrow call your family physician. Have him examine her. That is the best I can say. Like I explained earlier, I am not an expert in this. I just finished my internship under a year ago."

"Please, Doctor," Maxine pleaded, "what are you not telling us?"

Dr. Hsu stood in silence, facing us, thinking. He began, "My best guess is that, judging from the blood test and the symptoms … my very best guess — and mind you, I am not a diagnostician — is that your daughter may have … leukemia."

✺

In Guangzhou

"Come sit with us, Poppa, Momma. Leong and I are discussing the wedding," Jan called to her parents.

"Didn't we discuss the wedding a few evenings ago?" Hi Bo questioned.

"Of course we did. But Leong was in Switzerland, taking care of your company." She smiled.

"This is very important to us," Jan said in an excited voice.

"First, Leong and I want to thank you both for helping Momma Chan by getting her a new home."

"Enough, enough," Hi Bo commanded. "How many times are you going to thank us?"

"I am never going to stop. You are both very good, Momma and Baba. I love your kindness and your generosity."

"And second, we appreciate the entry-level job you arranged for Nina," Leong added.

"Did I tell everyone that Momma Chan got herself a job as a cook and housekeeper near her new home?" Leong mentioned.

"Why did she do that? She certainly has enough to make her life a little easier," Hi Bo said.

"Mother is a strong and independent woman; she takes pleasure in your generosity," said Leong.

"But she insists on taking care of herself. It is very important to her and her self-esteem. And it was her decision."

"Poppa, I know you like a book," Jan interrupted. "You are proud of Momma Chan." He nodded a yes.

The new family sat in the library drinking tea, smiles on all their faces, except for Hi Bo.

"What's the matter, Poppa?" Jan Yee quizzed.

"Mother and I must confess a story to you." He gazed at his TaiTai. She nodded, as if giving permission. "When that terrible incident happened a long time ago, you were young, very young, and you were innocent. You became with child." He breathed deeply. "Twin girls were born. Mother and I, without asking, and in a state of bewilderment, took the helpless babies from you and brought them to the Catholic orphanage only a few miles from here. We gave the sisters at the orphanage money to help with the costs of care. We never returned."

"I never knew ... twins?" A baffled look fell on Jan Yee's face. "Oh my God!'

"Yes, twins," her mother replied. "With life's twists and turns and unforeseen conclusions, our friend and partner and his wife adopted the children. When? I cannot answer ... But it was soon after the children were born."

"Were they boys or girls? What did they look like? Please tell me what they looked like?" Jan Yee begged.

"We were filled such remorse, and a terrible sense of guilt, we did not pay attention to anything. We were distressed to the point that we believed we had sinned. Our misdeed was not asking you what *you* wanted. You were a mere fifteen-year-old girl with nothing, with no one in your life. It was a horror for you, and for us as well.

"Only a few months ago, your father and I discussed this, and we rationalized our sin and the guilt that we harbored by saying that our offense was truly a gift from Buddha. We adopted a child, we educated her, and we have given her a good life. Also, we have given ourselves the joy of having that girl — you, my daughter — in our lives. On the other side of this complicated history, the Landsmans adopted these two children, who are now happy and well educated and who also live a good life. Most importantly, like you, they too are happy, well, and loved."

All sat motionless. The room filled with tension. No one spoke or moved. Leong's finger tapped lightly on the table.

Poppa took a deep breath and expelled the air from his lungs, trying to ease his anxiety. "They were girls."

Jan Yee rose from her chair, took a few steps to her mother, took her hand, and turned to her father.

"Momma, Baba, you did the right thing. I was a baby having a baby. That is not what God wanted." Jan took a breath and sipped some water. She continued. "She wanted what we all are living right now. It was Her way of bringing us all together. It was Her guidance that put Leong and me on a path to meet, fall in love, and now to marry. Neither Leong nor I have committed a sin, as some will most probably say. And now that we are to marry, in a situation that some may call unorthodox, it is not immoral or evil because we are not in love as brother and sister; we are in love as a man and a woman. It was meant to be; otherwise, She would never have allowed it to happen. It is God's appointed course, and it is the path we are going to follow. Let's enjoy Her blessing that She has bestowed on us. We should take pleasure in our God's other gift: our upcoming wedding and lifelong celebration."

"What's the matter, Poppa Hi Bo?" Leong began. "You continue to look distraught."

"Jan Yee referred to God as a She. God is not a woman; God is a man." He was stunned, unable to believe his ears. He looked directly into his daughter's eyes. "Tell me, my child, where has all this come from?"

"Please, Poppa," she said, followed by a pause. "I have no disrespect for your belief in Buddha."

Jan Yee began to explain softly, with respect and caution. "You have traveled the world. You have seen this amazing earth. You have crossed its rivers, its oceans, and most beautiful, its mountains. Think for just one moment, my father, and you will understand why my God must be a Woman." She resumed. "Who but a woman can take a barren, lifeless earth and make it into the splendor we all value and respect? Think, my father. You are a most intelligent man. Who fills a home with comfort? Who ensures the strength of a family? Who has prearranged the beauty of flowers, fish in the sea, rice on the earth? A man? I believe not. It is the heart and the feeling of a woman that brings the safety into your life and mine.

"My beloved and most respected Baba, each time I enter our home and move to the stairs that take me to my room, I gaze upon our beloved Buddha, one at our entrance and the two guarding our home at the foot of the stairs. What do I see in the eyes and the faces of each one? I see a Woman.

"Look for yourself sometime soon. Look closely. Tell me if you see a man or a woman. I see a woman and her face engulfs me."

Each fell into a very long moment of silence. Leong did not move. Madame Hi Bo gazed with a newfound calm in her heart. What she heard was truth and clear honesty from her daughter. Her eyes turned to her husband.

Hi Bo was bewildered. *What am I hearing? What is my child saying? Did we fail in our instruction to her when she was a young woman? Does she not understand and know that men rule and is they that are made in the image of God? How can I possibly accept this blasphemy?*

"I sit here and listen to my daughter, and I cannot believe what my ears are hearing," Hi Bo began. "I will not order you to stop your unthinkable philosophy. Still, all my life, my prayers have always gone to Buddha. It has been this way not only for me, but also for my father and his father before him for centuries. It is our way. It is the only way." He challenged.

Hi Bo thought for a moment. He could not contain himself. "Had I confronted *my* family's beliefs, I would have been disowned, barred from our home — this very house that we sit in now. This, my father's and grandfather's home for two lifetimes." He touched his teacup to his lips. He looked at his daughter's face. Tears slipped from her eyes.

"I refuse to bring pain into your life, nor will I ever commit such a deed, my father. I value the life we have as father and daughter more than your Buddha or my She-god. You and my mother are my most valued. And whether it be Buddha or She who has brought us together, I am thankful for it all and will remain grateful all my life."

Jan Yee stood, walked over to Hi Bo, and embraced him, letting her tears fall onto his shirt. "I love you. I love you." She wept. "And from my understanding and faith, She has bestowed this love and this respect I have for you and Momma. It is Her gift to me for *my* life."

Quiet filled the room. "Tell Poppa what you have explained to me," Leong said quietly.

"May I, Poppa?" Jan Yee interrupted.

Hi Bo did not answer at first. Seconds passed, and then he nodded.

Jan Yee moved to a chair close to Leong.

"Poppa," she began, "if God is a man, why are men not the givers of life? Why did God give women the gift of perpetuating our species and our race? If God is a man, as you believe, why has your God given woman the power to feed the species from her body? Why is the beauty of the earth called Mother Nature? I have heard men look at a car and say, '*She* ... is a beauty.' From all the books in your library, many of which you have given to me, I read that men and men alone destroy each other and the splendor of our world. Poppa, it is not a He who has given all of us this life we enjoy and our love and health. For the twins I brought into this world, they too have a wonderful life. For all that, and for all the advantages and the good things in life, if not for that alone, *God must be a woman!*" she said emphatically.

Hi Bo stretched his arms, placed his strong hands on his knees, and lifted himself from his chair. He went to the bar at the end of the room and poured himself a whiskey.

This must be serious, Leong mused.

Hi Bo stood in silence, gazing at his daughter.

"For centuries, it has been written that God is a man. Now my own daughter, in my own house, wishes to change the world. You shame me. This is not how your mother and I raised you. This libelous speech you have just given to me and your mother is a sin according to everything we believe. You must — and on this I insist — apologize for this reproach to our belief and our way of life."

"I love you, Poppa. Please forgive me. I respect you and your beliefs. You say that for centuries it has been written that God is a man. Those scriptures were written only by men. Men created and wrote that philosophy. How could men possibly write about my belief that God is a Woman? Women have always been victimized, enslaved, lost their lives perpetuating their families. Please understand that I shall never apologize or ask for forgiveness for what I believe in. It will shame me more than the assault inflicted on me … by your guest in this house while I was under your protection. It was my God who saved me. As a woman, She understood my disgrace and the humiliation a woman has to carry with her for life because of such a horrid incursion when one is a helpless child."

"I insist. This is not the way a daughter speaks to her father." His voice rose.

"I am speaking in a respectful tone. There are no harsh words coming from my lips to disgrace you or Mother. I am only expressing my own point of view."

The room was still. Mrs. Hi Bo stood close to her husband, her hand on his arm. Leong sipped his Scotch. His mind was racing; he could not retain any memory of his thoughts, as they vanished from his mind the moment they entered. And then involuntarily, he reached out for Jan Yee's hand, pulled her close, and asked, "Why are we having this political conversation? I was under the impression that we were going to discuss the wedding. What has changed?"

"May I say one more thing?" Jan Yee inquired.

"Of course you may," Momma Hi Bo inserted.

"Allow me to share with you what my God has taught me," she began. "There are two kinds of people on our earth: the givers and the receivers." Everyone remained silent.

"My most honored father, you are a giver. You, my father, my Da Loban, have given all your life from the time you were a young man. I know your history. She has told it to me. She has put me in your care. You have given me love. You have given me a life filled with kindness, education, fairness, and truthfulness.

"You are a giver, not only to me and my mother, but also to our entire community. You give all your employees a sense of safety, a future, and most of all an honest wage. It is all part of your giving life. Giving makes you happy and content, as all givers experience."

Jan Yee sipped a little water. She reached out to touch her father's hand. She turned to her mother, tilted her head ever so slightly, and pursed her lips, as if sending her a kiss. Momma glowed, admiring her daughter's intellect and her perception of life.

"My dearest father," Jan Yee resumed, "the receivers are also good people. She has taught me and counseled me that the confusion of the receiver is the result of the gratitude they feel along with a touch of anger that they are a receiver and not a giver. The giver has more joy than the beneficiary of the kindness. It is sad but true. I will never forget the simple but interesting story you once told me about your trip to New York to visit your partner Daryl Landsman."

Everyone looked around. Hi Bo could not remember any such story about New York.

"Your story was that Daryl offered to have his car drive you to NYU hospital. But it is your nature to take risks. You wanted the experience of taking the subway, which as I understand is an underground train. You boarded the train and sat down, when an elderly woman came through the door carrying a cane. You stood and offered her your seat. You told me that instead of showing gratitude or even surprise, her face reflected anger. Still she sat. It puzzled you. To be sure, your experience in New York was a mystery, to you as well as to me. I could not get it out of my mind.

"Months later as I lay in my bed, She came to me and, in all Her wisdom, solved the puzzle.

"Father, you as a gentleman gave your seat to a lady, as is your style. You are a giver. In her angry life, she has always been the receiver. So even in a most innocent moment of kindness, that elderly woman with the cane resented the giver.

"When you told me this story, it was not to demonstrate in any way your lifelong kindness. Your story was about your inability to comprehend the anger." Jan Yee rested, sipped more water, and then continued. "You have taught me to show kindness to others without judgment. She has guided me to be generous with understanding. Why is God a woman? Because She is not a God of revenge, anger, or retribution. She is a God of mercy and love and generosity. And my beloved Baba, that is why I believe that God is a woman.

"We, as women, always forgive, but we never forget. That is a woman's way of life. She has blessed us with Her teachings. As She explained to me, the givers have joy in giving; the receivers are grateful in times of need and angry because they need and want. We as givers must continue to give and forgive their anger."

Hi Bo returned from the bar with another Scotch, three ice cubes swimming in a circle at the rim of his glass. He sat next to his wife, sipping his drink. He was calm and did not appear angry. He looked at his daughter sadly.

"I know how deeply you love me. I can feel it. I can feel your hope for my happiness. I am a woman who sees the truth of your strength in your wishes for my life. I can also see a sign of betrayal stemming from my belief. Let that pass. She has placed me into your life for as long as you shall live. You have not failed with me. You have won."

With eyes shut, Hi Bo took a deep swig of his ancient tranquilizer, leaving two cubes resting alone at the bottom of his glass. He snapped a napkin from the coffee table, dabbed his lips, and began speaking.

"Daryl Landsman, in New York, called and asked us to find out if you would be willing to meet their daughters. They as parents think it would be good for the girls to meet and know their birth mother, and perhaps it may be good for you to meet the twins."

What happened? Why has he changed the subject? Or did the Da Loban understand there would be no winners in this debate? It was important for him to get to his original reason for the conversation.

Hi Bo sighed. He sat back in his chair and stared into his emptied glass. Jan Yee turned her head to Leong, who stretched out his arm, leaned toward his bride to be, and touched her open hand.

"Your mother and I decided that we could not make such a decision without your permission. We did that once before, and we have regretted it for many years. We refuse to make the same error again with anyone, especially our daughter." That phrase as spoken by Hi Bo indicated the end of his anger.

"Poppa, I have no answer for Mr. Landsman right now. I must think about it. I promise, I will decide after the wedding and our honeymoon."

Jan Yee rested for a moment, and then in continuous thought began again. "Please, Poppa, pardon me. I am sincerely sorry for surprising you with the religious concept I have come to accept. Do not judge me for having a different take on the status quo. I have learned new ideas, and I have a new appreciation for unorthodox philosophies. I learned, and I believe, that change is inevitable. And it happened to me, here in this very house. Allow there to be two Gods in our home, yours and mine. Above all, please know that I love you and mother very much ... and forever."

We Return to New York City

Maxine and Daryl, back at home, moved quickly. LangPi was in bed, her skin with a claylike, yellowish look. Her eyes were pink, and her forehead was warm. They waited until 9:30 a.m. to call Dr. Freid, Daryl's friend and medical advisor.

"How did that half-brother-half-sister issue resolve itself?" he recalled.

"It's still in process," Daryl replied. "I am reaching out to you about another, more serious issue."

"And that is?"

"My daughter is ill," he answered in a voice of despair.

"What can I do to be of help?"

"LangPi became ill at school. We rushed up to Dartmouth. She had, and still has, a temperature. The girl looks horrible. We rushed her to a local hospital up in northern New Hampshire. After a thorough examination and a blood test, the young resident intern gave us a guess diagnosis: leukemia."

The other end of the phone was silent. Then Dr. Freid explained, "What is most important is for you and Maxine to calm yourselves. It is probably a bad guess, but let's not underestimate the diagnosis. The sooner we know, the more comfortable we will feel, and the better we'll be able to identify what to do. I will call Dr. Zelda Altman. She is the most knowledgeable when it comes to leukemia diagnosis and treatment. She's at Sloan Kettering. I'll call her office now and try, if I can, to arrange for her to see your daughter today. I will call back as soon as I reach her."

"Thank you, thank you, my friend. We appreciate your sense of urgency."

24

The Joy of Youth and the Celebration of Promise

"You always said you wanted to go to the States. I have never been there. We could go to Las Vegas, or ski in Aspen, and then go to Disneyland — or do all of it. Let's plan on taking three weeks off. It's our honeymoon. Who would deny us that time together? It's once in a lifetime."

"Leong, my love." Jan Yee smiled. "I enjoy that you always want to please me and make me happy. A trip to America — what a wonderful idea," Jan agreed."It sounds like a great idea. I will tell Poppa our plans. He may not like that I will be away so long. But I have a feeling he will be okay with the long-overdue vacation we are planning. How about you? Think Mr. Landsman will approve?"

"I do. He is a good person. I can see him and his wife getting on a plane to Las Vegas just to take us out to dinner."

They rushed into the library. Jan Yee sat at the computer. "Let's see, the wedding will be on February 8, during Chinese New Year. We should gather our thoughts and stay with the family for a few days to relive the wedding party and enjoy all the people there. And then, my love, we will fly off to a magical and exciting three weeks of nothingness, fun, food, the shows of

Las Vegas. We'll sleep late, stay in bed as long as we want to, and then have breakfast in the room … and on to Aspen."

"Sounds like a great idea. Let's plan to leave around February eleventh or twelfth," her future husband agreed. "I believe we can take a plane from Hong Kong directly to Los Angeles and connect to Las Vegas."

"First class?" she questioned.

"Too expensive; we will do fine in coach," he answered.

"Oh, Leong, this is our honeymoon. We will probably have gifts from family and friends. Let's do it. Please, please?"

Leong was a smart and conservative businessman. They could do so many more good things with the money. He did not answer.

"Please." She reached out.

"Okay, okay. But not first class. Business class is almost the same. It's much less costly."

She threw her arms around him, snuggling her face into his neck. "I love you," she whispered.

"I am so happy."

The next few weeks were filled with excitement as they prepared for the wedding. Jan Yee had no idea of the complexity of putting together the details of a wedding ceremony and a celebration simultaneously. Dresses were needed for the mother of the bride and the mother of the groom, of course, the bride, and Leong's sister. Planning her wedding was Jan's most exhilarating experience, filled with a touch of anxiety.

A beautifully designed custom-made ivory lace dress was selected for the bride, with a sheer handmade veil for the ceremony. Most important was Jan Yee's shimmering red stretch satin cheongsam gown for the after-ceremony party. Leong planned to wear a simple white Mao suit and Poppa Hi Bo, a traditional black velvet tuxedo.

The wedding with its vast guest list was held at the White

Swan Hotel, a scenic location set amid the colonial architecture of Shamian Island and the Pearl River in Guangzhou.

Two hundred guests, including the master Sang Ye Piao and his wife, converged from all the provinces of China. Sitting next to them was Auntie Sun and her new husband, the brother-in-law of Piao. Sun Yang and the governor of Guangdong Province, the director of international commerce of Guangzhou, customers, and friends filled the hall. Missing from the celebration were Daryl and Maxine Landsman, who had explained that the illness of their daughter prevented them from attending. This was totally understandable. Four antique sterling silver candlesticks from Tiffany's in New York represented their presence.

The wedding ceremony was to be conducted by a Chinese Buddhist priest and a Chinese Christian minister. Simple wedding symbols chimed as the bride entered, followed by her parents, with Leong's sister and mother just behind them. The attendees were quiet as the priest and the minister began the ceremony. A small Chinese quartet played time-honored wedding music.

To honor Poppa Hi Bo and Momma, the ceremony was performed in the most traditional Buddhist fashion. In front of a shrine of Lord Buddha, surrounded by flowers and candles, the couple and the family joined together. Leong and Jan Yee recited the Tisarana Pancasila and the Mandan, he in Chinese, she in Pali. Both calming prayers told a story.

Tears filled the eyes of Madame Hi Bo. Momma Chan openly wept as their children made the vows of loyalty, love, and respect. It was customary for the groom, as the husband, to pledge to provide and protect, and be considerate and faithful. For Jan Yee, she vowed as his wife to please her in-laws, to be faithful to her husband, and to save money for the future. The bride commits to conscientiously fulfilling her household responsibilities and being a loving wife. Both Leong and JanYee, holding hands, lit two more candles and two incense sticks.

Thus, the Buddhist ceremony was concluded, only to be
followed by the Christian minister, whose unpretentious speech
counseled the couple to honor the vows they'd previously recited.
The minister asked the congregation, "Should there be anyone
present who in good conscience could present to this assembly
a reason why these two people should not marry, speak now, or
forever hold your peace." Momma Chan squeezed her daughter's
hand. Poppa Hi Bo and TaiTai pressed against each other. There
was silence in the assembly hall.

"In God's name, and in the name of our Lord Jesus Christ, I
pronounce you husband and wife."

The audience applauded and shouted, "*Kun Hai Fat Choy*
(Happy New Year)," with cheers of happiness and good health
and wishes for many children. Leong and Jan Yee gazed at one
another, crushed hands, and simultaneously rolled their eyes.
They tucked their hands under each other's arms. He leaned over,
his mouth close to her ear, and said, "I love you and wish us both
good fortunes."

She, a born Christian, whispered, "Awomen."

25

The Horror of the Truth

Daryl Narrates

Dr. Altman, wearing a white coat over a blue blouse and dark skirt, looked at us, two troubled parents, through her rimless glasses. In the very first moment, she attempted to calm us and ease our immediate concerns about Lauren. The doctor smiled, trying to look comforting and reassuring. I had vetted her before coming to the Sloan Kettering hospital, and found her credentials as a leukemia specialist to be impeccable. She was among the top two or three doctors at her level of expertise.

"I am so sorry to keep you waiting. We were giving your daughter several blood tests, plus testing her heart and urine, and giving her a body scan," the specialist explained. "Still there is no evidence to suggest your daughter is a leukemia patient."

Clutching hands, we struggled to keep our anxiety in check as we listened intently to Dr. Altman's words.

"In both acute and chronic leukemia," she said, "as the number of the leukemic cells increases, normal cells are crowded out of the bone marrow and warning signs begin to develop."

We listened carefully. "A major indicator is bruising and bleeding, resulting from low levels of platelets. Also, fevers, night sweats, weight loss, fatigue. Often a patient gets flu-like symptoms, which brings them to the doctor's office early. And, of course, early detection is the most important thing when it comes to a cure. So far, let me assure you that we have no serious reason to diagnose Lauren with leukemia."

I had a weak smile. Maxine quietly wept.

The doctor continued, "Lauren may have a heavy flu. We will need one or two overnight stays to take all the tests we need to be certain that Lauren does not have leukemia. We want to find out what is causing her discomfort."

We both stood there silent. We were thinking of how to respond to the doctor's no answer.

"What do we do now?" Maxine asked.

"Your daughter will be here for a few days. Please come and see her anytime it is convenient. Do not ask her too many questions. You should continue in your normal good mother and father roles. Bring her things to read. No sweets. If she likes pizza, that would be okay, but nothing more. I promise you, we will get to the bottom of this in a few days or sooner. I want you to be aware that you are in the best hospital in the world if she were to be diagnosed with leukemia. Let's hope that is not the case."

We stood and in turn shook the doctor's hand. I said, "Thank you, Dr. Altman. Please call us if you have any news as soon as possible. We will be back here tomorrow morning."

"Not to worry. She is in good hands. Oh, by the way, Mr. Landsman, are you the Landsman from Landsman Toyota and Honda on Northern Boulevard?"

"Yes, I am."

"I bought a car from you." She smiled.

"Nice." I smiled. "Here's my card. Call anytime."

The Author's Turn

Hi Bo and Tan Ha were quiet in their happiness as their daughter and her husband were about to leave for their honeymoon. The driver, parked outside the big house, was going to drive them from their apartment in Guangzhou to the Hong Kong airport.

"Momma, Poppa, why are you beaming and so hushed?" Jan Yee questioned.

"We are happy to see our daughter begin a new life with a fine man. Baba and I are thrilled for you. Please call us when you arrive in America." Momma Hi Bo bit her lip, holding back her tears.

The car pulled away. "Don't be angry with my parents. They are good people. It must be difficult for them to let go," Jan Yee quietly said to her husband.

"I am okay with that. Eventually Da Loban is going to have to remember that I am the man of this family, which at this moment in time is just the two of us." He grinned. "Your father is the patriarch of the whole family, including our mother and our little sister. I am good with him, and he is good with me."

After a sixteen-hour nonstop flight to Los Angeles on Cathay Pacific, the newlyweds arrived at LAX. They searched for the business-class lounge and sat down to rest in the comfortable room. In Los Angeles they had a two-hour wait for their connecting flight to Las Vegas. They were very impatient. Las Vegas was, for Jan, an unexpected dream come true.

Jan Yee walked to the restroom; she washed her hands and brushed her hair. Now she was ready for Vegas.

Back in the lounge, Jan whispered to her new husband, "I cannot believe I am in the US of A."

"It's simple. You get on a plane, you close your eyes, and in no time you are anywhere in the world."

"It's like a dream."

"It is more like a magic carpet," he answered.

Jan Yee hugged Leong's arm against her breast. She was happy, enjoying a full feeling of contentment. Four days in Las Vegas, a week in Aspen, and three days in Chicago: a dream she never could have conceived or thought possible. She was filled with bliss, with love, with something she'd never before experienced: the total and complete absence of stress, coupled with a sense of freedom. This was Her blessing for Jan Yee.

❧

On the second morning in their suite at the Bellagio, they turned to one another in their oversize king bed. "I love you," Leong spoke softly. Jan Yee snuggled even closer. "I want you to be happy and enjoy our honeymoon." He spoke with caution and tenderness. "But I sense something strange; you are not excited or are perhaps even a little unhappy about something. Have I said or done something to disturb you?"

"You have been wonderful, just perfect," she responded in a hushed voice. "I am blessed that you have a good sense of me. I am disappointed." She hesitated. "Las Vegas. It is not what I expected — the gambling, the people, the pushing, the noise. It's not my cup of tea."

The new groom remained thoughtful, and then he said, "I agree, let's leave. We will go to Aspen a few days early."

Jan Yee lay silently deep in her thoughts. *I have made such a good choice for my life. He is inside my mind. He knows me and considers my existence and my feelings. Oh, how I love my Leong. And most important, he hears me.*

"I read that Los Angeles and San Francisco are only a short flight from here. Let us leave this Las Vegas and go to one of those cities before we ski at Aspen."

"It sounds like a plan. But I think we should make another slight change. Los Angeles is only a two- or three-hour drive through the desert. We will rent a fancy convertible, go to that great movie city, and see the land from open car. And you, my dear wife, I will teach you to drive on the way." He laughed.

Jan Yee leaped from her lying position and moved on top of Leong. She kissed him and said, "Great idea, wonderful gift. But first, let us once again make love." She laughed, feeling his body beneath her. "I can tell you are ready."

26

The Diagnosis

Daryl Narrates

I crashed into a chair, my face in my hands. *No, no. It can't be true.* It felt like the doctor had pushed a knife right into my heart. I sat there listening to this so-called genius, not hearing what she was saying. The treatment, Dr. Altman explained to us, included heavy doses of chemotherapy, which would completely purge LangPi's immune system. Our daughter would have to be totally isolated for at least two weeks, and then she would undergo a bone marrow transplant.

It was crucial to find the perfect bone marrow match. The task of finding an equivalent bone marrow was vital and the most difficult undertaking. It was something that had to happen if our daughter was to be cured, or at least enter remission. The word *remission* gives one hope, but it does not indicate that my daughter is cured.

Doctors David and Altman, the two chief oncologists, suggested that LangPi's twin might be the easiest and probably most successful candidate. As a twin, opportunity had increased significantly the probability of finding an excellent match. Maxine and I looked at each other with trepidation. A sense of panic raced through every artery in my body. I felt like a strap had been wrapped around my chest, crushing me until I could hardly breathe.

"Please tell us if this transplant has any aftereffect for the donor. And is there a danger to LangPi?" Maxine probed.

Both doctors sat in silence. Dr. David broke the hushed moment. His voice was tender and sympathetic. "All medical actions have some degree of danger. The bone marrow transplant has almost zero negative repercussions, but marrow transplant dangers do exist. A transplant involves harvesting bone marrow from the donor, treating the marrow, and transplanting it intravenously into the recipient. Match errors exist but are infrequent. But understand that all surgery has its danger. Infection and a poor transplant result are only two of those dangers. Let me stress that the dangers are few and far between. The decision, of course, is yours," he explained.

I swallowed hard, trying to digest this new twist. Maxine and I tried to absorb each and every detail that was revealed to us. It was a dilemma we'd never anticipated or imagined in our lives. My life had been one of almost total control. I was always able to solve problems regardless of their complexity. Here, in this case, in this hospital, Maxine, Lauren, and I had to depend on the skills, experience, and knowledge of someone else; somebody I did not know, a person I could not totally or unconditionally trust no matter their credentials. I only trusted two individuals, the only ones I could depend upon: Maxine and myself.

In all my adult existence I'd never found myself vulnerable and defenseless. For the first time in my life I had to depend on an unknown quantity. The unfamiliar part of this equation was Dr. Altman. LangPi's life was in her hands.

I sat in silence. *Please, God* — the latter being a word I never used — *please help me make wise decisions that are essential for our daughter's road to wellness.*

"We believe the decision belongs to Sammy," I said. Maxine nodded.

❦

Later that evening, Maxine and I sat down with our daughter and explained in detail the process as we understood it.

"Mom, Dad, I can see on your faces how worried you are. My precious sister needs me. If the tables were turned and it was I who was ill, would Lauren hesitate for a moment? I think not. It is not a difficult decision for me to make. In fact, it is a very easy one. And you must allow me to make the choice that may help my sister. I am fully aware that it carries a slight possibility of danger. It is not your option; it is mine."

Maxine and I sat in silence, looking at Sammy. Surely she saw our fear and distress. Evidently, she had to end this taxing scene.

We were silent, not even a murmur. We just looked at Sammy.

"I can and I will, without hesitation, agree to be the donor. In fact, I insist that I be the one to help my sister."

Back at the hospital, tests were quickly taken: blood, bone marrow, and cardiogram. Sadly, Sammy's bone marrow was not a perfect fit. She could not become the donor. Sammy sobbed uncontrollably. "Why is this happening to us? Why am I unable to help my poor Lauren? I am her twin. Maybe it's an error. She needs our help. Daddy, we must do something. Daddy, you must do something."

I was crushed and Maxine devastated. We *were* depending on Sammy as an easy solution. It was a dead-end. Money was no object; we had the resources to find someone, somewhere in the universe — that single, unknown kind soul who would be a match for our daughter's bone marrow transplant and save her life. The doctors explained that it could be months before a proper donor could be located.

In our bedroom that evening, Maxine and I undressed in silence. She cleaned off her very little makeup and brushed her teeth, readying herself for bed. She craved and would be grateful for only a few hours of rest and escape from her emotional exhaustion. Otherwise she would not make it through tomorrow.

Both of us lay on our usual sides of the bed, staring at the ceiling. Together, in silence, we were thinking what to do. At last I rolled over to shut off the reading light and the switch to the chandelier.

I placed my eyeglasses on the night table to my right. I whispered, "Good night. I love you." Lying quietly in the dark, I was hoping for sleep. "Good night," I said again, and shut my eyes.

Within moments Maxine did the same. Here, in a sit-up position, she was eager for rest. Sleep would not come. She lay there, eyes wide open.

I looked at the clock next to our bed: 10:30 p.m. I remembered putting my head on the pillow at 9:30, now one hour later. Then it was 11:30, and 12:30 ... and now 2:30 ... four hours, four hours ... not a moment of shut-eye. I released a deep sigh.

"Are you asleep?" I questioned.

"No, I am not."

"What are we to do? What can we do?" I asked.

Lauren told me she was comfortable, but she was scared and very angry. "What did you say?" Maxine whispered. I reassured her that everything would be fine. We had arranged for the best doctors in the best hospital on this earth.

"The truth is, I am terrified as I have never been in my life," I answered.

"Wait a second, wait a second," Maxine interrupted. "I just thought of something right in front of our eyes that we could not see."

"What are you talking about? You are delirious." I sat up instantly. I was puzzled.

"It just occurred to me," my wife whispered.

"What occurred to you?" And suddenly we both thought the same as we have always done. "Oh my God ... how could we not think of that?" I shouted.

"But we did not forget. We didn't forget! We have to find our birth mother!"

"What time is it in Guangzhou?" I pleaded.

27

The Honeymoon Changes

The Author Brushes Daryl Away and Resumes

Jan Yee and Leong rented a yellow BMW convertible. Its seats were covered in plush brown leather. "What's this, a TV?"

"No, it's a GPS. You type in your location and your destination, and the voice of a woman directs you exactly to your final stop," Leong explained.

"Why is it in a woman's voice?" Jan asked.

"No doubt, women are better navigators and usually better drivers."

His bride smiled.

The trunk of the car was loaded with their luggage. They made a quick stop to buy four bottles of water and a large bag of M&Ms with peanuts and two baseball caps with the letters LA. Sitting in the Vegas desert sun with the convertible roof down, they were off on a new and unknown adventure. "Okay, GPS, take us to Route 15."

Jan Yee slept while her husband drove, listening to Dream Baby Dream. He couldn't remember the name of the singer. Their first stop was at Kelso Depot, a train station built in the early 1900s, about a hundred years ago, in the early days of the railroad going west. There was a restaurant, an information office, and a small museum. At the historic point, the couple took a break, rested, and had a cool drink. They returned to the road thirty minutes later.

They drove to the Kelso Dunes, almost 750 feet tall and 45 square miles wide. A look at the mountains surrounding the town makes the source of its name obvious. In the distance they could see the magnificent mountains of California and Nevada.

The young couple discovered they did not need the GPS map finder. It was a simple, straight drive from Las Vegas to Los Angeles. But they would need that clever woman's voice once they arrived.

The morning before their departure, Jan Yee had spoken to her father. She and Leong were not happy in Las Vegas, she told him, and were going to Los Angeles for a few days. She asked if he could recommend a decent hotel they could stay at. He suggested the Peninsula Hotel in Beverly Hills. It was the hotel he frequented when he traveled in the States.

More than halfway through the desert, the newlyweds stopped at another station to get some gas, stretch their legs, and use the toilet. They joked, laughed, and touched each other affectionately. They became children, free, away from their parents. No rules, just what they wanted to say or do. Jan Yee and Leong were two free lovebirds flying in the sky, like the lyrics to a song he loved: "You are the wind beneath my wings."

Back in the car, Leong said, "Sweetheart, you sit behind the steering wheel."

"Are you serious? Do you want me to kill us? We've only been married two days. Give us a week." Both smiled, and he shook his head. "I do not want to learn how to drive, at least not on our honeymoon," she moaned.

"Please," he pleaded. "Do me a favor and sit behind the wheel."

Jan Yee pouted as she nervously sat in the front seat on the driver's side. Leong patiently and gently explained how the car moves and stops and turns. He told his wife how simple driving was, mentioning that in the United States, sixteen-year-olds drive cars legally.

"I find it not surprising, after reading that there are many car accidents in this country," she said, her lower lip tight against her upper.

Leong calmly said, "First I strap in." Jan Yee, with a grin, connected the buckles as ordered.

Leong said, "Hold the wheel with your left hand. Put your left foot on the brake. Put your right hand in the drive position, over here on this handle." Again, Jan Yee followed his instructions. His new bride was smiling and taking deep breaths, trying to hold back nervous laughter.

Leong said, "Now pull the handle in your right hand and press it down to drive. Slowly take your left foot off the brake and put your right foot gently on the gas pedal." Jan Yee listened carefully to his instructions. She could feel her heart beating. Her eyes clenched tightly.

The car began to move.

"Open your eyes," he called nervously, momentarily regretting his loss of control.

Her lids opened wide.

The car began to move forward, at first by inches.

"Oh my God, I am driving, I'm driving." Suddenly, without warning, the car lurched forward. Her left foot crashed on the brake pedal. Leong was thrown forward, held back only by the safety belt strapped around his chest.

Leong strongly urged her once again to take her right foot off the gas. This time his voice was a little less demanding. She relaxed instantly.

"Oh my goodness, I will not do that again. Can I have a second chance?" she pleaded. "Did I hurt you?"

He nodded. "Just a little. Now relax and follow my high school driving teacher's instructions."

Jan Yee did not smile. She was serious now.

One hour later, the young bride was driving safely on the highway at thirty-five to forty-five miles an hour. Cars passed her going as fast as eighty miles per hour, the drivers glaring at the beautiful woman behind the wheel of the sleek vehicle. But that did not stop them from cursing her. In a moment of surprise, she lifted her hand with only the middle finger pointing upward. Leong grinned behind the hand he'd placed on his lips. "You are learning quickly how to be an American driver."

"Why?" she asked.

"That middle finger up in the air is an often-used symbol of aggression here in the United States."

"These Americans are so rude. I was driving safely, wasn't I? And," she continued, "I was not feeling aggressive. It was much worse. My way of thinking includes only four letter words."

"Yes, you were driving safely, my love," Leong replied.

It took almost four and a half hours to get to LA. The new driver had been behind the wheel for two hours and ten minutes.

Outside of LA city limits, Leong and Jan Yee changed seats. Leong took the wheel. Jan Yee flopped next to her husband on the passenger's side, exhausted, her body drenched with perspiration. A happy woman, she closed her eyes, not sleeping, just enjoying the success. Her eyes were tightly shut. There was a glowing beam on her face. She was delighted. "Oh, I am so happy."

Leong knew it was risky teaching and allowing Jan Yee to drive, but he was delighted he had taken the chance. "Now I have to teach you to ski." He rolled his eyes and had a self-assured smirk on his lips. She again had her lower lip pushed up, pouting, still totally content with herself.

She hugged him and put her head on his shoulder. The bride

opened her eyes and slipped her sunglasses back on. *How I love this man,* she thought.

"Now there is one very important issue when you drive a car."

"What is that?" she questioned.

"You must get a driver's license."

The entrance to the Peninsula Hotel was a right turn off Santa Monica Boulevard into a beautiful walled garden entrance. Bentleys, Rolls-Royces, and Ferraris were parked in the driveway. Two uniformed doormen, several porters, and two garage attendants were all dressed in a way denoting *you are at the entrance to the most elegant hotel in the United States.*

The doorman opened the car door. "Welcome to the Peninsula. Your name, sir?" he asked.

"My name is Leong Chan."

"Ah! Welcome, Mr. and Mrs. Chan. We have been expecting you. Our general manager, Mr. Johnson, will greet you." Leong was puzzled. He could not comprehend the greeting he had just received. Jan Yee had a knowing look on her face.

"Mr. Chan, Mrs. Chan, welcome to the Peninsula Hotel. We have been expecting you. You have been preregistered, and your room is ready and waiting. Here is my card. I am Adam Johnson, general manager."

"How did you know we were coming? We took a chance driving here without a reservation," Leong said in a strange, strained voice.

"Mr. Hi Bo is a longtime guest here. He telephoned me this morning and told me to expect his daughter and new son-in-law."

Leong stared at Jan Yee. "This is your doing?"

"No, darling, it is not my doing. I called Poppa and told him we were not happy in Las Vegas and we were going to drive to Los Angeles. I asked where we should stay. That was it and no more. Please, sweetheart, let's just enjoy the moment."

Leong was a captive of his intense feelings for this special person. "Do I have a choice when you look at me like that? Men are lucky that most women do not know how strong they are and the power they have." He loved his new partner very much. There was nothing he could do. He was powerless. He recalled Daryl telling him, "Men go where they love; women go where they are loved."

For the first time in his life, he began to understand the strength and the intellect of the opposite gender through the love he had for Jan. He felt fortunate to have such a wonderful, sensitive person like Jan on his side. "Maybe God *is* a Woman," he mused.

They walked out of the elevator and took a quick step to the right. The porter opened the door to their suite. Mr. Johnson explained the luxuries of the hotel. They stood in the large bedroom, which had an adjoining sitting room. He showed the couple the bath, the closets, and the fridge with drinks and snacks. On the coffee table were flowers, a platter of assorted cheeses and fresh fruit, a bottle of Moët &Chandon in an ice bucket, and two very elegant champagne flutes.

"Please enjoy your stay with us. By the way, you also have a reserved cabana at our pool every morning.

"Also, a Mr. Daryl Landsman has been calling you, and may I suggest you join us for lunch on the roof? It's quite pleasant, and dress is casual. Enjoy your stay, and happy honeymoon." The door closed and he was gone.

The newlyweds were speechless. "What does Daryl want? It must be a business thing," Leong casually mentioned to Jan Yee.

"We are on our honeymoon. Please return his call later," Jan Yee begged.

Here in their luxurious suite, both were focusing on this unique moment. Leong opened the bottle in the bucket and poured two short drinks. They toasted the good fortune of their new life partnership and then sipped their wine slowly. They put their glasses down simultaneously, as if some special signal had been given. Calmly and in silence, they undressed and stepped into a warm shower. They washed one another. He rubbed her back, her neck, and her buttocks with a soapy washcloth. His hands moved around her trim, svelte body. She kissed him and said, "Now it's your turn." He turned his body to face his bride. She looked down at her husband. Leong followed her gaze. Both laughed and were totally happy, the return telephone call forgotten.

28

The Hope for a Miracle

Daryl Interrupts the Author

"It's two thirty p.m. in China. Call Mr. Hi Bo right now, right from this phone by our bed," Maxine suggested to Daryl.

"You are a genius. You know something, honey? God gives women special gifts that men do not have. I think it's called women's intuition. You are all born with it."

After trying for more than an hour, Daryl was unable to reach Hi Bo on the phone.

At midnight in New York, Hi Bo finally answered the phone. "I am very glad to hear your voice," I said.

"Daryl, my friend, are you well? You sound distressed."

"My dear friend Hi Bo, our daughter LangPi has been diagnosed with leukemia. I must reach Jan Yee. Your daughter is the birth mother, and she is the only possible bone marrow match for my child."

Hi Bo was silent. I prayed that he could digest all of what I had to say. It was vital that Hi Bo understood the urgency and the need for him to assist my family. But, and it was a big but, I did not know that his Jan Yee was away on her honeymoon.

"I am so sorry to hear about your daughter. Leukemia is a difficult illness, and frightening."

"We must reach Jan Yee. She is our last chance to help her."

"What about her twin sister?" Hi Bo questioned.

"She turned out not to be the right match. As a last resort, the only solution we could think of was the birth mother."

"Daryl, Jan Yee is on her honeymoon. She and Leong were married last week. You were invited, remember?"

"Jan Yee is a good person. She is kind and understanding. You must contact her and tell her the circumstances. She can help our daughter and then spend the rest of her honeymoon in New York City. The trip will be on me."

Hi Bo assured me he would try to reach Jan and Leong and call him back as soon as possible.

It did not take Hi Bo more than a minute to decide to telephone the honeymooners. He quickly dialed the Peninsula Hotel and was advised that Mr. and Mrs. Chan had not arrived yet and were expected the next morning.

Hi Bo telephoned me within fifteen minutes of our last conversation. He told me the news and said that he would call the newlyweds as soon as they reached the Peninsula.

I could not wait for Hi Bo to reach Jan Yee. I called the Peninsula myself. She and Leong had not arrived yet. An hour later I called again. Still they had not arrived. Twice more I tried to get them on the phone, but they had not yet registered.

At three o'clock that afternoon, the telephone rang in my office.

"Hi Daryl, it's Leong. We missed you at the wedding. Now we are in LA on our honeymoon. I got a message you telephoned several times. Everything okay? What's up?"

Back to the Author

Freddie and Sammy sat in the kitchen at their parents'

apartment. Nancy prepared two chicken sandwiches for them. Sammy had been crying earlier in her room.

"I feel so inadequate," she began. "I hoped that I would be the perfect marrow match for Lauren. Wouldn't you think that twins would be able to help one another? I am so worried. I can't sleep at night or any time. I can't stand this. It's an impossible hurtful feeling. It is breaking my heart."

"Try to be positive. I heard from Mom that Dad is trying to reach your birth mother."

"What for?"

"She may be the solution. She may be the match that Lauren needs."

"May I tell you a secret?" Sammy asked.

"Of course you may," her brother replied.

"I always wondered what my birth mother was like. Is she married, does she have children? I used to think at night, is my birth mother smart? Is she pretty? You know, silly things like that. Lauren and I have often spoken about it. We both were troubled about why she did not want us. It sounds strange and cruel, yet it is how I feel, or rather how Lauren and I feel. And now when my sister needs me the most, we are far from the same. We are not a match. I thought twins meant twins. It seems that the word *twin* means looking the same, but not being the same."

"That sounds very normal to me." Fred responded."I believe that also. I would speculate not only about my birth mother but also about what my biological father might be like. Or what he was. From stories I heard, I think that Dad once met her," he said, trying to console her.

Sammy could not hold back. "Dad has spoken about her briefly, but he didn't say too much. And I was not comfortable asking too many questions. I never wanted Mom to think I was more interested in my biological mother than in my real mother, I mean our mom."

"Leave it to Dad; he will work this out." Freddie got up, opened the door of the huge refrigerator, and peered inside. "You want a piece of fruit?" he asked.

"No, thanks, I am not even hungry for this sandwich." Fred took an apple and shut the fridge door.

"What are you kids up to?" Maxine asked as she put two packages down on the kitchen table. It was cold outside, and her cheeks were shining red. She slipped her gloves off, threw her coat on a chair, and turned to Sammy. "Would you put a pot of water on? I am freezing. I would like a cup of tea."

"We were talking about Lauren and Sammy's birth mother," Fred responded.

"Very interesting," Maxine added. "She, the birth mother, is on her way to New York with her husband as we speak. Jan Yee is coming here, to New York, to help our LangPi. Thank God."

❦

Daryl's driver pulled the car up to the entrance of the Empire Hotel on Manhattan's West Side, convenient to Maxine and Daryl's apartment. Both were waiting at the hotel to greet Jan Yee and Leong as they got out of the car.

Daryl immediately recognized Leong and remembered Jan Yee slightly. He was not certain, but she looked familiar. Maxine ran up to them. "Welcome, welcome. We cannot tell you how much we appreciate your generosity and interrupting your honeymoon to come to New York and help our daughter." For a moment she caught herself. She cleared her throat and softly said to Jan Yee, "And your daughter also."

Jan Yee had a slight tic in her heart upon hearing the words "your daughter." She couldn't figure it out, but there it was. She thought for a brief moment, *what was that? That signal, my inner voice? Is it possible there is connection that I am unaware of? Is it from Her?*

Daryl looked into Jan Yee's eyes. He saw her pain. "We are all one family," he began. "We help each other when we are able to. The truth in life as I know it: You can have good friends everywhere. But when the chips are down, it is always family members who rise to the occasion. Thank you for your help. We thank both of you."

He knew that Jan Yee was a unique woman. "We can express our gratitude that we are as one family connected by our children," Daryl said.

Oh my, these are such wonderful people. How fortunate are the twins I mysteriously brought into this world. Please tell me, my God; you are a woman as I am. Give me the wisdom and the strength to help my birth child.

❦

The next morning, Maxine picked up Jan Yee and Leong at the hotel. She took Jan to the Memorial Sloan Kettering Cancer Center, leaving Leong in the car for a meeting with Daryl at the latter's office. Daryl knew that Jan would have to go through a series of tests before a decision is made about a possible match. If the tests were found to be a match, the next day would be the important procedure.

Daryl greeted his partner at the Landsman headquarters. Fred was also invited to join the meeting. The three men discussed the future goals of the company and the issues that had to be corrected. Fred suggested that he spend some time in Zurich and check out the sales approach the company was taking, and perhaps give his input using the experience he had gained working with his father. Daryl and Leong immediately agreed and proposed that Fred should plan to leave for Switzerland before the week was over. Daryl's son was nervous, happy, and breathless about the opportunity.

"Dad," Fred interrupted, "I'd like to wait a few days to see how things work out with Lauren."

"Absolutely, I am glad you said that." Daryl answered. Turning to Leong, he said, "I want to express my appreciation to you and Jan Yee for responding to our needs this quickly. You and Hi Bo are the best partners I've ever had."

"Sorry, boss, I am not a partner, although I do my job as if I were an owner. That is how I am. I have been trained to give a hundred and fifty percent of my effort to every project I am involved with, regardless of the rewards. In fact, my compensation is self-imposed. My incentive is always a job well done – how's that for a sales pitch?" Everyone smiled at hearing Leong recite to Daryl the Landsman philosophy.

"I could not have done a better job myself. You did well." Daryl went on, "Please believe what I am about to tell you. Our other partner, your father-in-law, and I had a long-distance conference call early last month. We decided that you have earned a partnership in the Swiss company."

Leong remained silent. The news of a promotion was something he had not expected. He'd expected something, perhaps the title of chief operating officer. A partnership was in his sights, but in the future. Leong's decorum allowed his feelings to remain undetected. He was calm on the outside, but inside he was screaming with joy. Still, he remained determined to handle this news with dignity.

"I am not going to respond to you or Hi Bo and tell you how grateful I am. I am confident you did not approach me with this partnership opportunity simply because I am married to Jan Yee. You and Da Loban have rewarded me with this unbelievable opportunity and promotion because I have earned your trust. And, most important, I am confident I have earned the promotion."

"You are utterly and absolutely incorrect." Daryl, Fred, and Leong laughed.

The three men sat back. All lit Havana cigars. At eleven o'clock in the morning, Leong, Daryl, and Fred were sharing a smoke, each of them also drinking a Scotch on the rocks.

The phone rang. "Mr. Landsman, your wife is on the phone," Daryl's receptionist advised.

"Hello?" he said.

"Sweetheart?" she questioned

"Yes, you sound terrible. What's wrong?" Daryl could hear the pain in her voice.

"Jan Yee is not a match."

It seemed like it took only seconds for Daryl and Leong to dash off toward the elevator and arrive at the hospital, where Maxine and Jan Yee were waiting. Fred followed an hour later.

Maxine was leaning over, her head in her hands, weeping. Jan Yee sat next to her, trying to comfort her new friend, as well as trying to hold back her own sobs and disappointment.

29

The First Sight

Lauren sat up in her bed reading a book. She looked better but was visibly not well. She did not know the news of the no match. "Come in," she called out, after hearing the knock on the door. She was expecting a nurse and was surprised to see a guest, not knowing who she was looking at. Finally, for the first time, she saw another Asian face, like hers, still different. Suddenly she gasped, a feeling she had never experienced ran through her body.

"I am Jan Yee. You may not know me. Allow me to introduce myself —"

"I know who you are. I know who you are," Lauren gasped. "You are our birth mother, both Sammy's and mine."

No words passed between them. The two women just looked at each other.

Lauren saw a beautiful woman who looked exactly like Sammy — same face, eyes, and nose, and the slight reflex on her cheek like Sammy had. The only difference was the blond hair she and Sammy shared.

LangPi could not take her eyes from the woman who stood before her. Her heart beat rapidly as her vision glazed over the view of her birth mother, which became unclear. She reached for a tissue on her night table to dry her eyes.

"You are so beautiful. This is love at first sight!" LangPi exclaimed.

Jan smiled. "Please forgive me; I am going to leave you now. It is important that you rest."

"No, no, please don't leave. We have so much to talk about," the young girl pleaded.

"We will have plenty of time tomorrow or the next day. I am staying in New York for a while," Jan reassured her.

Lauren pushed her head deep into the pillow. Sick as she was, she felt happy. Or was it completeness, or perhaps confusion? It was important, oh so vital, for her to love both her mom and her birth mother. But could she accomplish such a complex relationship? "Oh how I wish Sammy had been here to share this with me. I must call her." Her eyes shut as a deep sleep engulfed her. She was happy but strangely uncomfortable.

"Lauren is such a beauty, and very grown-up. You both are fortunate to have raised this winning young woman. We must figure a way to help her." The birth mother tried to sound reassuring once she entered the waiting room.

In the car returning home, Maxine invited Leong and Jan Yee up to their apartment for some rest and refreshments. They declined, advising the Landsmans that they also needed some rest. They were exhausted. Fred had taken a cab to his apartment. Maxine and Daryl arrived at their home and crashed.

They both sat in the den. Nancy brought a glass of white wine for Maxine and a Scotch on the rocks for Daryl.

"This is such a difficult time for Lauren and everyone who loves her," Daryl said. "I don't know how much more of this I can handle. For the first time in my life I have not a single idea, not a clue, of what next to do."

"Please be positive. You always told me that to accomplish something worthwhile, you have to step out of your comfort zone.

That is the only way to succeed and reach your goal," she recited. "Perhaps, and I pray, the hospital can find a donor."

Jan and Leong at the Hotel

Jan rested in a huge beige chair with overstuffed pillows. The room was filled with prints of New York scenes in years past. They felt that the hotel was a real New York blessing and in a perfect location.

Jan explained to Leong the very special and peculiar feeling she'd had looking at her birth daughter, knowing full well what their biological relationship was. "It's a miracle to gaze at another human who looks as you looked almost twenty years ago. LangPi and I are identical. It was an amazing moment for me when I had my very first glance at her.

"It is difficult to believe that LangPi came from my body. I felt like I wanted to cover her with kisses, put my arms around her frail body, and take her illness in exchange for my own wellness. I wished I could change places with her. I didn't care if I got sick. I was ready to do anything to give her my good health. I felt a very strong connection. It was love and fear at first sight."

She rested, fell silent, and welcomed Leong's arms around her. Her heart was bursting with the anguish of not being able to offer anything to ease Lauren's pain. She experienced that endless fear a mother feels for a child when illness strikes.

"It is simple to explain the connection I feel. What's strange is my fear for her."

Leong sat quietly listening.

"If LangPi does not survive … I refuse to accept that end. I know it will tear my heart apart. I pray to God, not the God of Judeo-Christianity, but the true God, the God who, I believe, is a woman. If LangPi dies, She will have taken my precious birth child away from me twice in one lifetime."

Leong said, "Her way or His way. It makes no difference to me at this moment. Your God or mine, who cares? We will do all that is humanly possible to keep Lauren alive and make her well again. I promise. Right now, you and I need to rest." Jan shut her eyes. "My dearest love, let's lie down, if only for a moment and take a nap. Let's close our eyes and plug our ears. We'll lock life and the world out. We must let this go for a while."

"I cannot wait to meet her sister, Sammy," Jan responded.

She gazed into his eyes and stroked his face with the palm of her hand. Jan lay down on the bed in the fetal position and quickly felt her eyelids falling.

Leong, with clothes and shoes on, collapsed onto the bed, lying next to his wife. His eyes searching the ceiling, he was deep in thought. *Please give me the strength and the wisdom to guide this woman. I love her with all my heart. And dear God, whether I am made in Your image or whether You are in the image of the woman next to me, please lead me to the solution to this difficult situation my wife and I and her birth child now face.*

❦

Jan Yee awoke first. Noiselessly she slipped her clothing off, walked into the bathroom, turned the hot and cold water on, and stepped into the shower.

Moments later, Leong's head popped up. He'd forgotten where he was. The bed space next to him was vacant. He heard the shower going.

He entered the bathroom and stood outside the shower stall. "Without me? You're in the shower without your husband?"

Jan Yee grinned, putting the washcloth over the front of her body. "Sorry, my darling, this evening without you; tomorrow morning, with you. Remember, we are still on our honeymoon."

꿎

She was in a white bathrobe and he, in his undershorts and watching the TV. "What are we going to do about dinner?" the bride asked. "Let's not go to one of those fancy New York restaurants. Let's try the Italian place across from the hotel, Café Fiorello. I hear from Daryl it's very good."

"Great idea. I am going to dress and make myself handsome for you."

Jan left the room, shook her little ass, teasing him, and laughed. She was sad and happy simultaneously. *Strange, very strange, that young woman is Maxine's daughter, not mine.* Jan saw Lauren's face in her mind and questioned, *are Sammy and Lauren also mine?*

Café Fiorello was the choice. It was close to the hotel. Daryl said they should just mention his name to Mike Vitanza, the general manager, and everything would be okay.

It was exactly as Daryl had predicted. Mike welcomed them with open arms. They were quickly led to a comfortable and private booth. At the side wall of each booth were names engraved on bronze plaques, mostly New York people who frequented the restaurant. The dining room was filled with visitors from every walk of life. Most of the waiters were unemployed actors and singers. Birthday guests or anniversary celebrants were entertained with a candle-lit cake, and a song in Italian. The entire restaurant joined in with the melody in both English and Italian.

The young couple sat there, wineglasses in their hands, relishing a well-earned momentary reprieve. Leong and Jan Yee, savoring their dinner, chatted away about their future. Suddenly Leong put his hand up. "Wait! Wait!" He interrupted. "I forgot to tell you. This morning Daryl advised me that he and our Da Loban discussed promoting me to partner."

"Congratulations. I am so happy for you. Better still, I am happy for both of us. That's good news."

She raised her glass, and they clicked. "I love you," he said.

"I love you back."

They ate slowly, first some pasta with clams, and then veal Milanese, the house special. The portion was large enough for three people, perhaps more. They laughed at its size.

The meal was extraordinary. They sat quietly for a while, listening to the singing and the noisy conversations around them. A waiter approached. "Our house favorite is a pail of chocolate mousse with another pail of whipped cream." Both laughed. "With compliments from Mike."

"Thank you, and please thank Mike." Leong answered.

It was green tea for Jan Yee and espresso for Leong, as well as the chocolate mousse and a mountain of whipped cream for dessert. The bride and groom sat and talked. "I am so proud that you are now a partner. And let me add, I know my father, he would never under any circumstances, give you anything you did not earn."

"Daryl said the same thing at our meeting this morning. He too would never do anything like that. He said I earned my partnership. But he added, being married to you did not hurt."

"That Daryl, I didn't know he was such a bad boy," she joked.

She glanced around the room, looking at the diners, who were eating, laughing, and talking loudly. The couple sat quietly enjoying the scene. Jan Yee was pleased that Daryl had made this suggestion.

Without warning, her face paled and suddenly changed. She lifted her hand to her open mouth, startled.

"What's wrong?" he questioned.

"No, nothing," she responded, remaining quiet and thoughtful.

"Let's have our dessert," Leong suggested. "Are you okay?" he asked once again.

"I am fine. Only a few minutes ago, I stopped to think ... I thought I saw a ghost. Well, I saw someone I believe I recognized."

"Who was it?"

"Perhaps my vision is going out on me. Do me a favor. Quietly and without fanfare, turn to the far right." Leong turned his head, puzzled. He gazed in the direction of the table. "No, not yet, there in a booth on the other side of the restaurant. A heavy-looking man, see, more to the right of you. He is with a woman and two children. Look at him carefully. Whom does he remind you of?"

Leong slowly turned his head to the right and looked at the booth. He saw the people Jan was pointing out. He did not recognize them.

"I do not have a clue. Whom did they remind you of?"

"No, not they, he; that man makes me shiver. That man reminds me of the disgusting animal who assaulted me in my father's home many years ago."

"That is not possible. He has been dead almost two years, perhaps more."

"I know, I know. And though the sight of that person gave me a feeling of revulsion, something caught me inside. My instincts stopped me; my feelings gave that little signal. Now this is just an idea, a hope, perhaps the answer to our prayers. That man sitting over there with his kids gave me this insane idea."

"Please, please, give me an inkling, a hint, of what is in your mind."

"Hans Leopold," she whispered. "Hans Leopold had two children, a boy and a girl."

"I know them," Leong interjected. "They both work at our office. His son, Bernhard, is quite accomplished and a good young man. Nora, his sister, is in production. I don't know her too well. Where are you heading with all this?"

"Can't you see what I am driving at? Those kids, Leopold's kids, could be possible bone marrow match donors."

Leong was in awe. He observed his wife with eyes staring and squinting. He looked at her carefully. "You're amazing. It is an idea. But let's not get too hopeful. The Landsmans and Lauren have been disappointed before. However, I think you are a genius. And I don't want to be a pessimist because it *is* a great idea."

Jan's heart beat loudly; she could hear it. She tried to catch her breath, turning her head upward and closing her eyes. *Let this be a message from Her, that She, my God, has heard my prayers.*

Jan looked across the restaurant to the booth with the family in it. They were gone.

"Let's telephone Daryl and Maxine. They are upset now. I think this may give them hope."

Back at the Hospital

"Am I going to be all right, Mommy?" Lauren asked in a frightened voice

"Of course, you will. Everyone is searching for that special generous donor. Please, darling, keep your usual spirits up and the optimistic attitude you learned from your dad. He will never give up. He feels positive we will find someone."

"I felt sad that Jan Yee was not the right one, the good match. I was hoping so much she would make me well again."

"Me too," Her mom answered.

"Do you like her?" Lauren whispered.

"I do like her, very much. May I tell you something? I saw a tiny cleft in her chin that you and Lauren both have," Maxine observed.

Lauren laid there, a closed-lip smile on her face. Her eyes were shut, not for sleep, but because she was in thought. She too had noticed the cleft in the birth mother's chin. She'd seen other signs too. Although Jan Yee's hair was black and straight, it had the same texture as she and her sister's. It was amazing for her to see her own genetic heritage. Her eyes opened. "Mommy, do you look like your mother?"

Maxine was silent. She thought, *I do have the same nose and eyes as my mom, but mostly I look like my dad.*

"That's an interesting question. What made you think of that?"

"I don't know. When I saw Jan Yee, I was searching for some sort of sameness. I was looking for something that connected us. The only likeness I saw was our Asian face."

"How did that make you feel?" Maxine questioned.

"I was disappointed."

"Disappointed? That's strange. First, you missed so many important virtues that you and your sister share with Jan Yee. The three of you have the same body shape and similar facial structure. And Jan Yee is very beautiful, as you and your sister are. And most important, I am told how smart she is."

A grin crossed the daughter's face. "You are wonderful, Mommy. You took the sadness of my illness away from me. But I wish I looked more like you."

"You may not look like me, my darling child, but you are exactly like me in every way."

A knock on the door shook Maxine out of her deep thoughts; she opened it and welcomed the surprise visitor. It was Sammy. She'd returned home from school a day earlier than expected to spend a long weekend with her parents and her sister.

"Hi, Mom, and how's my big sister?" She smiled and leaned over to kiss Sammy. Mom quickly moved to Lauren, holding her back.

"We can't have any physical contact. Lauren is going to be in total isolation beginning tomorrow. We don't want to take the slightest chance that anyone of us gives her even a sniffle."

Without hesitation, Lauren began. "You are my older sister. Remember, you were born three minutes before I was."

Mom laughed. The girls smiled. It was an insane moment. The realization came to everyone that starting tomorrow and going forward, Lauren was going to be treated with heavy doses of chemotherapy. The treatment would deplete her immune system, and she would be in total quarantine for more than two weeks. By that time, they believed, a donor would be found and the bone marrow transplant would be done. It was a serious gamble, but the family and the doctor agreed it was worth the risk.

Daryl walked in. He hugged Sammy and Maxine.

"Lauren, I am going to have to pass on you, my love. I think I may be getting something. I feel a tiny cold sore creeping on my lip and about to greet me. How about if I throw you a kiss?"

"That works for me, Daddy," she called. "We will have a lot of hello and goodbye kisses in the future." The child saw her father's worried look.

"I have some medicine at home for that lip. You used it before; it worked," Maxine added.

"Sweetheart, let's leave the girls alone for a while. They haven't had a chance to gossip for more than two weeks, except on the phone."

"Thanks, Dad. Mom, we'll be all right."

The door closed. Daryl led his wife down the hall to the family waiting room. His face was unshaven; he looked like he hadn't slept in days. It was a physical metamorphosis. From out of nowhere, this usually attractive, healthy man suddenly appeared aged, fatigued, and depressed. Maxine had never seen her husband so distressed and helpless. He appeared beaten and lost. He was a stranger to his wife. This was not the man she'd married or the man she had lived with these thirty-two years. His body slumped; he was slightly bent over as he walked. They entered the waiting room. He did not sit down on the chair in his normal way. He crashed down into it, exhausted. He leaned forward, his hands covering his eyes. Daryl turned to his wife.

"I do not have a clue or an idea where to go for a donor or where to seek help. For the first time in my life," he said, beginning to whisper, "For the first time in my life, I prayed to God, to the God I do not believe in. I pleaded with Him." Daryl wept. "I promised to do anything God wants me to do, if only our daughter can be saved." He sobbed silently.

Maxine sat, not moving, not uttering a word. She put her arm around her husband. He'd always been the strong one. He always knew what to do, what course to take. As soon as he figured it out and knew the answer, the task was completed.

To see him this way was alarming. He was in a panic, and his panic was contagious.

"Listen to me, Daryl Landsman. Yes, this is a difficult health issue, and we are in strange territory. You must pull yourself together. If you think for one moment that our daughter cannot see what you look like, you are greatly mistaken. You always told me that a glass is half full, not half empty."

"What the hell do I look like?" Daryl asked.

She stood up right in front of him and slowly descended, her knees bent, looking straight at his knuckled hands covering his eyes.

"Daryl, look at me, look at me. Take your hands down. Please look at me," she commanded. Slowly, he lifted his face from his hands and raised his head to look her in the eyes.

"Daryl, you look like you have been to hell and back, like a train hit you. What you don't look like is much more important. You do not look like our daughters' father. They're both frightened to see what they saw. The resemblance between you and Fred is gone — disappeared. More important, you're not like the guy I fell in love with a long time ago." She sounded angry to see her husband this way.

"I know my husband. I know your strengths and your weaknesses. I can't stand to see you this way."

She plunged an arrow into his vanity, into his ego. "You were always my young and handsome lover, constantly self-assured, and most of all, smart — very smart. Go back to being that man. That's the guy I want around me. That's the father your children need. Having one person in our family with health problems is more than enough for us to handle. If you are going to fall apart, I cannot deal with all this alone. I need you."

Daryl's lips opened slightly. He knew she was right. His wife clutched his hands. She'd gone right for the jugular and directly for his heart.

"Our daughter isn't going to die."

Maxine knew her husband. She understood that he had built a case for the tragedy that he and his family were experiencing. But in truth, she knew that *he* was the disaster.

"I have heard you say a thousand times that only the customer has that privilege of the word *no*. May I remind you of how you often have preached to me and our children that in order to get what we want, there is no other choice but to step out of our comfort zone and go for it? This is not a time to crumble," Maxine said in a very tough voice.

Daryl wept. He completely lost it.

"Stop it," she commanded. "Neither of us wants to experience the death of a child, *our* child. How could we live with that? But we're nowhere near that. We have options that we're searching for to help our Lauren."

She reminded him of the pain they experienced when they heard of another parent who lost a child.

"That will never happen to us. No, never, it will not be. We refuse to allow that to take place," Maxine assured him. "Do you remember my father's only wish? It was to predecease his children? Do you understand now what he was praying for? It is a gift in a parent's life to leave this earth before your children," she said in a firm voice.

Maxine reached down and slowly helped raise her husband up from his chair.

"I know why you are my best friend, my partner, my everything. I want you to be that all-powerful husband who joined hands with me a long time ago."

There was silence. It took a few moments for Daryl to slowly return to himself. He had gradually come back. He was weak, exhausted, but back.

"Thank you," he quietly said. "Thank you for those punches in the stomach. I needed each and every one. But it didn't have to be such a hard blow. It really hurt," he complained.

"I don't understand you. You are a very confusing man. You always loved hard blows."

They both smiled. Maxine put her arms around her husband. She closed her eyes. They kissed. And in that moment, they gave strength to each other. That was the partnership that matured over the many years, each in their turn giving the support needed.

30

Hope Was Coming

Several Days Later

Daryl and Leong arrived at Kennedy Airport at 2:15 p.m. to pick up Leopold's son and daughter.

Leong alone went into the arrival station inside the baggage room. He looked up at the flight schedule screen. The plane from Zurich, Swiss Air flight 4332, had arrived twenty minutes early. His eyes raced around the room, looking for the two adult children from Switzerland. After a slight panic, ten minutes later there they were: Bernhard and Nora. Both were gazing in every direction, searching for Leong, who had promised to meet them. Leong waved.

"Bernhard," he called. "Nora, here I am." They turned their heads and waved back. Grins on their faces, they rushed to him.

"How was the trip?" The young people smiled. "We have never been in business class. It was great. Lunch was terrific. Wow! Rich people sure know how to live." Glancing at the luggage carousel, Bernhard said, "I see one of our bags. Let's get the luggage."

Daryl moved into the front seat next to the driver. The car moved slowly, leaving the airport on to the Van Wyck Expressway. No one spoke except for polite greetings.

At some point into the drive, Bernhard began. "We are so

pleased that there is a chance that we might be able to help you with your daughter, Mr. Landsman."

"My family and I can't thank you enough for coming to New York and cooperating with us," Daryl began.

Without a hello and without any warning whatsoever, Nora said, "My brother and I have some clue that our dad may have fathered your daughter. Is that true? Is that the reason we are here?"

Daryl was caught off guard by the first words he'd heard from Nora. "Don't think about your father or anything bad. That was a long time ago. If there is any truth to it, we will know soon enough. If it's true, there exists a very high chance that your genetic makeup will end our search for a bone marrow match for my daughter."

"What's your daughter's name?" The young woman asked.

"LangPi is her Chinese name and Lauren is her English name, but everyone calls her Lauren. She's nineteen years old, probably a few years younger than you are. How old are you?"

"I am twenty-two. I will be twenty-three in three months," Nora replied.

"I hope we can be successful for your daughter and your family, Mr. Landsman," young Bernhard added. "You and your family have been very kind to us."

Daryl nodded in silence.

The two young visitors marveled at the sight of the New York City skyline as the car sped across the Triboro Bridge. They gazed out the window of the moving vehicle, looking at a plethora of sky-high buildings. The moment was both exciting and worrisome.

"It's hard to believe what a wonderful city New York is," Nora exclaimed excitedly. "It's a combination of not believing and that we are actually here," she explained. "We've seen this miracle in the movies and on TV hundreds of times. But to be here in real life is just amazing."

Her brother added, "Still, we understand the reason you invited us, and we hope we can be of help. May we ask you a question?"

"Of course you may. Please, tell me what's on your mind."

"Is what we are here for, is it — what do you call it, a bone marrow transplant?"

"That is right," Daryl replied.

"Is it painful? Are there any aftereffects?"

"To be honest, I really don't know. Many people have donated, with few or zero bad results. I'm sure that there could be a slight pinch of pain from an injection. I'll ask the doctor to explain everything to you. If for any reason either of you are uncomfortable, we'll end it without any questions," Daryl replied.

"We must confess that this is very special for us, that our boss has asked us to be of help to him. It gave us a feeling of being special. We were excited that you asked us to help you."

"Here we are," Leong announced. "This is the Empire Hotel. It is the same place where my wife and I are staying. We know you will both be comfortable here."

The bellman took their luggage into the hotel. Leong got out on his side of the car and told Daryl not to worry. He said that he would attend to all the details of registering the Leopold children at the hotel, providing them with dinner, and ensuring that they arrived tomorrow morning at eight o'clock at the Sloan Kettering Hospital.

The next morning, Maxine and Daryl waited in the family room. The doctor entered. "Mr. and Mrs. Landsman?"

"Yes," Maxine answered.

The doctor's report was simple and straight to the point. He began, "Both Bernhard and Nora were very cooperative.

Unfortunately, neither is a match for your daughter, I am sorry to report."

The room echoed the silence and the pain of the parents. Maxine shook her head. Jan Yee moved close to her and put her arms around her. "We must figure this out. There has to be a match somewhere," she whispered.

Daryl was silent; his eyes closed briefly. He held on, trying to be strong. He had placed all his hopes on these two children. His disappointment was beyond description. He became short of breath. His left hand shook. He thought, *hold on, hold on. There must be a solution. Oh God, oh God, please don't take her away from us. She is only a child … a baby.*

Leong put his hand under Jan Yee's arm and led her away. He signaled to Bernhard and Nora to follow. In the taxi everyone was hushed. There was nothing to say.

Arriving at the hotel, Leong said, "Let's rest a bit. We'll meet in the lobby at noon and go for lunch. As for you two, please remain in New York for a couple of days. Enjoy the city, go to museums and perhaps the theater, or just walk around. Have a good time. You did your job. You tried. You were good. Tell me what you want, and I will take care of it. Remember, you are the guests of Mr. and Mrs. Landsman."

In their room, Leong and Jan Lee looked at each other, totally beaten and disappointed. "I haven't a single idea of what the next step will be for the Landsmans," Leong said, breaking the silence.

Jan Yee did not respond. She was in thought. Her feelings were in conflict. *Why do I feel this way? Do birth mothers have only a biological connection? Is there a possibility of a psychological tie as well?* Her thought process continued. *I'm the birth mother, and I failed to help, as has her full sister and the half-siblings. None of us match. Why? Why?*

She closed her eyes as sleep quietly streamed into her spent mind and body. Jan rolled over on her side, bringing her knees up to her chest. She glanced at Leong as sleep embraced her body and put her mind to rest.

She slept for no more than ten minutes. Her eyes opened wide. She sat up, thinking she had been asleep for hours. It was a moment of surprise. A smile crossed her face. "I've got it, I've got it," she announced excitedly.

"What have you got?" Leong asked.

"I have a final slim shot, a last-chance hope of a match to help *my daughter.*" The "my daughter" was a mental afterthought that surprised her.

"And please say, what is this last chance?" Leong questioned.

"Sweetheart, the last hope is … you."

"Have you lost it?"

"Not at all. Listen, please sit down next to me. I'm too excited. What a fool I've been."

"Please explain. You're making me crazy. I see that look in your eyes," he said, raising his voice.

"Lauren has one last biological connection."

"Who is that? Tell me."

Jan Lee was still. She looked into her husband's eyes and responded, "You are, my love. You are. We have the same father."

Leong was stunned by her statement. He was in total silence for about thirty seconds. And then, taking a deep breath and a gulp of air, he responded, "You're right. You are right. Why didn't we think of it before? Shall we call Daryl and Maxine?"

"No, not yet. Call the doctor. Ask him for an appointment for another test today or tomorrow."

One Week Later

At their apartment, the Landsman's kitchen was filled with the smells of two roasted chickens and Grandma Yetta's special brisket recipe. In the oven, a peach pie gurgled with tiny pops, and a fresh challah was warming up. And finally, there was a large pot of matzo ball soup with noodles. Nancy had done her usual delicious magic. The dining room table was set for nine people: Maxine, Daryl, Fred, Lauren, the two young visitors from Switzerland, Leong, Jan Yee, and Maxine's mom, Yetta. Lauren was at the hospital, asleep.

"You are amazing, with unbelievable natural intuitive skills. I wondered about it. Thinking about you kept me awake all night. How did you ever think that Leong would be a perfect bone marrow match for Lauren?" Maxine was asking, speaking so rapidly that she had to gasp for air.

"She told me. I heard Her voice. Our God in heaven and on earth, She told me Herself."

"Who *is* She? I don't understand," Maxine questioned.

Jan Yee looked at Maxine. The color of fear had disappeared; the furrowed brow was gone. As Maxine peered at Jan, she put her hands to her cheeks. The young woman was glowing. She was now finally at peace. She had done Her work — God's work.

"The moment of silent communication I had with Her was humble and guileless." She continued to describe the encounter. "It was like two caring women with a lifelong friendship were engaged in a simple conversation, each speaking to one another with genuine attachment and respect. She saw my face; I saw Hers. It was dreamlike, a pure out-of-body experience."

Maxine remained calm, quiet, and attentive. She wanted to know more about Jan's encounter. She did not question the authenticity of Jan's vision. The older woman waited for more details about this mysterious woman, a woman who felt safe, calm, and confident. Maxine sensed that Jan Yee had instincts far above those of anyone she'd ever met. She wanted to understand if her daughters, or one of them, had inherited that heaven-sent genetic gift, *the inner voice,* and the voice that many believe is God reaching out to them.

If God is truly speaking to her, which God is it? Is it the God we have worshiped for centuries, or is it the God that Jan Yee calls "Her" and "She"?

"I'm hungry," Jan Yee said in a happy voice. "I have never eaten Jewish food before."

"You have never eaten the Chosen People's food?" Fred questioned. "It's blessed and filled with magical smells and strength. Do you know why we have existed as group for more than six thousand years?"

"Why?" Leong popped in.

"Jewish food," Fred exclaimed. "And it takes that many years to cure the heartburn." The room roared with laughter.

The honeymooners spoke simultaneously, "Yes, yes, now we know, Jewish food." Neighbors could hear the voices of a happy family, enjoying the sound of elation and laughter. It was an occasion of thankful happiness for everyone.

31

A New Adventure

Nora and Bernhard left for Switzerland. Grandma Yetta returned to her apartment, and Sammy departed for school. Daryl and Maxine asked Leong and Jan Yee to remain in New York for an additional week, in case Leong was needed for additional bone marrow.

The newlyweds spent three great days at museums and wonderful restaurants, and saw two Broadway shows recommended by Maxine. Neither had ever seen a live show before. They found it amusing and interesting. They loved the ballet and the New York Philharmonic. At Carnegie Hall, they'd experienced the greatest treat when they heard Itzhak Perlman play the Beethoven violin concerto. Their unexpected trip to New York had been thrilling. They valued the experience, believing they would never return.

On the fourth day, Daryl asked Leong to spend some time with him in the office. "Hey, Daryl, this is my honeymoon. I don't want to leave Jan Yee alone. It isn't fair to her."

"Let's meet in the morning only, and Maxine and Jan can have lunch together in some swanky, trendy restaurant." Leong thought for a minute, pulled out his cell phone, and walked out of the room.

"Jan, tomorrow morning Daryl wants me to spend a couple

of hours with him at his office. He suggested that during that time you and Maxine have lunch and then go shopping. What do you think?"

"Sounds like fun. But I will miss you. See you at two in the hotel?"

"It's a date."

❦

Jan Yee met Maxine at the Bergdorf Goodman department store at 10:30 in the morning. Maxine turned to her guest. "We can do a lot of damage here." They both laughed. It was the beginning of a strange friendship, the birth mother and the adoptive mother.

Jan loved everything she saw, but declined to make any purchases. "These are all beautiful, but they are not for me. Where I live, it would be out of place."

"Please allow us to buy you a gift; it would make Daryl and me very happy."

"I do not need a gift — for what?" she demurred.

"I just want you to have something to remember how you helped in the miracle of our daughter's return to health. For that I must thank you." *What an interesting and unpretentious young woman she is. Young yet mature. She stands there with her thoughts, silent and deep. I like her.*

Jan Yee looked at Maxine. "The gift you already have given to me is you and Daryl and your daughters, or perhaps, with your permission, our daughters. Every one of you is now in our lives forever. We are a family." She laughed.

They entered the elevator. Maxine pushed the button to the seventh floor, where the Bergdorf coffee shop and lunch area were located. It was almost noon. It was obvious to both women their date would include no more shopping, only the lunch and polite girl talk.

A waiter showed them to a quiet booth in the corner overlooking Fifth Avenue. A fine white cotton tablecloth covered the table, atop which was sparkling silverware, matching napkins, two water glasses, and two wineglasses. A tall, cylindrical flower vase sat in the center of the table, with one white rose standing above the lip. A young woman server came to the table; she poured water and asked, "Would you like plain or bubble water?"

"Regular water with no ice, please," Jan said.

They had a bit of conversation with the waitress, soon discovering that she was from Croatia. Maxine knew two words in the woman's language from a trip to Yugoslavia she'd taken many years ago. She took quick advantage to say, "*Dobra dan* (Good day)." The young woman smiled and responded in her native language, speaking at a hundred miles an hour. The two mom friends laughed. Neither understood a single word.

Jan Yee is so charming and easygoing. I think we are not only joint mothers; we are going to be friends, Maxine thought.

She looked at Jan. *What an interesting young woman she is, elegant but quiet. Still, I wonder, I wonder. In truth, I like her. Nevertheless, I do feel something, a twinge of anger, or perhaps envy, that she, and not I, am the birth mother of my daughters.*

"Tell me, Jan, a few days ago you spoke about God being a woman. Is it possible that you actually believe that?" Maxine began in an incredulous voice. "Both the New Testament and the Old Testament, and the Koran, clearly state that God made us in His image. Doesn't it make sense that God is a man when the facts are written in the holy books?"

Jan sat quietly, fingering a croissant. She put a small smear of strawberry jam on the roll, took a bite, sipped her tea, and looked at Maxine. She saw love in Maxine's eyes, and something else. Jan saw a woman in deep thought. *My new friend wants to believe what I believe. She is seeking, as I have sought and found. I am feeling something else. Is she their mother or am I? I sense disappointment. No, not disappointment. Perhaps regret.*

The room was filled with an elegant lunch crowd. People were focused, speaking in many languages. The sounds of Russian, Italian, and Arabic — the global music of language from every part and every port in the world — filled the room. Wine was poured and food served. All were talking to one another. An occasional cell phone interrupted the diners. The restaurant was a party in a department store in midtown Manhattan. Jan's mind and body were like a sponge as she took in the wonder of the United States and especially New York. The Big Apple experience was immense. She picked up the napkin at her left, dabbed her lips with it, and responded.

"I believe that God created us in *Her* image," Jan Yee started. "I continuously ask this question of myself. If we are all made in God's image as a male, why are women the perpetuators of our species?" A momentary pause. "And why did God give women the gift of feeding children from their bodies to sustain a child at birth? Why did God grant women the body for providing the ultimate pleasure to man, which makes man the pursuer of all that a woman has to offer to fulfill his needs, wants, and dreams? That gift is the gift that uniquely gives us the power and the patience to teach men about the right path they must take. I ask you," Jan Yee continued, "why do they call nature 'Mother Nature' or our unique globe 'Mother Earth?' Why is the symbol of freedom in your great country called Miss Liberty? Why is justice a blindfolded woman holding the scale of judgment?

"Still men, to overcome the fear of female supremacy, have created by themselves a world of misogyny. They act not in God's way, as She planned. They make war and destroy other living creatures. Men produced a bomb so dangerous, so horrific, that one day it may destroy the earth. It will be up to women to exert the power and strength that She has given us to begin using our

rightful God-given intuitive strength to create an era of life and
peace as She visualized and planned for all life here on Her earth."

Jan sipped more tea. Maxine sat, digesting the logic of Jan's
perception of God.

"I cannot deny that your belief and your arguments express
serious truths, but how do women change thousands of years of
history?"

"Maxine, my dear and new friend, misogyny is centuries
old. Even when men pray to their God, they say 'amen.' Why?
It is to the exclusion of women, whose power they fear. When
Eve was created — I believe she was born first from Her womb,
God's womb. Adam came from Eve's body. In the men's version
of the creation, it is said that Eve was formed by Adam's rib. How
ridiculous. Adam could only have come from a womb. Otherwise,
how could he have existed? He survived from the milk of her
breasts. The tale that Eve urged Adam to take the apple from the
tree cannot be true. That was a tale to make women the evil one.
Eve did not need to seduce Adam to eat from the tree of wisdom;
she was able to feed him from her bosom filled with milk. The
male author who created this fictitious Bible described the anxiety
and the beginning of what men fear the most. It is the power of
women."

Jan placed her water glass to her lips. She took a sip and caught
her breath. "Let me assure you, all this has nothing to do with
any hatred of men. I love the man I am married to. I love my
father. I find your husband and your son nonthreatening. They
are fine and sensitive men loving you, and they give much love
and kindness to our twin children, both women.

"Look at all the great art. Van Gogh, Picasso, Rembrandt,
and more — all the greatest artists — painted and sculpted the
great beauties on earth: women. Still, I will not refute the beauty
of men in Michelangelo's *David* or da Vinci's magnificent *The
Last Supper.*

"One of my favorite stories," Jan Yee continued, "is one that some people find amusing. The male God, as is written in the Old Testament, instructed Abraham to sacrifice Isaac, his only son at the time, to honor Him. A man might do that, but a woman?" Jan paused. "A mother would never sacrifice her child ... *never!*" she said emphatically.

"As Abraham was about to make the sacrifice of his only son, he heard the voice of his God praising his attempt to obey by making the supreme sacrifice, that of his son Isaac. Suddenly, from nowhere, Abraham heard the voice of his God, who commanded, '*Stop!*' It appeared that God was satisfied with Abraham's commitment to obey." Maxine sat in silence, with lips apart and eyes gazing in intensity. "Here is the twist. As the story continues, the voice that Abraham heard was not that of his God. It was the voice of Sarah, Isaac's mother, with a message from She who would never sacrifice a son or a daughter. A mother would sooner take her own life than take her child's life. And there Sarah stood, high on the mountain with a goat in her arms, and released it to Abraham to offer his God a sacrifice. Ah, a goat ... but not her son.

"In the New Testament it is written that when Jesus was on the cross, he looked down at his mother and told her, 'Forgive them, for they know not what they do.'" Jan looked into Maxine's eyes. "Jesus was not talking to his Lord; he was talking to Mary and through her the true God, the She-God. The New Testament states that Jesus is the son of God. And that is true. Since Jesus could only have come from the womb of a woman, his mother Mary ... is that God."

Both women were quiet now. Maxine picked at her omelet, while Jan Yee hungrily devoured her very first turkey club sandwich.

"I've never eaten anything this delicious. What do you call it?"

"It's called a turkey club." Maxine smiled and called the waitress. "May we have a dessert menu?"

"I hope I haven't bored you. My father disagrees with me on every point I told you. And often he gets very angry with me."

"Why?" Maxine was puzzled.

"Because I am a woman, and in Chinese culture, women are to be obedient, do our husband's bidding, and fulfill their every wish. Tan Ha, my mother, is that person in my father's life. But she has a mind of her own. She disguises it with tiny manipulations. Although my father capitulates to her maneuvers, he knows exactly what she is doing. It amuses him. However, he never anticipated that I would be different. He could never anticipate my being an independent woman. I have disappointed him with my philosophy. Still, I know he and my adoptive mother love me. And I love them very much. They saved my life. Or should I say it was my mother Hi Bo's idea for me to be part of their family. Here again, She spoke to my mother's heart and helped to give me the life I have."

"Living in that kind of untraditional environment, where your beliefs are different than your father and mother, must be difficult for both your parents," Maxine added.

"It's not difficult at all, not in China. It is traditional. And everyone plays their role. My biological father took me to an employment agency when I was fifteen years old. He arranged to borrow money to help cure my half-brother, Leong. My birth father, to be perfectly truthful, sold me to an employment broker to save his son. Boys in China and all of Asia and much of the world are more valuable than girls. And that is why I say that when you and Daryl came to the orphanage and found your daughters — that tiny spot, out of all the places in the world — it was She who led you there. There were only girls for adoption. Some are not so lucky as Sammy and Lauren. Many die. Some go to bad homes. On occasion, some go to a good home. The point of my story is that my mother would never have sold me. Only a man, my biological farther, could and would do that. I am not saying that men are without heart. I am saying that men act on urgencies and women respond with heart."

"I do not know the whole story. It is very sad, but I am grateful that you are able to share your history with me," a teary-eyed Maxine answered.

Jan continued, saying, "The true sadness is that women are treated poorly and used throughout history. In many countries, life for a female is more horrid than you can imagine. In most parts of the so-called third world, many women are actual slaves."

"If God, as you say, is a woman, why has She permitted this kind of history to perpetuate itself? Wouldn't the woman God rise and strike down those whose immorality is revolting? Where has this tradition stemmed from?" Maxine questioned.

"Every book about God and religion, including the New and the Old Testament and the Koran, was written by men. It has been preached by men and confirmed by men that the history in these books are the word of God. This has been going on for centuries. It's difficult to undo. But She sees all things, and the world will change. In fact, it is changing as we sit here. Women are rising and are being elected or appointed to strong political positions. Women are now educated and are breadwinners. And most of all, She has given women, made in her image, the most valued role on earth, that of the endless nurturer of peace and love. I am certain you have heard the phrase, 'Behind every successful man is a strong woman.' That is not an accident. That is Her way of guiding men, who need the gentle managerial skills of women. All God's doing — all from Her.

"Moses led the Israelites out of Egypt and thousands followed him. They came to the Red Sea. He looked at his wife, Zipporah, and told her that they would never be able to traverse the sea. She turned to him and said, 'Let us all rest. In the morning, the tide will take the sea out and leave us a space to cross.' Moses questioned his wife's knowledge. Zipporah responded, 'Each morning when I wash the clothes in the sea, the tide is down.' That is history, where a woman changed the course of a nation. Moses never reached Palestine, but he could see it on the horizon. He was too weak to go any further. And though never said in the Old Testament, it was Zipporah, his wife, who led the entire congregation to a new home and a new life."

For Maxine, this was a unique conversation. It was a topic that she had never discussed with anyone. The plight of women and struggling female populations everywhere were issues that were not new to Maxine. She was very smart and educated. Stories about the migration of women searching for a better life were well known to her. She knew that people, all people, viewed life and religion in their own ways. Many were committed to the orthodoxy of their beliefs. Others just wanted to live and survive. She'd never thought about God being a man or a woman.

Jan reached across the table and put her hand on top of Maxine's. They looked into each other's eyes with an understanding and a new kinship.

The two women from dissimilar parts of the world, separate cultures, and different times in life, were the mothers of the same children, now totally bonded. They were as close as sisters; they were as one.

"When I travel and view all the oceans, the rivers," Jan maintained, "and the mountains, I ask myself, could a man have made this earth so beautiful? A man could not. Only a woman can create such beauty," Jan stated. "When I married Leong and we moved into his apartment, his residence was comfortable. He asked me to make it into a home for both of us. Now, thanks to the natural feminine nature She has given me, our dwelling is beautiful, as yours is. Am I right?"

Maxine nodded and grinned. She was becoming a believer.

"Maxine, my new friend, I cannot recall the moment, but when I was just fifteen years old, two babies lay on my belly. I was a baby having babies. The pregnancy was not of my doing. I was young and had endured a horror that only a crazed man trying to demonstrate his masculinity could commit. Another woman on the other side of the globe took these children into her heart, as if they had come from her womb. And here we sit, loving each other. I love you for taking my birth children and erasing the ugly deed of my childhood. I admire you for adoring and caring for the children that I brought into this world. It was God at work, as only She can do. This is a portrait of our lives. We are separate but bound — not at the hip, but connected at our hearts. This scene of life was painted not by a man, but by the God I trust. For this experience that you and I have lived, I more strongly believe that our God is a woman."

32

A Good Deed's Reward

Lauren was recovering. The bone marrow transfer from Leong seemed to be bringing her back to health. Fortunately, she required no repeat transfusion. Lauren and her mom and dad were grateful. The entire family valued the gift that gave their child another chance at a full life.

The farewells at the airport were filled with hugs and kisses. Maxine and Jan looked into each other's eyes. The two women hugged and kissed each other's cheek. No words were said, but they knew in their hearts and their minds that ... God is a woman.

❦

The newlyweds were exhausted as they sat in the first-class cabin, the upgrade a gift from Daryl. Before the plane took off, Leong and Jan Yee were fast asleep.

Midway over the Atlantic Ocean, a flight attendant saw they had awakened. "May I bring you coffee or tea? You slept through dinner. We still have plenty of time. We arrive in Zurich at 6:30 a.m., in about four more hours."

The flight attendant returned a bit later. "May I serve you a drink?"

"I will have some red wine," Leong replied.

"And you, Mrs. Chan?" Jan Yee opened a crunched eye, her mouth slightly ajar.

This was the second time she'd been called Mrs. Chan. It was an amazing, strange feeling — totally different from the time her father had asked her to change her name from Shan Di to Jan Yee. That first change had made her proud to please her father. This time was different. It made her feel completely grown up. And though there was joy in each new role, she felt a glimmer of resentment. On the first occasion she had changed her name to honor her father, and the second time she'd done so to honor her husband. *Why are women and men so fixed on the concept that the male is the leader, the protector, and men are those made in the image of God?* She thought for a few seconds. Then she pressed her forehead against the window, whispering, "You and I know different, my Beloved."

"I will have a bottle of water, no ice," Jan said.

"Don't you want a drink? You always have a glass of white wine," Leong asked.

"No thank you."

"Don't you feel well?"

"I do."

Leong shrugged his shoulders. *Women are a puzzle, and still their instincts are amazing. Yet in the brief time I have been with my bride, I have never been happier, so this is a good time to tell her the news.*

"Jan, my love, I have some interesting news to tell you. Do you recall having lunch with Maxine?"

"Yes I do. It was interesting. And she is an intelligent and delightful woman. I like her very much."

"I am pleased to hear that. Daryl has invited me to join him and his son to work in New York on a new and very exciting

project. I would partner with them in a new real estate venture.
It's huge." The words jumped from his lips in complete excitement.

The news was a total surprise to Jan. It was a turn in her life,
one she'd never imagined. Leong never expected this event.

"I must confess," she said, "on this trip, I fantasized about
living in New York. It is such a wonderful city, better than Paris
or Shanghai. I believe I would be happy raising our family there."

"Yes, that would be a good place for children to grow up.
There are great schools, many cultural opportunities, and excellent
health-care facilities. And it is safe. I am so pleased you and I are
in the same place."

"Ah, my love, we are not in the same place, but soon we
will be."

"I don't understand."

"I, my darling lover, am pregnant." She smiled.

"Oh my God, oh my God!" Leong exclaimed. "Did this
happen on our honeymoon?"

"No, it occurred about six weeks ago in our apartment."

"But how could you know it so quickly without testing?"

"I know. I just know. My body is telling me. She is telling me.
And to be scientifically accurate, I purchased a pregnancy testing
package at the pharmacy when we arrived in New York. Each
morning I would put a touch of urine on it. If the strip changed
color, I would be pregnant. This morning, we won."

Sammy Landsman, interning at Johns Hopkins Hospital, was
having the time of her life. She was devouring everything placed
before her, gobbling up each assignment and every experiment.
The professor at the Laboratory of Medical Health found her to
be a miracle, an intellectual sponge when it came to absorbing
facts. Having been a teacher for more than two decades, Professor

Bovard found the young woman to be a dream student and scholar.

She had two new and special friends at school, Zack and Jennifer. Both were smart and on equal footing with Samantha. These two young people and Sammy had a unique friendship. They were each other's confidants; she shared everything with Zack and Jennifer. They knew about her parents, and especially about her birth mother, who had married her half-brother. It was complicated. They were nonjudgmental, and above all, they thought it to be very interesting.

"Why do you use the term *birth mother*? She is your biological mother, which is equally accurate as a title, but just a bit more scientific," Zack stated.

"I believe *birth mother* states my case more accurately."

"Tell me about her," Zack asked. He, Jen, and Sammy were sitting outside the medical school. It was early April. The day was comfortable, in the high sixties. Trees were turning green. Tulips and small daffodils were beginning to sprout. Students, sensing the warm weather, were wearing shorts and lightweight clothing.

At the university it was a season change. As for the rest of world, who cared? They were at school. That was their life.

"Jan, my birth mother, is a very elegant-looking woman. She is beautiful, soft-spoken, educated, and smart. Jan and my mom, instead of creating a competitive situation, have both accepted their roles in our lives. I believe they have become good friends. She is married to a man who is a partner in my father's business in China. And now that Lauren is well again, all is okay. But there is one thing that makes Jan stand out. She believes that God is a woman."

"I never thought of that concept," Jennifer inserted. "Why is that her belief?"

"I do not know all the details, but she says she gets premonitions and believes it is a woman God speaking to her."

"That's weird," Jen responded.

"I don't agree with you," Zack joined in. "Why is it not possible for God *to be* a woman? There is no scientific evidence that God is a man or a woman. It is just the word of men. Men wrote the fiction that God is a man."

"Don't be silly, Zack. Believing in God is not a science. It is faith."

"Well, I never had any faith in religion or God anyway."

"You sound like my father," Sammy said.

The reorganization began. Leong spent months flying between Zurich and New York. In their new office in Switzerland, Leong methodically explained the hundreds of details to Karl about how to make the business machine run. His new assistant would be Bernhard. Karl would be the CEO in Europe, while Bernhard would be managing director. Nora was registered at the university in Geneva to study business and finance. She would return to the company as an accounting supervisor, someday to be the CFO. The plan was in place.

When back in New York, Leong worked closely with Fred and Daryl, meeting with banks, real estate investors, and business executives. He was learning the complexity of real estate. In fact, he and Fred were forming a special alliance as they learned the nuances of the new enterprise.

Jan Yee flew to Guangzhou to visit her parents. She was in her sixth month. She felt that at any later point it would be more difficult to make such a long trip.

Hi Bo and Tan Ha were delirious about her visit. Friends

and family from everywhere in China came to go see the mommy-to-be.

Jan Yee's stepmother and her sister, Nina, dropped in as well. Auntie Sun and Ting came from way up north in Manchuria. But this time they took a plane. Everyone brought gifts, piles of baby things all wrapped and unopened. Mother Tan Ha would not allow Jan Yee to open or look at any of the presents. Jan Yee was not allowed to even think of taking the plethora of gifts home. Hi Bo and Tan Ha would bring them to New York when the child was born. Then all the gifts would be opened. The families were superstitious: no baby gifts until the baby was there to receive them. That settled, Jan Yee asked, "May I open one gift, please?"

"Ask your lady God. If She says yes, we will still not let you open even one," Hi Bo ordered.

Jan smiled. "You are so right, Poppa. I will wait until your grandchild is with me to show how he or she brings honor to the Hi Bo family."

When Sammy finally left the Johns Hopkins research department, she took her doctorate at Harvard. She was offered positions at universities in the UK, elsewhere in Europe, and in the United States. For a brief period she went to work at Pfizer Laboratories as chief of research for birth control medicine.

She left the commercial world to take a professorship at her alma mater, the Johns Hopkins University School of Medicine, where she remains today.

33

A Fresh Life

The wire transfers arrived; the real estate deal was closed. Leong received a generous bonus for having raised the funds, along with a letter from Sang Ye Piao. The letter read as follows:

Dear Leong, Daryl, and Fred,

> We appreciate your considering us as partners. We are open to additional investments with your group in the United States. Our experience has been straightforward, honest, and detailed. We have fifty million US dollars or more for any additional worthwhile investment opportunities. Thank you.

Best regards,
Sang Ye Piao

Leong took the letter into Daryl's office. A huge smile on his face, he asked, "How do you like that letter? Here is another fifty million or more to invest from Piao and his partners."

"That's great," Daryl answered in a strange and unusually weak and gasping voice. Normally Daryl's voice was strong.

"Are you okay? You look pale."

"I just feel tired." In one lightning-quick moment, Daryl's head slumped to his chest. He collapsed in his chair.

Leong feared the worst yet remained calm. Instantly he dialed 9-1-1 and called Fred from the other office. An ambulance arrived in seven minutes. Daryl was immediately taken to the New York Hospital. A possible heart attack was the diagnosis of the medical aides. Daryl, on a gurney, was placed into the ambulance. Fred jumped in with his dad and called his mom.

"Dad is not feeling well. We are taking him to the New York Hospital emergency entrance. Please call Dr. Holly. I do not have her number."

"What's wrong? What happened?" Maxine was frantic.

"Mom, please, please keep yourself together. Make the call and have her meet us." He was abrupt and as frightened as his mother.

Within minutes after Daryl was taken to the hospital, Leong's cell phone buzzed. He heard Jan Yee's voice at the other end. "Hello, sweetheart. Are you all right?" he questioned.

"Come and get me. Our baby is ready to be born. My water broke."

"This is some day. This is some day." He slapped his open hand to his forehead.

The corporate office was on Madison Avenue at Thirty-fourth Street. An Uber car nearby was there to pick him up within three minutes. He met Jan Yee at the door of their apartment on Bleecker Street in Greenwich Village.

The car zipped uptown on the road hugging the East River, on the way to New York Hospital's lying-in division. The driver was fast and careful. "This is my f-f-first baby d-d-drive. I am n-n-nervous and excited. D-d-don't worry, I am a g-g-g-good d-driver."

Leong rolled his eyes. Jan smiled. Her contractions became stronger. Still she remained determined and in control.

They arrived at the hospital in just shy of eight minutes. Jan was immediately put on a gurney and whisked to the delivery room. Leong telephoned Dr. Bonner, Jan's obstetrician. "I will be there. I am dialing the hospital as we speak," the doctor responded.

Leong was aided by the nurse to be dressed in an operating gown, mask, hat, and gloves. Then he was led to join the medical staff in the delivery room. Jan was struggling with her abdominal pushes.

"Breathe," Leong urged her. "Just like they taught us in the prenatal classes." Together they breathed as a team. "Breathe in and now out. In and now out. Push, push," he whispered in an encouraging voice.

Four hours later, Jan Yee gave birth. It was a boy. The nurse placed him on the new mommy's belly. After a few moments, Dr. Bonner snipped the umbilical cord and placed the child into Leong's open arms.

The new father searched and saw two eyes, a healthy-looking head, ten toes and ten fingers, and finally the part that differentiates the sexes, that tiny but healthy-looking penis. The infant came into the world, and as expected, a little girl came flying out — no resistance, no pushing, no struggle. Her arrival was easy and comfortable. The nurse placed the baby girl next to her mother. Then the doctor again cut the cord and placed the child in her father's arms. Leong gazed at the girl. Her look was different. His baby daughter shone. She had a special glow, as if there was something extraordinary about her. He observed a beautiful head, ten fingers, ten toes, two ears, and two eyes. She was perfect, and the winner at five pounds, seven ounces. There she was, little Miss Chan. This new human being was not a baby girl. To her dad, a woman had been born. He turned his head to Jan Yee. A nurse had wiped her brow and brushed her hair. Two other attending nurses were cleaning the infants. Everyone was at peace and happy. There were no imperfections; the twins were healthy and beautiful.

Jan peered into Leong's eyes. They looked at each other, happy and loving. "Now, all four of us are a big family." Momma Chan smiled. "She gave us two special gifts," Jan Yee said, sighing, to Leong. "They are healthy and normal. This is a miracle because of our secret that only our special, wonderful God could bestow on us. We are grateful for Her kindness." The new mom wept.

Leong leaned toward his wife's wet cheeks and dabbed them with a tissue. Brushing away the tears from his own eyes, he quietly asked, "Are you well?"

"I cry from happiness and with joy. She has blessed us with two new lives to love and care for, two to replace those who were taken from me. She has returned to us twins, both beautiful, healthy, normal children. I am grateful. Thank You, my God," Jan murmured, looking above her to an imaginary heaven. The new mother closed her eyes, welcoming sleep, thinking of Her.

"Oh my, I almost forgot I must rush to the other side of the hospital to see how Daryl is doing," Leong whispered.

❦

Dr. Holly, Daryl's cardiologist, arrived at the emergency room at the same time as the ambulance. She was amazing. She took over the entire staff and moved Daryl along quickly. Everyone stood back and watched this brilliant physician at work. The hospital staff demonstrated total respect and admiration for the doctor's skills. Holly had the talent. The doctor was amazing and strong and knew how to save Daryl's life.

34

Fickle Lives

Lauren, now cancer free, was advised that periodic tests were required to maintain her health and to treat any new suspicious cells, if any ever appeared. She now was prepared to return to school. Almost a year had passed. She read for a little while, but fell asleep quickly.

On the fifth day of September, Maxine helped her daughter pack for her return to Dartmouth. Lauren knew her old classmates would be way ahead of her; however, inside her was the determination to catch up and do even better. Her choice of majors had changed. She always wanted to be a writer, and now that was going to be her goal. Her wish was to tell the story of her illness. She wanted to express in the many pages yet to be written her fear of dying and her fear of living. All this she noted mentally. She wrote every day in her mind. The pain, the search for the donor, and the transfusion were burned into her memory. She would never forget the anguish in her mother's face or the panic in her father's expression. Her strong, all-knowing dad had crumbled under the pressure of perhaps losing his precious daughter. This was a story that had to be told for all those who followed, and for the family and friends who stood by her side.

Lauren had a book inside her brain about her birth mother's

belief that God was a woman. The story in Lauren's head, this indeed was a book to be written. It would take hard work, determination, and truthfulness. That was Lauren's dream.

Back on campus, Lauren's friends greeted their missing classmate with cheers, saying, "Welcome back, Lauren!" They were wearing T-shirts that read, "I am a freshman." Lauren broke down and wept. All her classmates, young men and young women alike, gathered around her like bees to a flower. Maxine exploded in sobs of relief; her baby, almost lost, was now back to life. She took a deep breath as she heard the voice, her inner voice say, *Life is over when it's over.* Maxine questioned in silence, *was that Jan's God speaking to me, advising me? Am I becoming a believer?*

❧

Daryl struggled as his eyes opened. He had no recollection of where he was or how he had gotten there. Tubes came from above and entered his arm and nose. One penetrated his penis. He breathed air from a mask on his face. Outside the room his family had gathered, Maxine, Fred, Yetta, and Sammy. Lauren was away at school and had been urged to remain there.

Dr. Holly spoke directly to Maxine. "Your husband has had a heart attack. We see blockages in two areas. We cannot determine yet the extent of the damage. But we will know by tomorrow or within a few days. His history has been one of good health and fit body. Remember, he is sixty-nine years old. It would be better for the family and for Daryl if you all went home and returned tomorrow at about ten a.m. I will be here then, and I will have more details to give you his prognosis."

"I would prefer to stay overnight, right here, and sleep on this chair," Maxine told the doctor.

"If that is what you want, I will arrange a bed to be brought into the room. You need the rest as well."

Dr. Holly left the room. Maxine sat there gazing at her husband — the love of her life. *It's too soon, too soon. I want more, I need more time together. Please, God.*

Fred went to the office. Sammy went to her laboratory. Grandma Yetta went to her apartment.

Early the next morning Maxine awoke at 6:15 a.m. She raised her aching body and moved slowly to the side of Daryl's bed. He slept. She saw his chest rise and fall. It felt like a gift. Maxine turned to the bathroom. She looked into the mirror, saw unwelcome dark rings beneath her eyes, and shook her head. She brushed her hair, toweled her face, dressed, and went to church.

Having been raised as a Catholic, she'd gone to church every Sunday with her grandmother, yet she was not religious. She had a sickening feeling of betrayal just being in church. She felt disloyal to the God she'd grown up with. Still, here she was asking for God's help. As she was about to slip to her knees and pray to Him, she had a feeling in her gut. It was a signal sent once again to her inner voice. She stopped, stood up, and looked at the Christ on the cross, seeing his tortured expression. He had given his life for his God.

Maxine leaned back in her seat, feeling Christ's pain. The man she'd loved for her entire adult life could possibly be taken away. She recently had felt the agony of the prospect of losing a child. Now soon after that, so very soon, she was again being challenged to remain strong. Maxine was determined to be the powerful woman who befitted the life that was meant for her to live. She leaned back, shut her eyes, and began to pray in a strong and whispered voice.

"Please, dear God, permit me to be sturdy, solid, and resilient in this moment. In the name of my children's beloved birth mother, through You, who gave me two beautiful children, I pray to her God, the *woman* God, whom my new friend has led me to believe in. You are the God I trust because You are a *woman* and understand the trials of all women. To You I pray for the health of my precious soul mate, Daryl Landsman. Give him the strength to regain his health and to live many more years. *Awoman.*"

Maxine stood up, not making the sign of the cross. She turned and left the church.

❦

Dr. Holly carefully outlined the future care of Daryl. Two weeks had passed since Daryl's heart attack. "Your husband will survive. He most likely will be here at New York Hospital for at least four weeks. He must remain at home for another month. No work, no phone calls, no discussions about business. He has to be stress-free. I suggest that he dress every day and walk a little at home and then outside, weather permitting. We will discuss more details in a few weeks. The nurse will give you a suggested diet when he is discharged. And remember — and this is an order — let Fred and Leong run the business."

Daryl was lying in bed listening. He looked at Dr. Holly and asked, "What about sex? How long do we have to wait until we can we have sex?" He smiled.

Dr. Holly looked at Daryl. She remained silent for a moment, and then said, "Maxine, oh, she can have sex today or whenever she wishes. You will have to wait at least two months, perhaps longer. Can you handle it?" Everyone laughed, including the attendant who was cleaning up.

"I guess I have to."

Maxine kissed his cheek. "You guys are alike. You were inches away from death, and all you're thinking about is your penis."

"Soooo, what else is new?" Daryl shrugged.

35

The Blessing of Family

At Jan Yee's home in Greenwich Village, the children were taking their nap when the phone rang.

"Hello, Jan. It's Maxine."

"Hi, my sister. Good to hear from you. How is Daryl doing?"

"Fairly well. He should be coming home in about a week."

"That's good news. When are you coming over to see *my* twins?" she asked, placing emphasis on the word *my*.

"That is exactly what I am calling about."

"Come today or anytime. I would love to see you."

On the following Tuesday, Maxine stepped from a taxi at about noon. In front of the Bleecker Street home, she stood with a huge package in her hand. The concierge announced her. The elevator opened on the third floor. Jan heard the bell and ran to the door. She greeted Maxine with enthusiasm and a warm welcome. It was a sisterly feeling for both women.

Maxine placed the package on a table near the entrance. "First I must see the children, and then I'd like a tour of your beautiful apartment."

The children were laying in their cribs, the girl all cuddled and the boy with his nose down and his backside straight up. They were almost four months old. They looked healthy and adorable.

Maxine stared at both. *How fast time flies. I remember my girls so little, so helpless. Life is amazing.*

"They are beautiful. I am so happy for you. Have you given them any tests yet?"

"No, not yet. The doctors prefer to wait until their immune systems are more mature."

"Please forgive this observation, but your son, Matthew, looks a lot like my Lauren. Your daughter, Alexandra, looks like Leong."

"You are 100 percent accurate. Leong and I think the same. Come — let me show you our home." Jan called Na Tie, one of the nannies. "Please watch the children. I have company." The young woman acknowledged the request in Chinese and moved to the room where the children were asleep.

The Bleecker Street structure was close to eighty years old. It had been declared a New York City historical site. The exterior of the building could not be changed in any way except for cleaning. The original site had to be permanent. The building was a five-story walk-up with four apartments on each floor. On the outside was an all-brick façade and an old-fashioned metal fire escape. Leong and Jan had bought the entire renovated duplex one year before the renovation was complete.

Jan said, "Our home feels like the great house in Guangzhou."

"This is a beautiful apartment, a perfect family nest to raise the twins, and who knows who else."

Jan laughed at Maxine's suggestion.

"Let's see how this works out. It isn't easy, even with the help we have. Would you like tea? Yesterday I baked some delicious chocolate chip cookies."

"Thank you. I would."

The two mothers sat in the living room, Maxine quietly sipping chamomile, and Jan drinking strong green tea. "How is Daryl doing?"

"He is getting better. In a few weeks he plans to go to the

office at ten a.m. and be home by three-thirty. He takes a nap, watches some television, and reads the paper, and then we have dinner. Three days a week, he is at the cardio gym."

"It was a scary time for the two of you."

"I was so frightened. I went to church to pray, but I couldn't. Instead" — Maxine paused for a moment — "I spoke to you ... and to Her."

"Did She answer you?" Jan whispered.

"I heard a voice, not in my brain or in my heart; I heard a voice coming from my gut. The feeling was deep, deep inside. It made me turn around and search the room. It was an out-of-body experience. It was if I was standing in one place and looking at myself from afar."

"What did She say to you?" Jan questioned.

"Our God whispered that Daryl would come through this health scare."

"You experienced the same as I did when I was struggling with many fears as a child and as a young woman." Jan responded. "Even now I pray that my children will mature and have healthy lives. I know She will guide me. And now, my friend, my sister, you too *have* heard Her."

Jan reached out to touch Maxine's hand. "Our friendship, our sisterhood, is now bound by Her love, and our love for each other. I think of this special gift we have been given. You have daughters, twins who came from my womb. Still, you and only you are their true mother. Please believe me. She blessed me, and blessed you, by leading me into your life. Giving life to Samantha and Lauren was Her gift to you. She led me to the path, bringing us together so I could discover that Leong was the perfect match. She blessed us by saving our LangPi. I am the birth mother, but in truth, you are the actual life mother."

"I believe you. This is too complex to be a coincidence. There are too many twists and turns, and accidental meetings from halfway around the world. I believe in Her. We, you and I, were all in Her plan." Maxine, teary-eyed, sat down on a sofa nearby.

"She rewarded and blessed me with twins, one of them a boy to please and repay my father. It was Her sign of forgiveness for his and my mother's error many years ago. My biological father is dead, and my momma Chan regrets not speaking up. With all my heart I accept and have faith that She had other plans for me." Jan spoke as if in a prayer.

"Do not forget you are blessed with a daughter to carry on Her work when our time has come," Maxine answered. She continued with, "I believe all you say is true. Please consider all the coincidental happenings that have connected our lives: Daryl meets Mr. Chen because of a business matter. Mr. Chen then arranges for the adoption of our daughters. Chen is a friend of your father. He takes Daryl to meet Hi Bo and Tan Ha. On the other side of the world, in Mongolia, Sang Ye Piao sends Leong on a mission to the big house. The family meets Daryl. Daryl meets Leong. All those occurrences are Her doing. How else could it all have happened?" Maxine caught her breath as her eyes filled with tears. "Life is strange. She guides us. All this is a miracle."

"No, my dear sister and friend, life is not strange. Life is wonderful. And we thank Her every day for the inner voice that counsels and guides us. We are blessed with this," Jan said softly.

The two women stood, their arms encircled in a deep embrace. Maxine whispered to her sister, "Jan, you are a wonderful teacher."

"You are an amazing mother, and an extraordinary friend and wife to Daryl."

And in a strange moment of fate, both said to each other simultaneously, "I love you. We shall be joined forever after today."

The author says in a commanding voice: "Daryl, please relax and stop looking over my shoulder. One heart incident for you is enough. Sit down and allow me to finish this final chapter. You paid me a great deal of money to write your family history. Please relax in that comfortable chair and allow me to finish." Daryl sat and the author began the final part of the Landsman story.

Ten minutes flew by, Daryl placed both hands on the arms of his resting chair and with all his strength, lifted himself up and quietly said to me, "Get the fuck out of there. This is my life, not yours."

I was more than surprised as he slowly began to write. Within a few moments his fingers danced across the key board; moving rapidly as the words flowed from his still sharp memory onto the blank computer screen. His recollection of his final night celebration with his family was perfect. He wrote:

"Maxine and I have invited all of you, our entire family, to celebrate Leong's return from Switzerland. To my wonderful friends, Jan Yee, our extraordinary and loving birth mother; to Leong and your twins — and a special greeting to you, Hi Bo and Tan Ta. It pleases all of us so very much that you have joined us in this celebration."

I recall the whole family sat quietly, listening to me. It was a unique party.

With a great deal of effort, I rose again, cleared my throat, and with a glass of water, only half full, I made a toast. Everyone listened, all eyes were on me. The children were quiet and at rest. A special stillness filled the room. I gazed around, feeling grateful to be alive and well.

I continued with my remembrance, to the best of my ability.

"I am a happy man to be part of this great and tightly knit family. With all the strength I have in my body, I believe that of all my successes, each of my many risks, and all the challenges in my life, this family, my family, our family, is by far my most valued accomplishment." *I sipped a little water and put the glass down on a small table nearby. The group was silent, and the twins, with eyes wide open, lay quietly.*

"My best friend and the love of my life, Maxine, my three children, and all the people here, each one of you, all make me feel safe and strong. The power of life is family, the family you are born into and the family you choose. They are the most significant reward that one can have. And to Leong, my partner and my friend, I will never forget that you have saved the life of our daughter. Jan Yee, you are a very special woman. Your presence in our lives, and all the astonishing gifts you have given our clan, confirm to me, unquestionably, that through you, we all have learned and believe that it is quite possible ... God must truly be a woman."

Five years later, Daryl passed away at the age of seventy-seven — reluctantly.